A Spring
Bouquet

BOOK YOUR PLACE ON OUR WEBSITE AND MAKE THE READING CONNECTION!

We've created a customized website just for our very special readers, where you can get the inside scoop on everything that's going on with Zebra, Pinnacle and Kensington books.

When you come online, you'll have the exciting opportunity to:

- View covers of upcoming books
- Read sample chapters
- Learn about our future publishing schedule (listed by publication month *and author*)
- Find out when your favorite authors will be visiting a city near you
- Search for and order backlist books from our online catalog
- Check out author bios and background information
- Send e-mail to your favorite authors
- Meet the Kensington staff online
- Join us in weekly chats with authors, readers and other guests
- Get writing guidelines
- AND MUCH MORE!

**Visit our website at
http://www.zebrabooks.com**

Janet Dailey
Debbie Macomber
Rebecca Brandewyne
Jo Beverley

A Spring Bouquet

Zebra Books
Kensington Publishing Corp.

http://www.zebrabooks.com

ZEBRA BOOKS are published by

Kensington Publishing Corp.
850 Third Avenue
New York, NY 10022

First Printing: May, 1996
10 9 8 7 6 5 4 3 2

Printed in the United States of America

CONTENTS

Castles in the Sand

by
Janet Dailey
and
Sonja Massie

One

"I see a man stepping from the mists of time . . . into your future . . . your *near* future . . ." The fortune-teller squinted her dark eyes, staring at the row of cards spread on the red satin tablecloth before her. Her gold hoop earrings glittered in the flickering candlelight as she moved her graceful hands over the card to her right—a knight riding a black horse, his sword brandished high above his head.

Bridget O'Dwyer chuckled, propped her elbows on the table, and breathed in the heavy sandalwood perfume of the incense smoke that curled from a nearby burner. "Ah, come on, Joleen," Bridget chided, "I suppose the next thing you're going to tell me is that he's tall, dark, and handsome."

One carefully tweezed eyebrow arched indignantly, the seer looked up from the cards. "As a matter of fact, Miss Smartie Pants, he *is* tall and handsome."

"Not dark?"

"Hey, two out of three ain't bad. And it's *Madame* Joleen when I'm giving you a reading."

"Oh, right. Sorry."

Smiling, Bridget leaned back against the satin and velvet cushions and felt a wave of fatigue sweep over her. It had been a tough day. The smile faded from her pretty face, to be replaced by a look of concern. Running one hand through her bedraggled strawberry blond curls, she realized she hadn't even taken the time to brush her hair. Her old tee shirt was spattered with paint, as were her arms and the backs of her hands. Her last manicure was a distant memory.

"Please, Jo," she said softly, "pull one more card for me."

The older woman's eyes glistened with affection and kindly understanding. "Why?" she asked in a tone that suggested she already knew the answer.

"I want to know if Mike is going to be all right."

Joleen sighed and shook her head. "I don't think it's such a good idea to ask the cards right now."

Bridget searched her friend's face, trying to see what wisdom lay behind that enigmatic expression. "Why? Do you know something I don't?"

Bridget's heart began to pound. Mike Sullivan had been like a father to her, her best friend, her business partner. His recent stroke and subsequent fall from the Sand Castle Pier, where they lived and worked, had left him with an impaired mind and a broken leg. And had left Bridget in a state of shock.

In spite of his advancing years, Mike had always been a strong, healthy bull of a man, invincible . . . or so she had thought until four days ago, when she found him unconscious on the sand beneath the pier, his leg twisted at a cruel angle.

"Did the doctors tell you something that you haven't told me?" she asked again, wanting to know but fearing the answer. "Did they—?"

"No, nothing like that." Reaching across the cards, Joleen laid one soft, time-lined hand on Bridget's and patted her fingers. "It's just that there's no point in asking yet. The matter hasn't been decided."

"What do you mean?"

As Joleen shrugged, the silver threads of her flamboyant robe glittered and her earrings tinkled. "If Mike wants to recover, he will. If he doesn't, he won't. I don't think he has decided yet."

"Not want to recover? Mike? That's ridiculous!" Bridget declared, dismissing the very idea. "He has too much to live for."

"Does he?"

"Of course! He has the pier, its shops and arcades, and the carousel. This place is his life's work." Bridget felt tears sting her tired eyelids. She fought them off. She had already cried several times today. "And there are all of us who love him . . ."

Squeezing her hand, Joleen said, "That's true. If love alone can bring Mike health, he'll be up off that bed and dancing an Irish jig at the wharf's fund-raiser next week."

Bridget closed her eyes for a moment, picturing the way Mike Sullivan had looked in his hospital bed, his leg in traction, so pale and helpless, so unlike himself.

"Mike *has* to be all right, Jo. I'm not sure I could make it without him."

"You could, sweetheart, but I'm praying that you won't have to. None of us is ready to give up on Mike yet." She gathered the cards into a stack and placed them in a small wooden box with an inlaid top. "You should get some sleep. Tomorrow is Saturday, and that means the crowds will descend on us like a swarm of hungry Mississippi mosquitoes at a Red Cross blood drive."

Bridget stood and eased the kinks out of her back. "You're right. Six o'clock comes early when you've got a hundred little kids hanging from your arms, crawling through your legs, trying to steal carousel rides. Plus, I've got a thousand things to do before the benefit next Saturday. Thanks for the reading."

She paused at the door and looked back over her shoulder at Joleen, who was dousing the incense. "Tall, dark, and handsome, huh?" she asked playfully.

"Nope, just tall and handsome. Don't push your luck."

As Bridget stepped outside the fortune-teller's parlor and onto the boardwalk she paused to listen to the hypnotic splashing of the waves against the pier. Beneath her feet she felt the slight shudder of the wharf and heard the moans and creaks of the aged wood.

Savoring the moment, she breathed deeply of

the salty ocean air. The atmosphere inside Joleen's tiny cottage might have been exotically aromatic, but Bridget had always preferred the tangy freshness of the onshore breeze that swept the Southern California coast. That pungent scent borne on the sea mists had been part of Bridget's life for as long as she could remember, as had this fanciful wharf known as the Sand Castle Pier.

Stretching from the silver sands over fifteen hundred feet into the moonlit waters, the pier was a mystical, magical place, a fairyland where Bridget had been born and raised.

Thirty years ago, the ancient pier's reconstruction had been conceived in the fertile imaginations of two immigrant Irishmen, Michael Sullivan and Patrick O'Dwyer, Bridget's father. Best friends since childhood, Mike and Pat had left Ireland together as young men. In their new country, they had worked hard to succeed, married and raised their families in an enchanted world of their own making—the Sand Castle Pier.

Badly neglected and falling apart, the old wharf had been long forgotten by the town's citizenry. But Mike and Pat had nurtured a vision, the dream of restoring the pier and transforming it into a recreational landmark that would provide pleasure for generations to come.

Through natural disasters, political opposition, and overwhelming financial challenges, they had persevered until their fantasy had become a magnificent reality.

But, like the Camelot of old, the Sand Castle

was a paradise too idyllic to continue indefinitely. When Bridget was thirteen years old, Patrick O'Dwyer and his wife, Helen, were killed in an airplane crash while celebrating their wedding anniversary in Puerto Rico. A year later, Mike's wife, Irene, left him and their fifteen-year-old son, Reese. She had disappeared one evening, leaving a brief goodbye note that was vague about her reasons for going.

Michael, Reese, and Bridget—who had been awarded to the Sullivan's custody—had been devastated by her abandonment.

Mike had withdrawn even farther into his self-imposed isolation, and, several months later, Reese had followed his mother's example by leaving without a word of explanation or even a farewell.

Now, twelve years later, Bridget strolled along the edge of the pier toward the seaward end and glanced over the railings at the beach below. One by one, the waves rolled gently on shore, then returned to the sea, leaving behind a thin sheet of water that sparkled like a layer of shimmering gold dust before sinking into the sand.

She recalled happier times when she and Reese had played in the sand, two happy children building castles and dreams—before the tides had swept everything away.

She thought of the night before Reese had left, how they had walked along that same beach, and what he had said to her.

"I can't take it anymore, Bridget. First, your folks get killed, then my mom runs out on me.

Then my dad crawls into a shell and won't come out. Of course, that's nothing new. He's never been there for me . . . or for my mom. All he's ever cared about is a full whiskey bottle and this stupid pier. That's why she left us, you know."

Even then, Bridget knew that his fury was only an outward manifestation of a pain buried deep in his heart. But she had her own feelings of abandonment. In such a short time she had lost both her parents and Reese's mother. Irene had been like a beloved aunt to her.

Now Reese, her childhood friend, was running away.

"Will you miss me, even a little?" she had asked, her heart in her eyes as she stared up at him, trying to find the answer on his face.

But his expression was hard and unreadable as he said, "Sure. Don't worry; I'll write to you once in a while, and you can come visit if you want. Mostly I just want to get away from this rotten place. You do understand, don't you?"

She hadn't understood then. She didn't understand now.

As she stood at the pier's end and looked back at the old wharf with its dimmed, golden lights, the sleeping shops, the stained glass windows of the carousel house like jewels gleaming against the night sky, she opened her heart and embraced the fantasy as she did almost every night of her life.

She loved the Sand Castle—every inch of it. The perpetually rotting boards beneath her feet, the barnacle-encrusted pilings, the peeling paint

on the arcade's walls and the shops' roofs that
were certain to leak again with the next heavy
rain. She adored it all, and so did the community. That was why the city was organizing a
fundraiser, a massive beach party to assist in yet
another badly needed restoration of the beloved
landmark.

Could she understand why Reese had left the
Sand Castle, his father, and her, or why he had
never written that promised letter . . . not even
a note . . . a postcard . . . ?

No.

Not now. Not ever.

"Your dad is sick, Reese. He's hurt," she whispered, sending the words into the night wind in
search of the heart who might hear, who might
forgive after so many years. "He needs you. And
I nee—"

She swallowed the words. Angry, she wondered
at how she could have nearly spoken them. She
didn't need Reese Sullivan or even care if she
ever saw him again. Not on her life.

As long as she had the pier, her friends who
shared it with her, and of course, Mike—strong
and healthy again. That was all she needed to
be happy.

Reese Sullivan glared across the polished ebony
surface of his desk at his business partner and
tried his best not to let the guy's smug grin get
on his nerves . . . as he was sure it was intended
to do. "Tex" Yarrow might hide the brain of a

brilliant financial genius beneath that ten-gallon Stetson, but he could be a pain sometimes. His enormous body dwarfed the wingbacked leather chair where he sat, ankle propped on his knee. His physical opposite, Reese was slender and trim in a charcoal Armani suit that was as tasteful as Tex's ostrich skin cowboy boots were garish.

Older than Reese by about ten years, Tex had begun to lose much of his hair and strongly resented Reese's leonine mane. He begrudged Reese his trim physique, too, but wasn't willing to give up the beers and barbecues to have it himself.

Their offices reflected their differences, as well. Tex's revolved around a well-stocked bar and big screen television, while Reese's looked like the reading room of a gentlemen's club with wainscoting, dark leather, and Oriental rugs.

For the first five years of their association, Reese had wondered how the combination could possibly work. During the last five, enjoying overwhelming success, he had simply been thankful that it had.

"*You,* Reese Workaholic Sullivan, taking a whole week off!" Tex said in that thick drawl that Reese found charming once in a great while and irritating the rest of the time. "A whole week! Now that's about as unusual as a snake with three tails and a dozen rattles on each one."

"Wipe that smirk off your face and try not to sound like a red-necked jackass," Reese said, but his teasing tone softened the insult.

Tex wasn't accustomed to taking offense, even

when it was intended. He laughed and continued his badgering, lighting up a non-filtered, guaranteed-extra-tar-and-nicotine cigarette. "Well, now, next thing you know, you'll be goin' on deep-sea fishing trips to Mexico, learnin' to do the hula in Hawaii, weavin' baskets in the rain forest and—"

"I'll plan my own vacation itinerary, if you don't mind," Reese said, scowling through the smoke. He shuffled the remaining papers on his desk, trying to tie up all loose ends before leaving town.

"You ain't gonna get it all done, you know," Tex said, crossing his arms over his ample belly.

"I can try." Reese knew Tex was right. In the land development business, new crises arose with every sunrise, no matter how many you had put to bed the night before. He shuddered to think what chaos would await him on his return.

"You know, buddy . . ." Tex leaned forward in the chair, his jeans squeaking against the leather. ". . . I can run the place for a week without you. Lord knows, you're God's gift to Wall Street, but we'll get along."

"You'll call if anything comes up? Anything at all?"

"I've got your pager number tattooed on my right arm, next to the heart that says 'Mom.' If I need you, I'll just pick up the nearest phone and buzz your butt. Okay?"

Reese laughed in spite of himself. "All right. I've got the point. I'm not indispensable, so get out of here and go have fun. Right?"

Tex grinned and puffed a perfect circle into the air. "I would."

"Yeah, I know *you* would. You could have fun in an airliner that was hurtling, nose first, toward the ground."

"Hey, everybody's gotta go sometime. Just lift your arms over your head, pretend you're on the world's biggest rollercoaster, and holler, 'Whee-eeee!' "

"Yeah, right."

After shaking Tex's ham-sized hand and receiving a few more instructions about how to "live it up," Reese ushered his friend out of the office. He needed a moment of privacy before he left. A moment to gather his thoughts and his resolve.

He might not be quite the daredevil that Tex boasted to be when it came to savoring life's assorted thrills, but he had never thought of himself as a coward, either. At least, not until this morning when he had opened that letter.

Picking it up from his desk, he unfolded the page and read the short message that he had already memorized. It had been written with a flamboyant, feminine hand, a scrawl that brought memories—warm and cold—to his heart. The note read:

Dear Reese,
    Your father is very ill. We need you here at the Sand Castle. Please, come quickly.
                                            Love,
                                            Joleen

Reese wasn't afraid of the world's largest roller coaster, planes crashing, volatile business negotiations, or anything else that crossed his path day by day, so why was his hand shaking as he read the letter for the thirteenth time? Why were his palms moist and cold, and his mouth dry?

He strolled over to the window of his New York City office, his dark green eyes surveying the bustling Park Avenue traffic thirty stories below.

Prime real estate. Prestige. A thriving business. More money than he knew how to spend. That meant he was successful. Right?

He had always welcomed challenges and savored dreams of the future. But the past? Reese Sullivan had hoped it was gone forever. He didn't want to remember, to experience the anger, the guilt, and the pain again, as though it had all happened the day before.

Funny, how one little letter could open the steel door of that carefully sealed vault, allowing all those demons to escape.

Yeah, really funny, he thought as he turned from the window and picked up the airline tickets from his desk. He tucked them inside his jacket and grabbed his briefcase.

But there was nothing in that case to help him face the dragons that waited for him in California.

Exactly what weapons do you use, he wondered as he left the office and headed for the elevator, *to slay the monsters from your past?*

Maybe it wasn't the dragons he was most concerned about, he realized with a pang of unwelcome self-awareness. Maybe the entity he dreaded most was a certain damsel, left behind by a rather foolish and egocentric young man. The last time Reese had seen her . . . she had definitely been a lady in distress.

And he had only himself to blame.

Two

Like a circus performer, Bridget stood, barefoot and delicately balanced on the saddle of a prancing white stallion. The carousel horse wore a jeweled bridle and a blanket covered with red and pink roses, its right front foot lifted daintily in a perpetual, flirting pose.

Every morning, before the carousel house doors were thrown open to the public, Bridget polished each of the brass poles that supported the animals. It was astonishing how many fingerprints could soil the glistening surfaces during only one day's use. Her motto: Never let it be said that the Sand Castle's carousel didn't gleam like the soul-light it ignited in the eyes of its riders.

"Bridget, I've finished with the mirrors. Can I wipe off the horses now?"

Glancing down, Bridget saw that ten-year-old Kevin Dixon had, indeed, done a fine job on the gilt-edged mirrors that decorated the center of the carousel. They were spotless. Better than she would have done herself.

Kevin was dressed in baggy, faded surfer shorts and an adult's tee shirt that swallowed his skinny body. The charming ragamuffin gazed at her through a mop of uncombed hair, the glow of infatuation shining in his chestnut eyes.

For just a moment Bridget felt a pang of guilt. She knew why he appeared every morning in the carousel house, polishing cloth in hand and an eager-to-please look on his face.

Kevin Dixon would do anything she asked, just for the opportunity to be near her. It was sweet, it was touching, and right now—with Mike in the hospital and the fund-raiser only days away—it was a tremendous help.

"Sure." She rewarded him with her warmest smile. "The horses are next. You start over there. I'll work in clockwise order, and we'll meet half-way. How's that?"

She had planned their itinerary in such a way that he would have the sacred and coveted privilege of polishing Trojan, the carousel's largest and most beautiful horse.

Classic merry-go-rounds had one special animal—called a "lead" or "king" horse—crafted and signed by the master carver himself. It was more ornate and elegant than all the rest. On this machine, the king was Trojan, a magnificent black horse clad in medieval armor.

Bridget wasn't surprised that he was Kevin's favorite. Children would wait in lines ten deep for the pleasure of sitting on Trojan's broad back.

But as she watched the boy gliding his felt cloth over the horse's gold and silver trappings, she noticed that he seemed distracted, worried, not as absorbed in his work as usual.

"So, how's it going?" she asked.

He shrugged and continued to polish. Bridget did the same to the small pinto with the flying mane and Navaho blanket.

"How's your dad?" She asked the question with a nudge of misgiving. Frank Dixon lived with his son in an RV park beside the pier. Their one-room trailer was woefully inadequate to house the twosome—as inadequate as the parental attention Frank provided for his son.

More than once, Bridget had asked Children's Protective Services to intervene on the boy's behalf. As many times, she had been told that the situation was "unfortunate, but not bad enough to take legal action."

"Frank's okay," Kevin muttered, moving to the front of the horse, where he lovingly caressed the broad chest.

Bridget had never become accustomed to the way Kevin referred to his father by his first name . . . like someone else she had known . . .

Clearing his throat, Kevin walked to the other side of Trojan, out of view, then said, "How's old Mike doin' anyway? I asked Eugene, but he just said, 'Don't know. Ain't my business and don't reckon it's yers, neither.' "

Bridget chuckled. That sounded like Eugene Lewis, the pier's ancient handyman. In his usual curt manner, he tended to be more sparing with words than he was with people's feelings.

But at least now she knew what was bothering Kevin.

"Mike's doing better," she said. "His leg is

mending, as well as can be expected. He's talking, and he's regained the use of his left hand."

"He's right-handed," Kevin replied. She could hear the sorrow and concern in his voice. Mike doted on Kevin and vice versa. Each seemed to have filled an aching space in the other's heart—one for a lost son, the other for a father.

"That's true," she said, "but you know Mike. He's a fighter. He'll spring back."

"I wish I could go see him, but they won't let kids in the hospital. I don't think it's fair."

"Neither do I." She thought for a moment. "Maybe we could work something out. I'll see what I can do."

"Really?" His head popped up from behind the horse, his eyes brighter than they had been since Mike had been taken away in the ambulance.

"No promises. But I *will* try. It would do Mike good to see you, too."

"Oh, no!" The head disappeared again behind the horse. "It's *her!* Don't tell her I'm here!"

Bridget turned around to see what had caused his reaction. But she knew, even before she spotted the blond hair plaited in perfect French braids and fastened with lace-trimmed, lavender barrettes.

"Good morning, Miss Bridget," said a sweet Georgia-peach voice that was far too sophisticated for its nine-year-old owner.

"Good morning yourself, Miss Amanda."

A living testament to her southern mama's

charm and femininity, the little girl never had a stray wisp of hair escaping from her French braids. She wore frilly dresses, white stockings, and shining black patent leather shoes, whether she was playing on the beach or on her way to Sunday school.

As impeccably groomed as Kevin was tousled, the girl sashayed into the carousel house. "Okay, where is he?" she asked in a sing-song tone. "I saw him come in here a while ago."

Bridget swallowed. "Who?"

"Who? Who? You know who."

"She sounds like a stupid owl," whispered a voice from behind the armored horse.

"I heard that!" Amanda brightened and hurried toward him.

Bridget smiled. How typical of a boy, to hide and then make sure he would be found. To hear Kevin tell the story, he hated all girls and especially this one.

"There you are!" Amanda exclaimed as she rounded the row of horses where he was hiding. Suddenly, her joy at finding him evaporated and her bottom lip protruded. She turned to Bridget. "He's polishing the horses! He's polishing *Trojan!* How come he gets to do that? It's supposed to be *my* job!"

"It ain't either your job, and you weren't here!" Kevin exclaimed. He puffed his shallow chest out proudly. "Besides, I did all the mirrors for her first, so I got to do it."

Quickly, Bridget tossed Amanda a felt cloth.

"There, you can do Rosie. She's your favorite anyway, right?"

Amanda's lip receded a bit as she glanced lovingly at Rosie, a beautiful white pony covered with garlands of roses and rows of silver bells.

"Yeah, you're a girl," Kevin said without bothering to hide his disdain. "*You* do Rosie. She's just a bunch of sissy stuff like you."

"Kevin . . ." Bridget gave him a warning glance, and he grinned.

But Amanda didn't appear to be offended. Quite the contrary, she seemed to consider being called a sissy a compliment.

For the next half-hour, Bridget watched as the twosome jockeyed for position around the circle of horses, fighting for the chance to polish their favorites, arguing over which were girl horses and which were boys.

Bridget enjoyed their banter, although she also experienced a wave of melancholy, an ache of longing. She recalled having done the same thing years ago with another young lad . . . one with sun-bleached hair and eyes the color of tourmalines.

Like Amanda, Bridget had been smitten early. Reese had been her first infatuation, the first boy to hold her hand and stroll on the beach, the first to kiss her . . . and the first to break her heart.

She seldom thought of him anymore, rarely gave him a moment's consideration. Only when she saw a young man with blond hair, or walked along the beach in the moonlight, or heard an old love song, or watched someone building a castle in the sand, or spotted an old Chevy similar to the one he had driven, or . . .

No, she scarcely remembered him at all.

But now, with Mike lying in the hospital bed, possibly never to recover completely, Mike's son seemed to be right there on the edge of her mind all the time. And with her memories so bittersweet, she wasn't sure that she welcomed his intrusion into her fantasies.

As she was finishing the last horse, closing the circle with the children, Bridget heard the door on the east side of the carousel house open and close. The sea breeze swept in, bringing with it the aroma of freshly popped corn from Tesla Montoya's concession stand next door.

Bridget paid no attention, assuming the door had been opened by Eugene, the handyman. It was time for him to arrive and help her open the carousel house for the day's business.

But after a moment, she felt someone's eyes on her, a disturbing but strangely pleasant warmth that seemed to emanate from a source behind her. Turning around, she looked into the eyes of a stranger.

He was tall, his lean body nicely filling a dark gray suit which, even to her untrained eye, appeared to be of high quality and expertly tailored. Although he was staring at her as though he knew her, she recognized nothing in the hard lines of his face, the dark emerald eyes, the thick hair the color of harvest wheat.

"Miss Bridget, that man's looking at you," she heard Amanda say as though from far away.

"Yeah, who is he?" Kevin asked.

"I don't know," Bridget replied, but even as she spoke the words, her heart was remembering what her eyes could not.

"Bridget . . . ?" His voice was deep, sensual in the way it caressed her name. But his eyes were guarded.

"Yes." She took a step toward him, and another, then she stopped and waited. For what, she wasn't sure.

There was something about those long, black lashes, the only softness that remained in a face of harsh lines and sharply cut, masculine planes. For a moment, he glanced down, a hint of shyness, a touch of vulnerability showing through the facade. A faint blush crept over his chiseled cheeks.

She knew.

"Reese?"

He lifted his eyes to hers. "I need to talk to you, Bridget, if you have a minute . . ." he said, as though having to force each word.

She drew a deep, shuddering breath, then nodded. "Yes. It's definitely time for the two of us to talk."

Reese followed Bridget up the stairs to the apartment over the carousel house. The last time he had seen her, she had been a gangly teen-ager, showing only the promise of beauty. Now the denim shorts and red tank top revealed how completely that promise had been fulfilled.

The woman four steps above him had the well-rounded calves and solid, muscular thighs of an athlete, but her body was softly curved and decidedly feminine.

Her hair hadn't changed and, for that, he was grateful. He had always been fascinated by those strawberry blond curls that danced in the wind or caught and held the California sunlight. Moonlight, too, he recalled, though he preferred not to remember that at the moment.

"You still live up here?" he asked as they approached the top of the stairs.

"Still," she replied.

He was surprised, though he realized he shouldn't be. His life had raced forward while hers seemed to have been frozen in time.

He didn't realize how much until they entered the apartment.

"This is like a time capsule. Nothing's changed since the day I left," he said, feeling a rush of bittersweet memories. "You even have your parents' furniture." He nodded toward Pat O'Dwyer's old easy chair, a tattered, overstuffed affair of green and red plaid with a matching ottoman.

"Of course," she replied. "I could never get rid of Dad's reading chair."

"Or his books?" He walked over to the nearby end table and picked up a volume by James Joyce.

"Certainly not."

Replacing the book, he glanced toward the bedroom door which stood open, revealing a white, wrought-iron bed with a royal blue duvet, topped by a snowy lace coverlet. "Your Irish grandmother's bedspread," he said softly, trying not to imagine this beautiful woman lying on that bed . . . *her* bed. Long ago, he had forfeited any chances of pursuing that path with her. For all he knew, she was . . .

He glanced down at her ring finger. No sign of a wedding band. Not even a telltale white circle or indentation of any kind.

When he raised his eyes to hers, he saw that she was staring at his hand, as well.

"I'm glad you came, Reese. It's good to see you," she said.

"Well, I got the message, and . . ." He shrugged, trying to appear nonchalant.

"You did?" Her amber eyes widened as a look of surprise and wonder crossed her face.

"Ah . . . yeah. Joleen's letter didn't say much, but—"

"Oh." She seemed almost disappointed. "I see. Joleen wrote to you." Then she chuckled. "So much for the 'two out of three' routine."

"I beg your pardon?"

"Never mind. It's just something Joleen told me during my last card reading." She motioned to a comfortable green sofa, scattered with needlepoint pillows, of the same rustic vintage as Pat O'Dwyer's chair. "Have a seat, and I'll get us a good strong pot of Irish tea."

Irish tea, he thought, *how quaint.* He hadn't

had Irish tea since . . . since Bridget's mother had served him here in this very room. Many an afternoon he had climbed the stairs to this apartment to enjoy tea and "biscuits," as Helen O'Dwyer had called the delicious, chocolate-dipped cookies she had served on a china plate delicately bordered with roses.

Almost instantly, Bridget appeared with a tray, balancing a cobalt blue china teapot, matching mugs, and the ubiquitous rose-trimmed plate with chocolate cookies.

"It's a bit early in the morning for sweets," she said, as she set the ensemble on the coffee table before him, "but it seemed the thing to do . . . you know . . . in honor of your home-coming."

So, she was remembering, too. Again, he was flattered, but somehow discomfited by the intimacy that seemed to pass so easily between them, despite the years of separation.

She sat on the sofa next to him, and for the briefest moment, her bare knee brushed his thigh. He could feel the contact through the charcoal wool, the sensation flowing through his body like a liquid hotter than the steaming tea she was pouring.

"I didn't know Joleen had written you," she said, as she handed him the mug of the strong, aromatic brew. "But I'm glad she did. I'm also glad you came."

"How is my . . . how is Mike?"

He could feel those amber eyes searching his face, though he refused to meet them.

"What did Joleen tell you about him?" she asked carefully.

He sensed she was trying to avoid hurting him; it must be worse than he had thought. "She didn't say much. Only that he was very ill. What's going on?"

Bridget took a deep breath and leaned back into the corner of the sofa, her long fingers wrapped tightly around the blue mug. "He had a stroke about two weeks ago, Reese. A bad one. And he fell off the pier onto the sand. He broke his leg just below the knee. The bottom line is: He's in the hospital, his leg in traction, and he's partially paralyzed. His right side. His speech is seriously affected and—"

"How is his mind?"

Bridget's eyes filled with tears and her lower lip trembled. "He's extremely depressed."

"I'm sure he is," Reese said. "Mike never could sit still. He's miserable if he can't be running the show."

One look at Bridget's face told him she was offended. But that was nothing new. She had always taken Mike's side. Why should things be any different now?

"I really miss him," she said, her jaw tight. "I wish he *were* here, 'running the show.' He did a lot better job than I seem to be."

"I'm sure you're doing fine," he replied, trying to smooth things over a bit. The last thing he needed right now was to make an enemy of Bridget.

He decided to backtrack; there were things he

had to know, even at the risk of alienating her. "Other than being depressed," he ventured, "how is he . . . mentally, I mean?"

"Are you asking me if he has all his carousel horses in a circle?"

He searched her face to see if she was teasing, but he couldn't be sure.

"Yeah, I guess that's one way to put it. Is he . . . is he mentally competent?"

Her eyes narrowed. "To do what?"

Shrugging his shoulders, he tried to appear nonchalant. But it wasn't easy. He could feel his face growing hotter by the moment, and he could hear his pulse pounding in his ears. He cleared his throat. "Oh, I don't know . . . whatever . . ."

"All he has to do right now is lie there in that hospital bed and get better," she replied. "I'd say he's still got enough between his ears to accomplish that."

All of a sudden, the tea wasn't settling well and Reese decided it was time to end this conversation. He placed the mug on the tray and stood.

"Is Mike still living in the apartment over the arcade?" he asked, walking toward the head of the stairs.

"Of course he is," she said.

"Of course," he echoed. "Nothing ever changes around this place."

She stood and folded her arms across her chest. "Maybe we don't want things to change. Maybe we like them just the way they are."

"Things always change, Bridget. It's a fact of life. People change."

"*Some* people change. Whether you want them to or not."

He decided to leave that one alone. "I need a set of keys to Mike's apartment," he said, abruptly changing the subject. "I'll be staying for a while."

She stared at him for what seemed like a long time, then turned, walked to an old oak cupboard, and took out a set of keys. Tossing them to him, she said, "I promised Kevin, one of the local kids, that I'd try to get him in to see Mike at the hospital this evening. Do you want to come along?"

"What time?"

"About six."

He nodded. His throat felt constricted, as though he were hanging from a lamppost by his Hermes silk tie. "Okay. See you then."

When he had taken four steps down the staircase, he heard her say softly, "Thanks, Reese. Thank you for coming. It's going to mean the world to Mike."

He didn't trust himself to look back at her, to meet those eyes that seemed to look straight through him. So he kept walking . . . only faster. "Yeah, sure," he said over his shoulder. "No problem."

Three

Bridget didn't like hospitals. Certainly, she realized that they were necessary, a God-sent blessing when you needed them. But she didn't like walking into the imposing white building, spending time inside those pale blue walls, or walking those highly polished floors that squeaked beneath her sneaker soles. Mostly, she couldn't bear the thought of anyone she loved needing to be here.

But today she had Kevin on one side of her and Reese on the other as she headed down the hallway toward Room 307, and their presence was comforting. It wasn't that she didn't want to see Mike. She did. But it was so difficult to witness his helplessness. Having Reese and Kevin along made her feel less alone, and she was grateful.

On the ride over in her Land Rover, Reese had kept up a steady patter of conversation with Kevin. They had debated the pros and cons of their favorite baits, hooks, and casting techniques. Reese had agreed with the boy that "prissy" girls were a pain, and surfing was the only thing on the face of the planet better than fishing.

Bridget was surprised and touched at how much attention Reese had paid to the boy, who was starved for male companionship. Although Reese had admitted to Kevin that he wasn't married and had no children—a question which Bridget had been reluctant to ask herself—Reese seemed at ease with the boy. Much more at ease than with her.

"Well, here we are," Bridget said as they approached Mike's room. She couldn't wait to see Mike's expression when he looked upon his son's face for the first time in so many years. She was already anticipating his joy.

Reese hesitated, then placed his hand on her forearm. His touch was warm and firm, imparting a strength that was welcome.

"Bridget," he said, his green eyes dark with emotion as he stared at the closed door, "you and Kevin go ahead. I'm going to find the doctor and have a chat with him about Mike's condition. Let's say we meet downstairs in the main lobby in . . ." He glanced at his watch. ". . . Thirty minutes or so?"

"What are you talking about?" Bridget glanced down at Kevin, who looked as confused as she felt.

"Aren't you going to say 'hi' to your dad?" the boy asked.

"Later," Reese said. "For now, I just want to talk to the doc. See you guys later."

He disappeared around the corner, leaving a

heavy silence between Bridget and Kevin . . . and an even heavier stone in her heart.

Once again, Reese had run away—from his father, from her, from those who loved and needed him.

"Why should I be surprised?" she muttered.

"What?" Kevin was watching her carefully.

Bridget could tell that he was waiting for her reaction to see if he should be angry at Reese on her behalf. After only a moment's consideration, she decided to let the boy off the hook emotionally. Just seeing Mike was going to be hard enough on the kid, without her being out of sorts.

Thanks, Reese, for nothing, she thought, sending the thought down the hall after him. She imagined her words giving him a swift boot in the rear when they caught up with him. *Who needed you anyway?*

Mike needed Reese. That was evident by the hurt look in his eyes when Kevin mentioned that Reese had come to the hospital with them.

"What the lad said . . . is it true, Bridie?" Mike asked, his lips twisting awkwardly as he fought to speak in a normal way with only the left half of his body responding as it should. In spite of his challenge, the charming Irish brogue remained. "Is my boy back in town?"

"Yes, Mike. He arrived this morning." She reached for Mike's right hand and squeezed it, but, as it had been since the stroke, she felt no response.

His Irishman's complexion was usually ruddy and robust, his skin crinkled from too many years in the California sun. But he looked sallow, an unhealthy shade of gray against the stark white of the hospital pillowslip. Every one of the few remaining red hairs on his head stuck straight up, but that was nothing out of the ordinary for Mike Sullivan. Vanity had never been a prominent trait in his character.

"Well, if my Reese is here, why isn't he *here* with the father that loves him so?" he asked, his heart shining in his eyes.

"He will be," Bridget replied with a conviction she didn't feel.

"And when will that be?"

"Soon, Mike. Soon. He was anxious to talk to your doctor, to find out how you're doing."

Mike sighed deeply, as though having just accomplished some exhausting task. He twisted slightly on the bed, but the cast on his leg and the sling from which it was suspended limited his movement. He grimaced from the pain—whether from his leg or his emotions, Bridget couldn't tell. "I'd think . . ." he said, ". . . that if he truly wanted to know how I was doing, he'd come in here and see for himself."

"He will, Mike. Really, he will. I promise." She turned to Kevin. "I think we'd better go now. Mike looks like he needs to take a nap."

"It seems that's all I'm about these days,"

Mike mumbled, his eyes fluttering closed. "Take naps, take pills, take more naps . . ."

As Bridget guided a troubled Kevin from the room, she thought of her promise to Mike. Reese *was* going to come in here and see his father. If she had to light a fire under him that was hot enough to singe those fancy clothes.

Shaking the water from her hair, Bridget walked across the cool sand, picked up a giant beach towel, and wrapped it around her waist. The sun had sunk behind the hills, which were now black silhouettes against a peach and turquoise sky. A perfect California postcard sunset. She shivered as a twilight-cool breeze swept over her damp skin, chilling her even through her swimsuit.

Any minute now, Eugene Lewis would announce that the swimmers were to leave the water for their own safety. In another hour, the pier's shops, arcade, and carousel house would close. The merchants would empty their cash registers and count the receipts. The restaurant and food concession owners would begin to scrub and disinfect every gleaming, stainless steel surface.

Fishermen would have to leave, settling for their day's catch, lovers would abandon the benches where they had watched the sunset together, and tired, sunburned children would trudge home, reluctant to surrender their sand castles to the tides.

Bridget knew how they felt. With the end of such a beautiful day, she always experienced a slight feeling of loss. Lately, she had come to realize that such a feeling—this deep appreciation for every minute, hour, and day of life—was the closest thing to a definition of "happiness" that she had ever found.

Tonight, as on most evenings, she was infinitely grateful for the life she led.

"Is sundown still your favorite time of day?"

Bridget looked up, searching the pier above her for the male voice that had called down to her. She knew its owner before she saw him, lounging against the rail, a fishing pole in his hands.

For a moment, the years rolled away and she saw the scruffy young man Reese had been back then. The tee shirt and cut-offs were the same. So were the battered sneakers. His golden hair, which had been carefully combed earlier that day, had succumbed to the salt wind and was hanging in his eyes, like that of any ordinary surf bum.

"Yes, I still love the sunsets," she called back as she pulled on her leather sandals and headed for the stairs that led from the beach to the boardwalk. "And I see you're still dedicated to holding up that rail."

"Hey, somebody's gotta keep it from floating out to sea . . ." he replied. Then, in a lower tone she barely heard, he added, ". . . like the rest of this decrepit structure."

Bridget felt her temper start to flare, but

fought to keep it down. Dealing with Mike's illness had taken a toll on her nerves, and she didn't have the energy to argue with Reese anymore. Besides, she wasn't inclined to start a fight that she might not win. She had lost enough battles lately.

Five days had passed, and still Reese hadn't seen his father, in spite of her shaming, blaming, and cajoling. Finally, she had given up and resigned herself to the fact that Reese would visit Mike only when he was ready. If he was ever ready. She was beginning to have doubts.

These past days, the atmosphere had been rather tense between them with few civil words exchanged. She was surprised that he was speaking to her so freely now.

It was the fishing, she decided as she reached the top of the stairs. The simple act of casting a line into the sea seemed to bring out the best in a man's personality.

"Any luck?" she asked.

"Now, Bridie . . . it isn't what you catch that counts," he said, reeling in his line. A bare hook dangled at the end. "It's the quiet communion with nature, the spiritual renewal, the opportunity for soulful reflection, the—"

"So, in other words, you haven't caught a single fish."

He sighed. "Not a stinking thing."

Securing his hook to the pole, he reached for his tackle box. "Now, that kid over there—" He pointed a thumb in Kevin's direction. The boy stood at the end of the pier, reeling in yet another perch to add to the growing pile, flipping and flapping, at his bare feet. "The fish are practically hopping onto his hook. But you can tell by looking at him that he's not into the Zen of it. He's just catching those fish for fun, not for deep meditation purposes. What a shame."

Bridget snickered. "Yeah, ain't it awful."

Rod in one hand, tackle box in the other, Reese paused to look down at her, and his smile nearly took her breath away.

Oh, yes, she remembered now why she had loved him so much. Reese had a soft, humorous, affectionate side that had touched her young heart. After the loss of her parents, his kindness and companionship had made all the difference. She had desperately needed a best friend, and Reese had stepped into the role without hesitation, helping to fill the terrible void.

Unfortunately, she also remembered why her heart had broken when he had left so abruptly. The emptiness she had experienced because of his abandonment had been profound. It still echoed through her spirit, causing her to guard her heart with everyone, especially men.

"Will you walk me back to the shed?" he asked, his voice softer than she had heard it since he had arrived.

"Sure."

They strolled across the pier, toward Silas Vincent's bait and tackle shop. A retired merchant marine, Silas no longer went out to sea, but he lived as close as he could, here on the wharf jutting out over the ocean he loved.

Bridget waved and Reese nodded as they passed his shop. As usual, the old sailor sat in a wicker chair on the porch, mending rods, his supplies strewn around his feet. A slight quirk of one bushy white eyebrow was all the acknowledgment they received. Silas wasn't exactly known as Mr. Hospitality on the pier.

As long as Bridget had known him, Silas had worn a tattered white tee shirt, equally worn khaki slacks, and a battered pair of navy blue deck shoes that exposed his little toes on either side and the tips of his big toes. His weather-withered cheeks always sported a short stubble of beard. On his nearly bald head sat a faded Greek fisherman's hat, sprouting a wide assortment of lures.

"Did you ever wonder," Reese said when they had rounded the corner of the shop and were out of earshot, "how he always keeps his beard that length? He must shave it once in a while, or it would be down to his belt buckle by now. But you never see him clean-shaven."

"I know. And his clothes. He's worn the same outfit for at least twenty years. Those shoes and the tee shirt never seem to fall apart and you never see him in anything new."

"Amazing."

They reached the back of the tackle shop and the "shed," a ramshackle structure that housed tools and supplies for the pier's upkeep. Bridget was surprised to see that Reese still remembered the combination on the rusty old lock. He spun the tumblers deftly, then yanked it apart. The door squeaked as he pulled it open. He grimaced at the noise, and Bridget felt slightly embarrassed.

For a long time, she had known that the pier was in a state of disrepair. It was simply too much work for so few people. But since Reese's arrival, she had been even more acutely aware, seeing it through his eyes.

As he stowed his gear, Bridget decided to take advantage of his openness and press for some answers to questions that had haunted her for a long time.

"The old characters around here . . ." she began tentatively, ". . . did you miss them while you were gone?"

He paused for a moment, his back to her. Then he closed the door and secured the lock before answering.

"The characters?" he said softly, still not looking at her.

"Yeah. You know, Silas and Eugene, and Madame Joleen. I mean, they were all here when you were growing up. They were an important part of your childhood. I was just wondering if you . . ."

Her voice trailed away as she realized how terribly transparent her question was.

He turned to face her, and she was puzzled by his expression, a mixture of sorrow and something that looked like guilt.

"Of course I missed them, Bridget." Reaching out, he trailed his fingers along one of the damp, copper-gold curls that lay on her shoulder. "I missed you all, very much. Did you think I didn't?"

The unexpected caress was deeply unsettling. She wanted to push his hand away, and, in the same moment, pull him closer. Exercising all of her self-control, she did neither.

"I had no way of knowing," she replied with a shrug. Turning away, she walked over to the edge of the pier and stared across the water to the town of Buena Yerba. The city's buildings, with their ivory stucco walls and Spanish-tiled roofs, lay between the blue Pacific and the background of the black mountains. Orange and red rays from the setting sun glistened on a thousand windows, until the structures looked like braziers filled with glowing coals.

Reese walked up behind her and stood, too close for comfort. The crowd milled nearby, some visitors leaving, others buying snacks and wandering into the shops and the arcade. For once, Bridget resented their presence. This moment was difficult enough without having to share it with the public.

Several people glanced their way as they passed. Bridget was well-known and loved by the pier's frequent guests, and she knew they were wondering about this handsome fellow. Why was he standing so close to her? Why they were speaking so intimately?

The cool breeze swept around her, but the chill was gone. Her skin seemed inflamed and she was certain that her cheeks must be glowing even in the diminished light. Blushing was the curse of the redhead.

"I know I must have hurt you badly, Bridget," he was saying. She could feel his breath warm on her cheek. "Believe me, it wasn't intentional. Can you forgive me?"

She thought the question over carefully, then said, "Maybe, if I understood why you did it."

He sighed and leaned both hands on the rail, staring out at the darkening waters. "This place . . . everyone here . . . the things that happened in my childhood . . . I couldn't separate them. You were all pieces of the fabric of my 'previous' life. If I turned my back on one part, I had to leave the rest behind, too. Does that make sense to you?"

"But why did you have to leave *any* of us behind?"

His face hardened and she felt him withdraw. "We've been through that before, Bridget. I know you think Mike Sullivan is a saint, but you have to understand that I see him differently. My experiences with him weren't the same as yours."

Bridget thought of Mike and all the work he had done to improve his life in the past twelve years. Her temper rose, along with the heat in her cheeks.

"Mike was mentally ill," she snapped.

"He was a drunk."

"It's the same difference. The alcohol altered his brain chemistry. It made him a different person from the one he really is."

"Stop making excuses for him, Bridget. He put the bottle to his own lips and swigged the booze all by himself. He was responsible for his drinking and for what he did under the influence."

"Of course he was, and he realizes that now. Reese, give your dad some credit; he's been sober since the night you left."

"Impeccable timing. The minute I leave, he decides to become a human being."

Bridget stared at him, not wanting to believe the depth of resentment she saw in his eyes. But it was there, distorting his handsome face and making him look much older and more careworn than his years.

"Bitterness doesn't become you, Reese," she said softly.

"Maybe not, but you had good parents. You only saw Mike's 'company' manners. You don't know what he was like when everyone else was gone and it was just Mom and me."

"I know about the abuse. The physical stuff, the verbal assaults, the emotional neglect. Your dad wasn't that good at hiding it."

"Then why are you standing here preaching to me?"

Yes, she thought, why was she? Obviously, he didn't intend to hear anything she said. And besides, he might be right. Maybe she didn't know what she was talking about.

"All right, Reese," she said, gathering her towel more tightly around her. Suddenly, she felt colder and more tired than she had in days. "I have no right to judge you. I'm sorry. But I do know one thing: You can live in the past all you want, but the past never changes. No matter how much time you spend there, going over and over the things that happened, it never gets better."

She reached out and laid her hand on his arm, half expecting him to jerk it away. But he didn't.

"I . . ." She had almost said she loved him, but caught herself just in time. He wasn't the only one who had learned to guard his heart. "I'm very fond of you, and I hate to see you waste your energy on something so destructive. I need you, the pier needs you, Mike needs you. If you have fiery emotions to burn, please kindle them for the present, or the future. Don't let all that passion go to waste."

A second later, he had placed his hands on her shoulders, pulled her to him, and captured her lips with his. The kiss was far different from the ones they had stolen beneath the boardwalk years ago. The heat of it burned through her body, taking away the chill of the night and her breath with it.

Shocked, she didn't respond at first. But soon, she felt her lips, her hands, her entire body answering his. Heedless of passersby, the argument they had just had, the years of feeling abandoned, she circled his waist with her arms and clung to him, drawing the heat from his embrace and returning it with her own.

Finally, he released her and she had to grab for the rail to support herself. He chuckled and said in a deep, teasing tone, "No, we wouldn't want the passion to go to waste."

Then he turned and walked away, leaving her with weak knees and a flush on her cheeks that felt redder than her hair.

"That wasn't exactly what I meant," she said, when she had recovered her ability to breathe. But by then, he was long out of sight.

Four

"Just who does that man think he is anyway?" Bridget grabbed Madame Joleen by her red and purple paisley sleeve and pulled her aside from the crowd gathering in the carousel house. "Reese calls a meeting! A meeting of *my* people! And he doesn't even bother to mention it to me first!"

"*Your* people? Oh . . . so we belong to *you* now?" The fortune-teller's tone was soft and teasing, her dark eyes alight with mischief. But Bridget wasn't in the mood for humor—good-natured or otherwise.

"You know what I mean. This pier and the people who work on it are *my* responsibility. He's got a lot of nerve asking them to assemble like this without telling me what it's all about."

Silas Vincent—ears perpetually perked for any tidbit of gossip—was pretending not to be eavesdropping. Along with the other vendors, he sat on one of the metal folding chairs in a semicircle beside the carousel, waiting for Reese to appear. Even Tesla Montoya was watching Bridget and Joleen, her pretty face alert with interest.

As Amanda's parents, Constance and George

Weber, took seats beside Tesla, Joleen dropped her voice to a discreet whisper. "Did you ask him why he called the meeting? I've always found that asking is the best way to receive an answer to a question that's bothering me."

Bridget snorted. "Of course that's best, Jo. Give me a little credit here. I would have asked him—while I was strangling him, that is—if I'd been able to get my hands on him. But since His Royal Highness issued the imperial edict yesterday afternoon, Reese has been conspicuously absent."

"So, you haven't seen gorgeously tanned hide nor sunbleached hair of him, eh?"

Joleen's smirk irritated Bridget to the soles of her sneakers. "Just because he's gorgeous doesn't mean he isn't a pain in the rear, Joleen. I don't think your priorities are exactly in order."

"Well, now, if you ask me what I think . . ." drawled a voice nearby. Bridget turned to see that Eugene had insinuated himself into their conversation. He stood behind Bridget, leaning on the wall, sucking a toothpick and jingling the change in his pockets.

"I don't recall anybody pulling your chain," Joleen replied bluntly. "If we want your opinion, we'll ask for it."

"I'm gonna give it to ya anyhow." He moved the pick to the other side of his mouth. "I think it's got somethin' to do with all that pokin' around that Reese's been doin' these last few days."

"Poking around?" Bridget said, her anxiety level rising.

"Yep. I seen him under the boardwalk, checkin' out the pilings, givin' 'em the old eagle eye. Even put on a scuba outfit and dove off the end, he did."

"When?" Bridget asked.

" 'Bout eleven minutes after nine yesterday mornin'."

"Could you possibly be more specific?" Joleen asked sarcastically. She had never made any effort to hide her dislike of the surly handyman. On more than one occasion, she had expressed to Bridget that she considered him an interfering, nosy busybody. Bridget believed that the core of Joleen's resentment was the fear that her position of "Head Busybody" on the Sand Castle Pier was in danger of being usurped.

"Didn't you take any notes about the make and model of his scuba gear?" Joleen said.

He gave her a blank look.

"Well?" she pressed. "What kind of detective are you, anyway?"

He scowled but said nothing, for which Bridget was grateful. At least Joleen's and Eugene's arguments seldom lasted more than a couple of exchanges. Eugene simply couldn't keep up.

"Looks like we're going to find out soon," Bridget said as Reese sauntered through the door, acting like he owned the place.

For some reason, the memory of his kiss came rushing back to her, but she angrily pushed the thought away. Okay, so he could kiss like a dream . . . he was still up to something, and her intuition told her she wasn't going to like it.

"Good evening," he said, as he stood in front of the small semicircle of attendees. Casting a brief, noncommittal glance at Bridget, Joleen, and Eugene, he said, "If you would all please take your seats now, I'd like to get straight to the point."

"Yes, please do," Bridget said in a loud, clear, and irritated voice as she reluctantly did his bidding. "We all have responsibilities. We don't exactly have time to sit around and chat." She felt all eyes turn toward her and saw the surprise and curiosity registered there.

"I realize that," he said, "and I want everyone to know how much I appreciate you showing up like this. I won't take long—I promise."

His tone was so conciliatory, so kind and considerate, that he made her look like a jerk for being angry. For the moment she buried her displeasure. This might not be the time or place, but she would get even with him, sooner or later.

Sitting on the chair, she felt the cold metal against the backs of her thighs and wished she had changed from her shorts and tee shirt into slacks and a nice blouse. For once, her casual attire made her feel vulnerable. She was acutely aware that she didn't appear as "professional" as the urbane gentleman standing before them in his fancy sports jacket, linen slacks, and oxford shirt.

Besides, for some reason she couldn't explain, she suddenly felt cold, even though the room was quite comfortable. She crossed her arms over her chest and sat, staring at him, defying him to say anything she didn't like.

It didn't take long.

"I've known some of you for years . . . all my life," he was saying in that warm, winning tone that she was sure was a facade. "Some of you I've only met recently. But I can tell you are all good people, dedicated to this place and trying to make a living for yourselves and your families."

He took a couple of steps closer. Even with her pulse throbbing and her face burning with irritation, Bridget had to admit that he had presence. She could feel everyone in the room gravitating toward him.

"I understand what a hardship my father's illness has caused for you, and I feel obliged to help in any way I can."

"We're doing fine," Bridget said without thinking how rude she appeared by interrupting him. The eyes that turned briefly in her direction weren't particularly friendly.

"Yes, I'm sure you are," he replied, but he didn't even turn to glance her way when he said the words. Ignoring her, he continued, "And I want to do everything I can to make certain that you continue to do well. That's why I feel it is my duty to tell you of some concerns that I have."

He paused, took a deep breath, and plunged ahead. "I don't suppose it's any secret that this place is in a desperate state of disrepair. Thanks to the ravages of nature and years of extreme neglect . . ."

Bridget's fury soared and she could hardly hold her tongue. How *dare* he criticize the up- keep of this pier when he hadn't even shown his face in twelve years!

". . . As a result, the entire structure has eroded to a point where—in my professional opinion as an engineer and building devel- oper—it can no longer be salvaged."

The people in the chairs uttered a collective gasp. Madame Joleen muttered, "Oh, dear," and Eugene spat out a couple of expletives along with his toothpick.

"What are you saying?" Bridget jumped up from her chair, knocking it over backward in the process. It fell to the floor with a loud, metallic clatter.

"I'm saying that, for the safety of everyone here and the public at large, this pier needs to be demolished."

"That is absurd!" Bridget could hear the shrill tone of her own voice and realized she was screaming at him. But she didn't care. "The city sends an engineer out here every six months to check for stability, and after every major storm or earth tremor. They say there is certainly room for improvement, but the pier is fundamentally sound. Are you telling us that you know more than they do?"

He shrugged and gave her what she consid- ered a condescending smile. "I'm afraid so. It is quite possible that I have more experience in this field than the city's representatives. And if they consider this structure safe, I must say that I *do* know more than they do."

Bridget looked down to see that every face had turned toward her. These people, her friends, were frightened and looking to her for reassurance. She was quick to supply it as effectively as she could.

"We know that the Sand Castle needs some repairs . . . expensive repairs. That's why we organized a fund-raising benefit to help get the work started. The city council is providing the necessary promotion and—"

"Excuse me, Bridget." He held up one hand and shook his head sadly. "But the kind of repairs I'm talking about aren't going to be subsidized by one beach party fund-raiser. This structure simply isn't worth the fortune it would take to restore it to viability."

"Yeah . . . well . . . says you!"

Bridget blushed, as much from embarrassment as anger. In some sane, less enraged corner of her consciousness, she realized that she probably looked like a petulant five-year-old, standing there with her hands on her hips, feet spread, glaring at him. And unfortunately, when she was furious, her vocabulary seemed to desert her.

"A lot you know about it, Mr. Reese Sullivan!" *Boy, now that was telling him,* she thought with a sinking feeling. But she felt obliged to continue. "You come waltzing in here, the big shot contractor from New York City, and you have the gall to tell us that our pier isn't worth fixing.

Well, maybe it isn't worth it to you, but it is to us. So, just . . . butt out!"

For what seemed like forever, they stood there, staring at each other, Bridget red-faced, huffing and puffing, and Reese, as cool and collected as she was angry. Finally, he lifted both hands in surrender and shrugged his broad shoulders.

"Have it your way, Bridget," he said quietly. "I just thought I should offer a professional assessment of the situation . . . as I see it, of course. I wish you the best of luck with your fund-raiser and your restoration efforts."

She could hear his unspoken addition: "You're going to need it."

Two days later, Bridget realized that there might have been some truth in what Reese had said. But that worry didn't bear close examination. With the opening of the festival less than twelve hours away, her stress level was high enough already.

As she stood beside the carousel, admiring the meticulous polishing she and the children had given it earlier in the evening, her spirits rose a tad.

Tomorrow was the day. In twenty-four hours she would know if their efforts had been successful, if the money would be available to begin the repairs.

One more spin, she told herself with a satisfied smile, *just for luck.*

Long ago, she had formed the opinion that

there was nothing like a carousel ride to assure good fortune.With a flick of her wrist, she threw the lever which activated the magnificent machine. Jumping aboard, she zigzagged through the leaping animals to Trojan, then swung herself up on his broad back.

The great beast rose and fell in wave-like rhythm with the other horses to the hauntingly beautiful music of "Lara's Theme."

Closing her eyes, Bridget gripped the horse with her knees, moving with him, feeling the joy of being one with this marvelous mechanism.

Suddenly, a horrific, rending sound tore through the room. The carousel ground to a stop so abruptly that Bridget was thrown forward and nearly fell from her horse.

"Ow!" she shouted as her forehead banged against the brass pole. Then she uttered another curse as the reality of what had just happened struck her with more painful force than the pole.

"No! No, it can't be . . ."

She slid off Trojan's back and stumbled over to the housing in the center of the carousel. Throwing the door open, she peered inside, dreading what she knew she would find.

Only one thing could have made a deafening roar like that—metal grinding against metal.

One of the most integral parts of the motor, the drive shaft, had broken, snapped completely in two. Her heart sank as she fell to her knees and examined the hopelessly severed rod. Three inches thick and over seven feet long, the shaft of an antique carousel was a specialty item that was almost impossible to replace. And the machine could not operate without it.

This had happened once, years ago, when she was only a child. Her father and Mike Sullivan had considered it a catastrophe then, and it was no less so now.

"What is it, Bridget? What's wrong?"

She turned to see Kevin standing behind her. Tears of exhaustion and defeat sprang to her eyes, but she blinked them back for his sake.

"It's the drive shaft, Kev," she said, as evenly as possible, pointing out the problem. "It's snapped."

"What does that mean?" he asked, running his finger over the broken piece.

She drew a deep breath and looked at her watch. Nine-thirty in the evening. It was too late to begin the search that would probably take weeks.

"It means," she said, "that the carousel won't be running tomorrow."

"But it *has* to! It's the best thing on the pier! Everybody will want to ride it and if they can't . . ."

"I know."

"But . . . but . . . can't you fix it?"

"I'm afraid not. If we were to weld it, the mend would never hold. That shaft turns the entire weight of the carousel. It has to be extremely strong. Repairs are out of the question."

"Wow . . ." Kevin plopped down on the floor,

looking as dejected as she felt. "That's really awful."

"Ah, it could be worse," she said, realizing how lame her feeble attempt at consolation sounded.

"How?"

"Never say that again, Kevin." She reached down and tousled his already-mussed hair. "Never, never ask how things can get worse."

"Why not?"

"I'm not sure," she said with a sigh. "But it's a rule. Trust me. It's a *very* important rule."

Reese had decided to call it an early night and settle down with a good mystery novel before bedtime. It had been a long day . . . for everyone on the pier.

From dawn until well after dark, he had watched with agitated frustration as the pier's residents prepared for the fund-raising party.

Dreamers. Pie-in-the-sky dreamers. That's all they were. He could see that their efforts were futile.

Reese could foresee the future of the pier, and he didn't need Madame Joleen's crystal ball. His training and experience were enough.

But Bridget and the others wouldn't listen to anything they didn't want to hear . . . just like someone else he had known.

Yes, he had been down this road before with a dreamer, and the path was becoming well worn. As a child he had been forced to live in a fantasy land . . . Mike's fantasy. But as an adult, Reese had escaped all that. And even if his reality was dull and colorless compared to Mike's grandiose dreams, at least his world was stable, predictable . . . real.

Twenty years ago, he had stopped believing in magic. And he never missed it. Well, hardly ever.

He had just slipped off his shoes and poured himself a final cup of coffee when he heard the soft sound of knocking on his father's apartment door.

When he opened it, he felt a slight twinge of disappointment that his caller wasn't Bridget. It was just as well, he decided. These days, when they got together all they did was yell at each other like a couple of kids.

Not unlike the one standing outside his door.

"Kevin, what are you doing out of bed?" he asked, ushering the boy inside.

"Oh, I don't have a real bedtime," he replied with subdued enthusiasm. "Dad lets me do whatever I want."

That's too bad, Reese thought, but he kept his observation and opinion to himself.

"In that case, why are you here?" he asked, studying the boy's distressed expression. "What's up?"

"I think we need your help."

"We? Who's *we?*"

"Well, Bridget and me."

"I see." Reese walked over to his father's recliner and sat down, waving the boy toward the sofa. But Kevin refused the seat with a shake of his head. "Did Bridget send you?"

"Oh, no way! She'd be madder than a wet hen if she knew I was here. She said that nobody could fix it . . . the problem, that is. Not her, not you, not nobody."

"Not anybody," Reese gently corrected.

"That's right. Not anybody neither."

Reese felt the white knight rising inside him, that irresistible urge to rescue damsels in distress, whether they wanted to be rescued or not.

"So, Kevin, my man . . . tell me all about this insurmountable problem of Bridget's."

As the boy began to explain about the broken drive shaft, a plan began to form in Reese's brain. And with it came a sense of satisfaction that—he had to confess—had little to do with chivalry.

If he were honest, Reese would have to admit he wasn't all that interested in rescuing a fair maiden. His main objective was to show Miss High-and-Mighty O'Dwyer that he was one step ahead of her.

At least this once.

"You're going to owe me big time for this one, Sullivan," Dave Porter said as he removed his welding mask and wiped the sweat off his brow with the sleeve of his denim shirt. "I don't stay up all night, working like a danged junkyard dog, for just anybody, you know."

"I *do* know," Reese said. "And believe me, I appreciate it."

Reese bent over and examined the job so far.

Not bad. At midnight, they had started with the drive shaft from an old Ford flatbed truck. And now, five hours later, thanks to Dave's almost magical skills as a machinist, they had nearly transformed the part into a reasonable replacement.

"Yeah, yeah, talk's cheap. How *much* do you appreciate it?" Dave said teasingly. "That's what I want to know."

"I thought you were just doing this for old time's sake," Reese said with a grin, recalling the nights he and Dave had spent in Dave's father's garage, assembling old jalopies into semi-viable transportation. Back then, they had spun dreams about opening a restoration shop together. But they had taken different directions, and this was the first time he had seen or spoken to Dave Porter in all those years.

"Old time's sake?" Dave said with a snort. "Dream on, pal."

"Oh well, it was worth a try. I suppose you want cold, hard cash."

"Nope."

"Nope?"

Dave peeled off his welder's gloves and threw them onto his workbench. "That's right. I work all day long for money. I only stay up all night for love."

Reese lifted one eyebrow. "Say what?"

"It's gonna take more than cash to redeem this little jewel." He pointed proudly to his handiwork.

"Okay, what do you want?"

"Remember that '56 Chevy you were restoring?" he said slyly. Reluctantly, Reese nodded. "Where is it now?"

"I still have it. It's in a garage across town, been there for years. Why?"

A broad smile nearly bisected Dave's plump face.

Reese shook his head. "Now *you're* the one who's dreaming, buddy. I'm not giving you my Chevy in exchange for one lousy drive shaft."

"Hey, I took it out of that old truck, I cut it down to size, I welded the gear onto the end, I'm gonna help you install it, I—"

"I'll install it myself, thank you. You don't get my Chevy. That's it—that's all."

Dave shrugged. "Oh, well, it was worth a try."

He looked so disappointed that Reese couldn't stand it. The last time he had seen that hangdog expression on Dave's face had been when Sally Thomas had refused to go to a homecoming dance with him.

"All right . . ." Reese began, "you can—"

"Really?"

"No! But you can drive it."

"How long?"

"Six months."

"A year?"

"Nine months."

"Deal."

Reese had hauled Kevin out of his trailer at dawn and brought him to the carousel house. It had seemed only right that the boy witness the triumph.

Reese held his breath. "Okay, Kev . . . throw the switch and let's see what happens."

Kevin reached out one hand, then paused. "Did you, you know, take care of what we talked about?"

"That little . . . alteration . . . that you requested?"

"Yeah."

"I sure did."

"Wow! All right!" With a trembling hand, Kevin pulled the lever. "Here we go!" he shouted. "Let 'er rip!"

Upstairs, Bridget was wakened from a restless sleep by the sound of . . . no, it couldn't be . . . but it was!

The carousel!

Throwing on a robe, she bounded down the stairs, two at a time.

As she ran into the main room, her eyes saw what her heart had been praying for. The carousel was working. Beautifully. Spinning smoothly and effortlessly. In fact, it was . . . something was different.

"It's working!" she yelled to Reese and Kevin, who were sitting atop horses, whirling around at an almost breathless speed.

"It works," she whispered, walking toward the machine in a daze, not daring to believe. "How did you . . . what did you . . . ?"

"Does it matter?" Reese shouted as he whirled past.

"No, not at all. But . . ."

She was becoming dizzy just watching. Something was different. Very different.

"It's *fast!*" she said, as they whizzed past again, a blur of light and color.

"I know!" Kevin yelled gleefully, clinging to his mount. "I told Reese it was too slow . . . an old ladies' ride. So, he changed the gears. Cool, huh?"

"Ah . . . yeah, guys . . ." She gulped, swallowed, then grinned. "Really cool."

Five

If Bridget had custom-ordered the weather, she couldn't have chosen a more beautiful Southern California day for the Sand Castle Beach Party. A million diamonds sparkled on the turquoise tide, mingling with the lacy whitecaps that washed in rhythmic waves onto the golden shore. "Faeries' diamonds," her mother had called them. Bridget's superstitious Irish soul was convinced that only good things could happen on a day when the faeries scattered their gems across the sea.

The cloudless blue sky was filled with colorful kites, Frisbees, volleyballs, the laughter of children, and the aroma of the concessions' delectables. Standing on the ocean end of the pier, Bridget surveyed the crowded boardwalk, the packed shops and buzzing arcade, and the beach that was nearly covered with towels and browning bodies in fluorescent swimsuits.

The city police officers patrolled the boardwalk on bicycles, occasionally stopping to give directions and advice to the visitors. And the multitudes of fishermen, fisherwomen and fisherkids seemed to be having a great day. The pier was aflop with their plentiful catches.

At the opposite end of the wharf, the carousel house was encircled with an even longer than usual line of customers—ages eight months to eighty years—waiting their turn to ride.

Thanks to Reese.

Yes, thanks to Reese, she admitted with only a smidgen of resentment. She was delighted that he had solved her problem . . . and a bit peeved. The most important thing was that the carousel was spinning. That was all that mattered. She only wished someone other than Reese had found the solution. Right now, she didn't want to give him credit for anything.

"It appears that your fund-raiser is a rousing success," said a familiar voice behind her. "Congratulations."

She turned to see that Reese had materialized out of her thoughts. As usual, he was propped against the railing on one elbow, an easy smile on his face. In his cut-off jeans, black tank top, and deck shoes, he looked like any other gorgeous beach bum.

"Thanks," she said, feeling less irritated than she wanted to. No matter what he did, she had never been able to stay angry for long.

"I just had lunch at George's and Constance's, and their cash register was ringing constantly," he said. "And almost everybody on the beach is enjoying one of Tesla's waffle cones."

Looking around, Bridget was pleased, for once, to admit he was right. All of the concessions were doing gangbusters business. And with the special pier admission fee, they were raking in the much-needed revenue for the overdue repairs.

"I was wrong," he continued, glancing down at the toe of his deck shoe. "It looks like you're going to pull it off, after all."

"Thank you again," she said. "I know it can't be easy for you to admit that."

"Easier than you think. I'm truly happy for you . . . for everyone here." He paused to study the families nearby, as they cast their lines into the ocean, chatting with each other, enjoying the pier, the sunshine, and—most importantly—each other's company. "It's a good thing, this pier," he said softly. "It's important. For the people who live here and the community at large. I see now that demolishing it would have been a mistake."

Bridget took a step closer to him, then another, and her heart followed her feet. For some reason that she couldn't quite explain, she laid her hand lightly on his forearm. His skin was sun-warm and vibrant, like the man himself. The contact brought back memories of years ago.

It was too much, too intimate, at least for the moment, so she removed her hand and simply stood beside him, surveying the crowd.

"So, you've made friends with Kevin," she remarked, trying to sound casual.

Reese followed her line of vision to the raggedly dressed young boy who was expertly casting his line, constantly adding to the stash of halibut, perch, and bass in his old blue cooler.

"Couldn't help myself," Reese replied with a smile as he watched the child. "He's a nice kid. Reminds me of . . ."

He didn't say it. He didn't have to. "Yeah, me, too," Bridget added.

"He needs adult attention and affection." He looked at her with a special light in his eyes that nonplussed her as much as the touch of his skin against hers. She looked away. "You've done a good thing, spending time with him, Bridget. He's really fond of you—talks about you all the time."

"Yeah, well, I like him, too." She glanced around, eager to find another subject. "Amanda's not so bad, either," she said, nodding toward the girl who sat demurely on a nearby bench, watching Kevin fish.

As usual, the little Southern belle was inappropriately dressed for the occasion in a frilly pink dress, spangled with white and yellow daisies, and white patent leather shoes. Her long hair had been pulled tightly into French braids and fastened with giant daisy barrettes. She looked pristine, ladylike, and miserably uncomfortable.

"Naw . . . Amanda's not too bad . . . I guess," Reese agreed grudgingly, "for a prissy girl."

"You've definitely been spending too much time with Kevin."

They watched quietly for a moment as Amanda arranged and rearranged her skirts and braids, trying to present an irresistible picture of feminine pulchritude. But Kevin couldn't have cared less.

"If she wants to get on his good side," Reese observed, "she should forget the posing and join him at the rail with a pole in her hand."

"But then he would expect her to put bait on the hook . . . you know, something gross and wiggly and slimy."

Reese turned to her, puzzled. "Of course. How else could she catch a fish?"

"Catch a fish! That's the last thing she would want to do. I mean, if she actually caught one, she'd have to touch it."

"Yeah . . . so?"

Bridget sighed and shook her head. "You're a boy. You just don't understand these things."

"No, I guess not. Uh-oh . . . look at that. There's more to our fair damsel than meets the eye. She's up to no good."

Bridget watched, fascinated, as Amanda rose from her bench and strolled to within a few feet of Kevin. Someone had abandoned a pole there, propped against the rail. After a careful glance around to see if anyone was watching, she nabbed it.

There was one awful moment when the hook caught in the lacy trim of her skirt. But she quickly removed it and stood for a long time, studying the apparatus as though it were some sort of complicated machinery.

"She's going to do it," Reese whispered.

"Women . . . they'll do *anything* to get a man's attention."

"No way. I know Amanda. She would never put a hook through a living creature, let alone catch a real fish. Trust me. She's seen far too many Disney movies."

Gliding silently across the boardwalk in her white patent leather slippers, the miniature Cinderella sneaked behind her Prince Charming and leaned over his cooler full of fish.

"She's not going to . . . !" Bridget exclaimed.

"She is!"

Gingerly, the girl reached into the cooler and picked up a small perch by its tail. When it wriggled, she dropped it and jumped back, her hand over her mouth to suppress a scream.

Bridget giggled. "That's it. She's had enough."

"No way. Women are relentless in their pursuit of mankind."

Reese was right. As soon as Amanda had recovered her composure, she made a second attempt. This time the halibut she chose was very dead and long past caring if he was handled. Holding it warily between her thumb and forefinger, she threaded him onto the hook. The grimace that crumpled her pretty face told of her inner turmoil.

"Wow. I'm impressed," Reese said.

"You should be. You have no idea how difficult that must be for her. We are witnessing a shining example of true love."

"You mean . . . of feminine duplicity."

"Whatever. Same thing."

As inconspicuously as possible, Amanda crept to the rail, about ten feet away from Kevin, and carefully lowered her already burdened line into the water.

"Hey, Kevin," she shouted gaily. "How's it going?"

For the first time, the boy became aware of his admirer. As he turned to her, his expression collapsed into the same distasteful scowl she had worn only moments before.

"Just look at that face," Bridget said triumphantly. "He likes her."

"Yeah," Reese growled. "He can't help himself. It's one of the worst things about being a guy."

A second later, Amanda began to squeal with delight and jump up and down. "I caught one! Kevin, look! I caught my first fish!"

Kevin looked doubtful until she began to haul up the line with a fish dangling from the end. A lethargic fish, perhaps, but a fish nevertheless.

"Hey! You *did!* Good goin', Amanda!" He ran to her and peered over the rail. "Let's see what you've got!"

Reese and Bridget watched as Kevin helped Amanda pull her "catch" over the rail and onto the dock. After a brief examination of the halibut and an uneasy glance back at his own ice cooler, the boy congratulated her warmly on her success. Amanda beamed, basking in the glow of sportsman pride.

"I don't know what it is about fishing," Reese

said with a sigh, "that brings out the liar in all of us."

"Doesn't it, though," Bridget agreed as a deep, therapeutic laugh bubbled up inside her. It had been a long time since she had felt that lighthearted, and she silently thanked the children and Reese for the healing gift.

Heaven knows, she needed a bit of levity. In a few hours, she was going to pay Mike another visit, and the last thing she wanted was for him to see how worried she was.

At first glance, Bridget was encouraged to see that Mike was propped up in his hospital bed, his leg no longer in traction, and he was trying to feed himself with a spoon. Progress! Finally!

"Reese," Mike exclaimed joyfully as Bridget and Kevin walked into his room. "You've come to see me, son! It does my heart good to look upon your face after all this time."

Bridget's brief sense of elation plummeted as she watched a confused Kevin walk across the room and sit down on the foot of the bed beside Mike's plaster-encased leg.

"Aw, come on, Mike," the boy said. "I'm not Reese and you know it. He's a grown-up; I'm a kid."

Mike studied him through narrowed eyes for a long time, then looked down at his bowl of oatmeal with a painfully embarrassed expression. "I knew who you were, lad," he muttered. "I was just teasin' you a wee bit."

"Then what's my name?" Kevin asked.

Bridget could see the struggle on Mike's face as he searched his damaged memory files. Some days he seemed so alert, almost his old self in every way. Those were the good days, but Mike had the occasional bad day, too. Today seemed to be one of them.

"Well, what is it?" the boy insisted. "What's my name?"

"It's . . . it's . . ."

"You don't remember, do you?" The boy's face registered his disappointment. "You've forgotten who I am."

"No, he hasn't," Bridget intervened. She walked over to Kevin and laid a quieting hand on his shoulder. "Mike knows you, Kevin. He's having a little trouble right now recalling some things, but he knows that you're somebody he cares about. Don't you, Mike?"

"Aye, of course I do. I'm just not so sharp when it comes to names and such these days." His hand trembling, he carefully laid the spoon on the tray, his appetite apparently gone.

After planting a kiss on his cheek, Bridget sat carefully on the bed and handed Mike a box. "This is from Tesla. It's a dozen of her famous pecan brownies. I'm sure they aren't on your doctor's diet . . . which should make them taste that much sweeter."

Mike peeked inside and smiled. "They will, indeed, lass. Tell her I'm forever in her debt. And be sure to thank her for the balloons, too. They arrived a couple of days ago."

Bridget glanced over at the brilliantly colored bouquet floating on the ceiling nearby, their printed messages wishing him a speedy recovery. She knew they had been delivered only this morning.

"Those were from George and Constance," she said softly. "They send you their love, too."

"Yeah, everybody at the Sand Castle misses you," Kevin added, then grinned mischievously. "Even Silas and Eugene. They said they love you, too."

Mike snickered and for a moment the confusion seemed to fade from his eyes. "Not bloody likely," he said. "That old Silas is a donkey's right hind-quarter and Eugene is the left. They'll not be sending me any brownies, cookies, or best wishes, you can be sure."

"Now, that isn't true, Mike." Bridget laughed, glad to see that her friend had retained at least part of his sense of humor. "Eugene wants you to come back so I won't work him so hard."

"*That* I believe. He always was as lazy as a piper's little finger." Mike sobered and turned to stare out the window for a moment. Bridget wondered what was on his mind. "Hasn't that son of mine been giving you a hand, girl?" he asked.

"The carousel broke down just before the beach party," Kevin said, "but Reese got it going for us. He fixed it *really* good! It even goes faster now!"

Mike looked to Bridget for confirmation. She nodded. "It's true, Mike. Reese stayed up all night getting the machine going. It wouldn't have been much of a pier party without the carousel."

Mike laid his head back on the pillow and sighed. "Aye, Reese always was fond of the carousel. It was the only part of the pier he ever cared about. And it's happy I am that he got her spinnin' for you."

"The party was a great success, Mike." She reached over and covered his hand with hers. "We raised nearly all the money we need to do the repairs . . . the main ones, anyway. Reese is lining up the contractors, and we'll start working on it next week"

"That's fine," he said, as his eyelids fluttered closed. "I'm glad to hear it."

Bridget glanced over at Kevin and nodded toward the door. It was time to go.

As they rose from the bed, Mike didn't open his eyes, but he said, "Tell Reese it's proud I am of him. He's a fine boy, always has been . . . and tell him . . . tell him I said thank you for the balloons."

"I will, Mike." She placed his box of brownies on the nearby nightstand and gave him another kiss, this time on his forehead. "I promise, I'll tell Reese as soon as I see him."

"I haven't had the chance to thank you, Jo, for sending me the letter about Mike," Reese said.

Sitting across the table from the fortune-teller,

he marvelled that some women seemed ageless. There might be a few more silver strands in Madame Joleen's dark hair, and the tiny smile lines might be a bit deeper, but she was as vibrant and youthful as she was when he left the Sand Castle twelve years ago.

This kind woman had been part of his life for as long as he could recall. Her words of guidance had always been helpful . . . when he had been wise enough to heed them.

"I'm glad you came home," Madame Jo said as her hands deftly shuffled the cards and spread them on the table between them. "We missed you. *I* missed you."

Gazing down at the strange, mystical symbols of the deck, Reese felt a tiny thrill of anticipation. Of course, he didn't believe in such nonsense. Madame was nothing more than a wonderful combination of sleight-of-hand magician and down-home family counselor.

Wasn't she?

"Hmmmm . . . what have we here?" she said, squinting her dark eyes and moving the cards from one position to another. "The Five of Cups . . . very interesting."

"The five of what?"

"Cups. Each suit refers to different areas of our lives," she explained. "Cups reflect the issues of the heart, the emotions."

"Oh, great," he replied with subdued enthusiasm. He would have preferred to have drawn a card that promised a lucrative commercial venture. *That* he understood, *that* he could handle.

"Here, look closely at the card and learn its lesson," she said, lifting it from the table and placing it in his hand.

It wasn't a particularly cheery card; in fact, it was rather dismal. A man stood at the seashore, draped in a black cloak, his shoulders stooped, his head low. On the sand before him lay three golden goblets. They were lying on their sides and the red wine, which they had once held, had been spilled onto the ground. On a large rock behind him sat two other cups, filled to the brim.

"What do you see?" Joleen said, gently coaxing him.

"A guy who looks pretty bummed." The curt response sounded trite and sarcastic, even to his own ears. But Reese didn't want to admit that sometimes he felt as sad as that fellow looked.

"He *is* bummed," she replied with a knowing smile. "Remind you of anyone?"

He said nothing, but nodded.

"That's because he's looking at the three spilled cups. He is focusing on what was lost and will never be regained."

"Maybe it was really important to him . . . the wine in those cups, I mean."

"It's only natural that he should mourn his losses," she said. "But, no matter how long he stands there, looking at the spilled cups, the contents will never be retrieved. The past can never be changed. The day must come when he is finished grieving, when he is ready to continue his life."

Reese thought of his mother's smile, of all the nights he had prayed for her return, of all the mornings when he had wakened to find that nothing had changed. "How does he do it?" he asked. "How does he stop feeling like that?"

"Feelings follow actions, Reese," she said. "First he must act. He must turn away from those spilled cups, turn his back on the past. When he does, he will see the two cups that are still full. Then he can drink his fill of happiness."

Reese sat for a long time, staring at the card, experiencing a kinship with the man depicted there. Yes, the three cups were empty, but the other two were so close, right there within his grasp, if only he would turn around.

Placing the card in her hand, he leaned across the table and kissed her lined cheek. "Thank you, Jo," he said.

"Leaving so soon?" She looked a bit disappointed.

"I'm sorry, but yes. Let's just say I have to go check some cups, to see which ones are empty and which are full."

She watched as he left, closing the door quietly behind him. Nodding, she said, "Ah . . . trying to tell the difference. Now, that's the hard part."

Bridget stood at the end of the pier, staring out across the Pacific at the ominous clouds gathering on the horizon. A chilly wind blew inland, bringing the pungent smell of the ocean to the town.

A cool mist sprayed Bridget's face, and when she licked her lips, she could taste the sea salt.

"Not now," she whispered to the spirits of the Almighty, Mother Nature, Neptune, or any other benevolent being who might have influence over the elements. "Please, not a storm. Not until we get the work done."

Hearing footsteps behind her, she turned to see Reese, his tackle box and rod in hand. All the other fishermen had already deserted their posts; he was the last to go.

"You look worried," he said. He laid down his gear and joined her at the rail.

"I am."

"Well, don't worry. If you worry, I worry. And I'm not at my best when I'm worried."

She didn't reply, but continued to stare at the clouds that seemed to be rushing toward shore, driven by a wind picking up by the minute.

"Okay," he said, "just so I'll know for sure . . . exactly what is it we're worrying about?"

"The incoming storm."

"Well, I know that. I mean, what are you afraid is going to happen, specifically?"

"Specifically, I'm afraid that if it's a bad one— like the weather services are predicting—some of those questionable pilings may go. I was hoping we'd have good weather—no earthquakes, brush fires, or plagues of locusts until after the repairs were finished."

"Is there anything I can do?" he asked with

a degree of sincerity and compassion that touched her heart.

She turned to him and saw something shining in his eyes, a warm glow she recognized from years ago.

"Sure, you can help," she said.

"Name it."

"How are you at holding back the wind and the waves?"

He sighed. "Lousy."

She turned and looked back at the pier, at the signs already swinging in the wind, tarps that needed to be secured, windows that needed to be boarded. "Then maybe you can just help me batten down the hatches. I have a feeling this one is going to be a real doozy."

$\mathcal{S}ix$

The storm was much worse than the weather service had predicted. Bridget stood at the upstairs window of her apartment and watched the rain slice in silvered streaks that were nearly horizonal from the driving wind. Below, white-caps glowed against the black, churning sea.

Two hours ago, she had asked the tenants on the pier to gather here in the carousel house. The building was closer to the land, more stable and less dangerous than their apartments over their concessions. But in spite of her invitation and later insistence, they had elected to remain, though Constance and George did send Amanda to stay with Bridget, where she would be safe. Soon afterward, Reese appeared at her door with Kevin in tow. He had found the boy alone in the trailer on the beach.

The two children and Reese sat on the carpet around her coffee table, playing a game of Fish by the light of several votive candles. The power had gone out over an hour earlier.

Bridget stood vigil by the window. Like her tenants, she felt—foolish though the idea might be—that just by watching, she could somehow prevent any further damage to her precious pier. But the storm was intensifying by the moment. If she continued to stand here, she might see the end of the wharf crumple and fall into those dark waters.

"Are we all going to die?" Amanda asked in a small, frightened voice. Her fingers trembled as she clutched her cards.

"No, of course not," Kevin replied. "Don't be such a scaredy, sissy girl."

"You'd be scared, too, if you had the sense God gave a goose," Amanda snapped in classic Southern style. "Why . . . we could all get sucked right up into the sky and dumped back down again, just like in *The Wizard of Oz.* Huh, Miss Bridget?"

Bridget continued to stare out the window, unable to concentrate on the conversation. "I think that was a tornado, Amanda. This is more like a hurricane."

"Same thing," Amanda muttered.

"No, it isn't." Kevin sniffed his contempt. "Boy, are you dumb."

"Hey, nobody is being dumb, Kevin," Reese replied in a gentle but firm tone. "We're all a little nervous right now, and that's okay. But we're not going to die, or even get hurt."

Bridget turned from the window and saw that he was watching her, his eyes intent, the angular planes of his face accented by the flickering candlelight.

He smiled at her, and she returned it weakly. "The worst thing we're going to have to do tonight," he said, "is put up with each other's company for a while until the storm quiets down a bit."

Bridget left the window, walked over to the coffee table, and sat down on the rug next to Amanda. Stroking the girl's golden braids, she said, "That's right, Amanda. This old carousel house has stood proud and tall through storms a lot worse than this . . . even earthquakes."

Amanda nodded vigorously, eager to believe. "Yeah, I remember the earthquake. Now *that* was scary! It knocked me right out of my bed!"

"*I* wasn't that scared," Kevin said with a macho shrug of his thin shoulders.

"Were too!"

"Were *not!*"

A particularly strong gust rattled the windows, and the old building creaked loudly. Both children's eyes widened. Amanda gasped, and Kevin dropped his cards.

"Why don't we toast some marshmallows?" Bridget jumped up and hurried to the kitchen. After rummaging through the cupboard for a moment, she returned, plastic bag and bamboo shish-kabob skewers in hand.

"Toast marshmallows?" Reese asked, giving her a questioning glance. "Nice idea . . . but . . ."

"We got no campfire," Kevin observed.

Amanda shook her head in aristocratic distaste. "We *don't have* a campfire."

"That's what I said."

"It's okay, really." Bridget handed each of

them a skewer and tore open the bag. "We have miniature campfires . . ." She nodded toward the votive candles. ". . . And that's just perfect, because these are mini-marshmallows."

"You're kidding, right?" Reese said doubtfully.

"Do I look like I'm kidding?" She tossed a couple of marshmallows onto the table in front of him. "Here. Toast."

"This is silly," Kevin replied as he threaded the tiny white puffs onto the end of his skewer.

"No, it isn't," Amanda argued. "This is fun."

Daintily, the girl held hers over the nearest candle and began toasting it to a golden brown perfection. Less patient, Kevin stuck his directly into the flame and instantly produced a flaming torch.

"You're doing it wrong, dummy," Amanda said, swatting his arm. "You caught yours on fire."

He blew on the charred morsel, then popped it into his mouth. "Meant to." He promptly lit another.

"Kevin, be careful," Bridget warned him, trying not to giggle. "You're going to catch your hair on fire."

Reese laughed as he tasted his marshmallow. "That's okay. If he does, we'll just toss him out the window into the rain. No problem."

The foursome laughed together, and some of the tension began to melt away, in spite of the escalating storm outside.

As Reese began to toast another, he said, "Actually, this reminds me of another night, years and years ago . . ."

"Like back in dinosaur times?" Kevin asked.

"Not *that* far back. It was more like the Dark Ages. It was a famous event, a notorious natural disaster. It was called The Night of . . . of the Howling Wind from Hades."

Bridget smiled, sensing a bit of Irish blarney on the way.

"Hades?" Amanda looked puzzled. "What's that?"

"I know what that means," Kevin piped up, proud of himself. "It's the same as hell."

Amanda gouged him with her elbow. "Shush your mouth, Kevin Dixon! That's a bad word and you aren't supposed to say it."

"You recall that night, don't you, Bridget?" Reese asked with a teasing grin.

"What's that? Oh, The Night of the . . . what was it . . . the Howling . . . ?"

"Wind from Hades."

"Oh, yes, of course." She sighed. "As though it were only yesterday. A horrible, dreadful night, I'm sure. Tell them what happened."

"Maybe *you* should tell them."

She gave a shudder. "No . . . I can't stand to think about it. I'll leave it all to you."

"Well, I don't want to scare you guys any more than you already—"

"No! It's all right," Kevin interjected. "Tell us about it."

Reese took a deep breath, leaned back on the front of the sofa, and struck a bard's pose.

"Well, it was a night sort of like this one, only worse. Much, much worse. It wasn't just a little windstorm like this one. No way. It was a hurricane, a typhoon, a tornado, and a cyclone, all mixed up in one. Awful . . . perfectly awful, I tell you."

"Were you here? And Bridget?" Kevin asked, spellbound.

"Both of us. Right here in this very room. Bridget's mother and dad and my mom were here, too, seeking shelter from the mighty tempest."

"What's that?" Kevin asked.

Amanda lifted her pert nose a couple of notches. "That's the storm, dumb bunny."

"Shh-h-h . . ."

Reese continued, his voice low and conspiratorial. "Bridget's mother had made us cups of hot chocolate, topped with marshmallows, just like these. And we were just sitting here on the floor, drinking our chocolate when . . . suddenly . . . the power went out, plunging us into a darkness that was blacker than the blackest night."

"You didn't have a flashlight or candles?" Amanda asked.

"Nope, no candles. They hadn't been invented yet."

"Oooo, cool." Kevin shivered deliciously.

Scooting closer to Reese, Amanda said, "Yeah, cool. And then what happened?"

As Reese continued to weave a story to distract his young audience, Bridget silently thanked him. But she couldn't lose herself in the tale, as they had. Outside the window, the storm was continuing to grow.

The weather service had predicted that the worst would occur about midnight.

She glanced at her mother's anniversary clock on a nearby end table. The brass balls on the pendulum glimmered, catching the candlelight as they spun right, then left.

It was only nine-thirty.

Two and a half hours to go.

After hearing the wharf groan for hours during the night, Reese knew that a sad sight would greet them by the gray light of dawn. But he hadn't realized how devastating it would be.

He stood on the beach, his arms folded against the chill of the early morning fog. The cold mist swirled among the spectators who had gathered on the beach to view the destruction. The haze floated on the surface of the quiet water, weaving a ghostly path between the shattered pilings and the crumbled deck that dropped and disappeared into the ocean. At least two hundred feet had been lost to the sea, and what remained of the Sand Castle Pier was unstable, ready to collapse at any further provocation from Mother Nature.

Bridget stood ten feet away, shivering in the cold despite her heavy cable knit sweater. Tears were streaming down her cheeks. For the first time ever, Reese could see defeat in those beautiful, expressive eyes. After all she had been through, she always landed on her feet; Reese found that her most endearing quality. But, apparently, this was one blow too many, even for a woman as strong as Bridget O'Dwyer.

He wanted to reach out to her, take her in his arms and try to offer some degree of comfort. But, instinctively, he knew this wasn't the time. She wouldn't welcome his advances.

Turning her eyes from the pier, she faced him with tired defiance. "Well, Reese, go ahead and say it. Say, 'I told you so.'"

Not knowing what to say, he said nothing, but stared down at the sand. He moved a rock aside with the toe of his deck shoe, feeling lower than he could ever remember.

"You were absolutely right," she said, not bothering to hide her bitterness or sarcasm. "You must be feeling pretty smug with everything happening exactly as you predicted it would. Right down to the number of pilings giving way, the deck crumbling . . . and, of course, the issue of public safety."

He took one step toward her and held out his hand. "Bridget, please, I. . . ."

She shook her head and turned her back to him. "They *were* at risk, just like you said," she admitted. "Everyone who has stood on this pier for the last few months has been in danger. I refused to see it, because I didn't want it to be true. But you were right all along."

"If it's any consolation, I wish I had been wrong. I'm truly sorry that this has happened."

"Really?"

His anger rose, along with a bitter taste in his mouth. She was angry, she was hurt, and she was directing her pain toward him. He couldn't really blame her—he had done the same thing to her before—but he found it most unsettling to have to be taking a dose of his own medicine.

"Of course I'm sorry to see this sort of thing happen," he said. "What kind of person do you think I am?"

She turned back to him and studied his face for a long time, searching, evaluating. Then she shrugged. "I don't know." Slowly, she began to walk away from him, toward the carousel house, the only building that remained completely intact. "I don't know anything anymore," she murmured, her head down, her shoulders slumped.

"Bridget," he called after her. "Please don't think that I would have wished this on you. On *any* of you."

He thought of the others on the pier—those who were, even now, packing their belongings, preparing to leave this place which had been their homes for years. It was like a family that was being split apart.

He thought of his father, lying in his hospital bed, his mind and body as devastated as his dream. When he found out what had happened here . . .

Reese couldn't bear to think of that right now. For the moment, he had to help those around him in any way he could.

Climbing the stairs to the deck, he surveyed

the length of the damaged pier from the top. Even he hadn't foreseen this much devastation. Gaping holes had been torn from the boardwalk, the railing was twisted and completely gone in places, the shops' roofs had been ripped loose and their shutters hung from the windows like broken sea gulls' wings.

Constance and George Weber trudged to and from their building, arms full of personal belongings as they evacuated their home of eight years. Even Amanda had been pressed into service. She struggled beneath a box full of stuffed bears, unicorns, and dolls. For once, her beautiful braids were untidy, and her frills seemed as limp as her spirit.

Madame Joleen had pressed Eugene into service on her behalf. She stood on the porch of her parlor, beneath the sign which bore the tools of her trade: a crystal ball, tarot cards, and the lined palm. He was following her directions, lugging overstuffed chairs and loveseats out of the building and onto the small veranda.

Only Silas remained, sitting in his rocker on his porch, watching the activity with a guarded eye. He simply gnawed on the end of his pipe and muttered under his breath. Reese had heard that the old sailor refused to leave until the city officials carried him—and his rocking chair— away by force.

Nearby, Reese saw Tesla pulling small trinkets from her window display. Carefully, lovingly, she was placing each cheap souvenir into a large cardboard box: Sand Castle banners, furry monkeys on strings, pinwheels, bubble pipes, and sun visors.

Reese hurried to her and felt a pang of deep sadness as she turned to him, her beautiful dark eyes red from crying.

"Tesla, are you all right?" he asked.

She flashed a bright smile. "Oh, yes, Señor Sullivan. I am fine." Waving one hand at her bedraggled concession, she said, "My small shop is very bad, but I am good. Thank you."

"May I help you carry some boxes, or—?"

"No, no." She nodded toward Constance, who was struggling with a box full of heavy kitchen utensils. "You help the others. I can do this. Thank you."

Reese watched as she stroked a small satin dolphin once before laying it in the box beside some stuffed sea lions. He thought of the stories he had heard about Tesla, of how she had escaped the horrors of Honduras to come to the United States. Her past life had been rife with hardship and it didn't seem fair that Fate had dealt her another blow.

"Tesla, what are you going to do now?" he asked. "Where will you go? How will you live?"

She laid one hand gently on his forearm and smiled up at him. "Ah, Señor Sullivan . . . you worry about Tesla. Thank you. But my God is with me." In a telling, but unconscious, gesture she touched the crucifix that hung around her neck on a silver chain. "The Madonna, she watches over me. I will be fine. When I come from Honduras seven years ago, I have nothing.

Now I have a little. I will begin again. It will be more easy this time, yes?"

"I hope so, Tesla. Good luck to you." Reese pressed a quick kiss to her cheek, then hurried away. He had to help Constance and George; besides, he didn't want Tesla to see the moisture welling in his eyes.

But even as he walked away, he heard her say, "And good fortune to you, Señor Sullivan. Go with God."

Go with God. Reese felt guilty even accepting the blessing.

Seven

When Bridget walked away from Reese, leaving him standing alone on the beach and calling her name, she realized that her words had been unnecessarily harsh. Sensing his grief over the destruction, she had known that although he had prophesied the tragedy, he hadn't been the cause of it.

But her confused emotions had come to a full boil, and Reese had been a convenient target when the mixture overflowed. And now she was too tired and emotionally spent to conjure much guilt over her reaction. There would be plenty of time to repent tomorrow, to apologize and maybe set things straight.

For today, she wasn't finished being hurt and angry.

As she strode toward the carousel house, she saw a dignified, silver-haired lady in a beautifully tailored suit standing beside the door. The woman was engrossed in conversation with another female whom Bridget recognized immediately. The younger of the two was Mrs. Timms, the social worker who had responded to Bridget's previous reports of Kevin's father's neglect.

Although Bridget had placed another call this morning, she hadn't expected such a prompt response. Perhaps, this time, Mrs. Timms had been as concerned as she that a young boy had been left alone during a violent windstorm. His father's trailer had been destroyed in the course of the evening and, had Bridget not sheltered Kevin, the boy could have been hurt or killed.

To Bridget's knowledge, Kevin's father still hadn't made an appearance.

Bridget approached the two women and waited to be recognized, assuming that the social worker would want to speak to her personally. But when both women continued to talk, huddled together and sharing what appeared to be a serious discussion, Bridget thought it best not to disturb them.

Unnoticed, she walked past them and into the building.

As soon as she stepped inside, Bridget saw Kevin. The boy was standing by the armored horse, his arms around its arched neck, softly crying.

"Kevin," she said, "what is it? What's wrong?" Gently, she stroked the boy's tousled hair. "Come on, Kev . . . tell me why you're crying."

He looked up at her with red eyes. His tears streaked the perpetual dirt on his cheeks as he tried to wipe them off with the back of his hand.

"They're taking me away," he said between hiccuping sobs. "Right now. I'm going to have to go."

Bridget led him to the gilded bench behind

Trojan and sat him down. Placing her hands on his thin shoulders, she said, "Who? Who is taking you away?"

"My grandma."

"Your grandmother? I didn't know you had a grandmother."

"Neither did I until a few minutes ago. That Mrs. Timms lady from the kids' protection place . . . she found out that I had a grandma in Santa Barbara and they called her. She came here to get me."

Bridget nodded. "Oh, I see. Is that your grandmother, the pretty lady standing outside with Mrs. Timms?"

"Pretty? Yeah, I guess so. She's kinda old."

Bridget laughed. The lady appeared to be in her early fifties. "Not as old as you think, Kevin," she said. "Well, she looks like a very nice person. Maybe it won't be so bad, living in a real house in Santa Barbara and having the opportunity to get to know your grandmother."

"I'll have to go to school . . . *all the time.*"

"Nobody has to go *all* the time. You'll still have plenty of vacations and weekends. I'm sure your grandmother would bring you back here to visit from time to time. It will be a new life for you, Kevin."

Even as she spoke the words, Bridget felt as though her heart were breaking. She would miss this scruffy, adorable child, probably more than he would miss her.

"I don't want a new life," he moaned, his lower lip trembling. "I like my old one just fine."

"But your life has to change, Kev. Everyone's life changes, whether we want it to or not." She thought of the pier, its inhabitants and visitors, and fought back her own tears. "Nothing lasts forever, good or bad. The old things pass away to make room for the new," she continued, speaking words that she knew were for her own heart as well as the boy's. "If something is changing—if something is going away—it's only because there is something better on the way."

"But I don't like the 'going away' part. It hurts to say goodbye," he said, losing the battle with his tears. They streamed unchecked down his face as he gazed up at her woefully.

"I know, sweetheart," she said, gathering him to her and hugging him tightly. "Believe me . . . I know."

"Excuse me . . . Miss O'Dwyer?" said a soft, refined voice.

Bridget turned to see Kevin's grandmother standing there, a look of excitement and happiness on her face. But her golden eyes—so like her grandson's—registered her sympathy.

"I'm Hilda Dixon, Kevin's grandmother," she said. "Mrs. Timms tells me that you've done a great deal for my grandson. I want you to know how very grateful I am."

Bridget choked back the tightening in her throat and nodded. "Thank you. But Kevin has given me far more than I've offered him. He's a very special young man; you're fortunate to have him in your family."

"Yes, I realize that. I'm looking forward to having him live with me on the ranch. I own a citrus farm in the hills north of Santa Barbara," she added, "and the place has been terribly lonely for me since Mr. Dixon's passing two years ago."

Bridget thought of Kevin, exploring his grandmother's groves, learning the character-building lessons a farm could teach. Yes, this turn of events was, indeed, heaven-sent.

Mrs. Dixon's eyes clouded with sadness. "My son and I . . . we haven't been . . . close . . . for years. The last word I had received was that he had left the state. I didn't even know about Kevin."

"You two have a lot of catching up to do." Bridget tried not to think of how much she was going to miss this little boy who had added his own rainbow of color to her life . . . how much she was going to miss everyone in her Sand Castle "family."

"A ranch?" Kevin whispered as though he was afraid to believe it. "You have a ranch?"

"Well, not the cowboy kind," Mrs. Dixon replied with a chuckle. "We don't raise cattle, only lemons, oranges, and avocados. But we do have horses."

"Horses? Really?"

"Three of them. Would you like to learn how to ride?"

Bridget had never seen a grin so wide. Her heart filled with happiness for Kevin.

"Give me another hug, Kevin," she said, reaching for the boy and pulling him to her. "Then get going. You're going to have *real* horses to ride, not wooden ones."

This time Bridget lost the struggle with her emotions, and tears filled her eyes. Seeing them, Hilda placed one hand on her shoulder and gave her a conciliatory pat.

"Please don't worry about Kevin," she said. "He's going to be fine. And we'll come to visit frequently. I know how important you are to him."

"Thank you." Bridget released the boy and was both pleased and slightly dismayed that he didn't seem so heartbroken to be leaving her anymore.

He's a boy, she reminded herself. *And he gets to live on a ranch with real horses.*

How heartbroken could she expect him to be? As Hilda Dixon led Kevin away, Bridget heard them discussing the fact that he would be expected to curry the horses after he had ridden them.

No problem, she thought, remembering how eager he had been to polish Trojan every morning.

Bridget turned and walked over to the handsome armored horse and wrapped her arms around his proud neck. The tears that Kevin had left behind had dried. But, *good ol' Trojan,* she thought . . . he didn't seem to mind getting wet all over again.

Reese knew this was the coward's way—standing here in the door of his father's hospital room, listening like a silent shadow. Unheard. Unseen.

How many times had he done this in the past two weeks? He had lost count. When the surgeon gave Mike Sullivan his latest checkup, Reese was there, shielded from view by the pale blue curtain that separated the cubicles . . . listening. When the physical therapist forced the recently-mended knee to bend for the first time, Reese heard his father's cries of pain, but said nothing. At the time, it seemed there was nothing to say.

Today was no different.

Stepping quietly, he took his usual place just behind the thin curtain that bisected the room. As before, the other bed was empty.

Reese heard Mike groan as the therapist removed the pads that had provided electrical stimuli to his thigh and calf. Reese listened as the therapist explained how this torture was, indeed, necessary to keep the muscles from atrophying.

"Who would have thought," Mike was saying, "that a lovely lass such as yourself would go around electrocuting souls with an evil gadget like that?"

A grim smile crossed Reese's face. Some things never changed; Mike Sullivan still had an eye for a good-looking woman. Unfortunately, his eye had been just as sharp when he was married to Reese's mother, Irene.

Reese couldn't help feeling a little bitter.

The attractive therapist offered Mike a few more instructions, a word of encouragement,

then left the room. On her way out, she saw
Reese standing behind the curtain and gave him
a questioning look.

"My dad," he replied softly.

"I see."

From the expression in her eyes, Reese had
the uncomfortable feeling that she could see
more than he wanted her to. What had the old
man said about him, anyway? Everyone in this
hospital probably thought him a horrible son because he had neglected his father.

Well, that was okay. They didn't know. How
could they understand the amount of animosity
that could build, year by year, brick by brick,
into an insurmountable wall dividing a father
and son?

Reese started to follow her out, but he paused
when he heard Mike say, "Is somebody there? If
you are, show yourself straightaway."

Drawing a deep breath, Reese crossed the
room and rounded the curtain.

He should have prepared himself for the
change in his father's physical appearance, but
he hadn't. How could he have anticipated the
difference the years would make? Even if he had
taken the time to think it through, he wouldn't
have guessed that so much of that burnished
copper hair had turned to silver. He wouldn't
have expected to see his father's hard, muscular
body replaced by this frail frame. When had the
slight worry furrows on his forehead turned to
jagged creases?

When had Roaring Mike Sullivan become an old man?

"So, what kind of misery are *you* going to inflict upon me?" Mike grunted as he shifted painfully on his bed.

"What?" Reese's head swam with the current of emotions washing over him. He couldn't think.

"I said, what are you going to do to me that the others haven't done yet? I've been stuck with needles, zapped with electricity. I've been poked and prodded like O'Leary's cow, until I'm sick to death of it all."

"Yes, I'm sure you are," Reese said, feeling an unexpected wave of sympathy toward the man on the bed. Of all the emotions he had expected to feel at this moment, he hadn't counted on sympathy being among them.

Anger, resentment, guilt, or sadness . . . maybe. But never compassion.

He watched Michael Sullivan's face for any sign of recognition, but saw none.

As Reese took a step closer, Mike turned his head and gazed out the window at the ocean view. Last night's clouds were receding, the skies clearing, but Mike seemed unaware and unconcerned about the weather.

"She was a lovely girl," Mike said, closing his eyes. "So lovely."

Reese thought of the pretty nurse. "Yes, she was," he replied.

"Eyes as green as the hills of Killarney, my Irene."

Reese's throat contracted and a curious moisture rushed to his eyes. "Irene?" he said softly.

"Aye. The most beautiful girl in County Kerry, she was, and I won her." His eyes remained closed, but a smile played across his lips. "That night at the Tralee Fair, I asked her . . . and she said yes."

Not knowing what to say, Reese simply stood there, listening to his father's reminiscing. He felt like an eavesdropper, invading a sacred, secret place, but he needed to hear the words of praise for his mother that his father had never shared with him before.

"I was so much older than she was," Mike continued, half asleep. "I wanted to make her happy, but . . ."

"What happened?" Reese wasn't sure he wanted to hear the answer, but he couldn't help asking.

"She left me. Went away with Pete. Was younger, paid her more attention than . . ."

Another man? This was the first Reese had heard of a third party's involvement. Vaguely he recalled an amusement operator named Pete, a dark-haired fellow with a hearty laugh and a playful smile. The guy had arrived from out of nowhere and disappeared the same way. Reese had never made the connection.

And, to his credit, Mike had never placed blame. Never once had he said an unkind word about Irene to her teenage son. Not even when Reese had openly condemned his father for her departure.

Mike's eyes opened and he looked, unfocusing, at Reese. "But she left me . . ." he whispered.

"I know. I'm sorry," Reese replied.

Mike shook his head. "No, she left me a son . . . the best part of her . . . she gave to me."

Reese bit his lower lip until he could taste the saltiness of his own blood. "Maybe," he said, "maybe she thought you would take better care of the boy than she could."

"I tried, but . . ." With a sigh, Mike closed his eyes again. Reese could see tears forming in their corners and spilling into the creases on his cheeks. "The other night," Mike whispered, "I dreamed Reese was here, at the foot of my bed, watching me with his mother's green eyes. But it was just a dream. He's many miles away, my boy."

Slowly, Reese walked to the bed and took the thin, freckled hand in his. The last time Reese had held his father's hand, it had seemed so large, so strong, dwarfing his own. Now, their roles had reversed, and it was he who was the strong one.

A sense of protection rose in him, the need to nurture, replacing the need to be nurtured. Another emotion he hadn't expected.

"It wasn't a dream, Big Mike," he said softly as he stroked the back of his father's hand. But Mike Sullivan had fallen asleep. "Your boy isn't so far away after all."

Eight

For the past week, Bridget had been plagued by an unrealistic but persistent hope that *something* could still be done to save the Sand Castle Pier.

Just one itty, bitty miracle, she had prayed nightly. *Just one . . . okay . . . one great big whopper of a miracle.* Surely, that wasn't too much to ask.

Until now, she had always considered optimism one of her strongest attributes. But idealism could be a failing when it had no basis in truth.

The discovery she had made this morning confirmed just how wrong she had been to believe this floundering Phoenix could ever rise again.

With the tide dipped to its lowest point, she stood beneath the broken shambles of the pier and surveyed the damage. The condition of the deck's underside made her sick at heart, but it wasn't merely the fact that the structure was in ruin. The storm had torn away part of the boardwalk, revealing an area which had been previously hidden from view.

Bridget couldn't believe the amount of deterioration that she saw in the exposed wood. This damage hadn't been done by the hurricane. Time, alone, had caused the decay.

"Oh, Mike," she whispered as she surveyed the section where he had taken his tumble. The newly replaced railing marked the exact spot where he had fallen; the boards beneath the place where he had been standing at the time were rotten nearly all the way through. The deck had probably shifted beneath his feet at the critical moment. No wonder he had toppled over the edge.

Of course, the stroke had been to blame initially, causing him to fall. But if he had been standing on a solid surface, he might have been able to regain his balance. Either way, he would have suffered the effects of the stroke, but he wouldn't have had to endure the agony of a severely fractured leg.

If they had only known.

We didn't, Bridget thought, trying to soothe her own aching conscience. Tears filled her eyes, blurring her vision. But it was too late; she had seen too much already.

"Now *I* know," she whispered. "And that's all that counts."

With knowledge came responsibility.

She knew what she had to do.

"Well, howdy, partner. It's about time I heard from you," boomed the deep, nasal voice over the phone.

"Yeah, Tex, things have been a bit hectic

around here, what with the storm and all." Reese shifted the receiver to his right ear and eased himself down onto Mike's favorite recliner. Leaning back against the battered leatherette, he took a deep breath and smelled the familiar combination of masculine scents that had always defined his dad's presence: tobacco, Old Spice aftershave, and . . . coffee.

That had changed. Years ago, it would have been Irish whiskey.

"I'll just bet you didn't call me in the middle of your vacation to talk about the weather," Tex said.

Reese chuckled. "You know, my friend, you aren't as stupid as you look."

"Why, thank you . . . I guess . . ."

"Did you close that deal yet, the shopping center in St. Louis?"

"Everything but signing the papers. Why? Are you getting anxious?"

"I don't want you to wrap it up until we get a chance to talk. We may need to invest that capital elsewhere."

"You're kidding, right? I mean, this whole St. Louis deal was *your* idea in the first place."

"I know. And I apologize for asking you to call a halt this far along in the game."

"So, why are you?"

"It's a long story." Reese sighed as he glanced around the room at the meager but distinctive memorabilia that chronicled a man's life: a rugby trophy won in Dublin in the summer of 1948; his mother's sheet music which still sat on the piano just below their wedding picture; Reese's own bronzed baby shoes; the awards and photos on the wall depicting the pier's first reconstruction and its importance to the community over the years.

Reese was grateful that, other than the carousel house, this building had survived the storm better than the others. To his surprise, he was pleased that these symbols of the past—*his* past—had been preserved.

"I need you to come to California, Tex. Right away," he said. "It's a family matter."

Usually, Tex wasn't the most receptive or sensitive guy on the block, but even he seemed to hear the quiet desperation in Reese's voice.

"I'll be there tomorrow evening," Tex replied. "But you better buy me one of them California Margarita Grande drinks, you hear?"

Reese laughed, feeling a burden beginning to lift. He had taken that first step in the right direction. And for now, that was all that mattered.

"Tell you what, ol' chap," he said. "I'll buy you a fine Mexican dinner and a margarita so big that you and two pretty señoritas could make a Jacuzzi out of it."

"Olé!"

Bridget felt as though she had just taken a bite of something incredibly bitter. *Who would have thought the flavor of "crow" would be so distasteful?* she thought as she left the carousel house and made her way to the arcade.

Yesterday, in the midst of finalizing the paper-work with the city for the pier's dismantling, she had discovered a legal barrier that made her furious: Reese had been granted Mike Sullivan's power of attorney.

More like he grabbed it, she added as she climbed the stairs to Mike's apartment. Halfway up the steps, she glanced down the remaining length of the pier and saw two people standing near the end.

Her heart thumped with fear and anger. What was the matter with them, anyway? They were adults . . . men. Hadn't they read the enormous sign warning them to stay away?

And where was Eugene? She had told him to keep an eye out for anyone foolhardy enough to venture past the sign.

Clasping the sheaf of papers in her hand, she stormed down the steps and out onto the pier.

"Hey, you two! Get back here!" she yelled, not bothering with the usual niceties. "The decking isn't stable, and you could be—"

The men turned toward her, and she swallowed the remainder of her words, along with her indignation.

It was Reese . . . and some big, burly fellow she had never met. The man was wearing fancy cowboy boots, an enormous Stetson, and a broad smile.

"Oh," she muttered, glaring at Reese, "it's *you.*" With the demolition documents clutched in her hands, she found that a few cliché insults crossed her mind. Comments about him taking a long walk on a short dock . . . since one was so readily available. But she decided not to say or do anything to humiliate herself any more than was already necessary. She couldn't believe she was actually going to have to ask Reese to sign papers that gave her permission to destroy the Sand Castle—something he had wanted to do all along.

Irony sure can be ironic sometimes, she thought as she tasted the bitterness in her mouth once again.

"Now don't tell me," the stranger drawled as they approached, "this is her in the fiery flesh. The Irish redhead who's been keeping you awake nights, right?"

Reese shot him a warning look.

Bridget took notice. Just what had Reese been saying about her? Keeping him awake nights, huh? She wasn't sure if that was an insult or a compliment.

Reese's eyes met hers, and she felt him reaching inside her thoughts, sensing the depth of her pain. His face instantly sobered. "Bridget, this is Tex Yarrow, my friend and business partner. Tex, meet Bridget O'Dwyer, the heart and soul of this place."

Tex enfolded her hand in his and gave it a painfully firm shake. "My pleasure, I'm sure. You're just as pretty as Reese said you were. Maybe more. I was wondering if you would—"

"Yeah, well," Reese said, cutting him off with a not-so-subtle jab to the ribs, "you were just leaving, right?"

"Actually, I was just going to ask Señorita O'Dwyer here if she wanted to join me in a margarita. Would you like that, ma'am? Reese is buying." Tex grinned and tipped his hat in a gallant gesture that was slightly diluted by the lusty gleam in his eye.

"You don't want to join him in a margarita or any other kind of drink, Bridget," Reese interjected. "Believe me. You don't know what this character has in mind."

Bridget turned to Tex. "Thank you for the offer, but I have some business to conduct with your *pardner* . . ." she said, mimicking his drawl, ". . . if you don't mind."

The moment Tex walked away, Bridget felt the heaviness, the sadness, sweeping back over her heart. A colorful character could only keep reality and despair at bay for a few moments.

"What is it, Bridie?" Reese asked, his tone surprisingly gentle as he used his father's old nickname for her. "What's wrong?"

She sighed and looked out to the ragged end of the pier. "Nothing new. Nothing that isn't obvious to me now . . . just as it was to you a long time ago."

Stepping closer, he placed one hand on her shoulder. She wasn't expecting the simple contact to feel so good, to offer so much comfort.

"I'm truly sorry about this, Bridget," he said. "I realize now how important this place is—"

"*Was,*" she corrected him.

"No, *is*—to you, to a lot of people." He paused and swallowed. "Even to me."

Her eyes searched his and found them filled with genuine remorse. Her heart warmed toward him, reached for him, needing a companion who would share this loss. It was almost too good to believe.

"The Sand Castle means a lot to you?" she asked. "Really?"

"Really. My vendetta against this place was foolish. My resentment of my father, immature and pointless. So, my childhood wasn't perfect. Whose was?"

His hand slid down her shoulder and arm to grasp her fingers. Leading her out toward the end of the pier, he continued, his voice heavy with emotion.

"I've been thinking a lot, Bridget," he said. "About the past, about the future. I thought that if I could erase this place from my memory, all the pain would leave with it. And maybe it would, if I truly could. But I don't want to forget. Memory can't be selective. If I throw away the sad times, I have to give up the happy ones, too."

When they reached the end of the pier, he chose a spot that appeared to be sturdy and pulled her down to sit beside him. Tucking the papers beneath her, she listened as he talked and stared out at the cloudless horizon.

"If I choose not to remember my parents and their problems, my mother's desertion, Mike's neglect, I have to forget the night I saw them kiss each other beneath the Christmas tree, and the times when my dad sang Irish folk songs to us and taught me how to cast a line. There were good times, too."

"Of course there were." She moved closer to him and wrapped her arm around his broad shoulders. The years seemed to roll back, and she recalled the evenings when they had sat here, watching the sun set and talking.

"I can't forget this place any more than I can forget the sand castles we used to build there on the beach." He pointed to the spot, further down near the jetty, which had been their favorite haunt.

His arm slipped around her waist, and she couldn't resist laying her head against his shoulder. "I'm glad you remember," she said. "As long as we both remember, it won't be completely gone."

"Gone?" He pulled back a bit and looked down at her. "What do you mean?"

She drew a deep breath. "That's why I came looking for you, Reese. I have some papers for you to sign, so we can start the demolition as soon as possible."

He glanced down at the documents she had shoved beneath her. "Is that—?"

"Yes. You aren't the only one who has been thinking things over. You may have been wrong to try to deny your past, but I've been clinging to mine . . . far too much. I placed this pier and its sentimental value above the safety and well-being of the people I love."

"But, Bridget, we—"

"No, it's all right now. I know what I have to

do. I just want to do it, to have it finished, before my stubbornness causes someone else to be hurt. That's why I want you to sign these papers." She pulled them from beneath her and shoved them into his hands. "Please, Reese. Now."

He looked down at the documents for a long time, then at her. "I can't."

"You *can't?* You can't what?"

"Sign them."

"But you have to! I can't begin the demolition without Mike's approval, and you have his power of attorney."

"I know, but—"

"Reese, there are no *buts.*" The tears spilled from her eyes and rolled down her cheeks. Of all the obstacles she might have anticipated, this certainly wouldn't have been one. "You have to do this. *I* have to do it, as quickly as I can. Why prolong the pain any longer than necessary?"

"No, Bridget," he said gently but firmly. She could see by the hard lines of his face that he had no intention of doing as she wished. "I won't order the Sand Castle's destruction. There's a better—"

She snatched the papers out of his hand and jumped to her feet. "You are the most difficult man I've ever known!" she shouted. "Leave it to you to make a bad situation worse. Are you just naturally cussed and bullheaded, or do you work at it?"

She wanted to hit him with the papers and scream at him some more. She wanted to give him a shove and watch him go flying off the end of the dock. She wanted to crawl back into his arms and feel that momentary but delicious sensation of comfort and companionship.

Unable to decide which to do, she turned and stomped away.

Nine

"You're trying to tell me that *I'm* cussed, that *I'm* the one who's being difficult here, that *I'm* stubborn?" Reese chased Bridget across the pier as she strode toward the carousel house. "Is *that* what you're trying to say to me, Bridget O'Dwyer?"

She stopped so abruptly that he collided with her. Whirling around to face him, she snapped, "That's right. I'd say you caught my drift. What an intelligent lad you are."

They glared at each other, eye to eye for a long moment, the only sound that of their accelerated breathing.

Bridget was far more conscious of his closeness than she wanted to be. They had fought some major battles over the years, but she couldn't recall when there had been so much tension between them.

But then, she didn't remember the stakes being so high either. They weren't exactly quarreling about whose turn it was to buy the ice cream cones.

She watched as the fury in his green eyes softened to minor irritation, then to compassion.

Reaching for her, he placed his hands on her shoulders and drew her a bit closer. At first, she wanted to pull away, to withdraw into her own anger and frustration. But she was too tired, too sad and defeated to put up much of a struggle. She surrendered to his touch and her own need to be held.

"I'm so sorry that you feel you have to do this, Bridie," he said. With one finger he stroked her cheek. "But you didn't let me finish what I wanted to say."

"You didn't have to. I know what you were going to say, and I couldn't bear to hear it all again."

Reese chuckled and tweaked her nose. "Kevin is right; you girls do think you know everything. And usually, you do. But this time, you're wrong. I have something I want to show you, Ms. Bridget O'Dwyer, if you'll crawl down off that high horse and come with me."

Ordinarily, she would have bristled. But his tone was soft and his eyes kind. Besides, she supposed she had been a bit unreasonable with him lately. Natural catastrophes had a way of bringing out the worst in a person.

"Okay," she said.

He held out his hand to her. Reluctantly, she took it.

What the heck, she thought as he led her toward the staircase behind the arcade. *At this point, what do I have to lose?*

* * *

Bridget sat on Mike's old sofa, holding a mug of strong coffee, which Reese had flavored with a dash of Bailey's Irish Cream. He sat on the bedraggled recliner, looking like a younger, golden-haired version of his dad.

Did he know how similar he and his father were? Probably, she decided. Sometimes the people most like us were the ones who could upset us most deeply.

"Thanks for the coffee," she said, attempting to accept his gesture of peace. "So, why did you bring me up here, really?"

His suggestive grin made her giggle. "To see my etchings?"

"You don't etch."

"No, but I do *sketch*. And I would like to show you some of my most recent work."

Without waiting for her permission, he stood and walked over to the dining room table. He gathered some of the large papers that had been spread across its surface and brought them over to her. Placing them on the coffee table, he took a seat beside her on the sofa.

"I didn't know you were an artist," she said, as he unrolled the drawings and weighted down the corners with some of Mike's detective novels from a nearby bookshelf.

"I'm not. I'm a land developer, remember?"

"Oh, yeah." At first glance, she could see they were blueprints of some sort. "Is this your next project?"

"I'd like it to be, but I've learned my lesson.

This time I'm going to consult my business partner first."

"Tex?"

"No, in this case, it's you."

"Me?" She gave him a curious look, but his face revealed nothing except suppressed excitement.

"Yeah, you. After all, you did inform me quite emphatically that you are half-owner of this place."

"This place?"

Catching her breath, she returned her attention to the maze of lines and figures, trying not to allow that bubble of hope to swell inside her.

The confusing puzzle began to take shape before her eyes. "It's the pier," she whispered, not quite believing. "There, that's the carousel house." She pointed to the octagon at the bottom of the map. "And here is the arcade . . . but it's so much larger and . . ."

"It would have to be to accommodate all the new video games and the virtual reality booth," he said, watching her face closely, his own expression anxious and eager.

"And The Crab House," she said, trailing her fingertip upward toward the top of the drawing. "It's a real sit-down restaurant, not just a fish stand."

"Do you think George and Constance would approve?"

For the tenth time that day, Bridget's eyes filled with tears, but this time they were born of hope, not regret. "Approve? Of course, they would be ecstatic, but . . . An ice cream parlor, Reese? Is this a soda fountain and wraparound counter?"

"Tesla seemed crowded in that little booth."

"Oh, Reese, it's wonderful." She read a special notation in the lower corner of the blueprint. "Cement pilings?"

"They have to be, Bridget," he said. "We can't risk trying to support all this on wood."

"Practicality over nostalgia, right?"

"In this case, I'm afraid so. But not always."

Her eyes sought out the bait and tackle shop and checked its dimensions. "Silas's place—it's still the same. And so is the carousel house."

"Some things, and some people, shouldn't change," he replied. "I don't believe ol' Silas would want to change any more than we would want him to. And I know I don't want one thing about the carousel house to change . . . or its present occupant, for that matter."

She blushed and chose to ignore his implication—for now. "What is this?" she asked, pointing to a ground-floor extension of the arcade.

"Mike's new apartment. He won't be able to climb stairs anymore when he comes home. But, knowing him, he wouldn't be able to sleep unless he could hear the racket of an arcade. So, I thought we'd better put him nearby."

"We? What are you talking about?" She reached over and grabbed his forearm, squeezing it tightly.

"We," he said with a mischievous grin. "You

know, as in *you* and *me. We*, two . . . and a lot of help from an army of subcontractors."

She caught her breath. "Do you really think we could do something like this? How?"

Placing his hand on hers, he gently stroked her fingers. "Our dads did it, Bridget, and they had a lot less to start with than we have now."

"But the money! It would take so much, and I don't even have enough for the basic repairs."

"I have some, and I understand you're a fantastic fund-raiser. If I match you, dollar for dollar, do you think you could go before the city council and swing some deals?"

The bubble inside her grew until she thought she could float up to the ceiling, maybe even out the window and into the sky with the seagulls and pelicans.

For once, the impossible seemed within her reach.

"I could try. I *will* try!" Alone, the task had seemed overwhelming, but with a partner, with Reese as that partner, she could see the future he had sketched on the plans before her. Her imagination was already taking wing, revising and magnifying what was there. "I'll do it! If you can do it, Reese Sullivan, *I* can certainly do it." Unable to contain her joy any longer, she threw herself into his arms, laughing and crying at the same moment.

"We'll rebuild it together. O'Dwyer and Sullivan," he said, placing a kiss on her wet cheek.

Wiping her tears away, she did something that her heart had wanted for a long time. It seemed like the most natural thing in the world; she placed her hands on either side of his face, drew him to her, and kissed his lips. A long, gentle kiss, filled with the passion that she felt for him in that moment, the passion for the dream that stretched before them.

"We always were good at building sand castles," she said when they had both regained their ability to breathe.

"The best," he said, pulling her to him for another. "The very best."

Ten

As Bridget stood on the beach and stared up at the gleaming white pillars—the new cement pilings—that supported the resurrected Sand Castle Pier, she missed the creak and groan of the old timbers. But not enough to interfere with the elation she felt, knowing that she and Reese had accomplished the impossible.

"We did it!" Bridget reached for his hand and gave it a hardy squeeze. "I can't believe it, but just look!"

"We certainly did!" His face reflected the pride welling inside her own heart. "I never had any doubts."

She looked up at him and quirked one eyebrow. "Not even when those first few pilings turned out to be three feet too long?"

"Well . . ."

"Or when the new planking had to be retreated, for the fourth time? Or when the plumbing—"

"Okay, okay, a *few* doubts, but all in all . . . it went smoothly."

"Smoothly or not, it *went*, and that's all that matters to me."

"I hear you." He sighed, but it was the tired, happy sigh of a contented man.

Bridget had never felt closer to another human being. Seventeen months of hard work had brought their dream into reality . . . a reality that would be enjoyed by countless people over the years to come.

Judging from the size of the crowd that lined the shore, creating a brilliant mosaic of beach towels, she estimated that over half of the town's citizens had flocked to the pier's grand opening.

The Sand Castle Building Contest had been a huge success. Over a hundred sculptures skirted the tide, everything from dainty Cinderella palaces to sturdy Moroccan fortresses, Rapunzel towers, and even a Tudor mansion.

"Hey, Miss Bridget, Mr. Reese! Come here and look at my pirates' treasure cave thing!" Kevin called to them from his construction site near the swing set area. He had assembled a formidable mountain of wet sand and was shaping it into something that looked like a cross between a castle and a skull. Though a bit grotesque in theme, the sculpture was startlingly creative.

Bridget couldn't adjust mentally to being called *Miss* Bridget, but the boy's grandmother had insisted on a number of changes in his manners. Wisely, Bridget had decided not to undermine her tutoring in any way.

"Wow, Kevin, that's . . . that's really something!" she said, as she and Reese bent over his handiwork.

Nearby, his grandmother sat on a canvas beach

chair, reading a novel. Her stylishly tailored suit
had been exchanged for capri pants and an
over-sized tee shirt. She glanced at Bridget and
the crossbones decor, grinned, and rolled her
eyes skyward before returning to her book.

"I suppose the treasure is in there." Reese
pointed to the skull's gaping mouth and ragged
teeth.

"Sure it is," Kevin replied.

"I think it's gross," piped a high-pitched voice.
Bridget turned to see Amanda skipping toward
them. She held a bubble pipe in one hand and
a bright red bottle of soap in the other. Gleefully, she was sending the glistening, iridescent
spheres dancing on the breeze before settling
onto the sand. She wore a bright pink swimsuit
with purple ruffles.

"Nobody asked you what you think," Kevin
growled without looking her way. "You're just a
dumb girl. What do *you* know about pirates?"

"Now, Kevin," Mrs. Dixon said, giving him a
reproving look over the top of her paperback.
"That is no way to address a lady."

"But she's not a lady. She's just 'Manda."

"All females are ladies," she said patiently, "because *you* are a gentleman."

Bridget watched, fascinated, as Amanda prissed
around him in ever-tightening circles, blowing
her bubbles in his direction. Obviously, she was
trying to be irritating, and she was doing an excellent job.

When a stream of bubbles bounced across the
bridge of his nose, Kevin's hand slipped to the

waistband of his shorts. Bridget could see the lime green handle of a plastic water pistol protruding above his belt. Reese had seen it, too. He gave her a knowing smirk. Trouble was imminent.

"The tide is coming in, you dumb bunny," Amanda cooed, stepping much too close to his precious creation. "It's gonna wash that all away, so what's the point in building it?"

Bridget couldn't stand any more; she had to intervene. "Your bubbles don't last either, Mandy," she told her. "But that doesn't mean you don't enjoy making them. Maybe that's what makes them so precious . . . the fact that they *aren't* going to last forever."

With her fingertip, Bridget touched one that was floating by her. It burst with a brief but beautiful explosion of rainbow colors. "That means you have to enjoy them as much as you can right now, while you have them."

"Like people," Mrs. Dixon said softly. The poignant expression on her face told Bridget that she was thinking of her late and beloved husband.

"Yes . . . bubbles, piers, sand castles, and people," Reese added. For a moment, his eyes scanned the pier railing, then lingered on the figure of Mike Sullivan, who stood at the end, a cane in one hand, a fishing pole in the other. Bridget saw Reese's slight smile soften his expression. The harsh lines had all but disappeared. Her heart warmed toward him, reached out to this gentle man whom her heart remembered from so long ago.

"Well, I don't know what you guys are talking about," Amanda snapped, irritated not to be the center of attention.

"That's because you're just a kid," Kevin muttered, "and they're talking about grownup stuff."

"Oh, yeah?" Amanda's delicate coloring blushed as brightly as her pink swimsuit. "Well! You're a . . . you're a . . . a . . . pooh-pooh brain!" she yelled.

Several heads turned, eyes on Kevin, waiting for his response. Bridget knew he had to avenge his honor. A pirate could only take so much.

A second later, the green plastic pistol had been drawn. A stream of cold water caught Amanda on the side of her face, soaking her pigtails and dampening her dignity along with her hair ribbons.

Reese exploded with laughter. "Aye, aye, matie! Ye've given the fair wench a taste of the brine!"

Amanda swelled like an indignant toad on a lily pad. Her freckles looked as though they were about to pop off her flushed, dripping face. "How *dare* you!" she shouted, shaking her finger at Kevin. "Mrs. Dixon, tell your grandson he shouldn't squirt a lady in the face either!"

With a bored but dutiful expression, Kevin's grandmother lowered her book and said in a monotonous tone, "Kevin, you shouldn't squirt a lady in the face." She paused as though reconsidering. "A couple of good shots to her backside should do nicely."

In less than a heartbeat, the ruffles on Amanda's rear were as limp and soggy as her hair ribbons. She ran away, squealing, with Kevin and pistol close behind.

The three adults watched, laughing, as the children raced down the beach.

"Ah . . . those wicked, wily wenches," Reese said, shaking his head and twisting the ends of an imaginary mustache. "We spend our lives chasin' after 'em. And when we finally get our hands on 'em, we haven't a clue what to do."

"Really?" Mrs. Dixon said knowingly, continuing to focus on her book. "Not a single clue?"

"Well . . ." Reese gave Bridget a lecherous, mustache-twirling grin, worthy of any blood-lusty pirate. "A few things come to mind."

He hesitated and glanced back up at his father, fishing on the end of the pier. "I have one thing to take care of, and then I was wondering . . ." He lowered his voice and leaned close to her ear. "If you could meet me you-know-where."

She returned his smirk, looking like anything *but* a virginal maiden. "I know where," she whispered. "And maybe we can . . . you-know-what."

"Exactly." His pulse rate accelerated, along with a sense of urgency. "This won't take long," he assured her.

"It had better not." She tossed her head and placed her hands on her hips. "You aren't the only pirate in the sea."

"But he's the only one for you," Mrs. Dixon added, when Reese was out of earshot.

Shocked, Bridget started to deny it, but she couldn't. "Well, maybe, but I don't want *him* to know that."

"Too late, dear," Mrs. Dixon mumbled into her book. "Trust me. He knows."

As Reese approached the figure at the end of the pier, he realized that he had never seen his father looking so relaxed, so totally at peace with himself and his world. It had taken a debilitating stroke . . . but, at last, Michael Sullivan had learned the importance of taking the time to savor the moment.

Better late than never, Reese thought, recalling some of the life lessons which he still had to learn. It didn't seem to matter so much anymore how quickly things were accomplished, as long as a person was moving, slowly but surely, in the right direction.

"Are they biting today, Mike?" he asked, after noting the impressive catch in the cooler at his dad's feet.

Mike beamed. "They are, indeed! They're waitin' in line down there for the privilege of throwin' themselves upon Michael Sullivan's hook!"

Reese laughed and joined Mike at the rail. Leaning forward on his elbows, he gazed down at the massive concrete pilings and felt a surge of satisfaction.

Mike seemed to be feeling the same thing. With a long, contented sigh he dangled his line in the gently rolling waves below. " 'Twas a fine thing we did, Pat, restorin' this pier," Mike said, his eyes dreamy.

Reese winced, feeling a brief stab of sadness that his father would confuse his son with his long-dead partner. Then he shoved the disappointment aside. Mike was happy . . . deeply happy, possibly for the first time in his life. And, although he might be a bit addled from time to time, Mike knew that he was speaking to someone he loved. That was what counted.

"Yes, Mike," Reese replied, "a fine thing, indeed."

"She's strong now." Mike nodded toward the concrete columns that gleamed golden in the afternoon sun. "Won't go breakin' up when the winds roar and the waves crash."

"Nope. She'll stand firm."

Mike nodded thoughtfully. "Aye, he's a clever lad . . . my Reese . . . a'thinkin' o' those cement pilings. Shoulda thought o' that meself, years ago."

A flood of joy went through Reese at his father's praise; he was astonished at how good it felt, at how much he had needed it.

"Ah, well, it doesn't matter who thought of it, Mike," he said softly. "As long as the work's done now."

Mike laughed. "Who would have thought that your Bridie would give the twinkle of her eye to my Reese? Now that's a fine turn of events, don't you think, Paddy?"

Reese felt another wave of pleasure that washed as deep as the first. "The twinkle of her eye? Do you really think so?"

Mike shook his head and chuckled. "Of course. If ye can't see that, ye've got stones for eyes and y'er blind besides."

For a long time, Reese said nothing, but stood, listening to the gentle splashing of the sea against the new pier. His pier. Her pier. More importantly, *their* pier.

"How do you feel about that, Mike?" he asked, his heart in his voice.

"About what?" Big Mike had a short attention span these days.

"About Reese and Bridget getting together."

"I think it's about bloody time. My Reese is a bit slow at takin' up the chase. And your Bridget is a good runner. Too good for her own good."

Reese grinned. Even with fewer brain cells, Mike could still call it the way it was.

A soft, gentle smile settled on Mike's face as he gazed out at the horizon . . . and across the years. "The lasses would have been proud of us, Patrick," he said. "Your Helen and my Irene. To see this fine pier, to know that our children cared for each other . . . they would have been proud, indeed."

Tears flooded Mike's eyes, but Reese noted that, this time, Big Mike Sullivan didn't bother to blink them away.

Yes. They were all learning.

Reese took one step sideways toward his father. To his surprise and delight, Mike took one toward him. And they were standing, shoulder to shoulder.

Only two steps.

One each, Reese thought. That was all it had taken.

Maybe the distance between father and son hadn't been so great after all.

Further down the shore from the pier, on the other side of the jetty, lay a lovely little cove with sun-warmed rocks, crystalline sand, and tide pools. The niche had long been Bridget's and Reese's own secret hideaway, where he had first kissed her all those years ago.

Over the past seventeen months they had found an occasional stolen moment to retreat to their cove, to talk, to touch, to sit quietly and allow old feelings to resurface and new ones to develop.

But in all those months, they had never discussed what was going to happen when the pier was rebuilt and Mike had regained his health.

As the sun sank on the mist-shrouded horizon, they sat with their backs against the rocks, their toes burrowed into the sand. Overhead a couple of sea gulls shrieked and dove, like ivory kites against the dark purple sky.

"Now that it's all done, how do you feel?" Reese asked. He reached for her and pulled her closer, leaning her back against his chest. She sat between his long, bare legs that were aligned, warm and comforting, against hers.

Bridget closed her eyes, savoring the closeness and the feel of his arms wrapped around her waist. "Tired," she said with a small sigh. "But good. Very good."

"Completely happy?"

She hesitated, then said tentatively, "Yes, of course I am."

I am happy, aren't I? she asked herself. *Yes,* came the unspoken reply. *But completely? No.*

Why wouldn't she be completely happy? The project of a lifetime was finished at last. The pier's opening celebration had been a spectacular success. The sunset was perfectly gorgeous, the moment exquisitely romantic.

After what had probably been the most perfect day of her life, she was sitting in the sand, enclosed in her lover's arms. What could be better?

Knowing that it won't be the last time, her heart whispered. *Believing that he won't run away . . . like he did before.*

"I'm not going to do it, Bridie," he said, turning her in his arms to face him.

She was shocked; it was as though he had read her mind. But that was silly, of course. The simple statement could have meant anything. "You aren't going to do what?" she asked, her pulse pounding.

"Abandon you."

"I never thought you would," she said, feeling like a hypocrite the moment the words left her mouth.

He laughed and placed a kiss on her nose. "Liar, liar, pants on fire."

Swatting his shoulder, she said, "I'm wearing shorts."

Slowly he trailed one fingertip down her bare thigh to her knee. "No kidding."

Again, he kissed her, but this time on the lips. She marveled at how the simple contact could still set her body afire with longing. Would she ever get over this man? She didn't see how.

Burying his hands in her thick, unbound curls, he leaned her head back so he could continue the trail of kisses down her throat. Sweetly, she surrendered to the caress of his lips and the feelings they aroused in her body and her emotions.

Maybe, like the sand castles on the beach, it would all be gone tomorrow. But Bridget pushed those fears aside and allowed herself to draw every drop of joy from the moment.

When they had both regained their breath, he reached for her hands and pressed them tightly between his. "Bridget," he said, "I have to return to New York."

Instantly, the fears came rushing back, overwhelming her like a tidal wave. So much for him not abandoning her.

Well, it wasn't as though she hadn't expected it.

But did one's heart ever really expect to be broken? *Not really,* she thought. *Hope springs eternal, and all that nonsense.* A fine line separated optimism from naiveté, and she felt she had crossed that line several times where Reese was concerned.

Instinctively, she pulled away and crossed her arms over her chest. Pitiful defense against the arrows of love, she realized.

"Of course you do," she replied, as nonchalantly as though she were discussing the coast guard's latest weather warnings. "You have a business to run, and now that the pier's finished and your dad is almost recovered, I understand that you—"

"Shh-h-h." He silenced her by pressing his fingers to her lips. "Kevin is right; you prissy girls *do* think you know everything."

"Whaddo-you-mn . . . ?" she muttered through his fingers.

"I *mean* that you think you have me all figured out. But you don't, Bridget O'Dwyer. I am far more complex a creature than you can possibly imagine. And it'll take a lifetime for you to comprehend all the marvelous idiosyncrasies that comprise my personality."

"Huh?"

"You heard me. Now, if I take my hand off your mouth, will you promise to be quiet and let *me* talk for a change?"

Confused, she nodded.

"Good." He removed his fingers. "Now, there's a very important question I need to ask you, and after I've asked you . . . *then* you can talk, okay?"

Again she nodded. Her heart began to beat so hard she could feel it in her throat. A question? He was going to ask her a *question?* Could it be . . . ?

"Bridget," he said, drawing a deep breath and squeezing her hands between his, "as I said, I do have to go back to New York for a short time to tie up some loose ends. And I don't want you worrying the whole time, thinking that I've done 'it' again, that I've run out on you."

A short time . . . The words echoed in her head, but she was afraid to believe them. *Tie up loose ends . . . ?*

"So," he continued, "my question to you is this: What would it take for you to believe that I'm not running out on you, that I will be back? And it won't take me twelve years, either."

Her eyes searched his and found the sincerity she required. She didn't have to push the fear away; this time it left of its own accord.

"Your word," she replied. "That's all I need."

A smile flooded his face, a smile of gratitude and relief. "You have my word. And thank you," he said. "I don't deserve your trust, but I'm thankful that you will give it to me."

"It's easy," she said, surprised at the realization. He had done a lot of growing up recently, and it seemed maybe she had, too.

"Okay, you say that now," he told her, "but I'm afraid that once I'm gone, you'll start to have doubts. You'll wake up one morning, about a week from now, and say, 'He's done it again, that rotten creep. He'll never be back.' And then you'll start shopping around for some other guy to toast marshmallows with you and tell you Irish folk tales."

She laughed. "I sincerely doubt it."

"But I can't take that risk. So, I was thinking that if I left you something to remind you . . . just a little token of my affection . . ." Reaching into his shorts pocket, he pulled out a small, dark blue velvet box.

As he opened the lid, her eyes reflected the sparkle of the diamond engagement ring nestled against the satin.

"Do you think this would do?" he asked, his heart in his voice. "As a reminder, that is?"

Wet, salty tears rolled down her cheeks as she slipped her left hand into his. Carefully, he slid the ring onto her finger, then pressed a kiss to her knuckle.

"Well . . . it's a lot better than a string," she said, laughing through her tears.

"Oh, I have one of those, too!" From the same pocket, he retrieved a bit of red embroidery floss, which he tied around the same finger, next to the ring. "Just in case," he said. "Some things are too important to take chances."

Bridget thought of the resurrected pier, of Mike's health, of Kevin's new home, and the future stretching before her and Reese, bright with promise.

"That's true," she said thoughtfully as she accepted his kiss and offered another in return, "and some things are too important *not* to take chances."

The Marrying Kind

by
Debbie Macomber

O_{NE}

Could it actually be Katie Kern? Katie, here in a San Francisco bar of all places? It didn't seem possible. Not after all these years.

Her hips swayed with understated grace and elegance as the sleek, sophisticated woman casually walked toward Jason Ingram's table. They'd been high school sweethearts in Spokane, Washington, ten years earlier. More than a lifetime ago.

Sweet, gentle Katie. That was what Jason had assumed until that fateful night so long ago. He'd say one thing for her, she'd certainly had him fooled. Then, without warning, without so much as a clue as to who and what she really was, Katie had brutally ripped his heart out and then trampled all over it.

He caught a whiff of her perfume and closed his eyes, trying to identify the scent. Jasmine. Warm and sensual. Seductive. Captivating, like the woman herself. Like Katie.

But it couldn't be Katie. It just wasn't possible. Jason sincerely hoped life wouldn't play such a cruel joke on him. Not now when he was three days away from marrying Elaine Hopkins. Not when it had taken him the better half of these last ten years to forget Katie. It would take much longer to forgive her.

Her back was to him now as she walked past him, making it impossible to identify her for certain.

Jason downed another swallow of beer. His fiancee's two older brothers sat with him, joking, teasing, doing their best to entertain him and welcome him to the family.

"Don't feel obligated to attend this potluck Mom's throwing tonight," Rich Hopkins said, breaking into Jason's thoughts.

It demanded every ounce of strength Jason possessed to stop staring at the woman. He wasn't the only one interested. Every man in the St. Regis cocktail lounge was staring at her, including Rich and Bob. She was stunning, beautiful without knowing it, the same way Katie had once been. She always had been able to take his breath away. But this wasn't Katie. It couldn't be. Not now. Please, not now.

"I'd get out of the dinner if I could," Bob added, reaching for his beer. He was Elaine's youngest brother and closest to her in age.

Jason watched as the woman approached a table on the other side of the room. The old geezer who occupied it promptly stood and kissed her cheek. Jason frowned.

"It's entirely up to you," Rich added. "You'll meet everyone later at the wedding anyway."

Wedding. The word cut through his mind like a laser light, slicing into his conscience. He was marrying Elaine, he reminded himself. He loved

Elaine. Enough to ask her to spend the rest of his life with him.

Funny, he'd never told his fiancee about Katie. In retrospect he wondered why. Certainly Elaine had a right to know he'd been married once before. Even if it was the briefest marriage on record. By his best estimate, he'd been a married man all of one hour. If it wasn't so tragic he might have been amused. The wedding ceremony had lasted longer than his marriage.

"You must be exhausted."

Jason's attention returned to the two men who'd soon be his brothers-in-law. "The flight wasn't bad."

"How long does it take to fly in from the east coast these days?"

"Five, six hours." Jason answered absently. He tried not to be obvious about his interest in the woman sitting with the old fart. It wasn't until she sat down that Jason got a decent look at her.

Dear, sweet heaven, it was Katie.

His heart pounded so hard it felt as if he were in danger of cracking his ribs.

In a matter of seconds, ten long years were wiped away and he was a callow youth all over again. The love he felt for her bubbled up inside him like a Yellowstone geyser. Just as quickly, he was consumed with an anger that threatened to consume him.

There had been a time when he'd loved Katie Kern more than life itself. He'd sacrificed everything for her. He assumed, incorrectly, that she loved him, too. Time had proved otherwise. The minute she faced opposition from her family, she'd turned her back and walked away without a qualm, leaving him to deal with the heartache of not knowing what had happened to her. To them.

"I believe I'll skip out on the dinner plans," Jason said, tightening his hand around the frosty beer mug. He deliberately pulled his gaze away from Katie and concentrated on Elaine's brothers.

"I can't say that I blame you."

"Make an early night of it," Bob suggested, finishing off the last of his beer. "It's already ten o'clock, your time."

"Right." The last thing Jason felt was fatigued. True, he'd spent almost the entire day en route, but he traveled routinely, and time changes generally didn't bother him.

Rich glanced at his watch and stood. "Bob and I'll connect with you sometime tomorrow, then."

"That sounds great," Jason answered. "My brother's set to arrive early afternoon." He could barely wait to tell Steve that he'd seen Katie. His brother was sure to appreciate the irony of the situation. Three days before Jason was to marry, he ran into Katie. God certainly had a sense of humor.

Rich slapped him across the back affectionately. "We'll see you tomorrow, then."

"You've got less than thirty-six hours to celebrate being a bachelor. Don't waste any time." Bob chuckled and glanced toward Katie suggestively. He stood and reached for his wallet.

Jason stopped him. "The beer's on me."

Both brothers thanked him. "I'll see you at the rehearsal."

"Tomorrow," he echoed, grateful when the two left.

If the woman was indeed Katie, and the possibility looked strong, he had to figure out what he intended to do about it. Nothing, he suspected.

Their marriage, if one could call it that, had been a long time ago. He wasn't sure she'd even want to see him again. For that matter, he wasn't sure he wanted to see Katie, either. She was a reminder of a painful time that he'd prefer to forget.

The cocktail waitress delivered Katie and her date's order. While still in high school, Katie had refused to drink alcoholic beverages. Her aversion apparently hadn't followed her into adulthood.

"Can I get you anything else?" the cocktail waitress asked as she approached his table.

"Nothing, thanks."

She handed him the tab and he signed his name and room number, leaving her a generous tip.

He toyed briefly with the idea of casually walking over and renewing his acquaintance with Katie. That would be the civilized thing to do. But Jason doubted that he could have pulled it off. He was angry, damn it, and he had every right to be. She'd been his wife and she'd deserted him, abandoned him and all their dreams.

Her family had openly disapproved of him

when they'd first started dating at the end of their junior year. He'd never completely understood why. He suspected it wasn't him personally that they objected to, but any involvement Katie might have with someone of the opposite sex. Someone not handpicked by them.

The man she was currently with was exactly the type her parents preferred. Older, rich as sin, and pompous as hell. Quite possibly they were married. It wouldn't surprise him in the least.

Ten years ago Jason hadn't been nearly good enough for the Kerns' only child. Her family had had no qualms about voicing their disapproval and so Katie and Jason had been forced to meet on the sly. Dear, sweet heaven, how he'd loved her.

As their senior year progressed, it became increasingly apparent that her parents intended to send her away to school. Then Katie had learned she was headed for a private girls' college on the east coast and they knew they had to do something.

The thought of being apart was more than either one could bear. They'd been determined to find a solution and eventually had. Marriage.

The night they graduated from high school, instead of attending the senior party the way everyone expected, Jason and Katie eloped across the Idaho boarder.

It had been romantic and fun. They'd been giddy on love, and each other, certain they'd outsmarted their families and friends.

During the wedding ceremony, when Katie read the vows they'd written themselves, her eyes had filled with tears as she'd gazed up at him with heartfelt devotion. He never would have guessed that her love would be so untrustworthy.

Jason's stomach clenched as he recalled their wedding night. He nearly snickered aloud. There'd been no such animal. If they hadn't taken time for a wedding dinner, they might have had a real honeymoon. Jason had no one to blame but himself for that. He'd been the one who insisted on treating Katie to a fancy dinner. She'd been cheated out of the big wedding she deserved and he wanted to make everything as perfect for her as possible.

He'd been nervous about making love and he knew Katie was, too. She'd been a virgin and his experience had been limited to one brief encounter with his best friend's older cousin when he was sixteen.

After he'd paid for the hotel room, they'd sat on the edge of the bed, holding each other, kissing the way they always did. In all the years since, he hadn't met a woman who gave sweeter kisses than Katie. Not even Elaine.

Just when their love for each other overtook their nervousness, the door had burst open and they were confronted by Katie's irate parents and the local police. The horrible scene that followed was forever burned in his memory.

Katie's mother wept hysterically while her father shouted accusations at them both. The police officer had slammed Jason against the wall

and he'd been accused of everything from kid-
napping to rape. The next thing he knew, Katie
was gone, and he was alone.

He'd never seen her again. Never heard from
her, either.

Correction. She'd signed the annulment papers in short order. No letter. No phone call.
Nothing. Not even a good-bye.

Until tonight. Thirty-odd hours before he was
scheduled to marry another woman. Then, lo
and behold, who should he see but Katie Kern.
If it was still Kern, which he doubted. Her parents had probably married her off to Daddy Warbucks a long time ago.

In the beginning he'd waited and hoped, certain she'd find a way of contacting him. He'd
believed in her. Believed in their love. Believed
until there was nothing left. Eventually he'd
been forced to accept the truth. She'd sold him
and their love out. She wanted nothing more to
do with him.

Briefly he wondered if she remembered him
at all. He'd wager she'd obediently followed her
father's blueprint for her life.

That was the way it was meant to be.

Jason stood and strolled out of the lounge as
if he hadn't a care in the world. He didn't so
much as glance over his shoulder. It gave him
only minor satisfaction to turn his back on Katie
and walk away from her. He'd go up to his
room, take a long, hot shower, and watch a little
television before turning out the lights. The next
couple of days were sure to be busy. He didn't

need the memory of another woman clouding his mind before he married Elaine.

He got as far as the lobby. If he could have named what stopped him, he would have cursed it aloud.

Katie, after all these years. In San Francisco.

He looked back just in time to see her leaving the lounge. Alone.

What the hell, he decided. He'd say hello, just for old times' sake. Ask about her life, perhaps bury some of his bitterness. Even wish her well. It would do them both a world of good to clear the air.

He waited by the pay phones.

Although the lighting was dim, it didn't take him but a moment to realize he'd been right. It really was Katie. More beautiful than he remembered, mature and sophisticated, suave in ways that had been foreign to them both ten years earlier. The business suit looked as if it had been designed with her in mind. The pinstriped skirt reached mid-calf and hugged her hips. The lines of the fitted jacket highlighted everything that was feminine about her. Her reddish-brown hair was shorter these days, straight and thick with the ends curving under naturally, brushing against the top of her shoulder.

Jason pretended to be using the phone. He waited until she'd strolled past him before he replaced the receiver. He spoke her name in a manner that suggested he'd recognized her just that moment.

"Katie? Katie Kern?" he said, sounding a bit breathless, surprised.

She turned and her eyes met his. Her lips parted softly and her eyes rounded as if she couldn't believe what she saw.

"Jase? Jase Ingram?"

Two

"Jase? Is it really you?" Katie raised her hand as if to touch his face, but stopped several inches short of his cheek. "How are you? What are you doing here in San Francisco?"

Jason buried his hands in his pants pockets and struck a nonchalant, relaxed pose, wanting her to assume he happened upon her just that moment and had spoken before censuring his actions.

"You look wonderful," she said, sounding oddly breathless.

"You, too." Which had to be the understatement of the century. He almost wished she'd gone to seed. She was more beautiful than ever.

"What are you doing here?" she asked again, not giving him time to answer one question before she asked another.

"I'm in town for a wedding. My own."

"Congratulations." She didn't so much as bat an eyelash.

His gaze fell on her left hand which remained bare.

"I've never . . . I'm still single."

He wasn't sure congratulations would be in order. He was tempted to blurt out something spiteful about making sure she knew what she wanted the next time around, but restrained himself.

"It'd be fun to get together and talk about old times," he said. But before he could claim that unfortunately, he simply didn't have the time, she nodded enthusiastically.

"Jase, let's do. It'd be great to sit down and talk." She reached out and wrapped her fingers around his forearm. Regret slipped into her eyes and she bit down into her lower lip and glanced toward the cocktail lounge. "I . . . I don't know that I can just now—I'm with someone."

"I saw," he murmured darkly. So much for playing it cool. She was sure to realize he'd spied her earlier now.

"You saw Roger?"

"Yeah." No use trying to hide it. "I was in the lounge earlier and thought that might have been you."

"How about dinner?" she suggested eagerly, her excitement bubbling over. He hadn't counted on her enthusiasm. "I haven't eaten and . . ."

"Some other time," he interrupted stiffly. He certainly didn't intend to join her and Daddy Warbucks for the night. He had never enjoyed being odd man out, and it wasn't a role he intended to play with Katie.

"But . . ."

"I just wanted to say hello and tell you you're looking good."

Her eager excitement died as she stiffened and moved one step back as though anticipating something painful. "There's so much I have to tell you, so much I want to know . . ."

Yeah, well, he had plenty of his own questions.

"Please, Jase. I'll make some excuse, tell Roger I've got a headache and meet you back here in an hour. I deserve that much, don't I?"

"All right." He may have sounded reluctant, but he wasn't. He had plenty he wanted to say to Katie himself, plenty of questions that demanded answers. Perhaps he should feel guilty—after all, he was marrying another woman in a couple of days—but God help him, he didn't. Maybe, just maybe, he could put this entire matter to rest once and for all.

"I'll meet you in the dining room," he said.

"I'll be there. Thanks, Jase," she murmured before turning and hurrying back to the cocktail lounge.

Jason headed up to his room and phoned for dinner reservations. It wasn't until he stood under the pulsating spray of the shower that his hands knotted into tight fists with a rare surge of anger. Katie had betrayed him, abandoned him, rejected his love. He'd waited ten long years to vent his frustration, and he wouldn't be denied the opportunity now. Once again he experienced a mild twinge of conscience, dining with another woman without Elaine knowing. His excuse, if he needed one, was that getting

rid of all this excess emotional baggage was sure
to make him a better husband.

At least that was what Jason told himself as he
prepared to face the demons of his past.

Katie couldn't quell the fluttery feeling in the
pit of her stomach. The last time she'd felt this
anxious about seeing Jase had been the night
they'd eloped. Her cheeks flushed with hot color
at the memory of what happened, or, more appropriately, didn't happen. Her heart ached for
them both, and for all the might-have-beens that
never were.

With her heart pounding and her head held
high, she walked into the hotel lobby, half expecting Jase to be waiting for her there. He
wasn't, and so she headed directly for the restaurant.

Although he'd approached her, he hadn't
seemed any too happy to see her. She understood his dilemma. By his own admission, he was
hours away from marrying another woman. Katie
should be pleased for him, glad he'd found a
woman with whom to share his life. What an
ironic twist of fate for them to run into each
other now.

He was almost married and she was practically
engaged. Roger had been after her to marry
him for months and his pleas were just beginning to hit their mark. The last time he'd asked,
she'd been tempted to give in. He was kind and
gentle. Affectionate. But what she felt for Roger

didn't compare with the hot urgency she'd experienced with Jase all those years ago. That had been hormones, she told herself. Good grief, she'd been little more than an eighteen-year-old kid.

Jase was already seated when she joined him. The hostess escorted her to his table. He'd changed clothes, and damn it all, looked terrific. Just seeing him again stirred awake a lot of emotions she'd thought were long dead, long buried. But then, she'd always loved Jase.

"So we meet again," he greeted with a telltale hint of sarcasm. One would think he'd already experienced second thoughts.

Perhaps it hadn't been such a good idea to meet after all, Katie mused, but damn it all, he owed her an explanation, and for that matter a hell of a lot more. She'd pined for weeks for Jase, waited, believed in him and their love. She'd literally been ripped from his arms and never heard from him again.

Katie made a pretense of reading over the menu, something Jase appeared to find fascinating. She made her selection quickly and set it aside.

"Tell me, what've you been doing these last ten years?" she asked, wanting to ease into the conversation. There'd been a time when they could discuss anything, share everything, but those days were long past. Jase was little more than a stranger now. A stranger she would always love.

Slowly, he raised his head until his gaze was

level with hers. She'd forgotten how blue and intense his eyes could be. What surprised her was how unfriendly they seemed, almost angry. She'd always been able to read his moods, and he hers. At one time they were so close it felt as if they shared each other's thoughts. Just when it seemed he was about to speak, the waiter approached with a bottle of Chardonnay.

Katie rarely indulged in alcohol, but if there was ever a time she needed something to bolster her nerve, it was now. The first sip, on an empty stomach, seemed to go straight to her head.

"Let's see," he said after their server left, sounding almost friendly. Almost, but not completely. "After I signed the annulment papers you sent me, I joined the Marine Corps."

He mentioned the annulment documents as if they meant nothing to him, as if it were nothing but a legal formality, one they'd discussed and agreed upon before the wedding. Surely he realized what it had cost her to pen her name to those papers. How she'd agonized over it, how she'd wept and pleaded and tried so hard to find a way for them to be together. It would have been easier to cut out her heart than nullify her marriage. Her fingers closed around the crystal goblet as the memories stirred her mind to an age and innocence that had long since died.

"When my enlistment ended with the Marines, I went back to school and graduated. I work for one of the major shipping companies now."

"West coast?"

"East. I'm only in San Francisco for the wedding."

She noticed that he didn't tell her anything about the woman he was about to marry, not even her name.

"What about you?" he asked.

"Let me see," she said, drawing in a deep breath. "I attended school, majored in business, graduated cum laude, and accepted a position with one of the financial institutions here in San Francisco." She downplayed her role with the bank, although she was said to be one of the rising young executives.

"Just the way Daddy wanted," he muttered.

Katie bristled. "If you recall, my parents wanted me to go into law."

"Law," Jase returned, "that's right, I'd forgotten."

That wasn't likely, but she let the comment slide. They'd both carried around their hurts for a long time.

The waiter came for their order and replenished their wine. Perhaps it was the Chardonnay that caused her to risk so much. Before she could stop herself, she blurted out, "Didn't you even try to find me?"

"Try?" he repeated loudly, attracting the attention of other diners. "I nearly went mad looking for you. Where the hell did they take you?"

"London . . . to live with my aunt."

"London. They don't have phones in England? Do you realize how long I waited to hear from you?"

Katie bowed her head, remembering how miserably unhappy she'd been. How she'd prayed night and day that he'd come for her. "She wouldn't let me," she whispered.

"And that stopped you?"

She swallowed against the tightness gathering in her throat, combating it with her anger. "You might have tried to find me."

"Of course I tried, but it was impossible. I was just a kid. How was I supposed to know where they'd sent you?"

"I told you about my father's sister before, don't you remember? We'd talked about her and how my parents wanted me to spend the summer with her before I went away to college. She's a law professor and . . ." She hesitated when the waiter returned with their salads.

Inhaling a calming breath, she reached for her fork. The lettuce was tasteless and she washed it down with another sip of wine. That, at least, calmed her nerves.

"Your aunt—sure, I remembered her, but I didn't have a name or an address. Someplace on the east coast, I thought. A lot of good that did me." He tossed his hands into the air. "I don't possess magical powers, Katie. Just exactly how was I supposed to figure out where you were?"

"You should have known."

His mouth thinned and he stabbed his fork into the lettuce. "Perhaps it'd be best if we left sleeping dogs lie."

"No," she cried emphatically.

He arched his brows at her raised voice. She wasn't the timid young woman she'd once been, shy and easily intimidated.

"I want to know what happened. Every detail. I deserve that much," she insisted.

The waiter, sensing trouble, removed their salad plates and brought out the main course. Katie doubted that she had the stomach for a single bite. She lifted her fork, but knew any pretense of eating would be impossible.

Jase ignored his steak. "I did everything I knew how to do to locate you. I pleaded with your father, asked him to give me the chance to prove myself. When I couldn't break him, I tried talking to your mother. The next thing I knew they slapped a restraining order on me. It wasn't easy for me, you know. Everyone in town knew we'd eloped, then all at once I was home and you were gone."

"I'd never been more miserable in my life," she whispered. He seemed to think being shipped off to a heartless, uncaring aunt was a picnic. "I loved you so much . . ."

"The hell you did. How long did it take you to sign the annulment papers? Two weeks? Three?"

"Five," she cried, nearly shouting.

"The hell it did," he returned, just as loud.

The entire restaurant stopped and stared. Jase glanced around, then slammed his napkin on top of his untouched dinner.

"We can't talk this out reasonably, at least not here," she muttered, ditching her own napkin.

"Fine, we'll finish this once and for all in my room."

Jase signed for their dinners and led the way across the lobby to the elevator. They stood next to each other, tense and angry on the long ride up to the twentieth floor. She paused, wondering at the wisdom of this, as he unlocked the room. She relaxed once she realized he had a mini-suite. They wouldn't be discussing their almost-marriage with a bed in the middle of the room, reminding them they'd been cheated out of the wedding night.

"All right," she said, bracing her hands against her hips. "You want to know about the annulment papers."

"Which you signed in short order."

She gasped and clenched her fists. "I signed those papers while in the hospital, Jason Ingram. I ended up so sick I could barely think, in so much pain and mental agony I was half out of my mind."

The color washed out of his face. "What happened?"

"I . . . went on a hunger strike. My aunt constantly stuck those papers under my nose, demanding that I sign them, telling me how grateful everyone was that they found me before I'd ruined my life."

Jase turned and stood with his back to her, looking out over the picturesque San Francisco skyline.

"Day after day, I refused to sign them. I insisted my name was Katie Ingram. I wouldn't eat . . ."

"You could have phoned me."

"You make it sound so easy. I wasn't allowed any contact with the outside world. I was little more than a prisoner. What was I supposed to do? Tell me!"

Her question was met with stark silence.

"I tried, Jase, I honestly tried."

"You ended up in the hospital?"

The years rolled away and it felt as though she were a naive eighteen-year-old all over again. The tears welled in her throat, making it difficult to speak "In the beginning I thought the stomach pains were from hunger. I'd lost fifteen pounds the first two weeks and . . ."

"Fifteen pounds?" he whirled around, his eyes wide with horror.

"It was my appendix. It burst and . . . I nearly died."

"Dear God." He closed his eyes.

"My mother was there when I came out of surgery. She looked terrible, pale and shaken. She pleaded with me to sign the annulment papers and be done with all this nonsense. She claimed it was what you wanted . . . I was too weak to fight them any longer. You're right, I should have been stronger, should have held out longer, but I was alone and afraid and so terribly sick. I remember wishing that I could have died—it would have been easier than living without you."

Jase rubbed his hand along the back side of

his neck. "I thought . . . assumed you wanted out of the marriage."

"No. I tried to hold out, really I did. More than anything I wanted to prove that our love wasn't going to fade, that what we felt for one another was meant to last a lifetime."

"Then I signed the papers," he whispered, "and joined the Marines."

"When I came back, you were gone."

The distance between them evaporated and he brought her into the warm circle of his arms. "I'm sorry, Katie, for doubting you."

"I'm sorry for failing you."

"We failed each other."

"I loved you so much," she whispered and her voice cracked with the depth of emotion.

"Not a day passed for five years that I didn't think about you."

His kiss was soft and sweet, reminiscent of those they'd once shared. An absolution, forgiveness for being young. For not trusting, for allowing doubts to separate them as effectively as her parents had once done. For giving in to their fears.

"If only I'd known," he whispered. His lips grazed her cheek, seeking her mouth a second time, and Katie tried not to think about this other woman Jase was about to marry. But when he kissed her again, any guilt she might have experienced died. She turned her head in an effort to meet his lips, expecting him to kiss her with the hunger she felt, the hunger he'd fired to life with the first kiss. Instead, his mouth simply slid over hers in moist forays, back and forth, teasing, coaxing, enticing.

Excitement began to build, fires licking awake the tenderness of what they'd once so freely shared.

After what seemed like an eternity, his mouth settled completely over hers and he kissed her in earnest. Jase groaned and wrapped his arms around her, lifting her from the floor, grabbing hold of the fabric of her suit, kissing her with a hunger that was so hot she felt the heat emanating from him like the warmth coming from a roaring fire.

"All these years, I believed . . ."

"So did I." She wept and laughed at the same moment.

"I loved you so damn much."

"I've always loved you . . . always."

He kissed her in a frenzy of hunger and breathless passion. When his tongue broached her lips, she was ready, her lips parted, welcoming the invasion, greeting him with her own.

He groaned again.

His hands unfastened her suit jacket, slipped it from her shoulders and let it fall to the floor.

She twined her arms around his neck, panting, breathless with wonder and shock. "Jase, oh, Jase, what are we doing?"

Three

"We're finishing what we started ten years ago." Jason repeated Katie's question without really hearing the words. He slanted his mouth over hers and devoured her lips with a hunger and need that had been buried deep inside him all these years. He sank his hands deep into her hair, loving the feel, the taste, the sense of her.

"Jase, oh, Jase."

She was the only person in the world who'd ever called him Jase, and the sound of it on her lips was more than he could stand. He took possession of her mouth before he could question the right or wrong of what was happening.

Her hands struggled with the buttons of his shirt while he fumbled with the openings to her blouse. They were a frenzy of arms, tangling, bumping against each other in their eagerness to undress. The raw, physical desire for her all but seared his skin. He sighed when he was finally able to peel the silky material from her shoulders and capture her breasts with both hands, fondling them while kissing her lips.

Their kisses became desperate as their hands caressed each other. Jason was never sure how they made it into the bedroom. He didn't stop to turn on the light or shove back the covers. He'd waited ten years for this moment and he wasn't about to be cheated a second time.

Their clothes were gone, disappeared, evaporated like the early morning fog over the bay. All that existed in that moment was their overwhelming love and need for one another.

He gently placed Katie on the mattress, then joined her, kneeling above her. She wrapped her bare, sleek legs around his thighs and raised her hips in unspoken invitation.

Through the haze of his passion, he saw her stretch her arms toward him, silently pleading with him to make love to her. In the dim light of the full moon, he watched as the tears rolled from the corners of her eyes and onto the bedspread. Her tears were an absolution for them both, for the hurts committed against them, for the long, lonely years that had separated them.

"Love me," she whispered.

"I do. God help me, I do."

His entire body throbbed with need as Jason eased forward, penetrating her body with one, swift, upward thrust. Katie buckled beneath him, sobbing with an intense pleasure as she buried her nails in his back. Her heels dug into his thighs as she rocked against him, meeting each pulsating stroke, riding him, pumping him.

He cried out hoarsely at the explosion of his climax, rearing his head back, blinded by the pure, unadulterated pleasure, breathless with the wonder and the shock.

He loved Katie. He'd never stopped. If anything the years had enhanced the emotion. He
didn't speak as he gathered her in his arms. He
was grateful when she didn't feel the need to
discuss what they'd shared. If they stopped to
analyze what had happened, they might find
room for regrets and Jason experienced none of
those now.

He eased next to Katie, keeping her wrapped
protectively in his embrace. Her head was on his
shoulder, her legs entwined with his. He stroked
the silky smooth skin of her back, needing the
feel of her to admit this was real. She was in his
arms the way she should have been all those
years ago. He dared not think beyond this moment, or look into the future for fear of what
he'd see. Eventually he felt his mind drifting toward the mindless escape of sleep.

Katie woke when Jase stirred at her side. She
rolled her head and read the illuminated dial
of the alarm clock on the nightstand. It was
three minutes after two.

"Are you cold?" he whispered, kissing her
neck.

"A little." She assumed he meant for them to
pull back the covers and started to climb off the
bed.

His hand stopped her. "No."

"No?"

"I'll warm you."

He'd already done an excellent job of that,

and seemed intent on doing so again, this time without the urgency or haste of the first.

"Jase," she whispered, unsure if they should continue. Her head, her judgment had been clouded earlier, but she was awake now, prepared to put aside whatever emotion had driven them earlier. "We should talk first . . . we need . . ."

"Later. We'll discuss everything later." He captured her nipple between his nimble lips and sucked gently.

Katie sighed and curled her fingers into his hair as the sensation sizzled through her. It didn't seem possible that he could evoke such an intensity of feeling from her so soon after the first lovemaking.

He loved her with a slow hand and an easy touch, whispering erotic promises as his lips explored the sensitive area behind her knees, then moved up the small of her back, eventually making his way to the nape of her neck. Shy and a little embarrassed, Katie couldn't keep from sighing. Again and again he coaxed a response from her, insisting she participate fully in their loveplay. She hesitated, reluctant, fearing recriminations in the morning on both their parts, but she held back nothing, including her head and her heart. She was his and had been from the time she was seventeen. His in the past, the present, always.

"I've dreamed of us like this," he whispered between deep, bone-melting kisses. "Some nights I'd wake and feel an emptiness in the pit of my stomach and realize I'd been dreaming about you."

Katie ran her fingers through his hair. "I can't believe you're here."

"Believe it, Katie, believe it with all your heart."

He entered her then and the sweetness, the rightness of their love was almost more than she could bear. Locking her arms around his neck, she clung to him on the most pleasurable ride of her life.

Eventually they did fall asleep, but it was from sheer exhaustion. Jase shoved back the sheets and they lay, a tangle of arms and legs unwilling to separate for even a moment. She'd never known happiness like this. She should have realized, should have expected it to be fragile. She just didn't know how breakable it truly was until the phone jarred her awake.

The piercing shrill sliced rudely through their lazy contentment.

Apparently jolted out of a deep sleep, Jase jerked upright and looked around as if a fire alarm had sounded.

"It's the phone," she murmured, only slightly more awake than he.

Blindly, he reached for the telephone, nearly throwing it off the night stand. It rang a third time, the loudness causing Jase to wince.

Katie looked at the clock and groaned aloud. It was nearly nine and she was due to meet with the vice-president of Great National Bank, Roger, and two other bank executives at ten. She couldn't be late.

"Elaine." Jase shouted the other woman's name and glanced guiltily toward Katie. "Sweetheart. What time is it?"

Sweetheart? He spent the night making love with her and he had the gall to refer to Elaine as *Sweetheart?*

"It's nine, already? Meet your Aunt Betty and Uncle Jerome for lunch? Sure. Sure. Of course . . . all right, all right, I'll say it. I love you, too." He rubbed a hand down his face and ignored Katie.

Katie didn't know if she could listen to much more of this without getting sick to her stomach. Tossing aside the sheet, she climbed out of bed and headed for the bathroom.

Slapping cold water on her face, she stared at herself in the mirror and didn't like what she saw. Her reflection revealed a woman who'd been well-loved. Well-used. She wasn't the woman in Jase's life any longer. Elaine was. Jase was engaged to marry the other woman.

A sick sensation assaulted her. She'd always been a fool for Jase, and the years hadn't changed that. But she wasn't about to become embroiled in an affair with a married man, or a near-married man.

"Katie."

Feeling naked and shy, she looked around for something to cover herself and grabbed a towel. Securing it around her torso, she walked back into the bedroom with her chin tilted at a regal angle.

"Mornin'," he murmured, yawning loudly. He sat on the edge of the mattress, a sheet wrapped around his waist, studying her. The appreciative look in his eyes said he wouldn't be opposed to starting the morning over on a completely different note.

How dare he act as if nothing had happened. "That was your fiancee?"

His face sobered and he nodded. At least he had the good grace to lower his gaze. "I'm sorry about that . . ."

"Not to worry—it's well past time I left." Doing her best to conceal her nakedness, she reached for her blouse, jamming her arms into it without bothering to put on her bra.

"What are you doing?" he demanded, as if it wasn't evident.

"Dressing." She glanced at her wristwatch and groaned. "I have to be in a meeting by ten. If I hurry I can get home, change clothes, and make it into the office before then."

He looked stunned. "Don't you think we should talk first?"

"I don't have time." She found her skirt and stepped into it, hastily tugging it over her hips and sucking in her stomach to fasten the button.

"Like hell. Make time."

"I can't. Not this morning." Then, realizing he probably had a point and that they did need to talk, she sighed expressively and suggested, "Meet me this afternoon."

"I can't."

"Why not?"

"My brother and his wife are arriving. Later I've got the wedding rehearsal and a dinner."

An unexpected pain momentarily tightened her throat. "That says it all, doesn't it?"

"Don't do this to me, Katie. We made love. You can't just walk out of here. Not now, especially not now."

"You're marrying Elaine." She made it a statement, unsure of what she wanted. They were different people now, not teenagers. He had his own life, and she hers. By clouding their heads with the physical they'd stepped into a hornet's nest.

"Elaine," he repeated and plowed all ten fingers through his hair, holding his hands against the crown of his head as if that would help him sort matters through. "Hell, I don't know what to do."

"Let me make the decision easy for you. *Elaine. Sweetheart. Of course I love you.*"

His face tightened. "I'm in San Francisco for my wedding. I told you that."

"I know." She sounded like a jealous shrew, but she couldn't help herself. Although it was painful to say the words, one of them needed to. It hurt, but it was necessary. "It's too late for us, Jase," she whispered, unable to disguise her misery. "Far too late."

"I suppose you're going to marry Roger," he accused, tossing aside the sheet and reaching for his pants. He jerked them on, stood, and yanked up the zipper. "He's perfect for you. Did your father handpick him?"

It was so close to the truth that Katie gasped. "Roger is generous and kind and caring and . . ."

"A pompous ass."

"I've never met Elaine but I know exactly the type of woman you'd marry," she cried. "She must be a simpering, mindless soul without a thought of her own."

Jase's eyes narrowed into thin slits.

"Let's just end this here and now," she shouted, throwing the words out at him like steel blades. Stuffing her bra, pantyhose, and shoes into her arms, she headed for the door.

"You're not walking out on me. Not again."

"Again?" she challenged. "That's the most ludicrous thing you've ever said to me." Turning her back on him, she took a great deal of pleasure in hurrying out of the suite and slamming the door.

"Katie! Don't you dare leave. Not like this."

As far as she could see, she didn't have a choice. Jase was marrying Elaine. He loved the other woman—she'd heard him say so only moments earlier. It was too late for them. Spending the night with him was quite possibly the worst mistake of her life. What a deplorable mess they'd created. She hadn't meant what she'd said about Elaine. She didn't even know the woman, but his fiancee certainly didn't deserve this. Katie was so furious with Jase and herself that she wanted to weep.

Despite the fact that her underwear was crunched up in her arms, she hurried down the hallway toward the elevator.

"Katie. For the love of heaven, stop."

Katie groaned aloud when she realized Jase had followed her. Barefooted, and with no shirt, he caught up with her at the same time the elevator arrived.

"Jase, please, just leave it."

The doors glided open and a middle-aged man wearing a pinstriped suit and carrying a garment bag stared openly at them. A blue-haired lady in a pillbox hat, who held a small dog under her arm, inhaled sharply.

Her dignity lay in a pool at her feet. Nevertheless, Katie stepped into the elevator and silently pleaded with Jase to let her go. He returned her glare and joined her.

"We've got to talk," he whispered heatedly, standing next to her as if nothing were amiss.

"It's too late for that."

"Like hell."

The two other occupants of the elevator moved as far away from them as possible. Fully aware of her state of undress, Katie wanted to crawl into the nearest hole and die.

"Jase, it's over."

"Not by a long shot. We'll discuss what happened now or later, the choice is yours."

"You're getting married later, remember?"

The elderly woman huffed disapprovingly.

Jase turned and glared at her. "Do you have a problem?"

The dog barked.

Never had it taken an elevator longer to descend to the ground floor. Katie was convinced she'd die of mortification before the doors opened to the opulent hotel lobby. The two other occupants left as if escaping a time bomb.

"We need to sort this out," Jase insisted in low tones.

She offered him a sad smile, and with as much dignity as she could muster, which at this point was shockingly little, she stepped out of the elevator.

"You're walking out on me again," Jase shouted, calling attention to them both. "That's what you've always done, isn't it, Katie?"

"Me?" She whirled around and confronted him, her voice tight and raised. "You're the one who abandoned me. You're the one who left me to deal with everything." Then, swallowing a sob, she turned and ran out of the hotel.

Four

Jason resisted the urge to slam his fist against the polished marble column when Katie literally ran out of the lobby. It was obvious nothing he said was going to convince her to stay and sort through their predicament.

Defeated and depressed, he walked back into the elevator and punched the button for the twentieth floor. Luckily he had his room key in his pants pocket or he'd be locked out of the suite, which at this point would have been poetic justice.

Once inside his room, he slumped onto the sofa and leaned forward, placing his elbows against his knees. It felt as if the weight of the world rested squarely on his shoulders. The last thing he expected Katie to do was run out on him. To prove how completely unreasonable she was, her parting shot was that *he* was abandoning *her.* That made no sense whatsoever. He didn't know how she could even think such a thing.

Fine, he decided, if that was the way she wanted it. Good riddance. He was better off without her. But he didn't feel that way. He felt the same empty sensation he had the night they'd eloped and her parents had literally ripped her out of his arms.

Although he comforted himself with reassurances, Jason didn't believe them. He'd loved Katie as an eighteen-year-old kid and God help them both, he loved her now. Nothing had changed. Except for one small, minute detail.

He was scheduled to marry Elaine on Saturday.

Elaine. Dear God, how would he ever explain how he'd spent the night with another woman? He didn't even want to think about it. Until now, Jason had always thought of himself as an honorable, decent man. He'd have to tell Elaine— there was no way around it.

Dread settled over him like a concrete weight. He expelled his breath in a long, slow exercise while he sorted through his options which, at the moment, seemed shockingly few.

He couldn't possibly marry Elaine now, not when he still loved Katie. Love! What the hell did he know of love anyway? Sixteen or so hours ago when he first arrived in San Francisco, he'd assumed he was in love with Elaine. He must love her, Jason reasoned, otherwise he'd never have asked her to be his wife. A man didn't make that kind of offer unless he was ready, willing, and able to commit the rest of his life to a woman.

Whether he loved or didn't love Elaine wasn't the most pressing point, however. He needed to decide what to do about the wedding. Really, there was only one choice. He couldn't go through with it now. But canceling it at the last minute like this was unthinkable. Humiliating Elaine in front of her family and friends would be unforgivable.

Elaine didn't deserve this. She was a wonderful woman, and he genuinely cared for her. The wedding had been no small expense, either. Her father had a good twenty grand wrapped up in the dinner and reception. Jason had invested another five thousand of his own savings.

He leaned against the sofa and tilted his head back to stare at the ceiling. It would be the height of stupidity to allow a few thousand dollars to direct the course of his life.

By all that was right he should put an end to the wedding plans now and face the music with Elaine and her family before it was too late, no matter how unpleasant the task. Again, the thought of confronting his fiancee and her family, plus the dozens of relatives who'd traveled from all across the country, boggled his mind.

Something was fundamentally wrong with him, Jason decided. He was actually considering going ahead and marrying Elaine because he felt guilty about embarrassing her and inconveniencing their families. First he needed a priest, then a psychiatrist, and that was only the tip of the iceberg.

No clear course of action presented itself and so Jason took the easy way out. As painful and difficult as it was, he'd confess to her what had happened with Katie and then together, Elaine and he could decide what they should do.

He showered, dressed, and still felt like he should be arrested. Actually, jail sounded preferable to facing his fiancee and her family. He'd deal with Elaine first and then find Katie. If his high school sweetheart, his teenage wife, thought she'd escaped him, she was wrong. As far as he was concerned it wasn't even close to being over between them.

With an hour to kill before meeting Elaine and her aunt and uncle, he drove the rental car around the streets of San Francisco, allowing his eye to take in the beauty of the sights while his mind wrestled with the problems confronting him.

He arrived outside Elaine's family home at noon.

Elaine stood on the porch and smiled when he parked the car. She was petite, slender, attractive, and as unlike Katie as any woman he'd ever met. His heart ached at the thought of hurting her.

Jason remembered the day they'd met a year earlier. Elaine worked as a secretary in the office across the hall from him, efficient, hard-working, ambitious. She'd asked him out for their first date, a novelty as far as Jason was concerned, but then he appreciated a woman who knew what she wanted. It didn't take her long to convince him they were good together.

As time passed, he discovered that they shared the same goals. Her career was important to her and she'd advanced from being the secretary to the vice-president to lower level management and was quickly making a name for herself. She'd surprised him when, two months before their June wedding, she'd decided to change jobs and had accepted a position with a rival shipping company. It seemed a lateral move to him, but her career was her business and Jason was content to let her make her own decisions.

"Did you sleep well?" she asked, wrapping her arms around his neck and bouncing her lips over his.

It was all Jason could do to keep from blurting everything out right then and there. He might have done exactly that if Elaine's mother hadn't stepped onto the porch just then. Helen Hopkins was an older version of Elaine, cultured and reserved.

"It looks like the weather is going to be lovely for the wedding," Helen announced, sounding pleased and excited. "It's always a risk this time of year, and I want everything to be perfect."

Guilt squeezed its ugly fingers tightly around his throat. Elaine was the only daughter and her parents had pulled out the stops when it came to her wedding. He wondered if it were possible for the Hopkins to get a refund at this late date, and was fairly confident that would be impossible. It was too late for just about anything but biting the bullet.

Elaine's Aunt Betty and Uncle Jerome were both in their early eighties and spry, energetic souls. They greeted Jason like family . . . which he was about to become, or would have if he hadn't run into Katie.

"I'm pleased to make your acquaintance," Jason said formally. He glanced toward Elaine, hoping to attract her attention. The sooner he explained matters to her, the better he'd feel. Or the worse, he wasn't sure yet. It might just be easier to leap off a bridge and be done with it.

"I thought we'd have lunch out on the patio," Helen said, gesturing toward the French doors off the formal dining room.

"What a lovely idea, Helen," Betty said, leading the way outside. Her husband shuffled along behind her. A soft breeze rustled in the trees as Jason followed along. He could hear birds chirping joyously in the distance, but instead of finding their chatter amusing or entertaining, he wanted to shout at them to shut up. As soon as the thought flashed through his mind, he realized his nerves were about shot. He had to talk to Elaine, and soon, for both their sakes.

"I need to talk to you," he whispered urgently in Elaine's ear. "Alone."

"Darling, whatever it is can wait, can't it? At least until after lunch."

"No." If she had any idea how difficult this was, she'd run screaming into the night. He was two steps away from doing so himself. The need to confess burned inside him.

"In a minute, all right?" She flew past him and into the kitchen, leaving Jason to exchange chitchat with her vivacious aunt and uncle until she returned with a pitcher of iced tea.

"What time did you say your brother was arriving?" Helen directed the question to Jason as she sat down at the round glass and wrought iron table. A large multicolored umbrella shaded the area, although the sky had turned grey and overcast. Jason's mood matched the gathering clouds. He felt as if he were standing under a huge cumulus, waiting for lightning to strike.

"Steve and Lisa should be here sometime around two," he answered when he realized everyone was waiting for his response.

"He had to be here to organize the bachelor party," Elaine explained.

"Naturally, Rich and Bob will help out. You met them last night, didn't you?" Helen passed the hard rolls to Jason and he nodded. He wasn't likely to forget Elaine's brothers. He'd been with Rich and Bob when he'd first seen Katie.

"They got him so drunk, Jason decided to make an early night of it, remember?" The salad bowl went from mother to daughter.

Jason was about to explain that the lone beer wasn't responsible for his 'early night,' then thought better of it.

"Don't pick on your fiance," Betty advised Elaine, winking at Jason.

"At least not before the ceremony," Jerome added, chuckling.

Helen spread the linen napkin across her lap. "You can't imagine what our morning's been like, Jason. Elaine and I were up at the crack of dawn, running from one end of town to another. It's been a madhouse around here."

"I can't believe you slept half the morning

away. That's not like you." Elaine dug into her shrimp-filled Caesar salad with a hearty appetite.

"I . . . I had trouble falling asleep," he muttered, certain her entire family knew exactly what he'd been doing.

Elaine gifted him with a soft, trusting smile. Not once since they'd decided to marry had she expressed doubts or voiced second thoughts. If she was experiencing any such notion now, it didn't show.

"Just think," Betty said, glancing fondly at her niece. "At three o'clock this time tomorrow, you'll be a married woman."

Married. Jason broke out in a cold sweat.

Elaine reached across the table and squeezed his hand. "I'm the luckiest woman in the world to be marrying Jason."

He actually thought he was going to be sick.

"Isn't love grand?" Betty murmured, and dabbed at the corner of her eye with her napkin.

By the sheer force of his will, Jason managed to make it through the rest of the meal without anyone noticing something was amiss, although he considered it nothing short of a miracle. He never had been much good at subterfuge.

He managed to answer Jerome's questions about the shipping business and make polite small talk with the women. Elaine glanced at him curiously a couple of times, but said nothing that led him to believe she'd guessed his true feelings.

"I want to steal Elaine away for a few minutes," he insisted when they'd finished with their salads. He stood and held his hand out to her.

"I keep telling him he'll have me for a lifetime after tomorrow, but he refuses to listen," Elaine joked.

Helen glanced at her watch and Jason knew what she was thinking. Steve and Lisa's flight was due to land in little more than an hour and he was a good forty minutes away from the airport.

"Ten minutes is all I'll need," he assured Elaine's mother.

"Take him out into the garden," Helen suggested indulgently.

Jason wanted to kiss his future mother-in-law. The more private the area the better. Elaine was known to have a hot temper at times and he was sure she'd explode. Not that he blamed her. Heaven almighty, what a mess he'd made of this.

The garden was little more than two rows of flowering rosebushes in the back side of the property. A huge weeping willow dominated the back yard. Elaine swung her arms like a carefree child as they strolled toward the cover of the sprawling limbs of the willow.

"I know you, Jason Ingram. You want me alone so you can have your way with me." Before he could stop her, she wound her arms around his neck and planted a wide, open-mouthed kiss across his lips.

"Elaine, please," he said, having trouble freeing himself from her embrace. She was making this impossible. The woman was like an octopus, wrapping her tentacles around him, refusing to let him go.

"Loosen up, sweetheart."

"There's something I need to tell you."

"Then for the love of heaven, say it," she replied impatiently. She leaned against the tree trunk and waited.

Jason's heart ached. He found it difficult to meet her gaze so he stared at the ground, praying for wisdom. "Before we go ahead with the wedding, there's something you should know about me."

"This sounds serious."

She hadn't a clue how serious.

This wasn't easy, and he suspected the best place to start was in the beginning. "You know that I was born and raised in Spokane."

"Of course."

"At the end of my junior year of high school . . ."

"Are you about to tell me you had a skirmish with the law and I'm marrying a convicted felon?"

"No," he snapped, thinking that might be preferable to what he actually was about to tell her. "Just listen, Elaine, please."

"Sorry." She placed her finger across her lips, promising silence.

"I started dating a girl named Katie, and we were deeply in love."

"You got that sweet young girl pregnant, didn't you? Jason Ingram, you're nothing but a little devil."

"Elaine," he snapped, growing impatient. "Katie and I never. We didn't . . . No."

"Sorry." She squared her shoulders and gave him her full attention.

"As I said, Katie and I were deeply in love." He could tell that Elaine was tempted to say something more, but he silenced her with a look. "For whatever reasons, her family didn't approve of me. Nor did they think we were old enough to be so serious." He glanced her way and found he had her full attention. "Her parents had plans for Katie and they didn't include a husband."

"I should hope not," Elaine said stiffly.

"But Katie and I vowed that we wouldn't let anything or anyone keep us apart." He experienced the same intensity of emotion now as he had all those years ago. "When we learned that her family intended to separate us, we did the only thing we could think of that would keep us together." He sucked in a deep breath and watched Elaine's eyes as he said the words. "We married."

"Married." She spit out the word as if it were a hair in her food. "That's a fine thing to tell me at this late date."

"I know . . . I know." Jason couldn't blame her for being angry.

"Jason Ingram, if you tell me that you've got a wife you never bothered to divorce, I swear I'll shoot you." Her eyes flashed fire, singeing him.

"We didn't need to bother with a divorce," he

told her quietly, sadly. "The marriage was annulled."

"Oh, thank heaven," Elaine murmured, planting her hand over her heart, her relief evident.

This was where it got difficult. Really difficult. Now was the time to mention how, through no one's fault, he'd run into Katie right here in San Francisco. Now was the time to explain how, when they saw each other again for the first time in ten years, they realized how much they still loved each other. Now was the time to explain how one thing led to another and before either of them was fully aware of what they were doing they ended up in bed together.

Now was the time to shut up before he ruined his entire life.

"Is there a reason you never mentioned this other woman before?" Elaine asked, sounding suspiciously calm. "You asked me to marry you, Jason, and conveniently forgot to mention you'd been married before."

"It was a long time ago." Canceling the wedding was as painful as anything in his life, including his own father's death.

"You should have told me."

He agreed completely. "I know."

"Well," she said, doing that sighing thing once more, as if to suggest she'd been burdened but not overly. She could deal with this. "We all make mistakes. It's understandable . . . I appreciate you letting me know now, but I must tell you I'm hurt that you kept this from me, Jason.

I'm about to become your wife, but then," she whispered, "we all have our secrets, don't we?"

It was now or never. Jason held his breath tight inside his chest. "I loved her. Really, truly loved her."

"Of course you did, but that was then and this is now." She frowned, but seemed willing to forgive him.

Now. He opened his mouth to tell her everything, but the words refused to come. His heart felt like it was about to burst straight through his chest.

"Elaine." Her mother called, and Elaine looked toward the house, seemingly eager to escape.

"I'm not finished," Jason said hurriedly, before she left and it was too late.

"I'll be right back." She kissed his cheek and hurried toward her mother's voice.

Jason clenched both fists and squeezed his eyes closed as he sought a greater source for the courage to continue. Swearing under his breath, he started pacing, testing the words on his tongue. Elaine had a right to know what had happened. It was his duty to tell her.

She returned breathless and agitated a couple of moments later. "Darling, it's a problem with the caterer. We specifically ordered pickled asparagus tips for the canapés, and now they're telling us the order came in without them."

"You're worried about asparagus spears?" Jason couldn't believe what he was hearing.

"It's important, darling. Mother's on the

phone with them now. Is there anything else, because this is important. I really need to deal with this. Mother thinks we may have to run down and confront these people right here and now."

"Anything else?" Jason knew he was beginning to sound suspiciously like an echo. "No," he said hurriedly, hating himself for the coward that he was.

"Good." She smiled broadly and then raced back to the house.

Jason stayed outside several minutes, condemning himself. Thanks to the years he served as a Marine, his swearing vocabulary was extensive. He called himself every dirty name he could think of, then slumped down onto a bench.

"Jason," Helen shouted from the back door. "Don't forget your brother."

"Right." He made his way back to the house. "Where's Elaine?"

"She's dealing with the problem with the caterer. It's nothing for you to worry about." She escorted him to the door. "We'll see you at five, right?"

"Five."

"The rehearsal at the church."

"Oh, right, the rehearsal." Jason didn't know how he would get through that, but he hadn't given himself any option. As far as Elaine and her family were concerned, the wedding was still on.

Five

A headache pounded at Katie's temple like a giant sledgehammer. Keeping her mind on track during this all-important meeting was almost impossible. She wanted to blame the wine, but she knew her discomfort had very little to do with the small amount of alcohol she'd consumed. Jase Ingram was the one responsible for her pain, in more ways than one.

Katie lowered her head to read over the proposal on the table, but her thoughts were muddled and confused, refusing to focus on the matter at hand. Her mind and her heart were across town with Jase.

"Katherine?"

She heard her name twice before she realized she was being addressed.

"I'm sorry," she murmured, "what was the question?"

"We were thinking of tabling the proposal until next week," Roger supplied, frowning slightly.

Katie didn't blame him for being irritated. She'd been useless as a negotiator this morning. Her thoughts were a million miles away with the girl she'd once been. At eighteen life had seemed so uncomplicated. She loved Jase and he loved her and their being together was all that was important.

"Tabling the proposal sounds like an excellent idea. Forgive me if I've been inattentive," she said in her most businesslike voice, "but I seem to be troubled with a headache this morning."

"No problem, Katherine," Lloyd Johnson, the first vice-president of Grand National, said kindly. "Your headache may well have given us a few more days' time, which is something we could all use just now."

Katie smiled her appreciation. "Thanks, Lloyd."

The men shifted papers back inside their briefcases. Soon the meeting room was empty save for Roger and Katie.

She knew she owed him an explanation, but she could barely find the courage to face him after her lie from the night before. She'd said she wasn't feeling well then and had him drive her home so she could sneak back to the hotel and rendezvous with Jase. It was an ugly, despicable thing to do to a man who genuinely cared for her.

"You're still not feeling well, are you?" Roger asked gently.

"I'm doing slightly better this morning." Another lie. She was worse, much worse.

"Tonight's our dinner engagement with the Andersons," he reminded Katie, eyeing her hopefully.

Katie groaned inwardly. She'd forgotten all about the dinner date which had been set weeks earlier. Had she arrived at her usual time this morning, she would have seen it on her appointment calendar. Instead she'd rushed into the office, barely in time to make the meeting.

The Andersons were longtime friends of Roger's. The couple was in town to celebrate their wedding anniversary and had invited Roger and Katie along for what promised to be a fun-filled evening on the town. They were going back to the Italian restaurant where they'd met fifteen years earlier. Fresh from graduate school, Roger had been with Larry that night as well.

Katie suspected Roger wanted to show her that he wasn't as much of a stuffed shirt as it seemed. With his friends he could let down his hair, as if that was what it took to convince her to marry him.

"You'll feel better later, won't you?" His eyes were almost boyish in his eagerness.

She couldn't refuse him, not after the callous way she'd dumped him the night before. The irony of the situation didn't escape her. She hadn't been eager to join him for drinks at the Regis. Roger knew she didn't indulge often, but he'd insisted they had reason to celebrate. They'd worked hard on this deal with Grand National Bank and would be meeting with the first vice president. It was a small coup and so Katie had given in.

She'd never thought of herself as a weak person. After her marriage was annulled she'd promised herself that she wouldn't allow anyone to control her life ever again. Yet here she was, trapped in a relationship with a man her father considered perfect for her. A man who constantly pestered her to marry him.

Marry.

By this time tomorrow Jase would be married. In her mind's eye she pictured him standing in a crowded church exchanging vows with a beautiful, sophisticated woman.

"You seem a million miles away." Roger waved his hand in front of her face, dragging her back into the present, which unfortunately was as painful as her dreams.

"I'm sorry."

"About tonight?"

She owed Roger this even if she did feel like staying at home, burying her face in a bowl of chocolate ice cream. But she couldn't do that to Roger, and it would do her no good to sit home and cry in her soup. Or in her case, ice cream. What was done was done. Jase would marry his *Sweetheart* and they'd both get on with their lives.

With time and effort they'd put the one small slip in their integrity behind them. Pretend it didn't happen. That was the solution, she realized. Denial. For the first time since she raced out of the St. Regis, Katie felt comforted. Everything was going to work out. She'd forget about him and he'd forget about her.

They'd gotten along perfectly well without one another this long. The rest of their lives wouldn't matter.

Now if she could only make herself believe that.

* * *

Standing outside the jetway at San Francisco International, Jason waited for his older brother and his wife, Lisa, to step from the plane and into the terminal. If ever there was a time Jason needed his brother's counsel it was now.

The minute he spied Steve and Lisa, his heart lightened. He stepped forward, hugged his sister-in-law, and impulsively did the same with his brother, squeezing tightly.

"That's quite a welcome," Steve said, slapping him across the back. "You ready for the big day, little brother?"

"Nope."

Steve laughed, not understanding this was no laughing matter. Jason felt about as far from being ready as a man could.

"I need to talk to you as soon as you're settled in at the hotel." His eyes held his brother's, hoping to convey the extent of his distress.

"Sure."

Jason led the way toward the baggage claim area.

Lisa eyed him skeptically. "Is everything all right?"

He longed to blurt out the whole story right then and there, but he couldn't.

"Jason?" Steve pressed. "What's wrong?"

He exhaled sharply. "I'll fill you in later. Come up to my room as soon as you're settled, all right?"

Steve nodded. "Something tells me you've gotten yourself into another fine mess."

Jason couldn't wait to see his brother's expression when Steve learned this "fine mess" involved Katie Kern. Three years his elder, Steve had played a significant role in advising Jason when he'd lost Katie the first time. The two had talked long and hard in the days and weeks following his and Katie's elopement. Frankly, Jason didn't know what would have happened if it hadn't been for his brother.

It seemed to take an eternity for Steve and Lisa to get checked in at the hotel. Jason returned to his own suite, but he couldn't sit still. He paced and snacked on a jar of peanuts out of the goodie-bar that cost more than anybody had a right to charge. And waited, impatiently, for his brother.

By the time Steve arrived, Jason had worn a pattern into the plush carpet.

"All right, tell me what's got you so worked up," Steve said and helped himself to a handful of peanuts.

"Where's Lisa?" Jason half-expected his sister-in-law to show. A woman's perspective on this might help.

"Shopping. It's only three hours until the rehearsal and she didn't know if she'd have time to hunt down those all-important souvenirs after the wedding. Mom's visiting Uncle Philip and he's driving her to the wedding tomorrow," he added unnecessarily.

Jason sat down across from his brother and

rammed his hand though his hair. "I saw Katie Kern."

"Who? . . . Katie?" Jason recognized the instant his brother made the connection. Steve's face tightened. "When? Where?"

"Last night. Here. The crazy part was she was sitting in the cocktail lounge downstairs having a drink with some old fart."

Steve watched him closely. "Did you talk to her?"

"You might say that," he muttered, rubbing the back side of his neck. "The fact is we did a whole lot more than talk."

"How much more?" Steve asked cautiously.

"We . . . ah, spent the night together."

Steve vaulted to his feet. "Oh, God."

"My sentiments exactly," Jason muttered. "I couldn't help it, Steve. Damn it all, I love her. I always have."

"But you're marrying Elaine."

"Maybe not." This wasn't exactly news to Jason. He'd wrestled with his conscience all day. The guilt was eating giant holes straight through his middle. He regretted cheating on Elaine, but not loving Katie.

"All right," Steve said, sounding calm and rational, "let's reason this out."

"Good luck," Jason said under his breath. He'd been trying to do exactly that all day and was more confused than ever.

"Where's Katie now?"

"I don't know. She ran out of here first thing this morning." He didn't confuse the issue by explaining Elaine's untimely phone call and how it had set everything off between them. "Get this. Katie ran out of here, claiming I was doing the same thing I'd done before by abandoning her."

"You? She betrayed you."

"She didn't," Jason returned heatedly. "Her parents shipped her off to her aunt's place in England. She had no way of contacting me." He didn't mention the hunger strike or that she'd nearly died when her appendix ruptured.

"You believe her?"

He nodded. Perhaps because he so desperately wanted it to be the truth.

"You were little more than kids."

"I loved her then and God help me, I love her now."

Steve sat back down. "What about Elaine?"

If Jason knew the answer to that he wouldn't be in such a state of turmoil. "I decided this morning that the only fair thing to do was tell her . . ."

Steve stopped him by raising his hand. "That would be a big mistake."

"I slept with another woman, Steve. I can't just stuff that under the carpet."

His brother jerked his hands back and forth in a stopping motion. "You might think confession is good for the soul, but in this case I don't think so."

"I tried to tell her."

"What does she know about Katie?"

Steve assumed that he'd confessed his teenage

marriage early on in their relationship, but he hadn't. "Only what I was able to relay this afternoon. I intended to tell her everything, but chickened out at the last minute."

"Thank God. The worst thing you could have done is tell her about what happened last night. Even the advice columnists think it's a bad idea. You read 'Dear Abby,' don't you?"

Jason stood and jammed his hands into his pants pockets. "Okay, so I don't say a word to Elaine about Katie. Don't mention a thing about last night. That doesn't change the way I feel."

"What do you mean?"

Jason took in a deep breath. "I . . . don't know that I want to go through with the wedding."

"What? You're joking. Tell me you're joking!" Steve was back on his feet. His brother had turned into a human pogo stick. He fastened his hand against his forehead and slowly shook his head.

"How can I marry Elaine now?"

Steve glared at him. For a minute, he seemed to be at a complete loss for words. "You're right, you're right," he said finally. "This is one of the most important decisions of your life and marriage isn't something to be taken lightly."

Jason felt part of the burden lifted from his shoulders. Steve understood. If no one else, his brother would stand at his side, support his decision, help him through this mess. Together they'd muddle through the same way they had as boys.

"But, Jason, have you considered the ramifications of canceling a wedding at the last minute like this?"

He'd thought of little else all day.

"Elaine's family has invested a lot of money in this." Why his brother felt it was necessary to remind him of that Jason didn't know. It was something he preferred not to consider at the moment.

"I know."

"Lisa mentioned that the wedding gown came from The Young Lovers. She said there wasn't a gown in the entire store under five grand."

Jason knew that, too.

"You're sure you want to cancel the wedding?"

"They're having pickled asparagus tips," Jason muttered, knowing it was a completely illogical statement.

"Pickled asparagus tips?" Steve repeated.

Jason shook his head to clear his thoughts. "Never mind." It seemed a damn shame to marry a woman he wasn't sure he loved because she planned to top the canapés with asparagus. He didn't even like asparagus. He'd never liked asparagus, and generally he enjoyed vegetables.

"I have to tell her, Steve," he murmured. "Even if it means ignoring Dear Abby's advice. Then Elaine and I can make an intelligent decision together." Surely his fiancee would realize that if he fell into bed with another woman only two days away from their wedding, something wasn't right. True, there were mitigating circumstances, but that didn't excuse or absolve him.

"I hate to see you let Katie do this to you a second time," Steve said, sitting back down and reaching for the peanuts. "There are people in this world who are just bad for us."

Jason had never thought of Katie in those terms but he didn't want to get into a verbal debate with his only brother.

"What's she like these days?" Steve inquired.

"The same." The outward trappings were more sophisticated, but it was the same wonderful, generous Katie.

"Daddy's puppet?"

Jason knew what Steve was doing and he didn't like it. "Leave her alone."

"Alone. I don't intend to contact her if that's what's worrying you. She ran out on you, remember? It isn't the first time either, is it?"

"I said stop it," he shouted.

"All right, all right." Steve raised both hands. "I apologize—it's just that I don't want you to make the biggest mistake of your life."

"Trust me, Steve, I don't want to either."

Six

The church was filled with people Jason didn't know. The priest directed traffic while the organist practiced the traditional wedding march. The musical score echoed through the sanctuary, bouncing off the ceiling and walls, swelling and filling the large church.

Everyone talked at once and soon Jason could barely hear himself think. Rich and Bob and their wives and children sat impatiently in the front pew. Bob's wife bounced a squirming toddler on her knee. A handful of kids raced up and down the aisles, refusing to listen to Elaine's mother, who chased after them.

Jason's stomach was so tight he didn't know how he'd make it through this rehearsal without being sick. He had to talk to Elaine, explain what happened with Katie, despite his brother's advice. He felt he owed her the truth.

Once he confessed the error of his ways, they could reason everything out like two mature adults and decide what they should do. The only clear answer, as far as he could see, was to cancel the wedding.

Steve elbowed him in the side. "Father Ecker

says you're supposed to step toward the altar as soon as Elaine starts down the aisle with her father."

At the mention of his fiancee's name, Jason turned toward the back of the church, hoping to find her. He hadn't seen her since lunch. Quite possibly she was still involved with the asparagus tip disaster.

When he finally did see her, his heart sank with dread. She stood just inside the vestibule with her bridesmaids gathered around her like a gaggle of geese. She wore a mock veil and carried a frilly bouquet made up of a hundred or more ribbons in a variety of colors and sizes. They came from her five wedding showers, if he remembered correctly. Oh, no. All those gifts would need to be returned.

"I have to talk to Elaine," he announced tightly.

"Now?" Steve asked incredulously.

"Yes." He wasn't putting this off any longer. He walked over to where Father Ecker stood. "I need a few minutes alone with Elaine." He didn't ask if the moment was convenient. He didn't care if he did hold up the entire rehearsal. This was by far more important.

Marching down the center aisle, he sought her out. "Elaine."

Giggling with her friends, she didn't notice him at first.

"Elaine." He tried again.

She glanced away from her maid of honor. "Jason, you're supposed to be in the front of the church," she teased.

"We need to talk," he announced starkly.

"Now?" Her eyes grew round and large.

"Right now."

Elaine cast a speculative glance toward her women friends before following him into the back of the church in the dim light of the vestibule. "What's going on? You haven't been yourself all day."

"I have something to tell you." The best way he could think to do this was to simply say it without offering her any excuses or explanations. He had no justifications to offer for sleeping with Katie.

"You need to talk to me again? Really, Jason, you're carrying this thing a bit far."

"What thing?" Maybe she knew more than she was telling.

"Nerves. Darling, everyone has them."

She didn't appear to be affected. "It's a lot more than nerves."

"You sound so serious." She laughed, making light of his distress.

"I *am* serious." He held her gaze for a long moment before he spoke again. "This afternoon I told you about Katie and me."

"Yes," she said, sounding bored. "We've already been through all that, Jason. Really, you don't have anything to worry about—I understand."

"I saw her last night."

"Katie? Here in San Francisco? I thought you said you met her in high school."

He nodded. "I did. I haven't seen her in ten years . . . the last time I did she was my wife."

Elaine's mouth thinned slightly. "But she isn't now, right?"

"No," he agreed readily enough. He paused because what he had to say next was so damned difficult.

She glared at him with agitation. "Jason, really, can't you see we're holding up the entire rehearsal? I'm beginning to lose patience with you and this woman from your past. So you saw your high school sweetheart after ten years. Big deal."

"That isn't all." His voice sank so low he wondered if she heard him.

Elaine crossed her arms and tapped her foot. "You mean to tell me there's more?"

He nodded, and swallowed hard. Lots more. "Katie and I had dinner together."

She laughed nervously. "So you had dinner with an old girlfriend. You should know by now that I'm not the jealous type. Frankly, Jason, you're making much more of this than necessary. I trust you, darling."

She might as well have kicked him in the balls. It was what he deserved.

"Katie came up to my room afterwards." It demanded every ounce of fortitude he possessed to face her, but he owed her that much.

"You don't need to tell me anything more," Elaine insisted tightly. "I already said I trust you."

She glared at him as if to will him to keep from telling her what she'd already guessed.

"Your trust isn't as well placed as you think." He ran a hand down his face and found he was shaking with nerves and regret.

"Jason," she insisted in a voice wrapped in steel. "Would you kindly listen to me? This isn't necessary."

"It is," he insisted. This was by far the most difficult thing he'd had to do in his entire life. "Elaine," he said, holding her with his eyes. "I wouldn't hurt you for anything in the world."

"Fine, then let's get back to the rehearsal. Everyone's waiting."

He didn't know why she was making this nearly impossible. "I need to tell you what happened between Katie and me."

"Must you really? Jason, please, this has gone far enough."

"Katie spent the . . ."

"Jason, stop," she snapped. "I don't want to hear it."

". . . Night with me."

It felt as if all the oxygen had been sucked from the room. The silence between them throbbed like a living, breathing animal. Jason waited for her to respond. To shout, to scream, to slap him. Something. Anything.

"I can't tell you how sorry I am," he murmured, his voice so hoarse with regret that he barely recognized it.

"Well," Elaine murmured tightly, "do you feel better now that you've bared your soul?"

"Yes . . ."

Her face tightened with a mild look of displeasure. "Do you have any other confessions you care to make?"

"Ah . . . no."

Her shoulders swelled and sank with a sigh. "Well, that's one thing to be grateful for." She started back toward the sanctuary.

"Elaine, where are you going?"

She tossed him a look over her shoulder that suggested he should know the answer to that. "The rehearsal, where else?"

"But doesn't this change things? I mean . . ." He hesitated and lowered his voice. "I made love to another woman."

"Okay, so you had a momentary lapse. Your timing was incredibly bad, but other than that I'm willing to look past this indiscretion. Just don't let it happen again."

Look past this indiscretion. She made it sound as if his night with Katie meant nothing, as if he'd used the wrong fork at a formal dinner. A minor faux pas.

She turned back to face him. "You aren't thinking of doing something really stupid, are you?"

"I thought . . . I assumed . . ."

"You thought I'd want to cancel the wedding?" She made the very idea sound ludicrous.

"Yes." That was exactly what he'd assumed would happen. He wouldn't blame her if she did decide she wanted out of the marriage. Forgiving him was one thing, but the ramifications of what he'd done went far beyond the obvious. He'd betrayed her faith in him, destroyed her ability to trust him ever again. Surely she understood that. His sleeping with Katie should have told them both something important. He wasn't ready for marriage.

"We're not calling off this wedding just because you couldn't keep your zipper closed."

"But . . ."

"Don't think I'm pleased about this, because I'm not. I'm furious and I have every right to be."

"I know . . ."

"What you did was despicable."

"I couldn't agree with you more."

"And it won't happen again."

"I still think we should . . ."

"Then I don't see what the big deal is," she said, cutting him off. "I'm willing to overlook this one incident. I have to say I'm disappointed; I never thought I'd have this sort of problem with you."

He gave her credit—she handled the news far better than if the tables had been turned. "Then you want to go ahead with the wedding?"

"Of course." She laughed, the sound grating and unnatural. "Of course, we'll still be married. After all the trouble and expense? You're joking, aren't you? I wouldn't dream of calling it off."

"Elaine . . ."

"But I want it understood that I won't tolerate this kind of behavior again."

"I wouldn't think . . ."

"Good. Now let's get back to the others before someone thinks there's something wrong." Without another word, she marched back into the sanctuary.

Rarely had Katie spent a more miserable evening. She enjoyed Wanda and Larry. Liked them. Envied them. Their love for each other was evident, even after fifteen years of togetherness, three children, a mortgage, and all the rest. Being with the couple, listening to them laugh with one another, made it all the more difficult to return to her own home, alone.

That was the crux of it, Katie realized. She was alone when she so desperately wanted the deeply committed relationship the Andersons shared. She longed for a husband, a family. It shouldn't be so much to ask. Nor should it be so difficult. Every man she'd met in the last ten years had fallen short of what she wanted in a husband. After seeing Jase again she understood why. She'd never stopped loving him. He was her heart. Her soul.

Mentally saying his name was like peeling back a fresh scab. The pain rippled down her spine. Within a matter of hours he would be forever lost to her.

"You're still not feeling well, are you?" Roger whispered. He'd been attentive all evening, and she knew why. When it came time to drop her off, he was going to bring out a dazzling diamond ring and ask her to marry him.

As tempting as the offer was, she couldn't. Roger was her friend. He'd never hurt her, never desert her or leave her emotionally bankrupt the way Jase had. Roger was kind and generous. But to marry him would be cheating this wonderful man out of the kind of wife he deserved.

Katie didn't love him. She was fond of him, cared about him, but she didn't love him. Not the way a wife should love her husband.

"I'm feeling much better," she assured him.

"More champagne?" He replenished her glass without waiting for her answer. He seemed to think a couple of drinks would fix whatever troubled her.

"You know that we met in this very restaurant, don't you?" Larry's gaze slid away from his wife's long enough to glance in Katie's direction.

"That's what Roger said."

Larry waved a breadstick in Roger's direction. "He was here, too."

"So I heard. In fact," Katie said, smiling, "he accepts full credit for getting the two of you together."

"No way." Larry chuckled.

"As I recall," Roger muttered, setting aside the goblet, "I had first dibs on Wanda."

"You make me sound like a piece of meat." Wanda pretended to be outraged, but she didn't fool anyone.

"You were such a cute little thing," Larry teased, and added pointedly, "then."

The other woman glared at her husband and

then laughed. "You try keeping your hourglass figure after three children, fellow."

Larry stood and undulated his hips a couple of times. "I managed just fine, thank you."

Katie couldn't keep from laughing. Roger's gaze captured hers and he reached for her hand, squeezing it gently. He was a handsome man, not the old fart Jase claimed. At forty-three Roger's hair was just beginning to show streaks of silver, giving him a distinguished air. While he did tend to maintain a businesslike attitude, she wouldn't call him pompous.

"Here's to another fifteen equally happy years," Roger said, toasting his friends.

"Here, here," Larry agreed.

Their dinners arrived and soon after they'd eaten, Roger made their excuses, surprising Katie.

After hugs and congratulations, Roger and Katie left the restaurant. She'd worked all day to keep the memories of Jase and the woman who would soon be his bride at bay. Her efforts had worked fairly well until that evening with Larry and Wanda.

For ten long years, Jase had been lost to her. Then life had played a cruel joke and sent him back for one all-too-brief interlude just so she'd know what she'd missed. One night of memories was all she would have to hold onto through the years.

"Thank you for a wonderful evening," she said, as she looped her arm in Roger's. He led

the way outside and paid the valet who delivered
his BMW.

"I was hoping you'd invite me up for coffee,"
he said, as they neared her condominium.

"Not tonight."

Although she knew he was disappointed, he
didn't let it show. He pulled into the crescent-
shaped driveway outside her building and kissed
her on the forehead. A touching, sweet gesture
of affection. "Sleep well, my love."

"Thanks for everything," she whispered and
slid out of the car. She waved when he pulled
away and then greeted the friendly doorman as
she entered the lobby.

By the time Katie stepped into the elevator,
unexpected tears had filled her eyes. Silly, unex-
plainable tears. She wasn't sure who she wept
for. Jase. Roger. Or herself.

Wiping the moisture from her cheek, she decided she was a mature woman, long past the
days of crying over might-have-beens.

She'd fallen in love with Jase far too early in
her life, and found him again far too late. Her
parents had taught her years ago that life was
rarely fair.

She let herself inside her condo and walked
over to the large picture window that revealed
the bright lights of the city. Her gaze wandered
to the thirty-floor tower of the St. Regis Hotel.

Hugging one arm around her stomach, she
pressed her fingertips to her lips. Fresh tears
filled her eyes as she stood and looked at the
bright, glittering lights of the city. Once more

her gaze returned to the St. Regis and Jase. Closing her eyes, she smiled and blew him a kiss, sending him her love.

Seven

"You're going to go through with the wedding then?" Steve asked Jason in the hallway outside his suite. It was well past midnight and he was scheduled to pick up his tuxedo first thing in the morning.

Elaine's brothers seemed disappointed that he'd cut his bachelor party short, but he wasn't in the mood to celebrate. He'd let the others have their fun, but hadn't participated much himself.

"That's what Elaine wants," Jason said, and slipped the plastic key into the hotel door.

"I can't believe you told her. You're a braver man than I am."

"I didn't have any choice."

"Sure you did. There are some things in life that are best left unsaid."

After the shock of Elaine's reaction, he was almost willing to agree. Frankly, he was sick of the entire matter. "I'll see you in the morning."

"You want me to pick you up?"

"Sure." He didn't show much enthusiasm for a man who was about to be married.

" 'Night," Steve said, hesitated, then added, "Jason, don't do anything stupid, okay?"

"Like what?" He resented the question.

"Contact Katie."

"No way," he said emphatically. "She was the one who ran out on me, remember?" As far as he was concerned, she'd done that one too many times. She had some gall, racing across the hotel lobby accusing him of abandoning her. No, he was finished with Katie Kern. He'd learned his lesson. Besides, she'd let him know the entire episode was a mistake and that she wanted him out of her life.

Elaine was right. They'd both put this unfortunate episode behind them and build a meaningful marriage the way they'd planned all these months. Katie had her life and he had his. It was too late for them, far too late.

Walking over to the picture window, Jason stared out over the lights of the city. He jerked his tie back and forth to loosen the knot. By this time tomorrow, he'd be on his honeymoon.

Sitting down in the large, comfortable chair, his feet on the ottoman, he reached for the television remote. No sooner had he found a sports station when the phone rang. He glanced at his wrist and saw that it was almost one. Not the time most folks would make a phone call.

"Hello."

Nothing. A wrong number or a crank call, he wasn't sure which.

"Hello," he said again impatiently. He was in no mood to deal with a jokester.

Then he knew. He wasn't sure how or why he recognized that it was Katie, but he knew beyond a doubt that the person on the other end of the line was his one-time wife.

His hand tightened around the receiver. "Katie?" He breathed her name into the mouthpiece. If he were smart he'd sever the connection now, but he couldn't make himself do it. His heart beat with happy excitement. He'd wanted to talk to her all day, needed her to help him make sense of everything—and she'd walked away.

"I shouldn't have phoned." Her voice was as fragile as mist on a moor. He heard the regret, the pain, the worry, knew her voice was an echo, a reflection of his own.

Jason clicked off the television, closed his eyes, and leaned back in the chair. "I'm glad you did."

Neither spoke. Jason suspected it was because they were afraid of what the other would say. Or wouldn't say.

Try as he might he couldn't push the memory of their night together from his mind. It had haunted him all day. Would stay with him the rest of his life.

"I . . . I wanted you to know how sorry I am," she whispered.

"Yeah, well, that makes two of us."

"I don't know how I could have let that happen." Her voice was so low, Jason had to strain to hear her.

"I'm not in the habit of that sort of behavior myself." He felt obliged to reassure her of that.

"Nor me."

That much he knew. "Why'd you run away from me this morning?" His day had been hell from the moment she'd raced out of the hotel.

He could hear her soft intake of breath against the mouthpiece.

"What made you say I'd abandoned you?" Jason asked. Her parting shot had burned against his mind all day.

She ignored the questions. "Does she know?"

He hesitated, then murmured, "Yeah, I told her."

"Oh, Jase, she must be so hurt. Hurting Elaine is what I regret the most. My heart aches for her. How . . . how'd she take it?"

He wasn't sure how to answer. Elaine had acted as if infidelity were no big deal. Certainly it wasn't a problem as far as their wedding was concerned. She knew what had happened between him and Katie, but she didn't want him to tell her.

Because he had no answer to give Katie, he asked a question of his own. "Did you tell Daddy Warbucks?"

"No." A bit of defiance echoed in her husky voice. "I'm not sleeping with Roger if that's what you're asking."

It wasn't. Then maybe it was.

"I should go." She was eager to end the conversation.

"No." There were matters that needed settling

first. He wouldn't let her break the connection when so many questions remained unanswered.

"The only reason I called was to tell you how very sorry I was. And . . ."

"And?" he coaxed.

"To wish you and . . ."

"Elaine."

"To wish you and Elaine every happiness."

Happiness was the last thing Jason felt. He was bone tired, weary to the very bottom of his soul. "Thanks."

He waited for her to disconnect the line. She didn't. He couldn't make himself do it. The telephone was the only contact he had with her. Would probably ever have.

"Katie?"

She didn't answer right away. "I'm here."

He already knew that. Knew she wanted to maintain the contact with him as long as she could, the same way he wanted to keep hold of her.

"She's all right?"

"She?"

"Elaine." Katie said the name quickly as though voicing it caused her pain. "If I learned you'd slept with another woman two days before our wedding, it would have killed me."

"She's fine." She'd been more upset with the caterers over the asparagus tips than she had been with what he'd done.

"Good . . . I worried about it all day."

So had he, but for naught. Elaine simply hadn't given a damn.

"Why'd you run out on me?" He wasn't going to let her off the hook so easily. His day had been hell and it had all started when she left him in a huff.

"I . . . don't know that I can tell you."

"Try." He rubbed his hand down his face. "I need to know."

She took her own sweet time answering. "You called her *Sweetheart.*" He heard the hesitation and the pain. "You'd spent the night making love to me and . . . and then you called Elaine your sweetheart."

"I was taken off guard by her phone call. You have to admit, the situation was a bit awkward."

"I know all that. Really, Jase, it doesn't make any difference now, does it? I suppose I was jealous, which is ridiculous in light of the circumstances." She tried to laugh and failed, her voice trembling as she continued. "All at once I was eighteen all over again and I felt," she said as she struggled to regain control of her emotions, "I felt so alone, facing an impossible situation, loving you, wanting you. Only this time it wasn't my family that stood between us, it was life."

"You ran away from me ten years ago, too."

"I didn't," she cried. "I explained what happened."

"This morning," he said, "I was that eighteen-year-old kid again, the same as you. I needed you to help make sense of what happened. Instead you walked out on me."

"All we seem to do is hurt each other."

He didn't disagree with her.

"Good-bye, Jase."

"Good-bye." He was ready to end it now. He'd gotten the answer to his question.

In the morning he'd be marrying Elaine.

Katie slept fitfully all night and was up mid-morning. Saturdays she generally did her shopping for the week and took care of any errands. This day would be no different, she decided. It wasn't the end of the world just because Jase was marrying Elaine. No matter how much it felt like it.

She dressed in jeans and a sleeveless blouse and headed for the local grocer's, but soon found herself wandering aimlessly down the aisles, her cart empty. Her mind refused to focus on the matters at hand. Instead it seemed focused on her short conversation with Jase the night before.

There'd been so much she'd wanted to tell him. Even now she didn't know where she'd found the courage to actually contact him. She'd gone to sleep, awakened, her heart heavy and sad. As she lay in bed, she knew she couldn't let it end abruptly with Jase like that. With her running out of the hotel never to see him again. And so she'd phoned, calling herself every kind of fool when he actually answered. She'd expected to wake him from a sound sleep. To her surprise he'd answered on the first ring as if he, too, were having trouble sleeping.

Instead of helping her bring some sort of closure to their relationship, their conversation created longing and wonder. To have found each other after all these years and still have it be too late.

She walked down the aisle and paused in front of the baby food section and was immediately assaulted with a sudden, unexpected flash of pain. Drawing in a deep breath, she forced herself to look straight ahead.

It wasn't until she was at the checkout stand that she realized her entire week's menu consisted of frozen entrees.

Back at the apartment, she noted the flashing light on her answering machine. It was probably Roger and she wasn't in the mood to talk to him. Not today. She was going to be completely indulgent, cater to her own whims and nurture herself. A long walk in Golden Gate Park sounded perfect.

The afternoon was cool and overcast as was often the case in San Francisco in June. Katie wore a light sweater and her tennis shoes as she briskly followed the foot path close to the water. Runners jogged past, daredevils on rollerblades, kids on skates. The breeze off the bay carried with it the scent of the ocean, pungent and invigorating.

When she'd completed her two-mile trek, she felt better. Her heart was less heavy. She checked her watch and noted that Jase and Elaine had been married all of two hours.

Because she was a glutton for pain, she went out of her way to stroll past the church where

Jase had mentioned he and Elaine would be married. The guests would have left long ago. Katie wasn't entirely sure why she was doing this. It wasn't wise, she knew, but she was indulging herself and she wanted to see the church where Jase had married his *Sweetheart*.

The church was situated on a steep hill overlooking the bay. By the time Katie had walked up the hill, she was breathing hard. She paused, leaned forward, and braced her hands on her knees.

Her gaze studied the sidewalk where she saw bits of birdseed left over from the wedding. A few small seeds had fallen between the cracks. The analogy between her life and those lost seeds didn't escape her. She felt as though her own life had fallen between the cracks. Mentally she gave herself a hard shake. She refused to give in to self-pity.

Slipping inside the darkened church, Katie's gaze went immediately to the huge stained glass window above the pulpit. A couple of older women were busy in the front, setting huge bouquets of arranged flowers around the altar.

Katie recognized that they were probably the very ones used for Jase and Elaine's wedding.

Walking up the side aisle, she heard the murmur of voices as the two women chatted, unaware she was there.

"Never in all my years as an organist have I witnessed what I did this day," the first woman said in hushed tones.

"From what I heard the bride threw a temper tantrum."

Katie's head perked up in order to better listen in on the conversation.

"While the mother dealt with the daughter, the father dealt with the groom. I don't mind telling you I felt sorry for that young man. Not that I blame him. Good grief, if he was going to change his mind, he might have done it a bit sooner than when he was standing in front of the altar."

"Excuse me," Katie said, making her way toward the two. "I couldn't help overhearing. You wouldn't by chance happen to be talking about the Ingram wedding, would you?"

The two women glanced at each other. "No," answered the first.

"Just a minute, Dorothy, I thought that might have been the name."

Dorothy shook her head. "Nope. It was Hopkins. I'm positive it was Hopkins. I played for the Ingram wedding earlier. Don't know when I've seen a more beautiful bride, either. Those two were so in love, why, it did my heart good just being here. Now that's a marriage that'll last."

"Thank you," Katie whispered as she turned away. For a moment she'd dared to hope for a miracle.

Katie speed-walked back to her condominium and took a long, hot shower. She hadn't eaten lunch and wasn't in the mood to cook so she slapped a frozen entree into her microwave. She wasn't sure when she got into the habit of eating her meals in front of the television, but it was well ingrained now. A voice, a friend, someone to share her dinner with so she wouldn't be alone.

Her favorite show was the evening news. The newscaster stood in front of a homeless shelter, a congenial soul who gave the weekend reports. "This evening the men and women dining at Mission House are enjoying Beef Wellington and succulent baked salmon fit for a king, or, more appropriate, a groom."

Groom. Great, she was going to be assaulted once again. Everywhere she turned people were talking about weddings.

"This groom experienced a sudden change of heart. Unfortunately, it was too late to warn the caterers. Rather than discard the dinner, the groom opted to serve the meal to San Francisco's homeless."

The scene changed to a group of ragged-looking men and women enjoying their elegant dinner. The camera zeroed in on a table of hors d'oeuvres, and petite canapés topped with asparagus spears.

"When asked about the wedding, groom Jason Ingram . . ."

"Jase." A flash of sheer joy raced through Katie as she roared to her feet.

Jase had called off the wedding.

Eight

Jason sat in the cocktail lounge at the St. Regis Hotel, wishing he was the type who found solace in a bottle of good whiskey. He never had been one to drown his sorrows in liquor, but if ever there was a time a man should drink, it would be after a day like this one.

He'd stood before the priest, Elaine at his side and the organ music surrounding them, and realized he couldn't do it. That very morning, he'd had every intention of going ahead with the wedding. Frankly, he couldn't see any other option. It was what Elaine wanted. What his brother, his own flesh and blood, advised. Everyone he knew seemed to think Elaine was perfect for him.

Everyone except him.

Then when he stood before Father Ecker and looked at Elaine, he knew otherwise. He remembered Katie's words on the phone from the night before. She'd claimed that if she'd learned that he'd cheated on her two nights before their wedding, she would have died. The pain of his betrayal would have killed her.

Elaine had barely been troubled by what she

referred to as his indiscretion. Not that he'd ever wanted to hurt her. He would have given anything to spare her this embarrassment, save his soul. But that was what marriage would have demanded. In that moment, he realized that no matter how painful this was to them both, he couldn't go through with it.

All this came down on him as the music swirled around them at the foot of the altar. Before the priest could start the wedding, Jason leaned over to Elaine and suggested they speak privately before the ceremony proceeded any further.

Elaine pretended not to hear him.

Fortunately the priest did hear and paused. Jason tried to tell Elaine how sorry he was, but he couldn't marry her. Then her father had gotten into the act and her mother. Soon the entire wedding party had gathered around them. Everyone seemed to have an opinion, but could reach no consensus.

When Elaine realized that he'd actually called off the wedding, she'd thrown down her bouquet, stomped all over the flowers, and then gone at him with both fists. It'd taken the priest and two ushers to pull her off him.

Jason worked his jaw back and forth to test the discomfort. He'd say one thing for his former fiancee—she packed quite a punch. But the beating Elaine had given him didn't compare with what her father had in store. Jason would almost have preferred a pounding to the financial burden facing him. Elaine's father had left

Jason to foot the bill for the dinner and reception. As best as he could figure, Jason would work for the next ten years to pay for the wedding that never was.

He took another swallow of beer and looked up to find his brother and sister-in-law. They looked pleased with themselves, as well they should. Jase had gifted them with his honeymoon. The two were scheduled to fly to Hawaii first thing in the morning. The honeymoon suite awaited them on Waikiki.

"We're checked out of the hotel," Steve said, pulling out the chair across from Jase and plopping himself down.

"I feel a little guilty having Steve and me go on your honeymoon," Lisa told him sitting next to her husband.

"You're turning down two weeks in Hawaii, all expenses paid?" Jason joked. His brother was no fool.

"No way," Lisa laughed.

"I had vacation time due me anyway. It's a little short notice, is all." Steve gave him a worried look, as if he wasn't square with this even now.

"But you swung it."

"We swung it."

"Enjoy yourselves," Jason said, meaning it. "I sure as hell won't be needing it." He wasn't sure what the future held for him.

"What about you and Katie?"

Jason mowed five fingers through his hair. "I don't know. We're different people now. I'd like to believe that we could make it, but she lives here and I work on the east coast."

"You can move, can't you? Or she can," Lisa advised. "Don't sweat the small stuff."

"Have you talked to her yet?"

"No." He'd tried phoning her twice, and each time reached her answering machine.

"What are you waiting for, little brother?"

It'd be nice for the swelling to go down on his eye, but he didn't say so. He raised his hand and tentatively tested the tenderness and winced at the pain.

Steve's gaze drifted toward the door. "Time to go, Lisa," he announced unexpectedly. "Jason's got company."

"Who?" He tossed a look over his shoulder and found Katie standing in the doorway. Her eyes lit up with warm excitement when she found him.

"Good luck," Lisa said, kissing him on the cheek as she followed Steve.

Jason had the feeling his luck was about to change. He'd found his pot of gold in his high school sweetheart.

"Jase?" Katie took one look at his face and bit into her lower lip. "What happened?" She gently cupped one side of his jaw and the pain he'd experienced moments earlier vanished.

"You don't want to know," he muttered.

"Elaine's father?"

"Nope," he said with a half-laugh. "Elaine."

"You look . . ."

"Terrible," he finished for her. He'd seen his

reflection and knew that his face resembled a punching bag. He had a bruise alongside his chin and one eye was swollen completely shut.

"Not terrible, but so incredibly handsome I can't believe you called off the wedding," she said all in one breath as she slid in the chair recently vacated by his sister-in-law.

"So you finally listened to your messages?"

"My messages. That was you? I thought . . . no, I didn't play them back. I heard about it on the six o'clock news."

There seemed to be no end to his humiliation. First Elaine punching him and now this. "They reported that I'd called off the wedding on the San Francisco news?"

"No, that you had the caterer serve the dinner at the homeless shelter."

"Oh." That salved his ego only a little. "I couldn't see any reason for all that expensive food to go to waste."

"It was a generous, thoughtful thing for you to do."

He smiled, despite the pain it caused. "I never did much care for asparagus canapés."

"Me, either." Now that Katie was here, Jason wasn't sure what to say or where to start.

"I can't believe I'm here with you. You actually stopped the wedding."

He shrugged, making light of it when it was the most difficult thing he'd ever done. "I had to," he said, taking Katie's hand in both of his. "I was in love with another woman. The same woman I've loved since I was a teenager. I've always loved you, Katie."

Her beautiful eyes welled with tears. "Oh, Jase."

"I don't know how many times I told myself it was too late for us, but I couldn't make myself believe it. We live on different coasts . . ."

"I'll move."

"I'm in debt up to my eyebrows for a wedding that never took place."

"I'm really good at managing money. In fact, I know a great place to get a loan. I've got an 'in' with the manager." She knocked down every objection he offered.

"Your 'in' doesn't happen to be Roger, does it?" he asked with a frown. He didn't want any help from Daddy Warbucks.

"No, me."

"You?" He knew she'd done well, just not that well. He felt a fierce pride for her accomplishment and at the same time was a bit intimidated. "You mean to say you'd be willing to give all that up for me?"

"Is this a formal marriage proposal, Jason Ingram?"

The question gave him pause—not that he had any qualms about marrying Katie. He'd already married her once, but his head continued to ring from his last go-around at the altar. The least he should do before considering it a second time was look at his options.

It took him all of two seconds. He was crazy about Katie and had been for more years than he cared to remember.

"Yes," he admitted, "that's exactly what I'm asking."

Her smile was probably one of the most beautiful sights known to man. Her eyes were bright with unshed tears and a happiness that infected him with a joy so profound it was all he could do not to haul her into his arms right then and there.

"I love you so damned much, Jase Ingram."

Her words were a balm to all that had befallen him that day. "I hope you're not interested in long engagements."

"How about three hours?"

"Three hours?"

"We can drive to Reno in that time."

"Are you suggesting we elope, Katie Kern? Again?" It didn't take him long to realize it was a fitting end to their adventure.

"I can be ready in say . . . five minutes."

He chuckled, loving her so much it felt as if his heart couldn't hold it all inside. "Are we going to have a honeymoon this time?"

"You can bet the house on that, Jase Ingram. My guess is it'll last fifty years or longer."

"I only hope that's long enough."

Jason paid for his beer and with their arms wrapped around each other, he brought her up to his room to collect his suitcase.

Eight hours later, they exchanged their vows. The very ones they'd promised each other ten years earlier.

Only this time it was forever.

Hasten Down the Wind

by
Rebecca Brandewyne

Prologue
The Schoolmarm

Tombstone, Arizona, The Present

A storm was coming on, Elizabeth Mulcahey thought as she glanced at the greying sky above the parking lot of the elementary school where she was a teacher. On the distant horizon, dark, swollen clouds were gathering, and the warm spring evening temperature had begun to cool quickly.

Not that it mattered. Unlike so many of her colleagues who looked forward to the coming summer, she had no plans of her own to celebrate the end of the school year.

Elizabeth enjoyed molding the young minds of children, helping to shape their futures. Orphaned in her late teens, recently divorced, and without any family of her own—not even a pet— she was always at loose ends during the summer. Usually, she whiled away her hours by puttering around her small house and garden, reading the stack of books—romances, mostly—that she had accumulated over the school year, watching old movies, and daydreaming endlessly.

These last two items were on her agenda for tonight. After supper and a bath, she planned to fix herself a big bowl of popcorn and settle down in her bedroom to watch her all-time favorite film. *Hasten Down the Wind* was about Billy the Kid and his reckless gang of Regulators. Elizabeth didn't know whether the movie was really an accurate portrayal of Billy the Kid's true-life story or not. She had researched his history at the public library, but she had been unable to track down any of the others the film depicted as members of his wild bunch. Maybe the scriptwriter had made them up. Or perhaps no one knew for sure who the rest had been.

That they might never have really existed had proved a crushing disappointment to Elizabeth, because one of the outlaws was the hero of all her daydreams. He was the handsome, mysterious, elusive Chaingo, a half-breed Apache who seemed different, somehow, from the others. Every time she watched the movie, she felt as though she and Chaingo shared some kind of bond. More than once, she had tried to tell herself what a foolish, even crazy, idea that was. After all, if the man had actually lived, he was long dead and buried, a hundred years in his grave— and in the film he was, of course, portrayed by an actor. Still, the feeling persisted, so strong that it had been a bone of contention in her marriage.

"You know, Elizabeth, I believe you're more in love with that damned movie savage than you are with me!" Michael had shouted one night. "All you do is sit around and watch that stupid film over and over, and moon around here, daydreaming. For God's sake, when are you going to grow up and get real, Elizabeth? This is the twentieth century—not the nineteenth—and it's not Billy the Kid you need to be thinking about. It's the bill collectors! Do you want us to lose our home and everything else we've worked so damned hard for?"

"Oh, Michael, no, of course I don't." Elizabeth had sighed heavily at the thought that all she and her husband seemed to do was argue. "But you knew when you left the accounting firm to set up your own office that things weren't going to be easy until you established a client base."

"That's right! Go ahead and throw that up in my face! *I'm* the one who's put us under a severe financial strain! It's all *my* fault!"

"I didn't say that, Michael."

"No, you didn't have to. Your implication was plain." He had glared at her furiously before storming away into his study and slamming the door.

Now, as Elizabeth remembered their unpleasant confrontation, she sighed as heavily as she had that day. Michael had never understood. He had been an ambitious pencil pusher, not a romantic daydreamer. She had never cared about their big, elegant house in Scottsdale, about being one of Phoenix's movers and shakers, or about climbing the corporate ladder as a social and financial success. She had just wanted to be loved.

Elizabeth would have been happy with the proverbial small white cottage with a picket fence, a husband who had paid attention to her and cared about her thoughts and feelings, who talked to her at the end of the day. A handful of wildflowers picked and offered spontaneously would have meant far more to her than the dozen long-stemmed red roses Michael had dutifully caused to be delivered every Valentine's Day and on her birthdays, along with a note purporting to be from him but actually scribbled by the florist.

Elizabeth, I love you, Happy Valentine's Day. Michael. Elizabeth, I love you, Happy Birthday. Michael. Until the divorce, when, thoroughly disillusioned, Elizabeth had thrown them all away, she had possessed a whole stack of florist's cards, each with one of those same two messages written on it. In retrospect, that pointed up how dull and plodding Michael had been in the romance department. His idea of a wild weekend was the nerve-racking one that fell before April 15 every year, when he would sit down at the desk in his study for a marathon session of numbers crunching to prepare his clients' tax returns.

During one such period, in a futile effort to gain her husband's attention for just a few minutes, Elizabeth had whimsically drawn a big num-

you'd better get a grip on yourself before you wind up a complete mental case, locked up in a sanatorium somewhere!"

Elizabeth tossed the TV dinner's empty styrofoam tray into the trash. She longed for a bath, but she was scared to take one now, since the rain had started to come down in earnest. Water attracted lightning, she had always heard, and she didn't want to be fried in her bathtub. So she changed into her long, frilly, sleeveless white cotton nightgown—which looked exactly like something from the 1800s—then popped herself a bowlful of corn. She would *not* watch *Hasten Down the Wind,* she insisted firmly to herself.

But despite her best intentions, that was the movie Elizabeth found herself inserting into the VCR in her bedroom a few moments later. The opening credits rolled, but she paid them no heed. She wasn't interested in the actors—only in the character Chaingo. He sat atop a huge black stallion as Billy the Kid and the outlaw gang rode over the crest of a scrubby desert hill, their figures silhouetted against a southwestern sky roiling with thunderclouds and lightning. The desperadoes' faces were young, hard, and resolute. Bandoliers stuffed with cartridges crisscrossed their chests. Rifles, carbines, and shotguns were jammed into their saddle holsters; heavy Colt revolvers—the Wild West's notorious "Equalizer"—rode at their wide leather belts. The handle of a big bowie knife protruded from Chaingo's boot.

As the men galloped down the hill, the storm

brewing on the horizon erupted, just like the
one that now enveloped Elizabeth's house. Rain
pelted against the French doors that led to the
deck off her bedroom, and beyond, lightning
forked across the sky that had turned eerily
blacker than black. On her television screen,
once the opening credits had disappeared, there
was some brief dialogue among the desperadoes.
Then the film flashed back in time to show the
events that had led to the formation of the
Regulators.

At that exact moment, a horrendous burst of
lightning shattered the heavens, the huge, jagged bolt seeming to come straight into Elizabeth's house and through her television set.
Fleetingly, she felt the hairs on her neck and
arms stand on end, warning her of the mon-
strous surge of electricity that was about to
strike. Then, abruptly, her entire bedroom appeared to explode in a blaze of brilliant, dazzling, white-hot light—and she knew nothing
more.

O_{NE}

Lincoln County, New Mexico, The Past

Elizabeth awoke in the morning to grey sunlight slanting drearily through her bedroom windows. As she lay there, still half asleep, listening to the birds chirping softly outside, she remembered that while she had slumbered, she had dreamed the strangest thing: there had been a thunderstorm sometime last night and while she was watching her favorite movie, a titanic bolt of lightning had struck her bedroom, blinding her and knocking her unconscious. At the memory, Elizabeth smiled to herself to chase away the vague, peculiar sense of uneasiness that suddenly assailed her. Really! What a bizarre, foolish dream that had been. If its events had occurred in reality, her entire house would undoubtedly have burned to cinders—and her along with it. Instead, she was alive and well, and her bedroom was just as it had always been, just as it should be—

As she glanced around to reassure herself, Elizabeth sat bolt upright, stricken. Good God! What on earth had happened to her? Where in the world was she? Bewildered and panicked, she took in the details of the unfamiliar bedroom. She *wasn't* at home—safe in her own bed. No, she was somewhere she had never been before, in a bedroom she had never seen.

She belatedly grasped the fact that the bed in which she lay was a high, old-fashioned tester with a small set of wooden steps leading up to the feather mattress topped by linen sheets and a gorgeous handmade quilt. A massive wardrobe towered against one flowery papered wall, and an ornate vanity with an ancient smoky mirror rose against another. Before a small fireplace stood a goose-necked love-seat upholstered in blue velvet. In one corner, there was a washstand with a white porcelain pitcher and basin, and on the table next to the bed, a Victorian lamp. Small Oriental rugs were scattered upon the hardwood floor, and lacy curtains hung at the windows.

Elizabeth's first thought was that she had been kidnapped. While she slept, crooks had broken into her house and carried her off. Even at this very moment they were probably in the room next door, telephoning their ransom demand to— To whom? Michael? He wouldn't pay a cent for her safe return, and she had no one else in her life. The elementary school where she worked certainly wasn't about to meet any ransom demand.

Before she could ponder her predicament further, there came a soft knock at the bedroom's heavily carved door. A young Mexican woman dressed in a crisply starched and pressed maid's uniform, complete with a frilly white apron and cap, stepped inside. She carried a copper bucketful of water in one hand.

"Good morning, Miss Elizabeth," she said cheerfully.

"Good morning," Elizabeth replied, shocked that the young woman—who was a total stranger—knew her name.

Still, despite the maid's apparent friendliness, Elizabeth decided it would behoove her not to ask any questions right off, to study her situation instead and learn as much as she could before taking any action. She watched closely while the young woman moved around the bedroom, pouring water into the pitcher on the washstand, then opening the wardrobe and withdrawing various garments.

Well, that explains everything. I'm not really awake yet. I'm still asleep and dreaming, Elizabeth thought as she gazed at the apparel. The clothes the maid was laying out were plainly Victorian: a chemise, a pair of pantalets, a corset, a set of voluminous ruffled petticoats, and a long morning gown.

Clearly, Elizabeth was expected to garb herself in this ensemble, and since she now understood that she was dreaming, she saw no reason not to comply. Flinging back the bedcovers, she rose, slightly surprised to find she was still wearing the nightgown she had donned last evening—except that she was naked beneath it, her panties having somehow disappeared. She climbed down the short set of steps at the side of the bed, mildly amused to spy the white porcelain chamberpot peeking from beneath the eyelet-lace dust ruffle.

After washing her face and hands in the basin, Elizabeth cleaned her teeth with the sterling silver toothbrush and tin of tooth powder that sat to one side. Then she dressed herself, grateful for the maid's assistance, as there seemed to be an inordinate number of buttons, hooks, and tapes that required fastening.

"I don't know how the women of the eighteen hundreds stood being constricted by these dreadful contraptions," Elizabeth complained, gasping for breath as the maid attempted to lace her into the corset. "It's sheer torture, pure and simple, and since this is my dream and I can do as I please in it, I simply won't wear this monstrosity. Take it off, if you please."

"M—M—Miss?" The maid glanced at her, obviously puzzled and horrified. "I—I not speak English so good. So I think maybe I not understand. What you mean . . . *dream?* And take off the—the corset, Miss Elizabeth? No . . . no, I cannot! What would your father say? Is not proper for young lady not to wear the corset. He be so angry, perhaps, that I lose my job here at the ranch!"

Father? Ranch? Elizabeth's dream was growing more complex by the minute. She couldn't remember the last time one had been so vivid and involved, so sharply in focus that it actually seemed to be happening in reality. The corset, for example, certainly *felt* real. She could hardly breathe as the young maid—obviously more fearful of losing her job than of displeasing her mistress—finished lacing it. On the other hand, Elizabeth thought as she studied her reflection critically in the dresser mirror, she had never looked so slender and curvaceous, especially after the remainder of the garments were in place.

Once Elizabeth was dressed, the maid indicated that she should be seated on the tufted satin chair in front of the dresser.

"What's your name?" Elizabeth asked as she sat down.

"Miss?" the young woman said nervously, once more eyeing her askance. Then the maid's brow furrowed with concern, and she laid her hand tentatively against Elizabeth's forehead. "You don't have fever. Still, you not feeling well, miss, I think. Maybe you fell sometime in the night . . . hit your head on bedpost? I'm Lupe, miss. I been your maid for last five years."

Five years! Elizabeth searched her mind diligently, trying to recall if she had ever had a dream in which time had been mentioned in such a fashion. She remembered a nightmare in which a giant, ominously ticking clock had hung on a crooked wall, and she had known she had only until midnight to accomplish some task that had consistently eluded her until, at last, she had awakened in a cold sweat, her heart pounding. But other than that, she could not recollect any dream in which time had been anything other than strangely out of kilter.

She didn't want to continue this particular dream. It had piqued her curiosity briefly, but now it was beginning to unsettle her. She told herself firmly to wake up. But nothing happened. She didn't suddenly find herself back in her own house. That disturbed her greatly, because she should have been able to rouse herself. Even when you were being chased in a nightmare and your legs seemed to stop working, if you simply turned and faced the monster, you would wake up. Something was terribly wrong—she couldn't seem to escape from this bizarre dream.

Lupe picked up the silver-backed brush that lay upon the vanity and began to brush her mistress's long blond hair. To Elizabeth's shock as she glanced down at the mirrored tray on the dresser, she observed that her initials were engraved upon the sterling silver lid of the powder box. Her distress escalated. Perhaps she was not really dreaming at all, but had somehow gone insane. Was she even now sitting in a padded cell somewhere, drugged, oblivious to reality, floating in the confines of her fantasies?

"Lupe," she began slowly, hesitantly, "maybe you're right and I *did* bang my head somehow last night, because to tell you the truth, I *do* feel . . . well, a little odd and—and mixed up. So please don't think I'm crazy, but . . . could you tell me where I am?"

"Oh, I just knew something was wrong, Miss Elizabeth! Your poor head!" The young woman ran her palms over Elizabeth's scalp, searching for a bump but finding nothing. "Maybe you just bruised. Or have ague coming on, even though you don't got fever—yet. You at your father's house, miss."

"And—and who is my father?"

"Why, John Chisum, miss. He be one of the biggest ranchers in Lincoln County!"

John Chisum! Lincoln County! Elizabeth thought, absolutely stunned by this news. No! That just couldn't be right! This was the twentieth century. There was simply no way John S. Chisum, the once-famous cattle baron of Lincoln County, New Mexico, could still be alive . . .

"Lupe, what's today's date?" she asked anxiously.

"Today? Why, is February 14, miss. February 14, 1878. Miss Elizabeth, maybe I should have your father send for doctor."

"No!" Elizabeth exclaimed, aghast. "No, please . . . I'm all right." She forced herself to take a deep breath, to continue more calmly as she realized how wild and desperate she had sounded. There was no way she wanted to see a physician, especially if—as she was now beginning to suspect—she had somehow been transported back in time. What other explanation could there be? She had been watching a movie in the twentieth century; the violent lightning had struck; she had awakened in the nineteenth century. "Really, I'm all right. My mind's clearing now. I think perhaps I was just momentarily faint and disoriented from being laced so tightly. I feel fine now. I'd better join Father at breakfast before he grows upset at my tardiness."

Much to Elizabeth's relief, Lupe, although a

tiny frown of worry still knitted her brow, accepted the explanation without protest. Plainly, she was accustomed to following orders.

The 1800s! Elizabeth nearly groaned aloud with dismay. This just couldn't be happening! This just couldn't be real! Things like this took place only in time-travel novels—not in the real world! She remembered thinking last night that perhaps she was slipping over the edge that separated sanity from madness. Maybe that's what had occurred. Still, she couldn't shake the eerie sense of *déjà vu* that gripped her as she followed Lupe through the house to the dining room downstairs. This *was* John S. Chisum's house—at least, the house he owned in the film *Hasten Down the Wind.*

Good grief! Elizabeth thought, stricken anew as yet another distressing notion occurred to her. Was it possible she had somehow been transported not just back in time, but also actually *into the movie itself?*

Her "father," John S. Chisum, the "Cattle King of New Mexico," sat at the head of the dining room table, reading a newspaper. He looked just as he did in the movie—like the actor who portrayed him. As she made her entrance, Elizabeth drew up short, half expecting to hear the director yell, "Cut! Let's try it again, people." Instead, her father merely glanced up from the newspaper, lifting one thick eyebrow.

"Elizabeth." He greeted her in a deep, dry

voice, pulling his pocketwatch from his vest and examining it pointedly. "You're late this morning. That's not like you. Did you have trouble sleeping again last night?"

"A little, Father," she managed to choke out. After helping herself to the breakfast arrayed in sterling silver dishes on the massive sideboard, she took what she hoped was her usual seat at the dining room table.

To her relief, she had apparently guessed right, for her father made no comment to the contrary. Instead, he resumed reading his newspaper. As Elizabeth applied herself to her breakfast, she studied the newspaper's headlines, noting that today's date *was,* indeed, February 14, 1878. She still found that fact difficult to assimilate—for if she were back in the past, shouldn't her father look like himself instead of an actor who had portrayed him in a film? And had John Chisum actually *had* a daughter in real life?

The only thing she really knew about him, in fact, was that he had sided with John H. Tunstall and Alexander A. McSween against Lawrence G. Murphy and Company in the Lincoln County Wars. Tunstall, a wealthy, twenty-four-year-old Englishman, had settled in the Pecos Valley, becoming a cattleman, banker, and merchant. McSween had been his attorney and partner. The Wars had begun when Murphy allied himself with J. J. Dolan and John Riley, who had co-owned a big general store, The House, in the town of Lincoln. As a result, they had held a virtual monopoly on trade in the county and the surrounding valley, and they had also controlled most of the extremely profitable government contracts for supplying beef to the Army posts and Indian reservations.

Because of that, the Chisum-Tunstall-McSween faction had sought to challenge the merchants' dominance. A group of small ranchers who loathed Chisum for having seized public grazing lands for the use of his own vast cattle herds had joined forces with Murphy and Company. Another circle of small ranchers and farmers—who had been refused credit at The House—had lined up on the side of Chisum, Tunstall, and McSween. Tunstall had further exacerbated the disagreement when he had opened a general store of his own in Lincoln, in direct competition with The House.

Eventually, after two years of escalating violence on both sides, Tunstall had been shot to death, and that became the spark that ignited the Lincoln County Wars in earnest.

The Lincoln County Wars! Oh, my God, Elizabeth thought, suddenly horrified. *February fourteenth!* It was just four days before the brutal murder of John Tunstall, who had given Billy the Kid a job as a cattle guard. Tunstall's killing had set off the savage rampage of Billy the Kid and the Regulators. She had to find some way to warn poor, unsuspecting Mr. Tunstall! No, she couldn't do that—because what if the result somehow changed history, wiped out the world as she knew it in the twentieth century? Wasn't that one of the problems with time travel—possibly altering the future? Elizabeth felt so torn that she didn't know what to do. Laying down her fork, she cleared her throat nervously.

"Father, how are your . . . difficulties with Mr. Murphy and Company going?"

"Not well at all, Elizabeth, I'm sorry to say. Dolan and Riley are a pair of merchants, for God's sake! So what in the hell can they possibly know about cattle ranching—the economic backbone of this very valley? I'll tell you what: Not a damned thing! Yet they've got every politician in the territorial capital building at Santa Fe in their back pockets—not to mention every law-enforcement official in the town of Lincoln. It's a disgrace, that's what! Now, Dolan and Riley have managed to obtain a court order attaching some of John's horses as payment for what they claimed was an outstanding debt. John has informed me that he has no intention of complying with that order and surrendering his horses—and I don't blame him one bit! No, sirree! Why, if even just one of those crooked sheriff's deputies attempts to set foot on my land, he won't live to regret it! But quite frankly, Elizabeth, I'm worried about John. He's too decent and kind-hearted to deal with men like Murphy, Dolan, and Riley. John's English. He doesn't understand the West, the code men live by out here."

From these last words, Elizabeth realized her father was, as she had suspected, talking about John Tunstall.

"I'm worried about him, too, Father," she declared. "Can't you at least warn him that he needs to hire some men to guard him as well as his cattle? I—I wouldn't put it past Murphy and Company to—to murder him. They're wicked men who will stop at nothing."

"Don't you think I *have* told him that, Elizabeth?" her father inquired, rustling the pages of his newspaper. "But John's as stubborn as a mule. He simply won't listen. He insists he won't have hired guns on his property."

It was all Elizabeth could do to restrain herself from blurting out that John Tunstall already had a slew of gunfighters on his ranch. He just didn't know it—and never would if she didn't tell him. But—especially in light of her father's failure to convince the young Englishman—how could she possibly hope to persuade Mr. Tunstall of the danger he was in? If she went to him and explained that she had somehow come back to the past from the future, he would think she was crazy. He might even suggest to her father that she should be locked away!

What could she do? How could she possibly avert the tragedy about to erupt in Lincoln County?

She was still asking herself that same question at dawn on the day John Tunstall was to be murdered.

Two

It was another grey, bleak day that broke on the horizon the morning of February 18, 1878. By now, four days into her drastically changed life, Elizabeth had grown accustomed to the fact that she had somehow been transported back in time—and possibly even into a movie that might actually still be running on the television set in her bedroom at home. This last seemed utterly fantastic, but she could not discount it. If she were back in the past, then the film, too, would surely be altered to include her in the tale of Billy the Kid and the Regulators, would it not? That only made sense—if anything at all about this incredible adventure could be said to make sense.

One thing Elizabeth was certain of: No matter the reality or lack of it with regard to her current situation, and regardless of the outcome of her meddling—it was simply not morally within her to stand idly by while John Tunstall was brutally murdered. Thus resolved, she had instructed her father's cook, Rosa, to bake half a dozen pies and was hell-bent on delivering them to the Tunstall ranch. It was the best—the only—

credible excuse she had been able to devise for getting herself to the scene of the crime before it actually took place. She could have just sneaked out, saddled up a horse from the corral, and ridden alone to the Tunstall spread. But having lived in Arizona all her life and rarely traveled, she knew little or nothing about the geography of New Mexico. She hadn't a clue as to where the Tunstall ranch on the Rio Feliz was, so she had arranged for Manuel, one of the grooms, to drive her there in the Chisum buggy.

Manuel assisted her into the vehicle's seat, then handed her the pies, which she carefully set beside her. Then he climbed in and, releasing the brake and gathering up the long leather reins, clucked to the two horses. With a lurch, the buggy rolled forward along the rough road.

Elizabeth wanted to urge the groom to hurry, but she couldn't think of any legitimate reason why he should—and if she told him the truth, he might think her crazy. So she bit her lip to hold back the words she longed to utter to Manuel about speeding up the horses—and worried silently that she might not arrive in time to prevent John Tunstall's killing.

Had he been shot in the morning? The afternoon? Elizabeth didn't know, and she sighed heavily at the realization that even in the "enlightened" twentieth century, there should be so much of history that was still as obscure as the so-called Dark Ages.

"It's chilly today, isn't it, Manuel?" she remarked, shivering a little and pulling her fur-trimmed cloak more closely about her as the brisk wind whipped across the cactus-dotted desert. For a moment, she thought longingly of her car, of its heater and its speed. Until now, she had never before grasped just how slow and uncomfortable travel in the past had been.

"*Sí, señorita,* is very chilly," Manuel agreed.

He did not seem disposed to talk to her, Elizabeth thought. In fact, her attempt to draw him into conversation had appeared to leave him ill at ease. Then, abruptly, it dawned on her that in the nineteenth century there had been strict social, racial, and gender barriers. It wasn't reasonable, she supposed, to expect the groom to engage in easy chitchat with her. After that, she didn't try to speak to him, but sat beside him in silence, lost in reverie.

It had been spring, nearly summer, when she had left the twentieth century. Here in the past, it was winter, advancing toward spring. Elizabeth wondered what else might be different. As they turned onto the winding dirt road leading up to John Tunstall's ranch, she saw that his house looked the same as it had in the film. And—galloping ominously over the crest of a knoll in the distance was the posse the sheriff of Lincoln County, William Brady, had sent to seize John Tunstall's horses. At the posse's vanguard was the sheriff's deputy, William "Billy" S. Morton. Both Morton and Brady were in cahoots with Murphy and Company and the territorial capital politicians who composed the notorious Santa Fe Ring.

"Oh, no! *No!*" Elizabeth exclaimed softly to herself. Then, turning grimly to the groom, she directed, "Hurry, Manuel, hurry! Something terrible is about to happen! I can feel it in my bones!"

"I think you right, Miss Elizabeth. So I take you home. We not get involved in this." Hauling determinedly on the reins, the groom began to wheel the team around, even as a group of Tunstall's ranch hands, also spying the posse, mounted up to flee.

From old daguerreotypes published in various books on the Wild West, Elizabeth recognized William H. Bonney—alias Henry McCarthy, alias Billy the Kid—at the fore of the ranch hands who were running away. Then her heart leaped to her throat, for behind him—unmistakably—was Chaingo, seated on the big, black stallion he rode in the movie. In that moment, as though she had made some gesture that had attracted his attention, the half-breed turned in the saddle and looked directly at her. A powerful current of electricity surged like a live wire between the two of them. But there was no time to analyze the strange, wild sensation, for just then, she saw John Tunstall riding out to confront the posse.

At that, without thinking, Elizabeth abruptly leaped from the buggy, paying no heed to Manuel's urgent cries as he fought to pull the horses to a halt. She had forgotten about her long skirts, however, and tripped and almost fell before she managed to run on toward the lone man cantering so unwittingly to his death.

"Mr. Tunstall! Go back! Mr. Tunstall! Your life is in grave danger!" Elizabeth shouted, cursing the corset that crushed her lungs and the high-button shoes, never intended for racing over uneven terrain.

He didn't hear her. He had already reached the lawmen and begun to protest their presence on his land. She was too late. Somehow, Elizabeth knew that in her heart even before she watched, horror-stricken, as Billy Morton pulled his pistol from its holster and cold-bloodedly shot John Tunstall. For an instant, she thought that maybe, miraculously, Morton had somehow missed. But then, as though in slow motion, blood spurted from Tunstall's wound and he crumpled from his saddle to sprawl upon the earth. He was still alive, struggling to rise. But before Elizabeth could run to his assistance, one of the posse members, Tom Hill—who she knew would later be killed while stealing some sheep—rode up. Placing his rifle against the back of Tunstall's skull, Hill fired point-blank, blowing out Tunstall's brains.

After that, all hell broke loose. With a cry of rage, Billy the Kid jerked his horse around and galloped back toward the scene, guns blazing. The rest of the ranch hands came hard on his heels, their own revolvers spitting bullets. Morton's men responded with a barrage of shots. Dimly, utterly terrified—because things like this just hadn't happened in her previously quiet, solitary life—Elizabeth realized she was caught in the crossfire. Instinct alone caused her to fling herself down, to hug the ground, praying she would not be struck by a stray bullet.

The sound of the shots was deafening, making her ears ring. The acrid smell of gunpowder filled her nostrils, and she could taste the gritty desert sand as she lay with her face pressed to the ground. She trembled uncontrollably, sobs rising in her throat. In her daydreams, she had never imagined anything like this—couldn't, even now, believe it was happening. She *must* be dreaming. Oh, she must be!

"Wake up. Oh, please wake up, Elizabeth," she murmured tearfully to herself, her teeth chattering from fear and cold, her heart hammering in her breast.

But she didn't wake up because this wasn't a dream. A bullet zinging past her ear brought that fact home all too graphically. Horses' hooves thudded on the earth. She wondered numbly if instead of being killed by a rifle or shotgun blast, she would be trampled underfoot in the melee. She could hear men hollering as they hurriedly sought cover. Bullets ricocheted off fence posts and barrels, splashed in water troughs. From the corners of her eyes, she saw that her father's team, spooked by the gunfight, had run away with Manuel. She watched the groom and buggy disappear over the horizon.

Then, as suddenly as it had begun, the battle was ended. The ranch hands successfully drove off Billy Morton and the posse, who cursed and yelled threats over their shoulders as they beat a reluctant but rapid retreat. After waiting several long minutes to be certain they didn't plan on returning, Elizabeth got to her feet, dazed and shaking, her heart still racing. Somehow, she had lost her hat. Her long hair, neatly swept up and arranged in an intricate French knot by Lupe earlier that morning, had tumbled from its pins. Stripping off her gloves to wipe at her tearful eyes, Elizabeth became aware that she had scraped her cheek on the sand and it was bleeding. Anxiety about infection assailed her. Had penicillin been discovered by the late 1800s? She was filled with despair to realize that despite her extensive education, there was still so much she didn't know about the past.

A short distance from where she stood, John Tunstall's body lay, his bloody face contorted in shock and disbelief. One hand flew to her mouth to hold back her sobs as Elizabeth turned away from the grisly sight. Why hadn't she come here yesterday? she asked herself dully. She might have prevented his murder. Or maybe she couldn't have, no matter what she had done. Maybe the truth was that the past couldn't be changed at all.

She wondered if Manuel had got control of the runaway horses, if he would be back for her. He believed her to be John Chisum's daughter, so surely he would be afraid to return without her. Limping a little in the tight high-button shoes, Elizabeth started to walk toward the road. But she hadn't taken more than a few steps when she abruptly found herself surrounded by the ranch hands, Billy the Kid at their head.

"Where do you think you're going, Miss 'Lizabeth?" he inquired as he sauntered toward her menacingly, obviously still caught up in his murderous rage.

"Home," she said quietly, studying him warily.

Why, he might have been some backward high school punk, she thought, surprised. He wasn't very old—eighteen, nineteen?—and he certainly wasn't big or handsome. Indeed, such was the overall composition of his face and the semi-vacantness of his eyes that she suspected he bordered on being simpleminded. He surely did not resemble the deadly desperado of history. Then she remembered that those stories depicting him as a swaggering, cold-blooded killer had circulated only during the weeks and months following his death. Later tales had portrayed him as being good-humored—always laughing—and of a generally obliging and polite nature. Near the end of his short life, he was rumored to have killed as many as twenty-three men, not including Mexicans and Indians. Historians, however, insisted the total was no more than nine at the most—and most of those, they declared, Billy had murdered by trickery or accident, not in duels at high noon.

His exact date of birth was unknown. Even his mother's and father's names were uncertain. Billy's real father had apparently died young, so he had never known him, and when his mother remarried, Billy had taken his stepfather's name.

When he was fourteen, Billy lost his mother, too. She died of tuberculosis in Silver City, New Mexico.

An older man who had stolen a Chinese laundryman's garments as a prank, had turned Billy into a fugitive at age fifteen when he asked Billy to hide the purloined clothes. To teach Billy a lesson, the sheriff locked him up in jail. Terrified after two days of confinement, Billy escaped by crawling up the jail's chimney.

Elizabeth realized that just a little over six months ago, in August, Billy would, if the tales about him were true, have killed his first man. His victim was a burly blacksmith by the name of Frank "Windy" Cahill, who had continually made fun of him and finally wound up calling him a pimp and then attacking him. Billy had seen no other way to defend himself except by pulling his gun and firing.

Elizabeth couldn't help but feel sorry for him. He had been dealt a rough hand in a hard time period—and in the end, he wasn't so very different from the troubled teens of the twentieth century, she thought.

"Home?" Billy repeated her answer to his question. "You ain't going home, Miss 'Lizbeth. I heard what you was hollering to Mr. Tunstall right before ole Morton gunned him down. Sounded to me like you knew what was about to happen."

"I did," Elizabeth replied.

"Aha!" Billy giggled abruptly, as pleased as punch at having his suspicion proved correct.

"You admit it, then! Well, maybe I can't read so good, but it 'pears to me like the only way you could have known that posse was going to murder Mr. Tunstall is if your daddy betrayed him, sold him down the river to Murphy and Company and the Santa Fe Ring! Ain't that right, boys?" He glanced around at the other ranch hands for confirmation of his theory.

Frightened by the accusation and by the young men's hard stares, Elizabeth instinctively sought the one face she thought would be friendly: Chaingo's. But to her distress, his dark, proud, handsome visage was inscrutable.

"No, that's not true!" she protested, licking her lips nervously. "My father didn't know what was going to happen to Mr. Tunstall. He doesn't even know I'm here. I—I came to bring Mr. Tunstall some pies our cook baked yesterday, that's all. And when I saw Mr. Morton and the posse, I just suddenly got a—a real bad feeling. That's why I was trying to warn Mr. Tunstall to go back, that his life was in danger."

"Uh-huh," Billy drawled, his skepticism plain. "Why should we believe you, Miss 'Lizbeth?"

"Because I'm—I'm telling you the truth!" she insisted, knowing instinctively that he and the rest would surely burst into laughter if she tried to explain to them that she was a visitor from the future. Still, the fact that she was not telling them the whole truth somehow communicated itself to the young men. Elizabeth realized then that they were as "streetwise" as any of the ghetto youth of the twentieth century and that it would behoove her to deal with them as such.

"Take her inside," Billy ordered the other desperadoes, motioning toward John Tunstall's house with one of his guns. "We'll keep her here until we can find out whether she can be trusted. If she can, we'll let her go. But if Chisum's sold out to Murphy and Company and the Santa Fe Ring, we'll hold her for ransom and make Chisum pay!"

Matters were not going at all as Elizabeth had imagined in her daydreams. She had invariably envisioned herself as a heroine, riding to John Tunstall's rescue and winning Chaingo's heart. She had not seen Mr. Tunstall lying dead on the ground and herself as a prisoner of these young men—whom she had always thought of as romantic heroes, not the counterparts of twentieth-century gang members. So it was with a great deal of relief that she spied Manuel returning in the buggy. Before the desperadoes realized what she intended, she hitched up her skirts and began to run frantically toward the groom, hoping to make good her escape.

Behind her, Elizabeth could hear the sounds of shouts and cursing and boots pounding on the hard earth, and they spurred her on, for she knew then that at least one of the young men had given chase. But she couldn't get her breath in the constraining corset. Her skirts and high-button shoes weren't any help, either. In moments, she was grabbed around the waist from behind and flung roughly to the ground.

Her assailant landed on top of her, the impact of his weight knocking the wind from her. Feeling as though she were being crushed to death beneath him, she fought wildly to free herself, gasping desperately for air. Realizing then that she couldn't breathe, her captor rolled swiftly to one side, turning her over as he did so, one long leg thrown across her to hold her down, one strong, sure hand pinning her wrists above her head, the other pressing a knife warningly to her throat.

Elizabeth's breath rasped, catching on a serrated edge as she stared up into Chaingo's fathomless black eyes, deep set in his finely chiseled face framed by long, sleek, black hair.

"Be still! Be quiet!" he growled, pricking her gently with the point of the blade. "Don't try to fight me. Don't make me hurt you. Don't you see how your running away has given the others even greater cause to doubt that you are worthy of their trust?"

Yes, now, in retrospect, Elizabeth *did* recognize that fact—and regretted her impulsive action as the rest of the desperadoes opened fire on Manuel, pelting him with a barrage of shots. Afraid for his life, he was forced to turn the buggy back around and drive away, leaving her behind.

Once the groom had gone, Chaingo stood, slipped his knife back into his right boot, and hauled Elizabeth to her feet. His hands, although slender and elegantly shaped, were nevertheless powerful, like iron bands around her wrists as he led her inexorably toward the house, initially ignoring her futile attempts to wrench away. But after a moment, he grew impatient, and jerking her to a halt, he gave her a small shake.

"You cannot escape from me, Elizabeth," he said softly, fiercely, a muscle working in his set, determined jaw as he stared down at her, his eyes smoldering like embers as they raked over her. "Not now. Not ever."

At that declaration, her heart began to pound so fiercely that she thought it would burst in her breast—and then, for the first time in her entire life, Elizabeth fainted.

Three

When she regained consciousness, Elizabeth found herself lying on the goose-necked sofa in John Tunstall's parlor. Chaingo sat beside her, pressing to her forehead a cool, damp cloth he had wrung out in a tin basin. The other young men—including Hendry Brown, Charlie Bowdre, and J. G. "Doc" Scurlock—slouched on the chaise longue, the fireside bench, the chairs, and the floor. Richard "Dick" M. Brewer, the ranch's foreman, was ensconced in what she guessed had once been John Tunstall's usual place in a big, burgundy leather wing chair at the head of the room. Billy the Kid lounged on a needlepointed footstool at the parlor's opposite end. From their competitive positions, Elizabeth knew—even if neither of them was yet aware of it—that Dick and Billy had already started to contend for control of the gang, which would quickly form itself into the infamous Regulators.

This was where and how it had all begun, she reflected as she glanced around the room, feeling as though she had a ringside seat at history in the making. Despite her shock and fear, she was fascinated by this glimpse into the past.

"My God, Dick! Mr. Tunstall's dead! Billy Morton and those other bastards killed him! What're we going to do? What're we going to do, Dick?" It was Hendry Brown who spoke, running one hand agitatedly through his badly cropped hair.

"Well, the first thing is, we're going to take care of Mr. Tunstall," Dick declared soberly. "He was a good man—the best!—and he deserves to be buried proper. Then we'll have to try to get help from some kind of law enforcement that hasn't been corrupted by Dolan and Riley."

"And just what law enforcement would that be, Dick?" Billy sneered, knowing—as they all knew—that The House faction had most of the local law officials in its back pocket. "I say we take matters into our own hands, go after them sons of bitches ourselves!"

There were stout cries of "Hear, hear!" all around, but Dick quickly shouted the speakers down.

"Listen to me!" he snapped angrily. "Billy Morton, Tom Hill, and the rest of that so-called posse murdered Mr. Tunstall—and we all saw it happen! We can get that bunch of bastards legally and testify against them in a court of law. That's better'n us turning to gunslinging ourselves. We'd be wanted men for the rest of our lives."

"Yeah, Dick's right," somebody muttered, and again, there was general agreement.

Billy the Kid had obviously lost the first round. Still, Elizabeth knew it was only a matter of time until the levelheaded, law-abiding Dick Brewer was killed in a shootout with A. L. "Buckshot" Roberts, and hotheaded, law-flouting Billy gained control. Perhaps she should warn Dick about his impending demise, but she hesitated to speak up. The young men would want to know how she could predict the outcome of an event yet to take place—and they were already suspicious enough. Besides, despite her presence on the scene, she hadn't managed to save Tunstall. It might be that her earlier supposition was correct: there was nothing she could do to change history, after all.

"Miss Elizabeth, since it appears you're going to be here a while, you might as well make yourself useful by going into the kitchen and rustling us up some grub," Dick said. "And, Chaingo, since you seem to have appointed yourself Miss Elizabeth's keeper, you can help her. The rest of us will go out and dig a grave for Mr. Tunstall."

Elizabeth got unsteadily to her feet to make her way with Chaingo to the kitchen. She could cook—on a modern gas or electric range. But other than what she had seen in movies, she hadn't a clue as to how to operate a cast-iron stove. Fuel. There had to be some kind of fuel, she thought, and it went inside what looked like an oven . . .

"There is a problem?" Chaingo asked as his eyes took in her confusion. "You don't know how to cook, perhaps?"

"No, it's not that . . . not exactly." Elizabeth peered into the oven-like cavity, trying not to tremble at his proximity, remembering his words before she had passed out. "I cook fine. I just don't know how to do it on a stove like this— Oh, never mind. You wouldn't believe me anyway if I tried to explain—"

"How do you know?"

"I just know, that's all. Does the wood go inside here?"

"Yes. But here, since you don't appear to know what you're doing, I'll start the fire for you. You can take care of the food."

Elizabeth turned to take stock of the cupboards, acutely aware of the way Chaingo's gaze followed her. She found a bag of potatoes, a sack of carrots. If she had some meat to go with the vegetables, she could make a stew. An electric potato peeler was out of the question, naturally. She would have to make do with an old-fashioned paring knife. Locating one at last, she sat down at the kitchen table to cut up the potatoes and carrots. Her long hair fell into her eyes, and she pushed it back impatiently.

She had had an appointment at the salon to get her hair cut for the summer, but, of course, she had missed it when she had been zapped back into the past. She wondered if her hairdresser had been angry when she hadn't shown up. She wondered if any of her neighbors had noticed she was missing, if all her houseplants were dead from lack of water, if her newspapers were piled up on her driveway, if her mail had overflowed her mailbox.

Chaingo had finished building the fire in the

stove, and now, observing how she kept trying to push her hair back from her face, he strode toward her.

"You have lost your pins, so your hair keeps getting in your way. I will fix it," he stated matter-of-factly. Then, before she could protest, he began to do just that.

His hands, rough when he had pinned her to the ground, were surprisingly gentle upon her hair as he used his fingers to work the tangles from it. Then, deftly, he braided it, Indian fashion, tying it with a leather strip he cut from the fringe of his buckskin jacket.

"Thank you." Elizabeth felt queer and tingling from his touch, as though she might swoon again. Unbidden came the thought that that was how she would feel if he made love to her. At that image, she flushed so brightly she could feel the heat creep into her cheeks. Quickly, she bent her head over the pottery bowl in her lap, hoping he wouldn't notice.

"You're welcome." Chaingo sat down beside her at the table, seemingly oblivious of her blush. "Is that all you're feeding the hands . . . potatoes and carrots?"

"No . . . actually, I was going to make a stew, if there's meat and onions, because I'll need those, too. And if there's any French bread . . . ah, no . . . I guess not . . ." Her voice trailed away at Chaingo's quizzical glance. "Any old bread will do, then. Or tortillas . . . You surely have those. And, well, I'm bound to think of something else. Beans!" she exclaimed as inspiration struck. "They always have beans in western movies . . . frijoles—"

"Elizabeth, you're not making any sense. Are you feeling all right?" Reaching out, Chaingo took the bowl and paring knife from her. "I think perhaps you're in shock. Mr. Tunstall's murder wasn't a sight any lady should have witnessed. You *did* faint, and you *are* being held here against your will—"

"No, it's not that. I knew all along that this was going to happen. It's . . . oh, what difference does it make if you think I'm crazy or not? The truth is that I'm not really John Chisum's daughter, and I don't really belong in this time. That's why I don't know how to do a lot of things here, like cook on that cast-iron stove. I'm from the twentieth century, you see, and during a storm a few nights ago, a bolt of lightning struck my house—I live in Arizona; I don't know if that's a state yet in this time or not—and when I woke up, I was here, in the past . . . well, past for me, I mean, not for you, naturally. It's the present for you. I'm from your future, which was my present, of course—only, now, it seems it's my future, too . . ." Elizabeth realized she was rambling, but she couldn't seem to stop. Then, suddenly, she was crying, and she knew everything had just caught up with her in that moment, that her nerves were utterly shattered by all that had happened to her.

Before she grasped his intention, Chaingo somehow had her in his lap, smoothing back a few loose strands that had escaped from her braid.

"Shhh, Elizabeth. Hush. That's the craziest story I ever heard."

"I told you that you'd think so."

"Yes, but that doesn't mean I don't believe you."

"Why should you believe me? How could you? You don't have all the scientific and technological knowledge here in the eighteen hundreds that we have in the twentieth century. It doesn't make sense that you would believe me. So you must just be saying that to make me feel better. What you probably really think is that I need to be locked up in a lunatic asylum. But I won't let you do that to me. If you tell anybody what I told you, I'll deny I said it."

"Don't worry. I'm not going to tell anyone. No one else would believe you—or me, either," Chaingo insisted calmly. "They'd think we were both deranged. But I know you speak the truth, because I have studied the mysteries of the universe. The day I went into the mountains to seek my vision quest, I foresaw that you would come to me—a woman with hair like the sun and eyes the color of the sky, a woman from out of a storm, from out of the future. You are my destiny, Elizabeth—as I am yours. You belong to me—now and forever. You know that. It is why you fainted, is it not?"

At those words, Elizabeth abruptly became aware of how Chaingo had his arms wrapped around her, holding her so close she could feel the strength of his hard, lean body, the steady beat of his heart. This was what she had dreamed of endlessly. But now that it was actually happening, it seemed too incredible to be true. Besides which, Elizabeth realized that although she knew him from the movie, Chaingo was, in reality, a stranger. On screen, he had appeared larger than life, heroic, but that had been only an illusion. He was a man—strong and virile—even if he wasn't like any other she had ever known. She had always imagined he would be different from men of the twentieth century, and he was. But now, that realization both frightened and excited her.

"I'd—I'd better get on with preparing supper." Flustered, she attempted to rise.

But Chaingo refused to release her; a smile curved his lips as he looked at her steadily, his eyes seeming to pierce her soul.

"As I told you earlier, you will not escape from me, Elizabeth—and in your heart, you know this, because you, too, feel the bond between us. So why do you fight me?"

"I—I don't even know you—" she protested lamely.

"Yes, you do. I'm not sure how yet, but somehow, you do. Come here."

Catching hold of her braid, he drew her head to his. Although Elizabeth understood his intent, she didn't try to resist as his mouth closed over hers. She was both afraid to defy him and curious to discover what his kiss would feel like—and in some dark corner of her mind, she was still

not quite certain all this was real. She thought
vaguely that if she lost control of the situation,
she would simply wake up to find she had been
dreaming all along.

Even though Elizabeth was shy, frightened,
and unsure in Chaingo's embrace, the same
could not be said for him. There was nothing
timid or hesitant about his kiss. His lips moved
on hers with the assurance of a man who had
considerable experience with women and lovemaking. His tongue traced the contours of her
mouth before compelling it to open for him and
thrusting inside—touching, tasting, delving deep.

Elizabeth moaned softly in his arms as his
tongue explored the warm, moist cavern. It was
incredible, the way he made her feel. It was
everything she had ever envisioned. A wild thrill
shot through her, setting every nerve to tingling.
Of their own volition, her hands crept around
his neck, her fingers threading through his long
mane of glossy black hair. At her response, he
increased the pressure of his lips on hers. His
tongue twined with her own, instinctively knowing every sensitive spot. His arms tightened
around her as he shifted her in his lap, so she
grew conscious of his arousal. His hand cupped
her breast, fingers circling her nipple, which
strained against the fabric of her gown.

"Hey! Where's that grub?" Billy the Kid
shouted from the dining room, startling Elizabeth so that she flinched in Chaingo's embrace
and abruptly jerked her mouth from his.

Realizing then that the other desperadoes had

returned and might come into the kitchen at any moment, she hastily scrambled from Chaingo's lap, grabbing the bowlful of potatoes and carrots. Her face was flushed, and she trembled so violently that she nearly dropped the bowl on the floor as she poured the vegetables into a cast-iron pot. She shoved the pot under the pump and filled it with water, only to find that it was so heavy she could hardly lift it. Behind her, she heard Chaingo, who had been watching her, push his chair back from the table and stand.

"Do women no longer labor at all in the kitchen in the nineteen hundreds?" he asked, one corner of his mouth twitching with amusement as he easily shifted the weighty pot from the sink to the stove.

"No, not like this," Elizabeth explained, unnerved by his nearness, and the thought that she had let him kiss her, touch her. She must be mad. Surely, all this was taking place only in her poor, muddled mind. "We still have cast-iron pots and skillets, but they're not used much anymore. Most of our pots and pans are made of much lighter materials—and we don't have to build fires in our stoves, either, or get water from a pump— Oh, God, I'm not crazy, am I? This is all really happening, isn't it? I'm truly here in the past, having this conversation with you— It all seems so strange, so unreal. I feel like I'm in a movie. I keep expecting the director to yell, 'Cut. Print.' "

"What's a movie?" Ripping the lid off a barrel,

Chaingo began to remove slabs of what she realized must be salted meat, handing it to her to slice into chunks for the stew.

"It's . . . it's, well, you know what a camera is, because there are pictures—daguerreotypes, we call the old ones—from this time period. There's one of Billy in many of our history books. Anyway, our cameras in the twentieth century take moving pictures, so they don't just record a single image, but things as they really happen. If I were filming us now, for example, you could watch it all later, exactly as it took place. Now, a movie—the kind I was talking about, anyway—is . . . well, it's like make-believe. It was in a movie that I first saw you, a movie about you and Billy and all the others, because Mr. Tunstall's murder today sets off a chain of events that become known as the Lincoln County Wars . . . Oh, I've only just now realized that the tortillas will have to be made from scratch—"

"From scratch? And you don't know how to do that—whatever that is?"

"No, we buy them already made, in packages at the grocery store."

Chaingo shook his head with amazement.

"It would seem that there are many marvels in the future," he observed as he opened another barrel and began to scoop masa flour from it. "Meals practically cook themselves. Women are apparently much freer in many ways." His eyes roamed over her in a fashion that brought another blush to her cheeks. "And Lincoln County is famous for its wars. Tell me, Elizabeth, are Billy and I and the rest going to die like Mr. Tunstall?"

"I—I don't know. Dick is killed in a shootout, and Billy is gunned down by a friend of his, a man named Pat Garrett. But perhaps none of that will happen now. Perhaps the past will change since I have come here, but I can't say for sure. Although I had hoped to save him, my presence didn't alter poor Mr. Tunstall's fate. As for you and the others, I honestly haven't a clue as to what becomes of you. They are but shadows in the pages of history, and of you, I could find no mention at all, Chaingo."

"So . . . you looked me up in your records, did you?"

"Yes," Elizabeth confessed, embarrassed, glancing away.

"Why?" When she didn't reply, he continued. "Because I was right. You knew, even in the future, that you belonged here in the past with me. It is all right, Elizabeth," he said gently when she made a little mewl of demurring, coming up behind her where she stood at the stove, adding the meat to the stew. His hands caressed her shoulders; he pressed his mouth lightly to her nape, sending another shiver through her. "I know what a shock all of this must be to your senses. I understand that you need time to adjust, to grow accustomed to me, to my touch. But this, you will do. I know it—and deep down inside, you know it, too. Otherwise, I would not make so free with you, nor would you permit me to do so, I think. Or have things changed so greatly between men and women in the twentieth century?"

"No, not really. In some parts of the world, women are still as subservient to men and strictly guarded as they are here in the past. In other places, such as the United States, women have equal status with men and are allowed many more liberties than they had in the eighteen hundreds. Even so, we have our moral standards, and a woman still hopes for a serious relationship when she becomes involved with a man."

"I *am* serious about you, Elizabeth. Never think that I am not. What will be is written in the stars, and we cannot change that. You must learn to accept that—as I have."

They spoke no more after that, for Billy, Dick, and some of the rest crowded into the kitchen, angrily demanding to know why there was no food on the table.

"Miss Elizabeth has been gently reared," Chaingo reminded them sternly. "She is not accustomed to serving in the kitchen. Leave her alone. The meal will be ready shortly."

After that, Elizabeth was not so scared, for she understood that because of the strange, inexplicable bond between them that Chaingo would defend her, would not leave her to the mercy of the others. She was grateful for that, even though as that feeling enveloped her, she wondered if it was because he was the man of her dreams—or because she had already been beset by the initial stages of hostage syndrome. All evening, she kept expecting John Chisum to show up, to demand her release. But he didn't appear. She wondered if his absence was due to the fact that he hadn't been home when Manuel had returned, or if time had somehow been distorted or displaced again, so that Chisum was even now unaware that she had ever been his daughter. But she had no answers to her questions.

That night, fearing an ambush, the ranch hands bedded down in Tunstall's parlor instead of the bunkhouse. Courteously, they gave Elizabeth the choice spot in front of the cheerily blazing fire, so she would be warm. Chaingo lay down protectively beside her, slipping his knife beneath his pillow.

It was a long time before anybody slept.

Four

Bright and early the following morning, Dick Brewer went into town, where he succeeded in getting himself sworn in as a special constable and armed with a warrant. He returned to John Tunstall's ranch and, with the rest of the hands, formed the posse that was to become known as the Regulators. Then they all hit the trail in search of Billy Morton and the so-called posse that had murdered Tunstall.

Since Elizabeth had ridden a horse only a few times in her life, Chaingo mounted her up before him on his stallion and held her close against him as they rode. So she was vividly conscious of his young, hard body, of his arm around her slender waist, of how his hand rested against the soft undercurve of her breast. The one thing she had done last evening before retiring had been to remove her corset, and she hadn't put it back on this morning. Instead, she had garbed herself in the clothes Chaingo had provided, which he had acquired from one of the Mexican women on the ranch—a loose, ruffled blouse and skirt and a pair of huaraches, all of which he had insisted would be much more comfortable. He had also provided a flat-brimmed sombrero to protect her pale skin from the sun. Even though it was still chilly in the mountains and valleys, spring was coming on, and the days would grow steadily brighter and hotter. Meanwhile, she had her fur-trimmed cloak for warmth.

"Elizabeth, I hope you are not planning to try to run away from me out here," he had warned before lifting her into his elaborate Spanish saddle, which he had informed her he won in a poker game. "Because while men may not do such things to women in your time, remember that this is *my* time, so if you attempt to escape from me, I will tie you up. I will not enjoy doing it, but I *will* do it. Do you understand?"

"Yes, Chaingo," she had answered, reminded that for all his kindness and the peculiar, incomprehensible force that leaped like electricity between them, she was still his prisoner. And he was still a man of the eighteen hundreds, a world in which men lived and died by the gun and women were second-class citizens. In reality, he could do whatever he wanted to her, and she would have no recourse against him. That thought had frightened her, even though she did not think he would hurt her. Besides, what other choice did she have but to trust and obey him? He was, she had realized, the only thing standing between her and the rest of the Regulators, and while Dick Brewer might be a decent sort, the same could not really be said about any of the rest.

They would perhaps have no compunctions about raping her and then abandoning her at some bordello—or worse. They could kill her out here in this desert—and who would know or care? She didn't exist in the nineteenth century—and in the twentieth, she would simply be another missing-person statistic. Maybe her entire life story would eventually wind up as a segment on "Unsolved Mysteries."

Now, as the thought recurred, she could almost hear Robert Stack announcing, *When we return, the tale of a young Tombstone schoolteacher, whose epitaph remains a mystery.* Cranks and crackpots all across the country would probably call in to report having seen her. No one would ever know the truth—and even if somebody did, no one would believe it.

She wouldn't have believed it if it hadn't actually happened. But as the days passed, Elizabeth could not go on telling herself it was only a dream or that she had gone mad. Her saddle sores and other aches in every part of her body were all too real for that. After more than a fortnight, the stiffness of her limbs was finally beginning to ease, but she still had difficulty walking and needed Chaingo's assistance to get in and out of the saddle.

"My poor Elizabeth," he said one evening as he assisted her down from his horse. "You are not used to this sort of life. It has been hard on you, I fear. No doubt you long for your twentieth century and the automobiles you have told me about."

"Yes, sometimes," she confessed. "But even if I wanted to return to my own time, I don't know how—because I don't really even know how I got *here* in the first place."

He helped her walk down to a stream that wended through the small arroyo in which the Regulators were pitching camp for the night. There, while Chaingo stood guard with his back turned to her, she stripped and bathed as quickly as she could, shivering violently in the chilly dusk. Then she donned her change of underwear and her cloak and washed her garments, which she would spread before the fire to dry. Afterward, he escorted her back to camp, then left her while he attended to his own ablutions. Although he'd been initially skeptical, he had been persuaded that germs existed, even if he couldn't see them, and that a daily bath would help to ward off sickness. The rest of the gang had teased him about his sudden penchant for cleanliness. But now, after more than a fortnight, they paid Chaingo and Elizabeth's evening ritual little heed. Seldom did they indulge in it themselves, however, much to her dismay.

They looked as disreputable as any gang of twentieth-century street thugs, she thought, their clothes travel-stained, their faces unshaven, their unwashed bodies stinking. She tried to stay upwind of them as much as possible. Her daydreams had never contained any of these harsh realities. Now, she realized how foolish and quixotic those fantasies had been.

Tempers were short, too, from the hard travel

and enforced companionship. More than once, Dick and Billy exchanged heated words. Once, Billy drew his pistol at the end of an argument and threatened to kill Dick; Elizabeth grew closer to Chaingo daily, coveting his protection. She quickly learned to speak only when spoken to and to draw the young men's attention to her as little as possible, especially at night. They would take liquor from their saddlebags and grow drunk and rowdy, hauling out their revolvers and firing wildly at bushes and rocks in the darkness.

"Chaingo, you don't have to be a Regulator. You don't have to stay with them," Elizabeth said. "We could just ride away, find someplace to make a life for ourselves. I'm afraid for you, Chaingo. If you stay, you're liable to wind up dead, the same way Dick and Billy are going to."

"And if I go—even for your sake—how will I live with my conscience, Elizabeth? You don't understand what John Tunstall meant to me, to all of us. He took us in when we had nowhere else to go. How can I turn my back on that, on him, and allow his murderers to go free? No, that I will not do. Besides, you said yourself that you didn't know for sure how events will unfold, now that you are here. It may be that just your very presence has altered what you know as the past."

"And maybe it hasn't," she pointed out.

"Well, we will just have to wait and see, won't we?"

Elizabeth had to be content with that, because she had no doubt that if she tried to run away,

Chaingo would catch her and would, in fact, tie her up thereafter. He was indeed a man of his word, just as he was in the movie. It was one of the reasons she had always admired him. She understood his feelings of loyalty toward John Tunstall, even while she worried constantly about what would happen in the days to come.

It was shortly afterward, on March 6, that the Regulators finally caught up with Billy Morton and four of his cohorts six miles from the Rio Pecos. Spying the posse, Morton and the others—most of whom were, unfortunately, unarmed—took off.

"Hang on, Elizabeth!" Chaingo spoke in her ear, roweling his spurs into his stallion's sides as, whooping and hollering, he and the rest of the Regulators gave chase.

She clung to the saddlehorn for dear life as Billy the Kid galloped recklessly past them to take the lead, his Winchester spitting bullets. Shots from the rifles, carbines, and shotguns of the other Regulators soon joined Billy's. But Morton and his companions were apparently too far distant, because none of them toppled from his saddle or even slowed down. At a fork, three of them split away, but Billy and the Regulators stayed hot on the trail of Morton and the other man, Frank Baker. At first, it appeared that the two men would get away. Then, without warning, their horses staggered and went down, whether because they were wounded, no one knew. The fleeing men took refuge in a sinkhole in the prairie desert, where they might have defended themselves for a long while. But as they had no supplies, they eventually opted to parley.

"Dick! Dick Brewer!" Morton shouted. "Are you listening?"

"Yeah, I hear you," Dick hollered back.

"Baker and I will surrender if you give us your word of honor that you and your posse will escort us safely to Lincoln."

"Go to hell, Morton!" Wildly, Billy fired off several more rounds at the two men, causing them to duck hastily back down behind the berm.

"Stop it, Billy!" Dick ordered angrily. "They're willing to give themselves up!"

"Hanging's too good for the likes of them two, after what they done to Mr. Tunstall! I say we ride in there and kill 'em!" Billy jammed more cartridges into his empty rifle.

"No! We're the law, damn it!" Dick insisted, and much to Billy's disgust, the rest of the Regulators sided with Dick. After he had sworn a pledge to take Morton and Baker safely into Lincoln, the two men came out and handed over their weapons.

"Well, now that we've got them two bastards, let's at least stop by Chisum's ranch on our way into Lincoln." Angry that he had been voted down, Billy shoved his rifle into his saddle holster. "We can find out whether Chisum's sold us down the river. If he has, we can haul his ass in, too. If he hasn't, I figure he owes us wages for all the hard time we've spent tracking down those two murdering sons of bitches. And if he doesn't pay up, we can take it out on his daughter." Billy's glance raked Elizabeth lewdly, making her shudder.

"Forget it, Billy." Chaingo's black eyes glinted like shards of obsidian. His low, silky voice held a menacing note. "The woman is mine, and I'll kill you if you touch her."

At first, Billy looked as though he couldn't believe Chaingo had spoken so to him. Then an enraged scowl darkened his face and he reached for his gun. But before the revolver had even cleared Billy's holster, Chaingo's knife was in his hand, poised to fly free.

"Don't even think about it, Billy. I meant what I said."

"Jesus! What in the hell's going on here?" Dick glared at the two men. "We've got Mr. Tunstall's murderers in custody—and the two of you are at each other's throats over a damned woman! No offense, Miss Elizabeth."

"None taken, Mr. Brewer," she choked out softly, thinking in some obscure corner of her mind that the sunlight reflecting off the blade seemed somehow like the lightning the night of the storm that had brought her here. She had never imagined this confrontation, not even in her wildest daydreams. In the movie, whenever Chaingo had killed someone, it hadn't been for real. But there was nothing make-believe about this. What was that old saying? *Never wish for things, because you just might get them.* Well, she had wished to be his woman, and now, she was. He had made that clear to everyone.

"Come on. Let's get to Chisum's," Dick said.

"Fine," Chaingo agreed curtly. "But I don't care what side Chisum's on these days. Either way, he's not getting Elizabeth back!" Shoving his knife back into his boot and shooting Billy a hard, challenging stare, Chaingo spurred the stallion forward.

From behind them, Elizabeth heard the sound of Billy's strangely childish giggle and devoutly hoped he wasn't preparing to shoot them in the back. But when she voiced her fear aloud, Chaingo only scoffed.

"He wouldn't do that, Elizabeth—at least, not to a friend. Billy's funny that way, loyal to the end. You should know that. After all, it was you who told me he found security in familiar people and places, so much so that he refuses to leave the territory, even when he has every chance to travel south to Mexico to escape the law. It's what kills him, you said."

"Yes, so I did. Chaingo, nobody ever knew for certain, but it was always believed that Billy killed Morton and Baker. Regardless of Dick's promises, they won't make it to Lincoln alive—at least, they didn't according to my history books."

"Well, I'll have to keep an eye on them then, and I'll warn Dick, too—because I want to see them stand trial and be hanged for Mr. Tunstall's murder."

In due time, the Regulators, their prisoners in tow, reached John Chisum's ranch. He stepped outside to meet them, his face as dark as a thundercloud; a group of armed men—obviously hired guns—accompanied him. Before working for Tunstall, Billy had been employed by Chisum, so the two men knew each other well and greeted each other congenially enough, despite the tension in the air. After that, tempers began to flare and things got ugly.

"Billy, where in the hell have you been?" Chisum queried sharply once the amenities were out of the way. "I've had men out all over the territory, looking for you! How dare you carry off my daughter?"

"Hey, that wasn't me, Mr. Chisum. No, sirree." Billy laughed, his eyes sly and amused. "You'll have to talk to Chaingo about that."

"Chaingo?" Chisum's eyes narrowed then hardened as he glanced at the young man seated upon the black stallion, his arm around Elizabeth's waist. "You half-breed Apache bastard! If you've touched her—"

"You'll do what, Mr. Chisum? Kill me? You can try, of course. But I promise, you won't succeed. If you cared for her, you should have been more careful with your daughter, sir. She's mine now." To emphasize that fact, he moved his hand slowly up Elizabeth's body.

"Why, you arrogant, insolent son of a bitch!" A blood vessel popped out alarmingly on Chisum's forehead, looking as though it might burst at any moment. He took a threatening step forward, and his hired guns drew their pistols.

Equally as swiftly, the Regulators pulled their own revolvers, and the next thing Elizabeth knew, shots were being exchanged right and left.

Chaingo was firing with one hand and hanging onto the reins with the other to control his horse, which pranced and reared at all the noise. Elizabeth was nearly thrown from the saddle.

"Damn it! Hold your fire!" Chisum shouted wrathfully at his men. "Hold your fire, for God's sake! You're liable to kill my daughter!"

"Chisum! You owed us money, Chisum!" Billy insisted, once all the shooting had ceased. "We worked for Mr. Tunstall, and he was in your camp. But you been disloyal, opening fire on us—and we won't forget it, neither! Chaingo was just funning you. He ain't touched your daughter. We were just holding her, in case you had decided to throw your lot in with Murphy and Company. And I guess now we know where you stand—and it sure as hell ain't with us! So we'll just be keeping Miss 'Lizabeth. Regulators, let's ride!"

The young men galloped away, carrying with them Elizabeth and the two hapless prisoners. It was now March 9, and the Regulators had thirteen in their ranks—an unlucky number, she thought. Five miles from Chisum's ranch, they rode into a small town, where Dick had said the captive Morton could mail a letter at the post office. Elizabeth started in the saddle as she read the wooden sign identifying the town.

"What's wrong?" Chaingo inquired, glancing around warily. "You said nothing of there being any danger to us in this place."

"That's because I don't know that there is any."

"Then what caused your alarm?"

"It wasn't alarm," she explained. "I was just . . . momentarily surprised, that's all. This town . . . Roswell—"

"What about it?"

"Nothing. It's nothing. You wouldn't believe me, anyway."

"Elizabeth, have I not believed you about everything else, incredible as it may have seemed? So why should this be any different? Do you not yet believe in the bond between us? Can you not trust me?"

"All right." Elizabeth sighed heavily. "But don't say I didn't warn you. When I saw the sign, I just found it difficult to grasp the fact that in sixty-nine years, this town will go from being a dusty, one-road watering hole frequented by you, Billy, and the rest of the Regulators to a place where a spaceship crashes and four alien bodies are discovered—a fact that will be covered up by the U.S. government for more than half a century."

"A spaceship? Aliens? What is all that?"

"Well, in my time . . . oh, never mind. I'll explain it all to you later. It's much too involved to go into at the moment. Is that the post office over there?"

"Yes, but Dick can take care of Morton and the letter. You and I are going to rent a room across the street for a while, Elizabeth."

At those words, she felt her heart begin to hammer painfully in her breast, for she did not know his intentions. In all the time they had spent together, they had never been alone, not really. So he had done little more than kiss her—and that on only a few occasions. But now, perhaps he meant to do more than that, and she didn't know what she would do if he did. It wasn't as though she had never had a lover. She was, after all, a divorced woman. And she certainly couldn't deny her overwhelming attraction to Chaingo. She had daydreamed about him endlessly, for heaven's sake. Even so, Elizabeth felt as shy and nervous as a virgin bride. In her fantasies, he had made love to her and responded to her however she had wished. In reality, she didn't know what to expect.

Although Chaingo, too, had sensed the bond between them, he had spoken no word of loving her, of where they were going together on this bizarre, fantastic journey. She tried to tell herself that that didn't matter, that surely, sooner or later, she would be whisked back to the future as suddenly and unexpectedly as she had been brought here to the past. Undoubtedly, some law of physics unknown to her would ensure that fact. But it didn't help. She wanted Chaingo to feel for her what she felt for him, that she was the other half of his soul, not just a woman—a possession—promised to him during a vision quest.

But Elizabeth said nothing of any of this as he dismounted and tied his stallion to the hitching rail, then lifted her down from the saddle. Taking her hand, he led her into the "hotel," which, to her mortification, turned out to be a bordello. Still, she couldn't restrain her curiosity as she gazed around, wide-eyed.

"I apologize for bringing you to such a place, Elizabeth," Chaingo declared after he had got a key to a room upstairs. "But there would have been difficulties had I tried to take you to a hotel. It is perhaps not a problem in your time, since you have not once remarked upon my heritage, but in this day and age, a half-breed Apache checking into a hotel with a white woman is just asking for trouble."

"Yes, of course. I should have realized— I'm sorry. I didn't think. It's so hard to remember what is and isn't acceptable behavior in the past. You're right. Our being together would cause hardly a comment in the future—at least, not among those who are enlightened and unprejudiced, although we still have our share of bigots."

The room into which he took her was, to her relief, clean, the bed obviously freshly made. The sheets, although mended, were newly washed and did not appear likely to harbor lice or bedbugs.

"I've ordered a hot bath for you, Elizabeth. I know from what you have said how much you have missed those. Meanwhile, I'll be down the street at the barbershop. I, too, could use a hot bath. And a shave." Chaingo grinned ruefully as he rubbed the coarse stubble. "Here is the key to the room. Don't forget that, like your own time, mine has its perils—many of which are at best unpleasant and at worst fatal. So don't let anyone in except for me and the servants who bring the water for your bath. Do you understand?"

She nodded, swallowing hard at the reminder of the dangers that lurked here—as they had and did in any time period, she realized now. And perhaps, in the end, none was more hazardous than another. The nineteenth century boasted no weapon more deadly than Sam Colt's "Equalizer," but medicine was not as advanced, either. In sharp contrast, the twentieth century was rife with lethal semi-automatic weapons, but medicine was also much more highly evolved. She thought that perhaps in the twenty-first century, Star Trek-type phasers would truly exist, but then, so, too, would medical tricorders, probably.

Her bathwater finally arrived, and after the tub was filled, Elizabeth sank into it gratefully, delighted by the fact that it was steaming. And although she guessed that neither the soap nor the perfume was expensive, she nevertheless viewed both as a real luxury—and laughed at the idea that she did. For these were all things she had taken for granted before she had been zapped into the past.

Elizabeth scrubbed herself vigorously, including her hair, laving away the stains of travel. Afterward, discovering that the servants had taken away her clothes, she had no choice but to garb herself in the robe that had been provided. She sat down on the bed, then abruptly leaped up anxiously, feeling that perhaps that pose was too bold and suggestive. Maybe a stiff whiskey would help, she thought, as she spied a bottle and two glasses, which the servants must have brought with her bathwater. Although she seldom imbibed, Elizabeth poured herself a shot and quickly drank it down, grimacing at the horrible taste.

"This must be rotgut," she observed to herself, wondering uneasily if it would come back up as fast as it had gone down. To her relief, it remained in her stomach, from where it shortly spread a warm, languid glow throughout her entire body, making her feel so much better that she poured another drink and swallowed it, too. After that, she wasn't nearly as nervous as she had been before. In fact, she felt pleasantly giddy and lightheaded as she stood before the window, gazing out at the street below.

Dusk was falling, the sun a huge, fiery ball sinking slowly on the western horizon, setting the earth aflame. Elizabeth supposed that by now, Morton had finished his letter to his cousin, Hon. H. H. Marshall, in Richmond, Virginia. It would be the last thing he would ever write, she thought, for even though she had warned Chaingo that Morton and Baker wouldn't make it to Lincoln alive, she held out little hope that their deaths could be prevented. Chaingo had said that what was written in the stars would be—and she was beginning to believe that was true, that there was nothing anyone could do to change it.

A soft knock sounded at the door, nudging her from her reverie. Drawing her wrapper more closely about her, Elizabeth crossed the room, wishing there were a peephole through which she could see who stood outside.

"Who is it?" she asked quietly.

"Chaingo. Open the door, Elizabeth."

It was his voice. She would have known it anywhere. Her hands trembled as she reached down to turn the key in the lock. Moments later, the silver spurs on his black boots jingling, he stepped inside, relocked the door, and pocketed the key.

"Alone at last," he drawled softly, taking her in his arms, whirling her around, and backing her up against the door, moving in so close that her heart raced uncontrollably.

His long mane of black hair was still damp and glistened like the pelt of a rain-soaked panther. Two slender braids plaited with thong, beads, and feathers adorned either side, framing his finely chiseled face with its strongly molded features. Thick, unruly black brows swooped like raven wings over deep-set obsidian eyes, an aquiline nose, a full, sensual mouth, and an arrogant jaw that marked him as a man accustomed to getting what he wanted. A black bandanna encircled his throat. His collar was open, his chambray shirt half unbuttoned, displaying a broad chest hard with muscle and dusted with fine black hair that tapered down his firm, flat belly to disappear into his denim breeches.

He was so handsome that Elizabeth's breath caught in her throat. Truly, there were no men like him in the twentieth century. How incredibly lucky she was to have been brought back to this time, to him. Because after all, how many women ever actually met their dream lover in the flesh, much less made love with him?

"Elizabeth, you are the woman of my dreams," Chaingo murmured, as though he had read her mind. "From the time I was fourteen years old and journeyed into the mountains to seek my vision quest, in which you appeared to me, I have thought of no woman but you. Since then, so much time has passed that I had begun to despair, to think my vision false. When I saw you that day at Mr. Tunstall's, I could hardly believe my eyes. You had come to me, just as I had imagined—my woman cloaked in sun and sky, borne to me on the wings of a storm from the future. It is one of the mysteries of the universe how you came to be here. But here, you are. And I want you, Elizabeth. I want to make love to you. Here. Now."

He was waiting for an answer, she realized. Yet such was the way her heart was beating that she couldn't seem even to get her breath, much less respond. She swallowed hard and opened her mouth to speak—but no sound came out. Chaingo's eyes darkened, glittering like shards in the dying rays of blazing orange sunlight that lanced through the windows. His nostrils flared slightly, and his voice, when he spoke again, now held a low, harsh note.

"Is your answer no, then, Elizabeth?" He reached out, trailing his fingers lightly down her throat, the valley between her breasts where her robe gaped a little, exposing her bare skin. His touch was like fire searing her flesh as, deliberately, he pushed aside the wrapper's edges and slipped his hand inside to cup her naked breast. His thumb rotated slowly across her nipple. "Is it no?" His warm breath fanned her face as his fingers glided on down her belly, unknotted the sash at her waist. When she still couldn't manage a reply, could only gasp softly, sharply, as her wrapper fell open wide, Chaingo swore hoarsely. "I'll take that as a yes," he growled. Then he swept her up into his strong arms and carried her to the bed.

He flung her down, then stepped back to strip off his clothes. His naked, coppery body was magnificent, long and hard and lean, corded with powerful muscle. He moved with the savage grace of a predatory animal as he stalked her, lay down beside her, his weight sinking into the feather mattress, causing it to dip so that she slid inadvertently into his embrace. He stared down at her intently, his black eyes searching, smoldering with desire. Gently, he smoothed her blond hair back from her face.

"You are so beautiful, Elizabeth," he said before his mouth took hers, possessively staking his claim to her, his tongue constraining her lips to part and shooting deep.

She sighed with pleasure as he kissed her; it was all happening exactly as she had always imagined it. It was nothing like what she had shared with her ex-husband, Michael. It was, in fact, like nothing what she had ever shared with any man. She had never known feelings like this.

It was as though she and Chaingo had always belonged together, been together, had known each other for a millenium. She did not understand the peculiar force that drew them together, that bound them to each other. But for her, it was enough that it did.

Like a flower unfurling, her mouth opened to him, yielded pliantly to his invasion. His tongue wreathed hers, and she met it eagerly, her hands, fingers tensed and splayed, creeping up his chest to clutch his shoulders, her nails digging into his skin. At her response, his lips grew harder, hungrier, more demanding. His tongue became rougher, bolder, more insistent. Tentatively, she touched her own tongue to his, an unbridled thrill coursing through her as he groaned against her mouth, his fingers tangling in her hair, as though to pull her even nearer, to hold her still so he could devour her. Dimly, she understood that she had never been kissed until now, not really, not the way Chaingo was kissing her—savagely, lingeringly, as though he inhaled her, consumed her, savored every taste of her.

"Sweet . . ." he muttered against her lips. "You're sweeter than I ever imagined, like wild honey melting on my tongue. I want to lick you and lap you, to swallow every last drop of you. And I will." His mouth slanted across her cheek to her temple, the strands of her hair. He breathed in her ear, nibbled her lobe, making her shudder with excitement. "Yes, you like that. I knew you would, Elizabeth, my girl."

He continued to whisper words of love she only

half comprehended, her mind dazed and reeling from his mouth, his tongue, and his hands, as well as the whiskey she had drunk earlier. She floated in a place that was neither future nor past, a place where time hung suspended—or did not exist at all—because it seemed that Chaingo was in no hurry to make her his completely, that he found as deep a pleasure in arousing her.

He buried his face in her hair. His lips sought her pale, slender throat, his tongue teasing the pulse that fluttered erratically at its hollow. His hands were at her shoulders, easing the wrapper from her, sliding it down her arms, momentarily imprisoning her wrists behind her back, so her body arched against his. Her breasts brushed his chest, and as his fine black hair caressed her responsive nipples, they flushed and hardened. His palm captured one breast, pressing it high for his mouth as he bent his dark head to envelop the stiff, rosy crest, sucking it greedily. Electric waves of delight radiated from its center, rippling through Elizabeth's whole body, leaving her every nerve raw and tingling.

At last, Chaingo slipped the robe from her totally, so she lay naked in his arms, bathed in the golden glow of the last vestiges of the setting sun before it vanished below the horizon, plunging the room into dusk. He pressed her down amid the pillows. Then, turning, he struck a match and lit the Victorian lamp on the nightstand, so the room was illuminated once more.

"I want to see you when I make love to you, Elizabeth," he murmured as he gathered her into his embrace again, kissing her mouth. "Your face, your body. You're blushing." He smiled down at her teasingly, although his black eyes burned, like twin flames, with passion. "Do men no longer look at the women they make love to, then, in the twentieth century?"

"Not the ones I knew," Elizabeth confessed softly.

"And did you know many, my sweet?" he asked between kisses, gently but inexorably stretching her hands up over her head, wrapping them firmly around the fencelike posts of the headboard of the brass bed.

"No, not many. Hardly any, actually. But I . . . I was married. We were divorced about six months ago. I know that probably sounds shocking to you, but it's not the scandal in my time that it is in yours. Half the population in the United States is divorced in the twentieth century.

"I wasn't shocked. I know your husband couldn't possibly have been right for you."

"How do you know?" she inquired, curious.

"Because for all that you are not a virgin, there is an essential part of you that is still inviolate, unawakened—and after tonight, you, too, will know that was so."

"Was?"

"Why, yes, my love. You are the other half of my soul—as I am yours. You know that. You feel it in your heart, as I do. That being so, do you truly think I intend to leave any part of you untouched, untasted?" His lips scorched her throat once more, found the sensitive place where her nape joined her shoulder. He bit her there, lightly, erotically, making her shiver violently as a surge of arousal and excitement rushed through her. "You see? You cannot tell me your husband made you feel these things—because I know he did not."

Chaingo's palms cupped her breasts, his thumbs sweeping across their peaks before his mouth seized first one and then the other, taunting, laving, teeth nipping gently. Elizabeth writhed beneath him, mewling and moaning softly as he kissed and caressed her. She let go of the headboard, her fingers snarling in his hair, gliding down his sweat-sheened back, tracing the curve of the muscles and sinews that bunched and rippled sensuously beneath her palms. His body was like a whipcord—hard, lean, powerful. She wanted to touch and explore every part of him, as he did her, to stake her claim upon him. But he lowered his head, his lips searing her belly, his hands spreading her thighs wide. His mouth trailed kisses along the insides of her thighs.

"Grab the headboard again," he demanded huskily before his lips found her softness, his tongue cleaving the mellifluous seam of her, tasting the fragile bud that was the key to her pleasure, inciting it to unfold its petals.

Elizabeth could do nothing then but whatever Chaingo wanted, her fingers curling tightly around the brass posts of the headboard, her body arching wildly in response to him as he kissed her, tongued her, stroked her, his fingers moving inside her, skillfully stoking the fire that had erupted inside her, the burning ache that had seized her, so she longed desperately to be filled by him. No man had ever done this to her before. She was both shocked and exhilarated by it—no matter how often in the past she had daydreamed about it. For the reality far surpassed the fantasy, the desire and tension building inside her until she realized dimly, in some dark corner of her mind, that for the first time in her life, a man was going to take her to the pinnacle of passion. The searing climax made her gasp and cry out, her head thrashing as the tremors rocked her.

Chaingo rose and poised himself above her, his black eyes glittering with triumph and satisfaction as he stared down at her. His breath came in harsh rasps that spoke more eloquently than words. She felt the tip of his hard, potent maleness find her. Then he drove down into her—swift and sure and deep, taking her breath. For a moment, he lay buried inside her, filling her completely. Then, with a low groan, he began to thrust, grinding his pelvis against her so that he brought her to a second orgasm hard on the heels of her first.

Feverishly, Elizabeth clung to him, wrapped her legs around him, enfolding him, taking him deep as he plunged into her. His hands were beneath her, arching her hips to meet his, harder, faster, until his own release came—as violently as hers, a shudder racking the length of his body as he spilled himself inside her.

Afterward, Chaingo lay propped up against the pillows, smoking a cigarette he had rolled and cradling Elizabeth against his chest, so their hearts beat as one.

"That's very bad for you, you know," she said quietly, sighing contentedly as she snuggled against him.

"What?" Tangling one hand in her hair, he tipped her head up to his. "Love?"

"No, smoking. It can kill you."

"Yeah, well, so can a Colt—but that doesn't mean I'm going to leave mine in my holster. Are you hungry, baby? Do you want some supper?"

"Yes, Please."

"Good." Taking a last drag off his cigarette, he ground it out in an ashtray, exhaling a cloud of smoke into the air. Then he kissed her and stood, pulling on his denims. "Let me go downstairs and get some food, then, so we can eat. After that, we'll entertain ourselves some more." His glance raked her in a way that brought a blush to her cheeks and made her draw the sheet up hastily to cover her nakedness. Chaingo laughed softly at that. "I have already seen—and very much enjoyed—all that you would hide from me, my love. And I will again before this night is through, I promise you."

"You're shameless—the most shameless man I've ever known."

"That's right. So eat your food—so I can show you just how much again."

When she was done with her meal, he did just that. Roughly stripping her robe from her and pressing her down upon the mattress, his coppery body moved determinedly to cover her own pale one, once more taking her to the heights of rapture and back.

Five

They left Roswell the following morning at ten o'clock, Morton having posted his letter. He and Baker were mounted on two scruffy horses, and Billy the Kid was as sullen as a stormy sky. Before departing from Roswell, Morton had told the postmaster, M. A. Upson, that he did not fear not reaching Lincoln alive, because Brewer had pledged his word to ensure the safe delivery of the prisoners. At that, one of the other desperadoes, McClosky, had spoken up, assuring Morton that he, too, would defend him if necessary.

Elizabeth had been glad to hear that, for she had thought that with Chaingo, Brewer, and McClosky on hand, Billy the Kid did not stand a chance at murdering Morton and Baker. But now, after pausing to greet Martin Chavez, a rider from Picacho, who was passing by, the Regulators turned off the main road to Lincoln, and her previous fear rose to haunt her once more.

"Chaingo, why are we leaving the trail?" Elizabeth asked softly.

"I don't know." He shook his head, his dark

visage sober. "Because this is the track to Agua Negra—not Lincoln. Dick! Hey, Dick!"

Before Brewer could respond, Frank McNabb and Hendry Brown moved their horses in close behind McClosky and John Middleton, who were guarding the two prisoners; before anyone realized what was intended, McNabb put his pistol to McClosky's head and growled, "Since you are so willing to die to protect Morton, you bastard, then do so." Then he pulled the trigger, blowing McClosky's brains out. McClosky twitched wildly in his saddle, then toppled to the earth, and chaos ensued.

Unarmed and terrified, Morton and Baker set their spurs to their horses' sides, galloping away as rapidly as the poor, broken-down nags could carry them. Shouting and swearing, the Regulators gave chase, guns raining a hail of lead. Billy the Kid and Charlie Bowdre had been riding point for the party, so they did not know what had happened, only spied Morton and Baker fleeing, getting away. Yelling, Billy roweled his grey forward, drawing up alongside the two prisoners. His revolver spat once, twice—and both Morton and Baker jerked and fell from their saddles. Hauling his horse to a halt, Billy dismounted and rolled Morton over.

"Is he dead?" Dick asked as he and the rest of the Regulators reached the scene.

"Yes," Billy replied shortly. "Baker, too."

"McNabb, you son of a bitch!" Dick pivoted angrily on his gelding. "What in the hell did you think you were doing? Murdering McClosky

like that? We're the law, damn it! And I had
guaranteed Morton and Baker safe passage into
Lincoln!"

"Yeah, right, like they'd have been convicted
there!" McNabb retorted scornfully. "When they
were in cahoots with Sheriff Brady and Dolan
and Riley! McClosky ought never to have said
he would defend Morton and Baker. They murdered Mr. Tunstall! We all saw it happen! So how
in the hell McClosky could have offered to lay
down his life for them is beyond me. Hell! He
was probably a damned spy, in Murphy and
Company's back pocket!"

"We don't know that," Dick insisted, still fum-
ing. "We had legitimate warrants for Morton and
Baker—and now, you've turned us into murderers just like they were, Frank! Go on. Get out
of here. Because from this moment on, you're
not one of us. You're not a Regulator anymore—
and if I see you again, I'll kill you myself!"

For an interminable instant, it seemed as
though McNabb intended to draw on Brewer.
Then, at last, cursing and spitting on the ground
to make his contempt for Dick plain, Frank
wheeled his horse around.

"You don't want me as one of you, fine!
'Cause I'm willing to bet that John Chisum will
pay me plenty to find out where the lot of you
are—especially you, Chaingo! 'Cause there ain't
a one of us what thinks you was just sitting in
a corner all night in that bordello, guarding Miss
'Lizabeth! We know what you did to her—and
don't think Chisum won't have your lousy, half-

breed Apache hide nailed to the barn door for
it before he's through, you bastard!" With that
Parthian shot, McNabb rode off, trailing a cloud
of dust in his wake.

As Frank disappeared over the crest of a knoll
in the distance, Elizabeth grew acutely, uncom-
fortably, aware of how the Regulators stared at
her and Chaingo, of the sudden tension that
filled his body, and of how his hand slipped
from her waist to the holstered pistol at the
leather gunbelt slung low on his hips. Hoping
to defuse the situation, she spoke quietly in the
strained silence.

"What happened between Chaingo and me last
night wasn't what you're all thinking," she told
them, flushing at the admission. She knew it
would be difficult for them, in this day and age,
to believe that she—a lady, a white woman—
would have welcomed Chaingo to her bed. "He
didn't do anything I didn't want him to do, I
swear."

"Is that the truth, Miss Elizabeth?" Dick queried sharply. "If it isn't, we'll hand Chaingo over
to Chisum ourselves—because we never intended
any harm to come to you, Miss Elizabeth. I hope
you know that."

"I do, Dick. And no harm has, I promise you."

"Well, all right, then. If you're sure." His tone
betrayed his doubt.

"I'm sure," she asserted firmly, laying her
head upon Chaingo's shoulder so they would all
know she had spoken truly. His hand moved up

to stroke her hair gently then, and he kissed her lightly on the forehead.

Startled but at last satisfied of her veracity, the Regulators said no more, regrouping and hitting the road again, leaving the bodies of Morton, Baker, and McClosky where they had fallen. Burying them would have taken precious time they didn't have, knowing that McNabb was on his way to Chisum's ranch.

"Elizabeth." Chaingo spoke softly in her ear. "What happened back there did not take place as you said it would. I thought it was Billy who needed watching, not Frank."

"So did I. But I see now what must have occurred after the incident—because it was McNabb who reported that Morton had yanked McClosky's pistol and killed him with it, and so you all had to kill Morton and Baker, because they had attempted to escape. That was the account that got printed in all the newspapers. Obviously, McNabb lied to cover his own part in the murders. I don't know what to do now, Chaingo, what to believe. There are so many tales about Billy the Kid and the Regulators that even the historians of my time often couldn't agree on just what was true and what wasn't. What if all the rest of the stories are as garbled as this one proved to be?"

"Then perhaps they were meant to be, so that when you were brought back here to this time, you wouldn't be able to alter the past, Elizabeth. Did you ever think of that?"

"No . . . but maybe you're right. I haven't

managed to prevent anyone from dying as he was supposed to. In fact, I don't seem to have changed anything at all."

"Yes, you have, my love. You have changed yourself—and me. And perhaps that was all that was intended. It was very brave of you to tell Dick and the others the truth about last night. Another lady, another white woman, would not have."

"An eighteen hundreds' lady, you mean. But that's not what I am, Chaingo. *You* know that, even if the rest of the Regulators don't. Besides, I don't care what they think of me. I couldn't let them turn you over to Chisum. He would have killed you—for something I very much wanted to happen."

"Did you?"

"Yes," she confessed shyly, blushing as she remembered all the things they had done—and how much she had enjoyed them. It had been everything she had ever imagined—and more. Whereas before, she had prayed to wake up and find this had all been just a dream, now, she feared that might happen. She didn't want this to be a dream, but reality. Somehow, sitting in her bedroom in the twentieth century, watching the movie *Hasten Down the Wind*, her heart had instinctively recognized that it belonged to Chaingo, that it had always been his. That's why she had not been happy with Michael or any other man. They had not been Chaingo, the only man for her, and deep down inside she had known that. She wanted to stay with him forever.

She worried constantly that he would be killed in the Lincoln County Wars.

"No, I won't be, my love," Chaingo insisted when she voiced her trepidation. "I can take care of myself—and you."

"But Morton and Baker are dead now, so I don't understand what the point is in riding on with the Regulators. It's not worth the risk!"

"Yes, it is. Morton and Baker were only the tools of Murphy and Company and Sheriff Brady. When they're dead, then it'll all be finished—and not before, Elizabeth."

She pressed him no further then, recognizing that his pride and loyalty demanded he follow the path he had chosen, no matter where it led. This was the man he was, and she would have him no other way.

Despite Brewer's apprehension that the murders of Morton and Baker would cause trouble for the Regulators, they rode on into Lincoln. There, the first thing they did was seek out John Tunstall's partner and attorney, Alexander McSween. Until Tunstall's murder, McSween had been a peaceable, law-abiding man. But now, he was righteously, passionately, outraged over the machinations of Murphy and Company and the Santa Fe Ring, and he thirsted for justice as much as Billy the Kid craved vengeance.

McSween gave the desperadoes what advice and information he could. The latter included a rumor that one of the members of the so-called posse that had killed Tunstall, an ex-soldier by the name of A. L. "Buckshot" Roberts, had hightailed it down to the Mescalero Apache Indian Agency at South Fork, approximately forty miles south of Lincoln.

"I know that region well," Chaingo announced. "It is the home of my mother's people. And we have a warrant for Roberts, don't we, Dick?"

"Yeah, we do," Dick confirmed.

"Well, then what in the hell are we hanging around here for?" Billy mounted his grey. "Let's go get the son of a bitch!"

He galloped off before anybody could stop him, and the rest of the Regulators saw no choice but to follow. Fortunately, thanks to McSween and his wife, they now had plenty of provisions in their saddlebags for the journey south; by this time, Elizabeth had become accustomed to their vagabond life on the road. In fact, she was surprised by how much stronger she grew daily. She had always known she needed more exercise and had kept telling herself after her divorce that one of the things she should do was join a gym, where she could get into shape and meet men at the same time. But somehow, she had never got around to it, and now, there was no need. The hard physical labor she endured was more than enough.

She continued to ride mounted before Chaingo on his big, black stallion, and she was glad of that, for she still didn't think she could have managed a horse of her own. Besides, she loved being close to him, cradled in his strong arms, safe and secure. He was solid and real, her anchor in this

wild whirlwind of an adventure she had so myste-
riously embarked upon. At night, he found sheltered places to shield them from the rest of the
Regulators. There in those desert refuges, he
pressed her down upon his blankets, claiming her
as passionately as he had in the bordello, mur-
muring sweet words of love to her. With every
passing day, she knew there was no longer any
doubting what he felt for her, that the strange ties
that bound her to him also bound him to her just
as irrevocably. There really was, she thought, such
a thing as love at first sight—and they had found
it in each other.

Unfortunately, they, along with the other Regulators, found Buckshot Roberts, too. He had
heard about the deaths of Morton and Baker
and he had determined that, unlike them, he
wouldn't be taken prisoner to be murdered en
route to Lincoln. As the desperadoes approached the Mescalero Apache Indian Agency
from the east, they spied Roberts galloping toward them from the west.

"Roberts! Buckshot Roberts! You're under arrest!" Brewer called out.

But the words were no sooner out of his
mouth than Billy the Kid yanked his Winchester
from his saddle holster and spurred his grey toward the ex-soldier. Roberts's response was to
haul forth his own Winchester and fire a round
off at Billy. The shot only narrowly missed him,
zinging past his ear. Billy's rifle blasted in retali-
ation—and his aim was a great deal better. His
bullet struck Roberts dead on, mortally wound-

ing him. Roberts, however, was a tough nut to crack and by no means ready to surrender. Amid a hail of lead, he swung down from his saddle and staggered into an outhouse. Inside was an old mattress and some bedcovers, with which he barricaded the door.

"Chaingo, this is where Dick gets killed!" Elizabeth hissed as he swiftly dismounted and snatched her from the saddle, roughly jerking her down beside him behind a pile of rocks.

"Understood," he rejoined as he took cartridges from his bandolier and began jamming them into his rifle. "Dick! Hey, Dick! Take cover, damn it! I think Roberts wants you especially, since you're the head of the Regulators." He turned back to Elizabeth. "There. I've warned him, and I don't know what more I can do besides that—except keep an eye out for him. Do you know anything about guns?"

"No—and I don't want to, either!"

"Elizabeth, you've got to learn, and I mean it. You may need to know how to use one if something should happen to me. Besides, you can load for me."

"Well, you certainly picked a hell of a time for a lesson!"

"I didn't mean right this minute. Elizabeth, get down, damn it! I don't intend to lose you!" Reaching out, he pushed her down flat on the ground, flinging his body across hers to protect her as Roberts let loose a barrage of shots.

Despite his makeshift barricade, the ex-soldier must be able to see out the cracks of the old wooden building, Elizabeth realized, her heart pounding. No one was safe from his fire. Even the slightest movement triggered another volley.

"Oh, Jesus! I'm hit! I'm hit!" Charlie Bowdre cried, blood spurting between his fingers as he pressed his hand to his side. He was severely wounded; his bandolier, which had partially shielded him, had saved his life. He lay where he had fallen, his moans unnerving the other Regulators and making Elizabeth long to press her hands over her ears to shut out the dreadful sounds.

She could hardly breathe with Chaingo lying on top of her, but she knew he would count that a small price to pay for her safety, as Roberts was clearly bent on killing as many of the Regulators as he could.

Directly across the street from the outhouse, in front of Dr. Blazer's sawmill, there were several big saw-boys. During the melee, unobserved by Roberts, Brewer had sneaked around behind these, bent on getting a clear shot at the ex-soldier. Unfortunately, despite Chaingo's warning to remain hidden, Dick poked his head up over the saw-boys, trying to get a glimpse of Roberts. The movement attracted the ex-soldier's attention. Taking aim, he squeezed off another round. To Elizabeth's horror, the bullet bored straight through Brewer's eye, the impact knocking him back behind the saw-boys and killing him instantly.

At their leader's death, the rage of the desperadoes knew no bounds, and they pelted the outhouse with a shower of lead that splintered the wood and shredded the mattress, sending shards and feathers flying in every direction. After a moment, the door fell off its hinges, and Buckshot Roberts tumbled out, dead. The battle was ended.

"Are you all right?" Chaingo asked, his brow knitted with concern for Elizabeth as he assisted her to her feet.

She was so weak and shaky from fear that her knees gave out beneath her, and she was forced to grab hold of him to keep from falling. Mutely, she nodded her head in response to his question, her eyes wide and stricken as she glanced involuntarily at Brewer and Roberts. Then, realizing Bowdre was still alive, she bade Chaingo help her attend to him. Together, they stripped him of his bandolier, jacket, and shirt, Elizabeth wincing when she saw the ugly, bloody puncture in his side.

"Chaingo, I'm not a doctor, but I *do* know there are certain things that are necessary if blood poisoning or gangrene is not to set in. Tell the others to build a fire and set some water to heating. Everything that touches the wound must be boiled, and we must have some kind of antiseptic, like alcohol or carbolic."

Taking charge, he gave the orders, understanding that her knowledge of medicine, even if she weren't a physician, was far more advanced than his. Because Elizabeth didn't trust herself to do it, Chaingo removed the lead ball lodged in Bowdre's flesh. Then she cleaned the injury and bound it tightly, trying to impress upon Charlie just how important it was that he wash the wound every day and cover it with fresh bandages. While she and Chaingo treated Bowdre, the rest of the Regulators took care of Dick Brewer's body.

Later that night, after Chaingo had made love to her and she lay in his arms, staring up at the stars in the vast, black-velvet sky, Elizabeth concluded at last that he *was* right, that each man's destiny was written there and could not be changed. Because so far, she had not managed to save anyone she knew had been killed in the Lincoln County Wars. Sighing heavily, she snuggled closer to Chaingo, who was always so much warmer than she.

Perhaps it didn't matter that her coming here had altered nothing. Before, she had had no one. Now, she and Chaingo had each other— and in the end, for her, that was more than enough.

Six

After the shootout at Blazer's sawmill, the Regulators returned to Lincoln to discover that their legal standing as a posse had been revoked and that they had become outlaws because of the murders of Morton, Baker, and Roberts. There were now prices on the desperadoes' heads. As a result, the posse officially disbanded. In reality, the Regulators were still determined to avenge the murder of John Tunstall. With Dick Brewer dead, they elected Billy the Kid as their leader and took to hiding in and around Lincoln, deftly eluding Sheriff Brady whenever he attempted to arrest them.

By now, Elizabeth had given up any hope of persuading Chaingo to abandon the Regulators and their quest for revenge, so she continued to live not only the life of a vagabond, but the life of a renegade. Despite herself, she had to admit it was far more exciting than puttering around her small house and garden, reading a stack of romance novels, and living in a fantasy world. More than once as she lay on the hard ground at night, cradled in Chaingo's embrace, she imagined returning to the twentieth century, to her job as a teacher at the elementary school, in time for the fall-winter semester, and writing a paper entitled "How I Spent My Summer Vacation." Every time that idea occurred to her, it brought a smile to her lips. She could just see the looks on her colleagues' faces.

At other times, when she thought of McClosky, Brewer, and the other men who had been murdered, she could not help but be saddened and horrified—even though she knew that, in all actuality, they had been dead more than a hundred years, that all the Regulators had lain in their graves for a century. Even she herself, if she never returned to the twentieth century, would long have been dust in the wind in her own time now.

"Why so pensive, my sweet?" Chaingo asked, his voice low, as, beneath the blankets they shared, he drew her naked body even closer to his own, kissing her gently but in such a way that she knew he was going to make love to her again.

"I was just thinking that in my time, we have both been dead for a hundred years."

"We all die, Elizabeth." He stroked her hair soothingly, continuing to kiss her. "In fact, it is death that gives meaning to life, because if there were no death, how, then, would we value life?"

"I don't know. *Do* we value it? Look how many men have already died in the Lincoln County Wars . . . in all the wars in the history of the world. Or perhaps it is only men who do not value life, for they are the ones always marching off to battle, killing one another, while women remain at home—and pray for peace. I suppose that is where I should be right now, what I should be doing. But I don't want to be left behind, Chaingo. I want to stay with you always . . . forever and ever. So please don't send me away. Because that *is* what you are thinking of doing, isn't it?''

Chaingo sighed heavily against her mouth, his breath warm upon her face.

"Elizabeth, before, when the Regulators were lawmen, I did not believe your life to be in any great peril, or that Murphy and Company would prove so vile and unscrupulous as to kill you—a lady and John Chisum's daughter. But now, we have been branded outlaws, and The House faction will know from McNabb that you are my woman. So I am afraid for you now, my love. I fear for your safety and well-being. I want to take you to live with my mother's people on the Apache reservation until this is ended and I can come for you.''

"No, I won't go. Oh, please, Chaingo, don't make me go. *I* am afraid that if we are separated, I'll be whisked back to my own era somehow, that I'll never see you again, never know what became of you, that I'll wake up one morning in my own bed, in my own time, to discover this has all been just a dream. And I couldn't bear that. I just couldn't!''

"All right," he murmured slowly after a long moment. "All right. Perhaps it is selfish and unwise of me, but I have to confess that the idea

of not being with you tears at my heart. But you
must promise that if a time should come when
I feel the danger to you is too great you will go
to the reservation."

"Yes, I will, I promise."

His lips claimed hers then, evoking a wealth
of emotion, strong and sweet as it swept through
her body, setting her atremble, setting her
aflame. His mouth was tender at first, and like
a desert rose unfurling, her lips opened to his,
yielding eagerly to his onslaught. Lightly, his
tongue followed the contours of her mouth,
then probed the dark, moist recesses within,
twining with her own tongue in a mating dance
as old as time. The night wind stirred, still cool
although it was now spring. But Elizabeth felt
only the warmth of Chaingo, sharing his body
heat with her, so it was as though a fire burned
between them, igniting her blood, her body, her
desire for him.

She melted like quicksilver against him, molding herself to fit the long, hard length of him
as he clasped her to him, his lips and tongue
and hands roaming where they willed, stirring
anew all the exquisite sensations he had wakened in her that night at the bordello. She felt
beset by a fever, while, at the same time, all her
senses were keenly honed, acutely focused, her
perspective narrowed so that she was intensely
aware of Chaingo—and only him.

With his mouth, he swallowed her breath, his
lips growing more savage, more insistent, his
tongue plunging deep. Roughly, his fingers bur-

rowed through her hair, tearing at her braid, loosing it, engulfing them both in a sun-gold cascade. Groaning, he buried his face in the blond mass, wrapped the silken strands around his throat, as though to bind himself to her forever. Her hair smelled of sunshine and wildflowers, scents of the desert earth, intoxicating him. Deeply, Chaingo inhaled the fragrances that mingled with the heady perfume of Elizabeth herself, making his loins tighten suddenly, sharply. Driven by his rising passion, his mouth slanted across her upturned face to seek her lips again, finding them pliant and willing as they clung to his, drinking him in.

Her heartbeat quickened like his own as they strained against each other, breast to breast, thigh to thigh, no space between, so Elizabeth did not know where she ended and Chaingo began. They were as one, and she reveled in the feel of him, his flesh as smooth as clay in places, as hard as horn in others, where old scars marred his coppery body she had come to know as well as her own. Every plane and angle of him was familiar now. Still, she explored him as he did her, kissing, caressing, arousing. The muscles in his broad back, his strong arms, and his powerful thighs quivered and rippled beneath her fingers. The fine black hair on his chest was as soft as down against her palms and the sensitive tips of her breasts as he brushed against them, a feathery touch that made her inhale sharply and moan low in her throat. With his mouth, Chaingo muted the sound, both of them ever conscious—despite the jumble of sheltering boulders that concealed the two of them—of the rest of the Regulators, who slept some yards distant.

"Shhh," he murmured against her lips, smiling down at her, knowing that the things he did to her were not designed to ensure her silence. "You don't want me to have to gag you with my bandanna, do you?"

"No . . ." she whispered.

"Then be quiet—and spread your legs for me. Wider, my sweet, shy love. Draw your knees up. Yes . . . like that . . . It pleases me to see you blushing in the moonlight as you open yourself to me, to watch your face when I touch you here . . ." Kneeling between her thighs, he slid his thumbs slowly up the delicate, wet cleft of her, parting the fragile, burgeoning folds of her, making her gasp. "Shhh," he warned again, his eyes dancing with deviltry and desire. "If you keep on making so much noise, I'll have to stop what I'm doing—and you don't want that, do you, my girl?"

"No . . ." she choked out breathlessly, for now, his thumbs were on the throbbing heart of her, circling and stroking, exciting her wildly, so that she bucked against him helplessly, wanting, *needing* more, aching desperately for fulfillment.

Without ceasing the sensuous movement, he lowered his head to her breasts, his black eyes still riveted on her countenance. His teeth captured one nipple, tugged on it gently, his tongue twisting about it, teasing and taunting before he drew the peak into his mouth, sucking hungrily. Waves of unbearable pleasure pulsed through her, so she could no longer think, could only feel, every inch of her so incredibly alive, so utterly responsive that his every kiss, his every touch was like lightning shooting through her body.

Time passed. Elizabeth didn't know how much as Chaingo continued to tease and arouse her until she was like a wild thing beneath him, whimpering, begging for release. Momentarily, he eased her longing with his fingers, pushing them deep inside her, thrusting them torturously in and out of her as he kissed her lips, her throat, her breasts, her belly, bringing her to the brink again and again, only to leave her unsated, frantic.

"Please," she entreated, biting her lower lip. "Oh, please, Chaingo! It's not enough . . ."

"You want more?" he asked thickly.

"Yes . . ."

"Then tell me. Tell me what you want."

"You . . . inside me . . . now. Please."

"Yes, Elizabeth, my heart, my soul. Yes!"

Groaning, he entered her then, piercing her to the core as her climax surged and exploded within her in a kaleidoscopic torment. From far away, it seemed, she felt Chaingo's hands tighten on her bruisingly in the heat of his own passion, his nails digging into her skin as he drove into her urgently until his own release came, leaving his breath rasping.

He collapsed atop her, his sweat-sheened skin

sliding on her own as his fingers tunneled through her damp hair. He kissed her eyelids, her nose, her mouth.

"Who is the shameless one now?" he asked huskily, an impudent smile curving his lips. "Wantonly imploring me for sex!"

"Hush! You're wicked—and the others might hear you!"

"If they did, they are green with envy—and cursing themselves for not chasing after you that day you tried to escape at Mr. Tunstall's ranch." Slowly, Chaingo withdrew from her, pulling her against his chest and stroking her hair gently. "But if they had, I would have killed them—for you are mine, Elizabeth, only mine, always mine. I love you."

"I love you, too, Chaingo."

He rolled a cigarette and smoked it silently in the starlit darkness, while she lay contentedly in his embrace, listening to their hearts beating as one.

Seven

Later, Elizabeth was to recognize the terrible irony of its being April Fool's Day. But that warm, spring morning, she was aware only of the pounding of her heart because the Regulators were once more in Lincoln, where they planned to ambush Sheriff Brady and as many of his cohorts as they could. Fronting on the main street of town was Dolan and Riley's store, The House. At the other end stood the courthouse. In between these two points, next door to John Tunstall's mercantile, was an adobe-walled corral, where the desperadoes intended to lie in wait for their prey.

After sneaking into Lincoln last night, they made their way to the corral. There, they carefully chiseled grooves into the top of the adobe wall in which to rest the barrels of their guns. Now, they waited impatiently for Brady to make an appearance. Many citizens of the town judged Brady an excellent sheriff, but Elizabeth knew this wasn't so. He was a close friend of all those involved with Murphy and Company, and for that reason, he had failed on numerous occasions to discharge his professional duties at all, much less with the objectivity of an officer of the law. Still, she was shocked and horrified that the Regulators meant to ambush and kill him and would have warned him of his peril. However, she was not only certain Brady wouldn't have believed her, but Chaingo also refused to permit her to tell the sheriff anything.

"You can bet that Brady was the one who told Morton and the rest of that so-called posse that they should kill Mr. Tunstall," he'd said. "Murphy and Company might have given the order, but by God, Brady's a lawman, and he ought never to have sided with them and carried out their instructions. He's worse than The House faction, as bad as those corrupt bastards in the Santa Fe Ring. Besides, Elizabeth, what good has it done to warn anyone else? They've all still died, haven't they, just as it said in your history books? No, if this is Brady's fate, there's nothing you can do to prevent it."

She crouched down behind the adobe wall of the corral, ashamed for not making more of an effort to halt the ambush, yet knowing that, realistically, this was the code of the West, that here in this time and place, men were as likely to settle their differences with a Colt instead of in a court. And who was to say that the twentieth century, with its gang wars and drive-by shootings, was any better?

Still, her heart hammered, her palms sweated, and the lump of fear in her throat was so big she could hardly choke it down. She prayed that Brady wouldn't appear. But that hope was in vain, for in due time, he strolled from The House along with two friends of his, George Hindman and J. B. "Billy" Matthews, and the three men headed down the main street toward the courthouse. Such was the lawless state to which Lincoln had by now degenerated that no man with any common sense at all went about town unarmed, and Brady and his companions were no exception. Each carried a rifle—although this circumstance availed them nothing in the end.

The corral not only provided an excellent view of the street, but it was also situated in such a way that Brady and his cohorts had to pass by it on their way to the courthouse, which was why it had been chosen as the ambush site. As the three men drew up level with the corral, the Regulators opened fire without warning. Brady and Hindman toppled where they stood, but Matthews managed to find cover behind some old houses on the south side of the street. His body riddled with bullets, Brady was killed instantly. Hindman, however, although fatally wounded, lived a short while longer.

Across from the corral was a saloon run by Ike Stockton, who was a friend of Billy the Kid. Witnessing what had occurred, Stockton hurried out from his saloon to check on the condition of the two downed men. Elizabeth heard Hindman calling weakly for water and watched as Stockton went to the bank of the nearby Rio Bonito, and dipped his hat in the water.

When Stockton rose, he spied Matthews hiding

behind the old houses and froze, because at that
moment, Billy the Kid and the other Regulators
leaped over the adobe wall of the corral, intending to seize Brady's and Hindman's weapons.
Stockton was caught square in the middle of the
gunfight and knew that as soon as the desperadoes came into sight, Matthews would unleash a
volley of shots at them.

"Billy," Stockton called out, lying, "Brady's
dead and Hindman will be soon, so there ain't
any rush to get their guns."

At those words, Elizabeth remembered reading
what Stockton's predicament had been, and she
caught hold of Chaingo's arm and jerked him
back quickly.

"It's Matthews!" she hissed urgently. "He can
see Brady and Hindman, and he's just waiting
for you all to come into view so he can shoot
you. Ike's going to be caught in the crossfire.
That's why he's trying to make Billy go back!"

Chaingo didn't need to hear any more. Reaching out, he knocked Elizabeth to the ground
and flung himself on top of her, shielding her
as he shouted, "Billy, it's Matthews! Get back!"

But the warning came too late. Even as
Chaingo spoke, Billy was bending over Brady's
body, intent on taking the sheriff's rifle. Before
Billy could rise, Matthews opened fire. The bullet buzzed through the air, slamming into
Brady's weapon and violently knocking it from
Billy's hand before plowing a painful, although
not mortal, gouge in his thigh. To have attempted to shoot Matthews while Billy himself

was injured and exposed would have been a fool-hardy act, and Elizabeth thought the Kid was not quite so reckless as history had painted him when he wisely opted to seek cover instead.

Some minutes later, the renegades were safely ensconced in the house of Alexander McSween. By then, Hindman was dead, although Matthews had escaped. Billy the Kid decided to remain hidden in town until his wound healed—and at one point, while a search for him was in progress, he concealed himself inside a barrel, on the top of which a Mexican woman prepared tortillas as her house was ransacked by The House faction.

For a short time afterward, Lincoln County was without a sheriff. But finally, a man named George W. Peppin agreed to undertake the job temporarily. He appointed a slew of deputies to assist him, as Billy the Kid and the Regulators were still continuing their rampage against Murphy and Company.

Still, the following weeks were almost idyllic for Elizabeth. Spring had come in earnest, and the desperadoes had chosen as their latest hideout the small town of San Patricio, which lay on the Rio Ruidoso some seven miles across the mountains from Lincoln. The Mexicans who principally populated San Patricio were friendly to Billy the Kid and the Regulators and kept them informed about any threat.

There was a small cantina in town where Chaingo had taken a room for himself and Elizabeth, so that for the first time in their relationship, it was as though they had a real home of their own. She kept the tiny room spotless and brought in desert flowers every day to brighten it up, placing them in clay pots on the window ledge and the dresser.

This last boasted a decent-sized, albeit smoky and crazed, mirror, and at first glance, she was shocked to see her reflection. It had been weeks since she had viewed herself in a looking glass, and she saw a woman so changed that she scarcely recognized herself. Her hair had gone untrimmed for so long that it fell below her shoulders and was streaked by the desert sun so it seemed a mixture of gold and silver. Her skin, too, touched by the sun, glowed like golden honey, making her blue eyes stand out startlingly in her oval face. There was in their azure depths a knowledge and sensuality that had never been there before; her generous mouth seemed somehow lusher, more voluptuous than it used to be.

"Do you find yourself so changed, then, my sweet?" Chaingo asked as he came to stand behind her, one hand encircling her waist, the other pushing aside her mass of hair to bare her nape, to which he pressed his mouth erotically.

"Yes. I look so . . . different somehow."

"Yes. This is the way you were in my vision, the way I saw you that day at Mr. Tunstall's ranch." His hand slid slowly along her shoulder, pushing the sleeve of her ruffled blouse down her arm, baring her skin for his lips as he dipped his fingers beneath the frilly, scooped neckline to fondle her naked breasts. His soft, mocking laughter rang in her ear when she closed her eyes, unable to go on watching the two of them in the mirror. He bit her lobe gently, whispering wicked things to her as heat crept up to stain her cheeks. She felt him pull her blouse down around her waist and cup her breasts, his fingers teasing her nipples until they stiffened. She knew without asking that he was still looking at their reflections, watching her as he kissed and caressed her.

After a moment, he turned her in his arms, lifted her, and settled her on the vanity. Rucking her skirt up about her thighs, he stripped off her pantalets and spread her thighs wide. Then he freed his hard maleness from his denims and pushed himself into the hot, honeyed core of her, knowing she would be ready for him. And she was. For after so many weeks in his bed, she was like clay in his hands. He had only to look at her for her to melt inside, to feel the sweet rush of moisture between her thighs.

He rocked her slowly, indolently, kissing her mouth and sucking her nipples until her climax welled and broke inside her, sending a flood of unbearable pleasure through her entire body. She cried out and clutched him to her, her nails digging into his back as the waves surged and crested, seeming to go on endlessly. They were still rippling through her when his own climax came. Groaning, he buried his head against her shoulder, his hands tightening upon her buttocks as he thrust into her one last time, hard and deep as possible, crushing her against him.

He bent his head and languidly licked the sweat from the valley between her breasts before kissing her lingeringly, his tongue shooting deep into her mouth. Then he withdrew and buttoned himself up, his drowsy eyes smoldering darkly with satisfaction, a lazy smile curving his lips.

"Hmmm. I don't think I'll ever get enough of you," he drawled softly. "It is a good thing the Mexican bandits who frequent this cantina learned their lesson the first night I brought you here, Elizabeth—because I would kill any man who dared to touch you, who tried to take you from me."

"I know." She shivered a little at his words, because on the night to which he referred, a drunken man had grabbed her and tried to kiss her in the cantina's common room.

Chaingo had yanked his knife from his boot and would have cut the man's throat had Elizabeth not intervened, insisting that her assailant had had too much to drink and pleading for his life. Chaingo had finally let him go, throwing him out of the cantina. The bandit had not returned—and no other man had dared to make so bold with her since, all of them afraid of her half-breed Apache lover.

"You are happy here, Elizabeth, are you not?" Chaingo asked as he helped her down from the dresser and rearranged her garments.

"Yes." She nodded. "Very much. It's almost like a home of our own."

"We will have that one day—soon—I promise you. Once I am sure we can get through safely, we'll ride south, across the border, into Mexico and start a small ranch of our own. There, we'll raise cattle and horses—and many children." He laid his hand gently upon her belly. "Even now, our first may grow inside you."

Elizabeth started at his words, for with all that had happened, she had given no thought to this. But it was true. After her divorce from Michael, she had stopped taking her birth-control pills, because she hadn't seen any point in continuing to use them. Now, she realized she hadn't had her period since she had arrived in the 1800s. She wondered if that was because time was out of whack for her—or because even now, she did, indeed, carry Chaingo's baby.

"I—I hadn't thought, but, yes, I could be pregnant," she confirmed.

"We will go to the small church here and have the priest marry us tonight. Yes?"

"Yes. Oh, yes, Chaingo!" Elizabeth cried softly, her heart overflowing with happiness.

And so they were married, the women of the town digging into their hope chests to produce a beautiful white wedding ensemble for the bride, the men decking Chaingo out like a Spanish grandee. It was nothing at all like her wedding with Michael had been. But to Elizabeth, nothing could have been lovelier than the simple church lit with dozens of candles and the ceremony performed by the priest as she and Chaingo knelt before him. Afterward, there was a gay fiesta, with food and drink contributed by all, dancing and firecrackers and a piñata stuffed

full of treats. In the wee hours, amid much
shouting and laughter, Chaingo finally swept her
up and carried her into their room at the cantina. There, he pressed her down upon their bed
and made love to her feverishly, and when they
lay together in the quiet afterglow, Elizabeth fell
asleep thinking that however strangely and inex-
plicably it had happened, all her dreams had
somehow come true.

Eight

It was impossible for the Regulators to stay in any one place too long, as Sheriff Peppin appeared to be taking his new duties seriously. Further, one of the deputies he had appointed, Marion Turner, who owned a store in Roswell, was a bitter enemy of John Chisum and was determined to see the Chisum-Tunstall-McSween faction destroyed. Learning that the desperadoes were on the move again, Turner gathered a huge force and set out in pursuit. He had heard a rumor that the renegades had started up the Pecos, toward Fort Sumner. He wasted a great deal of time, riding twenty miles in that direction, before he decided that the Regulators had caused him to go off on a wild-goose chase, and he turned back toward Lincoln.

It was there that the desperadoes were once more holed up in McSween's elegant adobe house in the center of town. Elizabeth had already warned Chaingo that this was to be the last stand of the Regulators, and he had promised her that after this, they would go to Mexico.

Outside the McSweens' home, Turner and his men, now joined by Sheriff Peppin, had positioned themselves all around town. For three days, they exchanged desultory sniper fire with the renegades, but nothing came of it—other than their accidentally shooting a horse and mule. Then, on the morning of July 19, Turner decided he was fed up, and, accompanied by his partner, John A. Jones, he approached the McSween house and demanded that Billy the Kid and his cohorts surrender. Elizabeth could have told Turner that this approach was doomed to failure, for no sooner had Turner stated his terms than Billy shouted back several of his own, and the battle commenced with a fury.

In the midst of the barrage, Lieutenant Colonel Dudley, of the Ninth Cavalry, showed up from Fort Stanton, nine miles distant. With him were one company of infantry and one of artillery. He positioned his cannon in the middle of the road, declaring his intention to fire on either faction who dared to shoot over the heads of his command. But neither side paid him any heed—and he did not ignite his cannon, his bluff having been called.

Inside the McSween house, Elizabeth cringed and took cover as the fusillade ensued, splintering doors, windows, and sending chips from the adobe walls flying. Some of the renegades climbed up onto McSween's roof to try to drive off the attackers. But Turner sent a dozen men up into the hills with long-range guns, and the Regulators were forced to retreat back into the house. While the marksmen were shooting at them, several bullets struck Mrs. McSween's piano, which rang discordantly. Later, reporters recorded that Mrs. McSween had inspired the desperadoes by playing battle songs and singing until their assailants had got close enough to the house to destroy the piano. But Elizabeth now knew that wasn't true, as Mrs. McSween left home before any of the fighting started. Chaingo had wanted Elizabeth to go with her, but she had refused, insisting he might need her knowledge of the future during the melee.

"Damn it, Elizabeth! You should have gone!" Chaingo said now as he observed Peppin's and Turner's men piling kindling around the house and setting it ablaze. "You didn't tell me they were going to burn the damned house down around us!"

"I was afraid you'd make me leave if you knew," she confessed, knowing from the muscle that worked in his jaw how angry he was as he dragged her toward the back rooms, the front of the house having been engulfed with flames. "You'd better make the others come with us. A man named Jack Long is going to sneak in and saturate one of the rooms with a gallon of coal oil."

"He has already done so," Chaingo replied grimly. "That's why the fire is spreading so quickly."

Although the house had eleven rooms, the Regulators were relegated to the kitchen by nightfall—and would have been burned out entirely had the home not been constructed of adobe. Watching his house go up in flames, McSween had grown increasingly dispirited and uncaring of the outcome. He had refused to pick up a gun and join the fray, on the grounds that his participation would invalidate his $10,000 life-insurance policy. He sat at the kitchen table, his head in his hands, as the renegades discussed how they could best flee.

"When the fire reaches the kitchen, we'll rush through the back door, through the flames, and take to the underbrush along the Rio Bonito. It's a fifty-yard sprint at most, and once we're there, we can head for the hills and make our escape," Billy the Kid declared.

No better plan was put forth, so that was the one carried out. A frightened Mexican in the house called out to the besiegers to halt their onslaught, saying that the Regulators would surrender, but Billy angrily pistol-whipped the poor man, knocking him unconscious. No sooner had that occurred than a man named Robert W. Beckwith, a cattle owner from Severn Rivers, and John Jones came around the house and up to the kitchen door and opened fire on the desperadoes. Billy shot Beckwith through the head. Then, leaping over the body, pistol in hand and yelling, "Come on! Come on!" he burst through the flames into the darkness, his revolver spitting bullets and the rest of the Regulators hard on his heels.

Elizabeth knew she would never forget that moment when Chaingo grabbed her hand and hauled her toward the river, with shots blasting all about them. Behind them, McSween, who had refused to surrender or flee, was riddled with bullets, blood spurting all over the white shirt that had made him an easy target when he had appeared in the doorway. He staggered out into the yard and collapsed, dead. Last out was Toni Foliard, a new recruit.

It was ten o'clock—and the Lincoln County Wars were over.

Reaching their horses, the Regulators mounted up, then split off, riding in all directions. Chaingo—Elizabeth perched before him—turned his stallion south, toward the Mexican border. Such was the adrenaline that still pumped wildly through her body that it was some time before she realized the fierce, unbridled tempest behind them was not McSween's burning house, but lightning.

"Chaingo, look!" She pointed at the shattered night sky. "A storm is coming—and it looks just like the one that brought me here!"

Glancing over his shoulder, he abruptly jerked his horse to a halt.

"It may take you home—to your own time, Elizabeth." His eyes searched hers intensely. "Do you want me to ride into it? It may be the only chance you ever have to go back."

"No! *No!* It might take me—and leave *you* behind! And I couldn't bear that. I'm your wife, Chaingo. I love you. Keep going south, toward Mexico. Hurry—before the storm catches us!"

"Oh, Elizabeth, I love you, too—with all my heart." His arm tightened around her waist, and he took her mouth feverishly, his passionate kiss speaking all that needed to be said. "Mexico it is, then, my own true love."

He spurred the stallion forward, Elizabeth clinging to him tightly as, together, they hastened down the wind.

Epilogue

In the small white house that had once belonged to Elizabeth Mulcahey, all was still and quiet, except for the television set playing in her bedroom. Had anybody been there watching it, they would have seen the ending of a movie entitled *Hasten Down the Wind* unfolding as the tape running on her VCR wound toward its finish. But there was no one present as, on the screen, a handsome, half-breed Apache riding a big, black stallion galloped south across the Mexican border—his beautiful, beloved blond wife mounted before him on his Spanish saddle.

Forbidden Affections

by
Jo Beverley

Anna Featherstone sat up in bed and fumbled urgently for her candlestick. Grasping it, she slipped out of bed to light it at the night lamp on the mantelpiece, then held it high and turned to study her peculiar new bedroom.

Her sleepy thoughts had been right. The Gothic monstrosity was exactly like Dulcinea's prison in the novel, *Forbidden Affections!* When the notion had come to her at a point between sleep and waking she had been sure she must have been mistaken, but now she wandered the room, convinced she was correct.

It was a wonderful discovery, but also very puzzling.

Anna had spent her sixteen years in the Derbyshire countryside and knew she was not *au fait* with the latest fashions, but even if dark, heavily-carved Gothic furniture was the rage in London, surely such morbid motifs as deadly nightshade and coffins were not. In the novel, Dulcinea's cruel uncle had caused her room to be decorated with symbols of death to remind her of her probable fate if she did not surrender to his evil passions.

Anna was not the least alarmed by the grinning skeletons and contorted gargoyles in the carvings. She was sadly lacking in sensibility. When her sister Maria had once demanded to know what Anna would do if actually confronted by a skeleton in a monk's robe, Anna had replied that she'd inspect it to find out how it held its bones together without ligaments or muscles.

Smiling at the memory of Maria's shudders, Anna wandered the room, appreciating the fine attention to detail. The heavy armoire boasted ivory knobs carved as skulls, and the rather pretty design in the wallpaper turned out to be a coffin shape. As best she could remember, it was all exactly as in *Forbidden Affections*.

She wished she had the novel with her so she could check each detail, but she had not been permitted to bring many books on this trip to London. Allowed only five, she would never choose *Forbidden Affections* over, for example, *Cruel Matrimony*, an earlier novel by Mrs. Jamison. Anna had always thought there was something unsatisfactory about *Forbidden Affections*, which had apparently been the lady's last work. Perhaps she had been ill.

Anna longed to know the history of this room for it must have been created by a wealthy and devoted admirer of the novel, and not that long ago. *Forbidden Affections* had first been published less than ten years ago, though Anna had only read it last year. After all, at the time of publication she had scarce been out of the nursery.

Would the servants know the house's history?

Number 9, Carne Terrace was just a house hired for the spring Season—part of a handsome row of houses in an excellent part of London. Her parents and sister had been delighted with it until this bedroom had been discovered. At that point, they had almost left to stay at an inn. The Gothic marvel was clearly the master bedroom, but Lady Featherstone had declared most absolutely that nothing would persuade her to sleep beneath a canopy of gargoyles.

Maria, who always copied Mama, had declared the same, adding that she could never even open a drawer if it involved touching a skull. She had gone so far as to collapse into a convenient chair to make her point, and had required a sniff of laudanum to overcome the shock.

Since there were only three good bedrooms in the house, and Maria and Anna hated to share a bed, there was only one solution. Anna and her father had shared an ironic glance and Anna had made the noble sacrifice, secretly delighted to have such a room.

Now she was even more so. Imagine having Dulcinea's chamber all to herself. Heavens, it might even turn her into a romantic heroine!

Anna caught sight of herself in a mirror surrounded by grotesque carved heads and laughed. Dulcinea she was not. Dulcinea—like all Mrs. Jamison's heroines—was slender as a willow-wand, had a complexion of pearly hue, and silky golden tresses. Anna possessed thick, dark hair which always fought the constraint of her plait, full rosy cheeks, and a round body that was the despair of her fashionable mama.

She remembered then that when Dulcinea had first seen her reflection surrounded by gargoyles she had screamed and fainted. Dulcinea—again like all Mrs. Jamison's heroines—tended to faint quite often. Anna had never fainted in her life.

She had always wanted to, and had tried various tricks to achieve it, including putting scraps of silk in her shoes, but she had never achieved so much as a slight sensation of dizziness.

With a grimace at her robust reflection, she hoped that sturdy nerves and common sense didn't rule out all possibility of a handsome hero one day sweeping her off her feet.

Still delighted by the room, Anna began to return to bed, but then she turned back to contemplate the huge carved stone fireplace guarded by armored skeletons on either side.

Surely not!

In the book, evil Count Nacre had constructed a secret doorway in the fireplace so that he could sneak into Dulcinea's room at night. One of the things about the book that irritated Anna was that Dulcinea's escape from his wicked plans was not of her own doing. Anna could think of any number of ways the silly creature could have escaped, but of course Dulcinea had waited for handsome Roland to find the secret door and rescue her.

Just before ancient, rat-infested Castle Nacre crumbled to the ground during an earthquake.

Now Anna eyed the ridiculous fireplace, refusing to believe that anyone had actually gone so far as to construct a secret door in a modern

London townhouse. Where could it go, after all? Number 9, Carne Terrace was solidly bounded by number 8 and number 10.

But she could not resist trying.

The lever, if it was there, would be the spear of the skeleton to the right of the grate. The spear was held across his body and extended into the chimney so that it wouldn't be accidentally moved by a servant.

In the book.

This was real life. This wasn't a book.

Anna seized the spear and pulled it toward her. At first—as she expected—nothing happened. Then it began to move.

Anna snatched her hands away and stared at the spear as if it had come to life. This was taking replication to extremes! After all, on the other side of this fireplace there assuredly was not an abandoned, rat-infested, ivy-covered tower.

Was there?

Her heart began to thump.

For the first time, Anna's very practical mind was toying with the fantastic.

On the other side of this fireplace, she told herself firmly, was number 10, Carne Terrace, a respectable modern house.

Well, not precisely respectable.

That had been another shock for her parents—to realize that Carne Terrace was named after the Earl of Carne, who had built it, and that number 10, the large end house next door, belonged to the notorious fourth earl.

Their housekeeper had revealed that fact when asked who their neighbors were. Mrs. Postle had hastened to explain that the house stood empty and had done so for over eight years—ever since *the incident*.

Those two words had been said with the sort of meaningful glance that Anna knew all too well. It meant that young ladies were not to hear about it, and of course that had left Anna in a ferment of curiosity. What on earth had the earl done? It was probably to do with carnal relations. *Incidents* always were.

She'd followed the subsequent conversations very closely, but all she had learned was that after *the incident* the earl had left England and had not been seen since.

Anna was surprised. She'd heard of a number of young ladies who had traveled abroad as a result of *incidents*. Gentlemen, on the other hand, never seemed to suffer the full consequences of their follies.

She had been delighted by this hint of murky mystery, however. Though her parents had brought both their daughters to London, only Maria was to make her curtsy this year, and Anna had expected to be a little bored. Digging out the whole story of *the incident* would definitely enliven her stay.

Now it seemed she had other amusements—if she dared pull the lever fully.

Was it truly possible that it would open a door into the house of the wicked Earl of Carne?

Curiosity was Anna's greatest weakness, and

she knew it. She generally kept it under control, but she could never return to bed and sleep without finding out if the door was there or not. After all, if Count Nacre could creep into Dulcinea's chamber, perhaps the wicked Earl of Carne could creep into hers!

She might be in danger . . .

But that was sophistry, and she knew it. She wanted to try the lever just because it was there.

She grasped it and pulled it all the way. It made only a slight grinding sound, but it clearly had done something. She took a deep breath, went to the right-hand part of the fireplace, and pushed.

Just as in the book, the panel swiveled slightly.

Anna stopped to consider. No, she was not dreaming. No, she had not been plunged into the pages of a novel. But there was, assuredly, a secret door.

Even Anna's prosaic heart was beating high and fast as she pushed the panel fully open. She told herself it had to open the way into number 10 . . .

But a small, less rational part of her brain was prepared for it to open into a rat-infested, crumbling castle.

Anna, therefore, was prepared to scream.

Once the door was open she cautiously peeped through. She laughed shakily and her heart rate began to steady. The room beyond was a perfectly ordinary bedroom shrouded in Holland covers.

The secret door, as expected, simply led into number 10, Carne Terrace.

Of course, that meant that it led into the home of the wicked earl. A proper young lady, assuming that she hadn't already fallen into the vapors, would at this point have run to Papa to have the door firmly nailed shut. Anna Featherstone, fairly bubbling with excitement, walked through to explore.

After all, the earl was not here, and had not been here for years. In confirmation, this room—which was probably the master bedroom—had the feel of a place long unused.

Anna turned to look at the fireplace and found it to be much more normal than the one on her side, though rather ornate for a bedchamber. It was of carved wood and had the heavy side panels necessary to disguise the moving parts.

Whatever the reason for this construction, there had obviously been a conspiracy by the residents of both houses, and she'd go odds it was all to do with *the incident*. Anna was not naive, and secretly-connected bedchambers told their own story. Although she still wanted to know why the bedchamber in number 9 was so peculiar.

Being a careful person, Anna checked the mechanism before moving away from the door. Once she was sure she could return at will, she prepared to enjoy herself.

She was wickedly at large in someone else's house, and it was an adventure impossible to resist, especially when the risk was so small. Since the house was unused it was unlikely that she would be found out. And if she did meet anyone, she would hardly be thrown into prison. A young lady of sixteen in her nightgown could not be mistaken for a housebreaker.

Anna crept barefooted across the carpet and gingerly turned the knob. It made no sound. She eased the door open and peeped out into a corridor rather wider than the one in number 9. This corner house, a nobleman's residence, was at least twice the size of the other houses in the terrace.

She was struck by the silence.

It took Anna a moment to think why this was so strange, and then she realized that there was not even the ticking of a clock. She'd never before been in a house which did not have a clock ticking somewhere.

She detected no smell of decay or mold, though. The house might be unused but it was not neglected. In fact, now that she searched for it, there was the faint smell of polish in the air. This meant there had to be some servants and so she must be careful.

It did not mean she would give up her exploration, though. This was like having an enormous playhouse all to herself.

She walked the corridor, shielding her candle and glancing at the pictures on the walls. They were not particularly interesting—mostly rather nondescript landscapes with no indication of the places they represented.

She peeped into the various rooms along the hall, but they were not interesting, either—some bedchambers and dressing rooms and a moderately-sized drawing room.

Then, in a large sitting room or boudoir, she caught sight of an intriguing painting. She wasn't sure at first why it had caught her eye, as it was only half-lit by the flickering candle. When she went closer, she decided it was a simple matter of quality. She did not know a great deal about art but surely this portrait had been painted by a master.

Even in the candlelight the young man's skin tones glowed with vitality and his dark curls sprang crisply from his brow. His expression was quite sober and yet she could *feel* that he desperately wanted to laugh. Perhaps it was the way his bright blue eyes were crinkled slightly with the humor he was trying to suppress. Was he trying to appear older than he was? She didn't think he was a great deal older than her own sixteen years. He reminded her in many ways of her brother James and his friends, full of the joy of life and ready for mischief.

Of course, she reminded herself, by now this young man could be ancient.

She didn't think so, though. The high collar and plain cravat fitted recent fashion.

Anna realized she had been staring at the portrait as if expecting him to move and speak, so skillfully had the fleeting expression been captured. With a smile of farewell, she made herself leave the room, feeling rather as if she abandoned someone to dark neglect.

When she had looked in every room on this floor, she came to her Rubicon, the stairs to the lower floor. A prudent miss would now return to her room and forget about this place. Anna had to admit as well that it was probably morally wrong to creep about someone's house like this, peeping and prying. It was almost like reading a private journal.

On the other hand, there were no secrets here. It was just an empty house and she wanted to see all of it.

She went cautiously down the stairs to the main floor.

All the windows she had seen had been curtained, presumably to keep the sun off the unused rooms, but here a handsome fan light over the door spilled moonlight into the hall, making it seem more alive, more as if someone might suddenly appear.

She stood still, her feet chilling on the tiled floor, listening for any sound.

She heard only silence. Any servants were fast asleep.

All the same, Anna decided to hurry through the rest of her exploration and get back to her bed.

A breakfast room, shrouded. A reception room, the same. A dining room, a library . . .

Anna halted, faced temptation, and succumbed.

Anna loved books. She loved novels, but they

were not her only reading. Her father said she would read anything, even a sporting journal if desperate, and he had always encouraged her. He had not, however, allowed her to bring more than a small box of books with her and to her dismay the library in number 9 was a skeleton of a room with empty shelves. She supposed no one would want to leave books for unpredictable tenants, but she had been disappointed. After all, her consumption of books was so large that trips to the lending libraries were going to take most of her days!

Here, however, was a supply, to hand and neglected. The books seemed to call to her, begging to be read.

No, no, her conscience argued. To borrow without permission would be like stealing.

Yet Anna was soon cruising the glass-fronted shelves almost without thought, drawn like iron to a magnet. Rows and rows of matched volumes—bound magazines, philosophical classics, eminent sermons. But also rows and rows of mismatched books likely to have been bought for love.

And organized. Here was travel. Here was science. And here were novels.

Just one row.

In fact, just the novels of Mrs. Jamison. That was intriguing, to be sure.

She opened the case and ran her fingers over the glossy leather covers, pausing at the three volumes that comprised *Forbidden Affections*. She wanted to read it again in Dulcinea's room to check the accuracy of the simulation. She wanted it so much it was agony to resist.

But Anna knew that if she took the books she would have gone beyond an intrusion of privacy to theft. She found the strength to close the bookcase doors and leave the chamber of temptation.

Frightened that she would weaken, Anna ran up the stairs and back to the secret door. Her candle blew out, but she knew the way. She groped toward the fireplace and squeezed through the door, easing it shut behind her. Then she was back in her own room again with that door firmly closed.

She jumped into bed and pulled up the covers, then lay there, wondering if what she had just done had been real. But she knew it had, and she knew she desperately wanted to explore again another day.

Anna awoke the next morning when Martha, middle-aged maid to the Featherstone daughters, drew back the curtains to let in sunlight. Anna's first thought was that she had had the most interesting dream.

It took only seconds to realize that it had actually happened.

The room was still the same, and in daylight assuredly Dulcinea's chamber.

"What a room this is!" declared Martha, setting the jug of hot water on the washstand.

"You're a braver lass than I am, Miss Anna, to sleep here so sound."

Anna sat up to hug her knees. "I don't mind. I like it."

Martha just shook her head. "Up with you, miss. I'll be back in a little while to button you up and fix your hair."

Anna popped out of bed and washed, then put on her stockings and petticoat. She was just working into her light stays when Martha returned to help her.

"How do you like it here, Martha?" Anna asked, holding her long plait away from the buttons down her back.

"Seems a decent enough house, miss. Sit you down now. Breakfast'll be ready in a moment."

Anna sat in front of the gargoyle-guarded mirror. "Have you found out anything about this place?"

"About it?" Martha was quickly unraveling the plait and brushing it out. "What do you mean, miss?"

"Well, about this room. It is a little strange."

"Who knows what they do in Lunnon, miss? The regular staff haven't said anything, but then, by the time we were here and unpacked, it were pretty well time for bed."

"I suppose so."

The Featherstones had arrived at nearly eight in the evening and had only taken time for supper before retiring. They were here until June, however. Time enough for Anna to unravel the

mystery this room presented, and to find out all
about the wicked Earl of Carne's *incident*.

As soon as Martha was finished, Anna ran
down to the breakfast parlor and kissed her parents. Lady Featherstone, slender and blond,
smiled in a slightly pained way at her younger
daughter's high spirits. Sir Jeffrey hugged her
warmly.

"Sleep well, Pippin, in your Gothic chamber?"

Anna had to suppress a giggle. "Very well,
Papa."

Lady Featherstone shuddered. "Anna, you
have no sensibility."

"Which is as well, my dear," said her husband,
"or the girls would have had to sleep together,
and you know they hate that." Sir Jeffrey was
ruddy-faced and robust. It was from him that
Anna got her looks and temperament.

"Maria tosses and turns all night," said Anna.

"Only in a strange bed," said Maria, drifting
in wanly. "I declare I have not had a moment's
rest! The mattress is decidedly hard."

If Maria was poorly rested, it had not affected
her looks. She, like Dulcinea, was a pale blond
beauty with pearly skin and a slender, elegant
figure. Lady Featherstone fussed over her, com-
miserating on her sensitive nature and plying
her with tea.

Sir Jeffrey grinned at Anna. "Well, what plans
for today, Pippin? Let me guess. An attack on
the book emporiums of the Metropolis?"

Anna grinned back as she helped herself to

eggs. "Most certainly. I am hoping you will direct me to the best lending libraries in town, Papa."

Since Sir Jeffrey was a Member of Parliament, he knew London quite well and obligingly wrote out a list of the best book suppliers while his wife and older daughter planned their assault on modistes and haberdashers.

Folding the list, Anna asked casually, "What was Mrs. Postle referring to when she mentioned an incident concerning our neighbor, Papa?" She had reason to hope that her liberal-minded father would give her a straight answer.

However, his only response was, "Never you mind, Pippin. London isn't like the country. It is quite possible to ignore neighbors."

"But Papa, the doors are only feet apart. What if we encounter people coming and going?"

Her mother had picked up the conversation and now a look flashed between her parents. Anna's curiosity expanded to bursting point. What *had* the earl done?

"Anna," said her mother, "if you should happen to encounter any of our neighbors, a distant nod will suffice until you have been formally introduced. Which is unlikely since you are not here to *be* introduced."

It was Maria who let the cat out of the bag. "Martha said that number 10 had a murder there some years back. Can you imagine? It makes me feel quite faint to think of it!"

Lady Featherstone began to say something sharp about the maid, but her husband overruled her. "It is perhaps as well, my dear, that the girls be prepared. Maria, Anna, it is true that an irregular death occurred at the Earl of Carne's house some years ago, but it was suicide, not murder. It is an old matter and need not disturb you at all, but you should know that the earl, despite his rank, is not the sort of man who is introduced to young ladies. I am assured that he lives abroad, but if you should encounter him, you will ignore him entirely."

Anna stared. "Cut an earl?"

"If the man has a scrap of decency that will not be necessary. But if he should turn up and approach you in any way, yes, you must refuse to acknowledge him."

This was hardly the sort of talk to calm Anna's bubbling curiosity, but she could see she would get nothing more out of her parents. She would have to hope the servants would be more forthcoming. It was typical, though, that Martha had told more to Maria than she had to Anna. It was so tedious being a schoolroom miss.

Immediately after breakfast Maria and Lady Featherstone embarked on matters to do with Society. Sir Jeffrey warned Anna to go nowhere without both maid and footman, then went out to Parliament. Anna obediently summoned Martha and a footman and set out for the best lending library in London, her main intent being to bring home a copy of *Forbidden Affections*.

As they walked, Arthur the footman pointed out the sights, and the occasional famous person passing by.

Anna was interested in London, but she could

not stop puzzling over the matter of number 10. "London seems so crowded," she said at one point. "I'm surprised the house next door to us is allowed to stay empty."

"Criminal waste of a house, I'd say," Martha remarked with a sniff.

Arthur shrugged. "It's the earl's to waste, Miss Anna, and he's rich enough not to care."

"But there must be servants," Anna probed.

"Just a couple who keep the place up. The Murchisons have got it easy, and that's the truth. The whole place is under covers, they say."

Anna waited, hoping for more, but it became clear that if she wanted more information, she'd have to dig for it. "And no one has lived in it for years?"

"That's right, miss. Ever since the earl's ladybird was found dead there."

"Arthur!" exclaimed Martha. "I'll thank you to remember that Miss Anna is still a schoolroom miss!"

Anna could have strangled Martha. Just as the conversation was becoming interesting!

The earl's ladybird? That meant lover. So the earl's lover had committed suicide in number 10? Embarrassing, certainly, but enough to send a peer of the realm into exile?

Hardly.

And why had Maria reported it as murder?

These thoughts tumbled around in Anna's head as she gathered an armful of books at Hatchards. She did not find a copy of *Forbidden Affections* so asked a clerk for assistance. He con-

sulted the large book which served as their cata-
logue. "I'm afraid we no longer have a copy,
miss."

"What? Why on earth not?"

At her sharp tone he looked rather harried.
"It is eight years old, miss. Possibly one of the
volumes was lost or damaged . . . May I recommend this one?"

Anna listened politely as he recommended a
number of the latest romantic novels, and even
took one to allay suspicion. She knew it was irrational to think that Martha and Arthur, who
were standing by chatting, would read anything
into her desire for a copy of *Forbidden Affections,*
but she felt compelled to disguise her feelings.

She wanted no one to discover her secret until
she had solved the mysteries of Carne Terrace.
And she wanted to solve them on her own.

She would have liked to go to another library
to continue her search for the novel, but how
could she with Arthur already burdened with at
least two days' reading? Seething at the stupidity
of a library that didn't have multiple copies of
every one of Mrs. Jamison's novels, Anna returned home.

Releasing Martha and Arthur to their other
duties, she sat down to read. The books she had
selected were interesting, but she could not concentrate on any of them. Her mind was full of
Lord Carne, his dead lover, and the Gothic
chamber of Dulcinea. In fact, Anna knew she
was merely passing time until that night when
she could explore again.

By mid-afternoon she could restrain her curiosity no longer and wandered into the kitchen where the cook, Mrs. Jones, and two maids were preparing dinner.

"Hungry, miss?" asked the wiry woman pleasantly enough. "There's maids-of-honor there that could do with testing."

Anna grinned at the cook and sat at the table to nibble an almond tart. "They're delicious," she said honestly. "Alas, I don't think my stay here will increase my chances of becoming thin and interesting."

"Let's not have any of that nonsense, miss. Some healthy padding serves a woman well. And there's many a gentleman likes an armful." Mrs. Jones pushed another cake over to Anna.

Anna did not actually want another one, but she took it with a smile. "I certainly hope so, since I am to have your cooking. I'm sure they should charge extra for this house if you come with it."

The cook preened. "Been here nigh on ten years, miss, and there's been no complaints. Maggie, stop beating those eggs now and put the water on."

A rather slack-faced maid put aside a big bowl of eggs and went to haul a copper pot onto the stove.

Anna decided on a direct approach to one part of the puzzle. "Were you here when my bedroom was made?"

The woman rolled her eyes. "That Chamber of Horrors? Aye. It was a fancy of the mistress of the time, Lady Delabury . . ." The woman broke off what she was about to say. "Maggie, the *big* pan!"

With a clatter, one pan was put down and another picked up.

"She must have been very fond of novels," Anna prompted.

The cook looked at her in surprise and with a touch of suspicion. "How did you know that, miss?"

"Oh, there are rooms like that in many novels." Anna dropped her voice and made it sound mysterious. "Usually in the less-frequented parts of moldering castles, hung with cobwebs and infested by rats . . ."

Both the cook and the two maids were staring at her.

"Well, there's no rats in this house!" declared Mrs. Jones. "It makes a bit of sense, though," she added more moderately, "since Lady Delabury wrote those sorts of books."

"*Wrote* them?" Anna almost choked on a pastry crumb.

"Not under her own name, of course. Mrs. Jamison, that was the name she used, even when she were a single lady . . . All right, Maggie, stop gawking and add those bones . . . ! She was a lovely lady, miss, very like your sister. Lord Delabury would have done anything for her, so when she wanted that room he had it made. Dreadful upset, he was, about her death."

A Dulcinea, in other words. No wonder Mrs. Jamison's heroines were always of that type. But then why the doorway into the other house? Lady Delabury had her Roland.

Perhaps. Perhaps the poor lady had been married to Count Nacre and had dreamed of escape.

"What was Lord Delabury like?" Anna asked.

"Oh, a very handsome young man and a good employer. He gave up living here, though, after the death, and stays at his estate in the north nearly all the time. A sad tale . . . Maggie, come cut up these turnips . . . Look, miss, we've got to get on with dinner now."

Anna took the hint, but instead of returning to the house, she chose to wander out into the garden, her mind churning with speculation. For Lady Delabury to have a room made in the image of a chamber in one of her books was eccentric but understandable. For her to incorporate a secret doorway into the house next door was another matter entirely. For one thing, it would surely require the consent of the owners of both properties.

And if the secret door was part of *the incident*, and Arthur had been right in what he said, then Lady Delabury had been the Earl of Carne's ladybird even though she was quite recently married to a pleasant young man who adored her. And she had killed herself.

It was all deliciously intriguing.

Anna played with ideas as she wandered the uninspired garden, pulling up a weed here or there. At the limit of the garden she turned to look back at the row of houses. They told her nothing, however. Number 10, with its blinds drawn, was particularly uncommunicative.

There was a gate in the back of the garden and Anna saw that it opened onto the mews. There was a gate from the mews into the garden of number 10, too. She resisted the temptation to explore. The garden was unlikely to hold the key to the mystery.

She returned to the house and her unsatisfactory books, and waited for night.

To Anna's frustration, her family was no longer tired from the journey, and they would never believe it if she claimed to be. If she tried to go to bed early, they'd send for the doctor.

It was very pleasant to play whist and read a little, but she was desperate to go adventuring.

The only progress she made with her mystery came from one comment by her father.

"I don't think we need worry about the earl. The general opinion seems to be that he died on one of his wild adventures. In fact his heir, a cousin, has started a court case to have him declared dead."

"I think that's rather horrid," Anna said, thinking of the young man in the portrait, for she suspected he might be the earl.

"It's practical, Pippin. Servants are all very well, but a large estate should not be left unsupervised for so many years."

Conversation turned then to another case of neglect and Anna learned nothing more.

At half-past ten, Lady Featherstone declared that it was time for her daughters to get their beauty sleep and they obligingly went to their bedrooms.

Martha came and went, Anna was officially in bed, and at last the adventure could begin. Even if the earl were dead, there was a mystery to be solved. She needed to do some research, and the library of number 10 was the place to do it. Anna had persuaded her conscience that if she didn't take the books away it was not very naughty, and so she slipped through into the next house. Once there, she crept quickly, carefully, down the stairs to the library.

Safely behind the closed door, she placed her candle on the marquetry table and surveyed the bound copies of magazines and journals. Somewhere among them would be mention of *the incident*.

She looked first at the yearly report called *The Annual Register*. It did not take her long to find a reference, though it was frustratingly brief.

May 25, 1809. On this night a great uproar was heard in the handsome environs of Carne Terrace, when a lady of gentle birth and fine family was found to have done away with herself by means of laudanum. This tragic event was made bewildering because the lady, wife of Viscount D******y, died not in her own bed, but in the bed of her neighbor, the Earl of C***.

Heavens! That certainly would have set the cat among the pigeons.

The noble earl, however, was not in residence at the time, being at his estate in Norfolk.

And that must certainly have saddened the scandal mongers. Still, many had clearly deduced that the lady was his mistress.

Unless it had been well-known before.

The circumstances were made yet more mysterious by the fact that the earl's heir, Lord M*******le, was hosting a bachelor party on a lower floor. Neither he, his well-born guests, nor the servants saw the lady enter in her nightgown. A doctor was summoned, but life had long since departed.

Anna stopped to ponder that. Who was the present earl? The one whose bed the lady had chosen to die in, or the heir carousing downstairs? She suspected the latter, and a glance at Burke's confirmed it. The current earl was now thirty years old and there was no Lord Manderville. What was more startling was that the earl had acceded to the title in May 1809, only days after Lady Delabury's death.

Anna returned the Burke's to the shelf and searched other publications for more details. She had almost given up when she found more in the London Report.

The account of the event was similar to that in *The Annual Register,* but this one continued on to cover the inquest.

. . . a doctor brought in by the lady's grieving husband stated that certain bruises on the arms suggested that the lady could have been compelled to consume the cause of her death, but since it was equally impossible that a murderer sneak into the house, and as Lord M******le and his friends all vouched for one another, that none had left the room during the eve-

ning, and in view of the fact that the lady was found clutching a farewell note to her poor bereaved husband, a judgment of suicide was made.

Anna closed the book. No wonder people thought the worst of the current earl, the then Lord Manderville. The death had been suspicious, and it was more than likely that he and his cronies would stick together.

What puzzled her was that no one seemed to know about the secret door or they would not wonder how Lady Delabury gained access to this house. It was particularly strange that Lord Delabury not know of it. Could he, in fact, have been the murderer?

She would dearly like to know what was in that note. What reason had the beautiful, talented young woman given for taking her life? Guilt because she was Lord Manderville's mistress?

But why had a recently-married woman sought a lover? Anna assumed Lord Manderville was the young man of the portrait, so she could see the appeal, but it did seem strange behavior, even for London. It suggested that her husband must have been a monster beneath his charming exterior.

But what of Lord Manderville, the prime suspect? Anna could believe that the young man of the portrait—a few years older—would have taken a neighbor's wife as lover. She could believe he had spent an evening carousing with his friends. She could not believe that he would have callously forced his mistress to drink laudanum.

She sat at the table, chin on hands, to ponder it all. What else might have happened? If Lady Delabury had been Lord Manderville's mistress, then she might have been at his party. Had it been some kind of orgy? Anna had read enough ancient history to know about orgies. She understood that quite sensible people could be carried into extremes of vice and passion.

Perhaps the young man had gone into exile out of grief and guilt because his wild party had turned into fatal disaster—especially if the events had led to the death of his father, perhaps from shame . . .

The candle was shrinking and it was time for Anna to return to her own room. She replaced the books thoughtfully, informed but dissatisfied. There was surely a great deal more to *the incident* but she was no longer sure what questions to ask.

Before leaving, she turned to the shelf of novels, wondering if there might be answers there. There clearly was some connection between *Forbidden Affections* and the unfortunate death, since the author had caused that room to be made.

Anna opened the glass door and hesitated. She would have to take the volumes back to her room to study them, and that was the line she had drawn for herself—she would not remove anything from the house.

But she needed to know the truth. She reached out for the first volume of *Forbidden Affections*—

With a click, the door behind her opened.

Anna froze, wondering in wild irrationality whether staying very still would make her invisible. But it wouldn't, so she turned slowly to stare, appalled, at the man staring back at her.

She was caught.

And surely she was caught by the wicked earl himself. Tall, dark, and authoritative, it was the young man in the picture some ten or more years older.

The astonished silence stretched, and then the earl closed the door and approached. "I was not aware that the Murchisons had hired staff. You do know you are likely to be on the street in the morning, girl?"

He thought her a servant intruding where she had no business to be. "Beg pardon, sir," Anna mumbled, thinking furiously. If she could just get out of this room without revealing her identity, he might never know who she was.

She was going to die of embarrassment if this got back to her parents!

He came closer, and her heart raced with even more immediate fears. Gracious, but he was tall and broad. Of course, that could be the effect of his heavily-caped greatcoat. But then he shrugged it off and dropped it on a chair and was still tall and broad. His dark jacket and leather riding breeches did not soften him one bit.

She remembered the portrait wistfully. That young man had seemed a friend, but this person was entirely different. There was no laughter in those blue eyes now and the lines of his face spoke of experience and ruthless ways. He even bore a scar down one cheek. Wicked or not, Anna feared the earl was most certainly a dangerous man.

Was he a murderer, though?

If he discovered that she had been looking into the death of Lady Delabury, would he kill again?

a was not of a nervous temperament, but s ed to think she knew when it was reasonable to be afraid.

She was afraid now.

He sat in a winged chair, stretched his legs as if he owned the place, and eyed her thoughtfully.

He does own the place! Anna told her mind, which was turning giddy with fear. *Think. Think. We have to get out of here!*

She considered running for the door but had no doubt that he could stop her. If she was to conceal her identity, she had to persuade him to let her leave peaceably.

He slowly pulled off his black leather gloves, watching her every minute. "Since you're here, girl, you can make yourself useful. Pour me some brandy." When she did not move, he added, "I suppose it's to your credit that you don't know where it is. In that table there. Raise the lid and there should be glasses and a full decanter unless my orders have been ignored."

Anna swallowed and went to the table to do as he said. Other reasons for fear were occurring to her. She was here alone with a gentleman—a

wicked gentleman—in her *nightgown*. With not a
stitch under it! Even though it was of thick cotton, high-necked and long-sleeved, she felt as if
he must feel her nakedness as she did, open to
the breeze of her movements across the room.
He would know from her bare feet that she wore
no stockings.

*Just see what a bramble-patch your curiosity has led
you to, Anna Featherstone! And you knew all along
it was wrong and foolish.*

Anna's hands shook as she opened the table
to lift the heavy-based tumbler and the cut-glass
decanter. She managed to pour the brandy without spilling any, then put the decanter down and
turned.

His brows were raised. "Do you think you're
serving a dowager? Fill it up, girl!"

Anna looked at the glass, at the modest
amount she had poured, the amount her father
would drink. A full glass would surely deprive a
man of his wits. But that might be good. She
filled it almost to the brim.

Then she had to take it to him. She wished
her arms would suddenly become ten feet long,
but they didn't and so she had to walk over to
stand by his chair.

She waited, but he made no attempt to reach
for the glass, and so she had to press against his
stretched legs to put it in his right hand. His
boots rubbed against her calves through the cotton and something—almost an emanation—set
her nerves jumping with panic. As soon as he

took the glass she stepped back but his left hand shot out to seize the front of her nightdress.

"Oh, no, you don't. What's your name?"

Anna leaned back, desperate that his hand not brush her body. "Maggie!" she gasped, plucking the first name that came to mind.

He gathered in more of the cotton, pulling her closer, bringing her body close to his fist. "Well, Maggie, were you going to steal the books, or can you actually read?"

"I can read, sir!"

He drank from the glass in his right hand. "My lord," he corrected. A glint in his eye told her he knew just how uncomfortable she was.

"Sorry, milord," she muttered, though she wanted to do the wretch a very painful physical injury. What right had he to tease a poor maid this way, even if he had found her in his library? And more to the point, what were his true intentions? Anna knew how the wicked part of the world behaved.

"You'll have to prove it," he said.

Anna jumped. "Prove what, milord?"

He abruptly released her. "That you can read. Choose one of those revolting novels and read me a passage."

Anna thought again of running, but knew it was pointless. Instead she accepted the test. Once he saw she was in here in search of reading material, perhaps he would let her go even if he did intend to dismiss her in the morning. Once she was out of this room unescorted, she could be back in her bed in moments.

She returned to the shelf. Avoiding *Forbidden Affections,* she chose *Cruel Matrimony.*

When she opened it, she realized with surprise that it had never been read. The pages weren't even cut. She could read the first page, however.

"Was any woman so profoundly miserable as beautiful Melisande de La Fleur when the dreadful news descended upon her? She was to wed the dread lord of Breadalbane? Never!"

"Enough," said the earl disdainfully, swallowing more brandy. "So, you *can* read, and with an educated accent, too. Who the devil are you?"

Anna cursed her carelessness in letting her servant's tones drop, and knew she was turning red with guilt. "I was raised gently, yes, my lord, but have no choice now but service."

"Plunged into dire poverty, are you?" His voice gentled as he said, "Perhaps we can find you an alternative to base service, my dear. Loose your hair."

It took a moment for Anna to guess his meaning, but then her breath caught. "No. Please, my lord—"

"Obey me." It was said without great emphasis, yet it chilled her protests.

Anna heard a whimper, and knew it was her own. She should scream, but who would hear?

What would happen if she told him who she was? Would the wicked Earl of Carne continue his vile seduction when he knew she was the gently-bred daughter of his neighbor?

If he did, said the logical part of her, then

he'd care as much later as now. Perhaps he was just playing with her and would let her go in a little while. After all, she was hardly the sort of girl to drive men wild, especially a man like this.

So Anna took off her ribbon and fingered her dark hair loose, knowing her naturally rosy cheeks were apple red.

He eyed her over the rim of the glass, studying her dispassionately from tousled head to naked toes. "Very pretty. How old are you?"

"But sixteen, milord."

"There's no use putting on that servant's burr again, sweetheart. Sixteen's a good age." He drained the glass and placed it on a table by his elbow. "Come here."

The slight slur in his voice alarmed her. She suspected he'd not been entirely sober when he came in, and was now worse. Any belief that he would be rational was weakening and she glanced around in search of a weapon. There wasn't so much as a penknife.

"Please, my lord, let me go. I'm sorry for having intruded—"

"But having done so, you must pay the toll." His eyes were hooded. "A kiss," he said with wicked softness. "No more, Maggie, or not yet. My word on it. Come here."

Anna discovered that her feet simply wouldn't carry her over to him. "I can't . . ."

He raised his brows. "I could threaten to dismiss you tomorrow. Yet why do I feel that wouldn't sway you? So, I'll make another threat. If you don't come here and be kissed, my sweet mysterious Maggie, I'll come to you and do much worse. And you have my word on that, too."

After a moment, he added, "That trembling innocence, the hands over the mouth, the eyes wide with panic, will not sway me. It's actually quite arousing, you know. We men are such perverse creatures. You'd do better to appear bold and willing. I'd probably dismiss you on the instant."

Anna realized she was reacting exactly as he said, but she *was* a trembling innocent. "I wouldn't kn . . . know how to act bold, m . . . my lord," she stammered. "Have mercy."

"Damnation, girl," he said without heat, "it's a kiss I'm demanding, not a life of sin. You'll be the better for getting over these nervous tremors. *Come here.*"

The snapped authority in the last words had Anna walking toward him before she thought. He caught her nightgown before she could retreat and pulled her onto his lap. She did scream then, and struggled, but it did no good. He just laughed. "Squirm away, Maggie. It's quite interesting, and in moments your legs will be naked as the day you were born."

Anna went very, very still.

"Wise girl," he said, and even smoothed her nightgown back around her legs—a touch that sent a jolt right through her.

He ignored it, and spoke soothingly. "There, see, the heavens haven't fallen. Satan hasn't appeared to drag you off to hell. Kissing is not a cardinal sin. You might even enjoy it. I suspect I will." He caught her chin, smiling as a thumb rubbed along her jaw.

Anna twitched. "My lord!"

"Oh, do stop my lording me, girl! If we're to share a kiss I'll make you free of my name for a while. It's Roland."

"Roland?" Astonishment temporarily overwhelmed even fear.

He continued to rub along her jaw, gently, confusingly. "Why the amazement, sweetheart? Perhaps my parents had high hopes of me."

"It . . . it's an unusual name, my lord. You are called for Charlemagne's hero?"

He grinned. "No. I'm called for a rich greatuncle who obligingly left me his all." His finger was tracing the edge of her lips now, as if learning of them.

Or perhaps he knew the extraordinary effect it could have on a woman . . .

"Roland was a noble character, though, my lord," Anna said desperately. In a moment she was going to have to tell him who she was. *"Roland est preux . . ."*

"She speaks French, too! *Chérie,* you are wasted in the kitchens. Let us proceed with your metamorphosis to a higher order." He deftly moved her more intimately to his body and dropped a light kiss on her tingling lips. "You're as tasty as a rosy apple, sweetheart. I think I'll call you Pippin."

At that use of her father's pet name, it was as if he were here, witness to her shame.

Anna burst into tears.

The earl froze, but did not let her go. To her astonishment, after a moment he held her closer and even rocked her a little. "Hush, Pippin. What the devil's the matter with you? We're talking a kiss here. It'll go no further today if you're not of a mind to it. I'm no rapist and we've plenty of time . . ."

His very reasonable and rather bemused tone calmed Anna's worst fears. She peeped up at him cautiously, sniffing.

But perhaps seducers always behaved like this . . .

"That's better," he said soothingly, thumbing tears from beneath her eyes and stroking strands of hair off her face. "Just a kiss, a taste, Pippin. And then I'll let you leave. This time."

Heart pounding, Anna held on to that. One kiss and she could go.

And she would never come back here again!

But when his lips brushed over hers—a gentle, brandy-flavored roughness—she flinched away instinctively. He was ready for it and trapped her head, preventing all effort to avoid the deepening of the kiss.

Anna tried to protest, but since her mouth was now covered by his, it came out as only a mewling sound. Her hands were trapped against his body and she truly feared that if she squirmed she would reveal all.

God help her, what would happen if her parents ever found out about this?

He ignored her struggles and protests, but released her mouth long enough to say, "You've the sweetest-tasting mouth I've known in a long time, Pippin."

"My lord, please—"

But then he was kissing her again, pushing her mouth open, touching her tongue with his so she squeaked and struggled violently. But then, abruptly, like a wave crashing over her, Anna realized there was pleasure in it.

There couldn't be.

But there was.

It was like the first time she had eaten oysters. She hadn't liked the thought of it at all, and hadn't liked the first attempt much. But then, somehow, she had overcome the thought that the shellfish were alive, and that they were a little slimy, and had discovered they were delicious.

She had never liked the idea of this kind of kissing, and hadn't liked the first mingling of his mouth with hers, but now she found that he, too, was delicious—sweet and spicy beneath the tang of brandy.

In moments the moist heat of his tongue seemed as natural as her own, and that acceptance spread downward through her body, relaxing her . . .

He released her mouth with slow, parting kisses, smiling more warmly now, more like the youth in the portrait. "That's it, Pippin, my rosy, juicy little apple. You see what's in store? You needn't fear I'll mistreat you. I'll take care of you . . ."

Anna suddenly realized that his hand was sliding *under* her nightdress and took in the meaning of his words.

She kicked against his touch. "No, my lord! Truly, I cannot be your mistress!"

Despite her squirming, his hand ventured slightly higher, up to her knee. "You didn't think you'd like kissing, Maggie. Let's see how you like this . . ."

"No . . . *Help!*" Anna tried to put the full force of her healthy lungs behind it but he clapped a hand over her mouth and laughed at her struggles.

So much for his promises!

As he looked down with interest at the leg her struggle was exposing, Anna saw the glint of the glass he had set down. She stretched out, seized it, and swung it with all her strength to crash against her ravisher's head.

With a cry, he relaxed his hold.

Anna tore herself free.

He was cursing now and holding his head. Anna was dreadfully afraid that she'd done him some terrible injury, but that was even more reason to flee.

She raced into the hall and up the steps, her heart thundering, her breath mere gasps of panic. In moments she was through the door and back in her bedroom.

She slid to the floor in limp relief, offering earnest prayers of thanks to the deity who watched over foolish virgins.

Which made her think of lamps.

Which made her realize a terrible thing.

She'd left the candlestick!

At that moment, Anna Featherstone nearly fainted.

She wanted to huddle under her covers and pretend none of the recent events had happened but if she didn't retrieve the candlestick, it would be obvious she'd been there. Quite apart from the fact that she would be short a candlestick, it was probably identifiable as from this house.

What on earth would happen to her? What if she'd done some terrible injury to the earl? What if he was lying on his library floor breathing his last?

Would they hang her?

At least, said a voice, if he's dead he can't identify his assailant.

But the candlestick could.

There was only one thing to do.

Anna's legs felt weak as wet paper, but she forced herself to her feet. Still shaking and struggling not to sob, she opened the secret door again to re-enter the Earl of Carne's cursed house.

She staggered out onto the landing, listening carefully for any hint of what was happening. She heard a voice. It was the earl, apparently calling for a servant.

Anna almost collapsed with relief again. He didn't sound at all dead. But in that case, how was she to retrieve the evidence?

Then she realized that he was heading for the lower floor, shouting for his servants. She leaned over the stair-rail and saw him, holding a white cloth to his head, disappear in that direction.

It almost demanded too much courage, but Anna forced herself. She ran down the stairs, tracking that distant voice all the time, dashed into the library, grabbed the candlestick, and raced back to her own room.

Once there, she flung herself into bed, pulled the covers over her head, and swore that she would never, ever, give in to curiosity again!

"Miss Anna! Miss Anna! Wake up."

Anna stirred, resisting the call to wake. She'd been sleepless half the night worrying over the consequences of her actions.

"Miss Anna! Are you all right?"

Anna forced her eyes open. "Yes, Martha. Of course I'm all right."

Martha frowned at her in grave concern. "I've never known you to be a slugabed. Are you sure you're not sickening for something?"

Anna struggled up, trying to appear her usual cheery self. "Of course I'm not! I must have just stayed up reading longer than I intended."

"The state of the candle tells *that* story, miss," said Martha with a glance at the candlestick.

Full memory rushed back and Anna winced at the thought of the story that candlestick could tell. Along with memory came anxiety. What would Lord Carne have done when he couldn't find Maggie? Had he called in the Bow Street Runners?

One thing was certain, Anna must make sure the man never set eyes on her. She leaned back against her pillows. "Perhaps I might be catching a cold," she said in a suffering tone. "My head aches a little . . ."

Martha came back to the bed and studied her. "You don't look yourself, Miss Anna, and that's the truth. Why, you've even taken off your ribbon and got your hair in a tangle. You must have been fevered in the night." She shook her head. "You'd best stay in bed for now. I'll bring you breakfast here and tell Lady Featherstone."

Martha left and Anna groaned. Her hair ribbon. She'd left evidence after all!

It wasn't a disaster, though. A candlestick was one thing, but a plain white hair ribbon could belong to anyone. It fretted her, though, so she was in danger of becoming truly ill through anxiety.

She took refuge in planning. The first thing was to stay out of sight for as long as possible, and being sick was an excellent excuse. It would be tedious, but far better than bumping into Lord Carne on the doorstep!

What was she going to do, though, if he intended more than a brief visit to his London house?

She rubbed her hands over her face. She should have known her mad behavior would lead to disaster. At the thought of what might have been, she shuddered. If that glass hadn't been to hand, she might have been ruined beyond all repair!

To a young lady raised in the country, known by all and well-guarded, it scarce seemed credible that a chance encounter—no matter how peculiar—could have ruined her life, but it was so.

Lord Carne could have stolen her virtue by brute strength. Truth obliged her to admit that he might have managed to steal it by clever seductions.

Anna stared sightlessly at a grinning gargoyle and absorbed the fact that she had almost been seduced by a stranger.

Lady Featherstone was no believer in innocence as defense against ruin. She had informed her daughters about carnal matters, and warned them that the perils of the flesh sometimes included the temptations of pleasure. Her instruction was to avoid occasions of intimacy in case their consciences turned weak on them.

"And that frequently happens," she had said. "Not many unfortunate girls *intend* their ruin. They are caught unawares and either forced, tricked, or seduced into depravity. And seduction means that they succumbed to pleasure. So be on your guard and avoid the very occasions of sin, girls. Prudent, well-behaved young ladies do not come to grief."

Anna had never really believed that she could be forced, tricked, or seduced into ruin, but then she'd never anticipated anyone like the Earl of Carne. Cautiously, she allowed her memory to bring to mind the man she had met last night, trying to decide what made him so dangerous. Handsome, yes. But not in a smooth, gentle way. He was lean, hard, and had proved to be alarmingly strong.

Anna shuddered at the memory of being as helpless as a struggling toddler.

Perhaps, however, that very strength was part of the seductive appeal that lingered even now as a spicy sweetness beneath anxiety. Certainly something about him had speeded her pulse and weakened her knees in a way she had never experienced before, and it hadn't entirely been fear.

Unless it was fear of the wantonness he had so easily summoned in her.

Yet another reason to avoid the earl. Anna was no fool.

Sometimes it was best not to put one's will power to the test.

She sat up straighter and turned her mind to assessing her situation and making plans.

With luck and caution, Anna decided, she might escape the consequences of her folly. She was not ruined, and it did not seem Lord Carne was seriously injured. He was doubtless puzzled as to the identity of Maggie, but if Anna stayed concealed for a day or two, all could be well. The earl would surely move on, either to travel again or to inspect his neglected estates.

Martha returned with a breakfast tray and Lady Featherstone, who laid a cool hand on Anna's brow. "You do not seem fevered, my dear. Are you in pain?"

"Just the headache, Mama."

Anna's mother studied her with intent concern and Anna felt sure she would read every secret. But eventually Lady Featherstone said, "I don't think there is anything much amiss. Perhaps it is just the excitement of the city. Or this horrid room. Do you want to share Maria's room?"

"No, Mama!"

With a shake of her head, Lady Featherstone dropped the subject. "Rest today, then, and I am sure you will soon be more the thing. But if you feel the need we will send for the doctor."

When her mother had left, Anna settled to her breakfast, then asked Martha to help her dress, saying she would sit quietly on a chaise by the window. It was true that she had no desire to spend the day in bed, but she had other reasons. Her room looked out onto the street, and she wanted to be able to observe the comings and going at number 10.

Preferably the goings.

What she hoped to see was the Earl of Carne entering a well-piled coach, clearly headed for foreign lands, or at least for the provinces. What she actually saw was two fashionable gentlemen stroll up and be admitted. Since they stayed about an hour, and neither looked like a doctor, Anna felt able to assume that the earl was not on his deathbed.

When two coaches arrived, Anna experienced a moment of hope, but then the chests and boxes were taken *into* the house. "Oh, no," she muttered. "The wretch is taking up residence!"

Anna looked at the fireplace in alarm, then hurried over to push a solid bench in front of the secret door. It might not prevent a forcible entry, but it would prevent a silent one.

But how was she to avoid a meeting if the earl was to stay next door?

When Martha came to offer her lunch, Anna said, "There seems to be some activity at number 10. Has the earl leased the house after all?"

Martha put her tray on the table and started to lay out the meal. "Nay, miss. Believe it or not, his lordship's come back. Arrived in the night without warning! And," she added in a whisper, "it's to be feared he's mad."

"Mad?" Dear heaven. Had her blow deprived him of his wits?

Martha looked around as if expecting an angel to come and silence her, then leaned closer. "He came knocking at the kitchen door this morning, miss."

"The earl?" Anna's heart started to flutter with panic. He knew! How did he know?

Martha leaned even closer. "The wicked earl himself! And the Lord knows what wickedness he'd been up to, Miss Anna, for he'd a mighty wound on his temple, all swollen and bruised-like. I tell you true, miss, none of us thought we were safe!"

"Whatever did he want?" Anna whispered back, wondering why the heavens had not already fallen on her.

"You'll never believe it . . ."

"What?"

"He wanted Maggie! Poor little Maggie, who might be a bit slow, but hasn't a scrap of bad in her!"

Anna didn't know what to say.

"Mind you," said Martha, straightening to rearrange a mustard pot on the small table, "the earl did come to his senses after a fashion. As soon as he clapped eyes on her he looked right bewildered. Apologized for disturbing us and took himself off.

"Sad, really," she said with a shake of her head. "Mrs. Postle says he was a right promising young man once, before . . . well, before. Certain it is though, Miss Anna, that you must keep out of that man's way. I'm sure your parents are going to be very concerned to know that he's settling in next door."

Lord and Lady Featherstone certainly were concerned, the lady rather more than the lord. Over dinner that evening she said, "You must be very careful, girls. Very careful. He has already shown his true flags."

Lady Featherstone left it there, so Anna decided to stimulate discussion. "You mean him crashing into the kitchen covered with blood demanding Maggie?"

Unfortunately, Maria had not heard the story. She shrieked and assumed her ready-to-faint posture, hand to heart.

Anna's father frowned. "Don't exaggerate, Pippin. And Maria, don't get into a taking. I am assured he knocked at the door and inquired after her in a fairly normal manner."

"Normal?" demanded Maria. "Papa, how can it be *normal* for an earl to turn up at the kitchen door asking after the scullery maid? He must be mad. We'll be murdered in our beds like that other woman!"

"Nonsense," said Sir Jeffrey. "I will not have such exaggerations, girls. Lady Delabury took too much laudanum and it was years ago. As for Maggie, though I did not like to do it, I called on the earl and asked an explanation. It appears he surprised an intruder in his house last night, a young woman who called herself Maggie. When he attempted to apprehend her, she hit him on the head, which accounts for his wound. When his servants told him a maid called Maggie served next door, he naturally assumed she would be the same."

"Then an honest man," said Lady Featherstone, "would have sent for a Runner!"

"A charitable man might not, my dear. I did not expect it, but I gained the impression that the earl was motivated by compassion. He admitted that he had frightened the girl into attacking him, and he thought she might have been lacking her wits . . ."

Anna almost choked on a piece of chicken. The wretch!

"So he decided to discover her," her father continued, "and speak to her superiors on the matter. Of course, since our scullery maid turned out not to be his quarry, he is no further forward in solving the mystery. And he did apologize for any upset he might have caused."

"So I should think!" Lady Featherstone declared.

"I must confess, my dear, that I was pleasantly surprised by the earl. He seems a man of sense. We know he indulged in some youthful follies, but time can heal. I gather he has spent his recent years in the Eastern Mediterranean and he speaks intelligently of matters there. I suspect he may have been engaged on the King's business."

Her father might be quite in charity with their neighbor; Anna was not. She did not believe for one moment that Lord Carne had been moved by compassion. He either wanted revenge, or wished to continue his wicked plan to set "Maggie" up as his mistress.

Perhaps both.

Perhaps he had been intending to blackmail the poor, powerless maid into surrendering to his vile lust.

"Is the earl to stay in London, Papa?" she asked.

"It would appear so, my dear. His cousin's efforts to have him declared dead have obliged him to return and prove his existence. It seems that he intends to stay for some time."

"I cannot like it," said Lady Featherstone. "It will stir all those old stories, and since there is a connection to this house, it will cause the kind of attention I cannot like."

Anna was hard put not to roll her eyes at the word "connection." If her mother only knew!

"Nonsense, my love," said Sir Jeffrey with a twinkling grin. "The earl's presence and those

old stories will assure you an excellent attendance at any entertainments you care to give."

And so it proved. When Lady Featherstone
held a small, informal musical evening a few
days later, her rooms were gratifyingly full, and
it was astonishing how often conversation turned
to neighbors, past and present.

As it was an informal affair, Anna had been
allowed to attend in her one good silk gown to
listen to the music. She knew she was not to put
herself forward in any way, and was quite content to sit quietly, watching people and keeping
her ears pricked for any snippets of information
about the wicked Earl of Carne.

Unfortunately, no one seemed to know more
than she. In fact she could, if she wished, give
them a clearer story than they had.

She heard one person murmur that he was
crippled by debauchery, and another report that
she had been reliably informed that he was hide-
ously scarred.

It was clear, however, that the *ton* was fascinated, and Anna suspected that the supposed
wickedness of his past would easily be white-
washed by curiosity about his present. Add to
that his status as a wealthy, unmarried peer of
the realm and she had the sinking feeling that
the dreaded earl would soon be accepted everywhere.

That was the last thing Anna wanted. Sitting
in her corner listening to Mozart, she seriously
considered taking up her investigations again in
order to prove that Lord Carne really had mur-

dered his inconvenient mistress. It would serve
the wretch right . . .

"Miss Anna Featherstone, I believe?"

Anna looked up to see a young man bowing
before her. She glanced at her mother, unsure
how to handle this, but Lady Featherstone was
deep in conversation with another guest.

Anna took refuge in good manners, smiled,
and admitted her identity.

The pleasant-looking, brown-haired young gentleman took a seat beside her. "I know I am
being a little bold, Miss Anna. My name is Liddell, by the way, David Liddell, and I am completely respectable."

Anna met his eyes. "You would be bound to
say so, though, wouldn't you, Mr. Liddell? However, since I cannot imagine being the victim of
seizure and rapine in my mother's drawing
room, I will not have the vapors just yet."

After a startled moment, he laughed. "What a
shame you are not making your curtsy, too, Miss
Anna. You would set London by the ears."

Anna twinkled at him. "I think that is what
my mother fears."

She held her smile even as her amusement
faded. Her mother was clearly wise, for Anna
had almost created disaster already. Perhaps bandying words with Mr. Liddell was a mistake, too.

He patted her hand. "Don't grow nervous
with me. Truth to tell, I wish to speak to you
about your sister."

"Ah," said Anna, relaxing. This was familiar

ground. "Have you fallen in love with her so quickly?"

He blushed. "Hardly that. We have only met a few times. But I would like to know her better."

"Then I suggest you speak to her, not me, Mr. Liddell."

"But I am being cunning, Miss Anna. If you will tell me the subjects that most interest Miss Featherstone, then I will be able to use my precious time with her to greatest effect."

Anna considered him approvingly. "Initiative should certainly be rewarded, sir. Maria is interested in fashion, Keats' poetry, and, on a more serious note, slavery. She is, of course, opposed to it. But I must warn you that we Featherstones are distressingly practical. Maria will not marry solely for money and title, but she is very unlikely to marry for love in a cottage. I do hope you have a comfortable situation."

His face rippled under a revealing flash of pique before he controlled it. "I have expectations," he said vaguely as he rose. "I must thank you, Miss Anna, and hope that perhaps one day we may be closer."

Anna watched him cross to where Maria held court, feeling mildly sorry for him. He seemed pleasant and intelligent, but she feared his expectations were not equal to the occasion.

Then Lady Featherstone swished to Anna's side. "And what, pray, were you doing conversing with a gentleman?"

"I could not avoid it, Mama. He introduced himself."

"Gentlemen do not introduce themselves!"

Anna grinned. "They do when they want to know the way to Maria's heart."

"Ah." Lady Featherstone frowned, but not at Anna. "It is unlikely to do, for all Maria seems to look kindly upon him."

"Why? What is wrong with him?"

"He's a Liddell. Which means he's related to the Earl of Carne. That cannot be to his favor."

Anna stared at Mr. Liddell with new interest. In her examination of Burke's, she had scarcely noted the earl's family name. "Is he the cousin, then?" she asked. "The heir?"

"Yes. Which now means he is a gentleman of limited means. 'Tis a shame, perhaps, that Lord Carne resurfaced, for as an earl Mr. Liddell would make an eligible *parti*. Without the title he is too small a fish."

"But if Maria favors him, Mama?"

Lady Featherstone patted Anna's head. "I will not force either of you to marry against your inclinations, dear, but nor will I permit you to follow some romantic fancy into hardship. It will be easy enough for a girl as pretty as Maria to find a husband who is both congenial and comfortable. Off to bed with you now, Anna. And tomorrow you are to cease this moping about the house or I will assuredly send for the doctor."

Anna considered David Liddell before she left. Any resemblance between him and the earl was very slight, though he was handsome enough in his own way. She was surprised by the fact that she had not the slightest wish for the earl to die so Mr. Liddell could be earl in his place.

Not the slightest.

Not even if Maria did favor him.

Not even if the earl had committed murder.

Anna feared she was a sad case.

She was finding it impossible to forget her encounter with Lord Carne, who was not marked by debauchery, and whose scar enhanced rather than diminished his appeal. Nor could she forget the feel of being in his arms, of his thumbs gently wiping away her tears, of his mouth exploring hers.

These were not suitable thoughts for a sixteen-year-old schoolroom miss. Anna was painfully aware that her parents would be appalled if they could read her mind, and that saddened her for she loved them very much.

For she now knew she was wicked.

Every night when she went to her room she had to fight the temptation to open the secret door and venture once more into the territory of the wicked Earl of Carne.

The next day Anna did venture outdoors, for otherwise her mother would send for a doctor and it was Anna's experience that doctors never admitted that a patient was healthy—there was no money in that. They always prescribed some medicine or treatment, invariably unpleasant.

She had no mind to be dosed with tonic or worse, blistered, purged, or have blood let.

What Anna wanted to do was to attack the lending libraries again. She had long since finished the books from her last trip, and more than ever she wanted a copy of *Forbidden Affections*. She quailed, however, at the thought of walking down fashionable streets where she might come face-to-face with the Earl of Carne.

Instead, she gathered Martha and Arthur and announced a walk in the park. She was sure wicked noblemen did not walk in the park at this unfashionable hour. The dangerous moment would be leaving the house when there was the slight possibility that the earl might be doing the same thing. All Anna could do to lessen that hazard was to wear her deepest-brimmed bonnet.

As it happened, her precaution was unnecessary and she and her escort left the house with no incident at all.

Anna delighted in the brisk walk in the summer sun after so many days of idleness. It was almost like the country. Trees were in heavy leaf and bright splashes of blossom broke the smoothness of daisy-speckled grass. Ducks and swans cruised the small lake, while at the edges children pushed out toy boats. She also had Arthur's gossip to enliven the day.

"Setting in for a regular stay," Arthur said. "New staff and all. The Murchisons don't much care for it if you ask me, Miss Anna. They've had an easy life all these years, living in comfort with no one breathing down their neck.

"Not but what they haven't done a good job," he added quickly. "And what a business about that young woman! Had a word with Jack Murchison myself, I did, and every word is true. They did think, as we did, that perhaps the earl had had a bit too much and imagined it, but Jack said he had clearly been hit a mighty blow on the head. And what's more, there was a ribbon. A female's hair ribbon!"

"Heavens!" gasped Anna, thinking such a response appropriate. In truth, she'd hoped that scrap of silk had been overlooked.

"No way to tell whose, of course. It'll be a mystery till Domesday, if you ask me, for she was doubtless just a sneak thief, thinking the house was empty. For all we know, she'd been in the habit of prowling the house, snitching things, for years . . ."

Anna stopped listening at that point because she was pondering the fact that the earl did not appear to have told anyone that the intruder was in her nightgown. It was true the weather was warm, but it was hard to imagine any woman going thieving dressed like that.

She wondered uneasily what the earl *was* imagining.

Then, as if summoned by her thoughts, she saw Lord Carne, elegant in blue jacket, buff breeches, and tall beaver, strolling along the path toward them.

Chilled by panic, Anna swung away from the path to stare at some trees. "Look, a kingfisher. How peculiar to see one here in town!"

"A kingfisher, Miss Anna?" asked Martha, shielding her eyes. "You must be mistaken."

"Oh, I could have sworn . . . Are there other birds of such bright color? It was a flash of the most remarkable blue! What other bright birds are there? Parakeets? Might one have escaped . . . ?"

She maintained this ridiculous chatter as long as possible, but eventually was forced to turn back to the path. With a wash of relief, she saw that the earl had passed them and was well ahead on the path.

She wished the wretched man in Hades. What possible business had a gazetted rake to be in the park at this time of day when only doddering ancients and nursemaids with children were supposed to use it?

And why did he have to look so very elegant . . .

"Miss Anna! Are you all right?"

Anna snapped her wits together. "Yes, Martha. I just had a thought, that's all. But it is doubtless time to return home."

By the time they arrived at Carne Terrace, Anna was well into the blue devils. She could not go on like this, afraid to step outside the door, gabbling about kingfishers in Green Park! Perhaps it would be best to confess all to Papa and have done with it. She wouldn't have to confess to that kiss, after all, for surely the earl must be as ashamed of it as anyone.

But her courage failed her.

Her parents would be so shocked by the fact

that she had invaded someone's home, never mind her brutal attack. And how was she to justify the attack without revealing the kiss?

No, she told herself, the chances of meeting the earl again were really quite slight since she didn't move in fashionable circles. Her mother had assured her that now the Season was well underway, the hours kept by the *ton* would not be those of ordinary people. The fashionable throng rose at midday and returned to bed in the early hours of the morning.

If Anna kept her outings to the morning, she should be safe.

It was most irritating that the Earl of Carne did not keep fashionable hours.

At least, as far as Anna knew, he danced the night away with the rest of Society, but it seemed he often rose at an early hour as well. Her careful observation of the front door of number 10 showed him leaving to walk or ride at nine or ten of the morning.

She was beginning to wonder if her mind were disordered, for it did seem to her that no matter what time she chose to leave the house, the earl was likely to appear, forcing her to hurry in or out to avoid giving him a clear view of her face.

And she was extremely tired of wearing her coal-scuttle bonnet.

She was also concerned for her sanity because she had a disturbing tendency to study the man when she could do so secretly.

At first, she had tried to persuade herself that she was merely studying the enemy, but she was not in the habit of deceiving herself. The truth was, she liked to look at him.

There was a presence to Lord Carne, an unconscious authority in every movement. He moved with remarkable grace, and she had the impression that at any moment he could respond to danger if need be.

From behind her curtains, Anna studied his features and was forced to conclude that they were completely perfect. Not perhaps as smooth as some gentlemen's, and there was that scar, but in her opinion they were everything a man's features ought to be. His bones were excellent, his nose straight, his lips well-shaped and neither thin nor pouty . . .

She was inclined to linger on the thought of those lips and how they had felt against hers. She very much wanted that sensation again.

But not, she told herself firmly, at the danger of exposure or ruin!

Her obsession was not improved by the fact that she now had a copy of *Forbidden Affections* to study. There could be no doubt that Roland— Lady Delabury had even used his first name!— was the earl. Or Lord Manderville, as he had then been. If Anna took the youth in the picture and merged him with the man living next door, she had an exact representation of Roland of Toulaine, Dulcinea's gallant lover.

That this merely confirmed the fact that Lady Delabury and Lord Manderville had been lovers was depressing indeed, especially when it suggested that the earl might have caused the lady's death, even if only by driving her to suicide.

There was nothing in *Forbidden Affections* to cast light on Lady Delabury's death, however, and Anna returned the book to the library and read Mrs. Jamison's other five novels. The rereading confirmed that she enjoyed them more, and it puzzled her.

The heroine was always the same—a variety, Anna supposed, of Lady Delabury herself, or Miss Skelton as she had been before her marriage. The heroes, however, were varied. Anna thought them a rather unrealistic lot. She had never known men to be so inclined to protest their extreme unworthiness to even touch a lady's hand, or to weep with grief at having dared to steal a kiss.

All this did rather incline Anna to remember a gentleman who would never weep over that stolen kiss, and would never for a moment imagine himself unworthy. She touched her own lips, remembering another touch, and was alarmingly aware that it would not take much for her to say to the Earl of Carne, "Kiss me again, please."

Lady Featherstone was not always right. Sometimes young ladies *did* plot their own downfall.

Perhaps it was just that the constant avoidance of the earl was so wearing, or perhaps it was a secret wish for ruin. One day, when Anna returned home and encountered the earl leaving his house, as close to face-to-face as two people twelve feet away could be, she did not duck her head and scurry. Instead, she stared at him, chin up, daring him to summon the constables.

He was startled, then a slight smile moved his lips before, with the slightest nod of acknowledgment, he went on his way.

Anna went into the house in a daze of horror and relief.

He knew!

It was as if he'd spoken to her and told her that he knew, and had known all along.

She was horrified that anyone knew what Anna Featherstone had done. At the same time there was tremendous relief. Clearly he was not going to call in the law, was not even going to inform her parents. And she didn't think the composed gentleman she had encountered today was going to lie in wait to have his wicked way with her.

She was just the tiniest bit disappointed about that.

By the time Anna had her bonnet and spencer off, reaction had set in, threatening tears. The great drama of her life had proved to be as substantial as a . . . a soap bubble! Rather than spending the past weeks searching for a mysterious, dangerous intruder, the Earl of Carne had known all along that it had been a mere schoolgirl neighbor, and had been amused.

It was intensely mortifying.

Anna would have liked to flee to the country or fall into a convenient fatal decline, but this being reality rather than a novel, she had to go on with life and try to put the whole matter out of her mind.

When she began to pay attention to events around her, she found that the wicked earl was being received everywhere. No one seemed to care any more about *the incident,* and Lady Delabury's death was being politely ignored.

Maria was a great success, and though she had not made her choice, it was likely that she would accept an offer within weeks. Mr. Liddell was still a constant attendant, but his chances of success seemed slim. Now that Lord Carne was back, his heir had no prospects beyond a small estate and a government post.

Anna returned to spending her time as originally planned, visiting historic places and educational exhibitions. In fact, she should perhaps have acted this way all along, for she never encountered the earl in these activities.

Then he began to show a marked interest in Maria, causing a great fluttering in the Featherstone nest.

"I have grave reservations," said Lady Featherstone at luncheon one day. "For all that the earl behaves quite properly, I cannot forget his past."

"Time heals," said Sir Jeffrey. "Morals as well as hearts. Since there is no evidence of anything but wildness in his past, I think Lord Carne should be judged on his present behavior. What do you feel, Maria?"

Maria raised a hand to her head as if dizzy. "I must be sensible of the honor, Papa. But I am not sure I can forget his past. Mr. Liddell has told me such things . . ."

"Mr. Liddell has his own ax to grind," Anna pointed out.

"I know that," said Maria, her expression a blend of irritation and complacency. She did enjoy being fought over. "But it is generally accepted that he . . . that the earl had an improper relationship with the woman who died. I cannot overlook that in a man."

"Then you'd best get yourself to a nunnery," Anna muttered.

Maria gasped, and even her father raised his brows in surprise.

"Anna!" exclaimed Lady Featherstone. "Go to your room at once, and study Bishop Stortford's sermon on unclean thoughts."

Anna flushed with mortification as she rose and curtsied. What had possessed her to say such a thing? "Yes, Mama. I beg pardon, Mama."

In her room, however, Anna didn't study the sermon—which she knew almost by heart—but contemplated the terrible reason for her outburst.

Jealousy.

She was jealous of Maria, and could not endure the thought of the Earl of Carne being her brother-in-law.

Which led to the next incredible step.

She wanted him for herself.

Anna laughed out loud. It was impossible, and exactly the sort of silly infatuation girls seemed prone to, but that did not make it any the less powerful at the moment. She ached with the loss of something she had never had, or had hope of.

She was honestly convinced, however, that Lord Carne and Maria would not suit. There was nothing wrong with Maria, but she needed a husband who appreciated sensibility and delicate feelings. The Wicked Earl would find Maria's airs a dead bore inside a month.

There was nothing a schoolroom miss could do about this, however, except be miserable and intensify her efforts to avoid the man. It would be the last straw if she made a fool of herself by acting like a lovesick moonling over him.

Anna thought avoiding the earl would be easy, but she hadn't considered the consequences of his interest in Maria. He now had the entrée to number 9.

In fact, he appeared at a small tea party Lady Featherstone gave two days later. It appeared he had been invited, though no one had expected him to attend. After all, it was an informal affair, so much so that Anna was in attendance.

When Anna heard him announced her heart began to pound, blood rushed to her head, and though she focused all her attention on old Lord Threpton, who was droning on about his problems with poachers, she didn't hear a word he was saying.

Once again she had this longing to become invisible, and that carried her thoughts straight back to a night in the Wicked Earl's library, and the things he had done to her then.

She knew color was flooding her face.

She wanted to die.

The mere sound of Lord Carne's voice—the first time she had heard it since that night—was interfering with her breathing, causing a perilous light-headedness.

Lord Threpton peered at her. "Hey, missie, I didn't mean to upset you with these matters!" He patted her knee. "You're a good girl to listen to an old man rambling on."

Anna kept her eyes fixed on his rheumy ones. "I don't mind, my lord. You are very interesting."

He pinched her cheek. "Some man's going to be very lucky in you, my dear. Now, why not go and find that plate of jam tarts and offer me another one. Very good, they are."

Thus Anna was forced out of hiding and set to walk across the room on unsteady legs. Which meant that her mother had to introduce her to the earl. "My younger daughter, Anna, my lord. She is not yet out."

He bowed with his typical grace. "Miss Anna. Charmed to make your acquaintance." He acted as if she was a total stranger, but Anna shivered as if he had stroked her back.

She wanted not to look to him, but couldn't help herself. He was even more perfect up close than he was at a distance. And what an actor he was. There was no hint of anything untoward about him except perhaps for a hint of intimate humor in his blue eyes, humor fighting to escape, just as it had in the portrait.

Anna wished desperately that he wouldn't look at her like that. It touched her heart and made her think of kisses.

Then she realized she was standing there red-faced and speechless, a picture of schoolgirl *gaucherie*. She hastily dropped a curtsy and he moved on to be introduced elsewhere.

Maria came over to hiss, "For goodness sake, Anna, there's no need for you to look at him as if you thought he'd eat you! You were the one defending him before!"

"I didn't!"

"Yes, you did. Oh well," she said with a superior smile. "I suppose you are unaccustomed to meeting earls. Don't worry, dearest, he won't expect much from a schoolroom miss."

Maria switched on a warmer smile and went off to greet new guests. Anna marched on in search of jam tarts, wishing fiercely that she were at least out and able to compete on equal terms.

Compete? she thought, as she picked up the plate. It was hard not to laugh like the madwoman in Mrs. Jamison's *Lord of the Dark Tower*.

Maria was a diamond of the first water, and Anna was a . . . mildly pretty pebble! Crossing the room with the plate, she flickered a glance at the earl. He caught her at it. Almost imperceptibly, he winked, and his mouth moved in a secret smile.

Anna jerked her gaze away, and hurried back to Lord Threpton. If she didn't know better, she'd think the Earl of Carne was *flirting* with her!

Nonsense, she told herself firmly. What he was doing was playing a rather cruel teasing game just to make her uncomfortable. Perhaps it was his way to pay her back for her assault.

Anna found herself busy handing out tea and passing plates of cake, and was glad of it, but inevitably this led to her offering a plate to Lord Carne. She had to stand quite close and was sharply reminded of the time she had brought him that glass of brandy.

And of all that had followed.

She watched him warily and prayed her hand wouldn't shake.

Again he met her eyes, but with no special expression. "Thank you, Miss Anna. I am spoiled for choice. Which cake would you recommend?"

Anna's throat went dry as if he had asked something private and significant. She swallowed. "The lady-cakes are very good, my lord."

He studied the plate, and Anna saw it start to tremble slightly with her nerves. "I wonder if a lady-cake would ˉmeet with me . . ." He appeared to trail off as if in thought.

Anna's heart skipped a beat. Had he really said, "me" rather than "my"? And had he swallowed the word "cake" so that he seemed to say, "I wonder if a lady would meet with me?"

Surely not!

"I doubt it, my lord," she mumbled. It had to be her imagination. Even the Earl of Carne could not be so bold. She remembered telling Mr. Liddell that she did not fear seizure and rapine in her mother's drawing room. Now she was not so sure.

He looked up at her rather seriously. "What a shame there are no maids-of-honor here to-day."

Anna flushed at the rebuke and the injustice of it. But inside her there was also a spark of delight at the sheer wit and effrontery of the man. He was using the name of the almond cakes and giving it another meaning.

"Perhaps there are maids-of-honor," she retorted. "Gentlemen-of-honor might be a little harder to find."

The lady sitting beside the earl tittered. "Miss Anna, you are too young to attempt barbed witticisms!"

Lady Featherstone came over quickly. "My lord, is there a problem?"

"Not at all, Lady Featherstone. I was merely inquiring as to maids-of-honor. I am particularly partial to them."

"Oh. No, I'm afraid we do not have them today, my lord."

"Alas. But as I like my maids-of-honor for a late supper, perhaps I can still order some for tonight. At about midnight, I think." He took a jam tart. "And, Miss Anna, I think you are quite correct. If we have maids-of-honor, we should have gentlemen-of-honor as well. I wonder what sort of cake they would be?"

Taking up his meaning of "cake" as "fool," Anna replied, "I don't see how any gentleman of honor could be a *cake*, my lord."

"Then it seems unfair that maids-of-honor be cakes, when it clearly is not so."

"Unless it means that they take the cake, my lord," said Anna, switching the meaning to that of victory. She was enjoying this clever wordplay immensely, but Lady Featherstone interrupted.

"You must excuse Anna, my lord. She is bookish."

As her mother steered her away, Anna heard him say, "I suspected it from the first."

Anna hated letting him have the last word.

Lady Featherstone drew Anna to the far side of the room. "It is most inappropriate of you to be bandying words with the earl, Anna, and it is fatal for a girl to become known as clever. Moreover, I still fear there is something strange about that man. Going on about his supper, indeed. Keep away from him."

"Yes, Mama."

Anna dutifully passed the cakes around the other side of the room, but her mind was running back over that conversation. She had just been invited to a midnight tryst with the wicked earl, and promised that he would behave as a gentleman of honor, and that he held her in the highest regard.

And he'd done it in front of a room full of people!

She couldn't help but admire a man like that.

She slid a glance over to him, and he smiled in a way that reminded her that she was a foolish, infatuated girl.

But how could a foolish, infatuated girl be expected to refuse such an invitation?

By the time she prepared for bed that night, Anna was still not sure what she would do, and she spent the next two hours pondering it.

Despite that talk of honor, logic said that it was more than likely that the earl was inviting her to a wicked encounter where he would kiss her again and try to do even more.

The alarming thing was that the idea was very attractive.

On the other hand, her instinct told her that the man she had met today had had no such intent, but some other reason for requesting a meeting. It was certainly true that there was little chance of them having a private *tête-à-tête* in a normal manner.

Of course, a silly little part of Anna's mind was dreaming that he had fallen desperately in love with her during that one encounter. If that was true, then perhaps he would go on his knees and protest his undying love for her even as he declaimed his extreme unworthiness to so much as touch the hem of her gown, just like a hero in a novel by Mrs. Jamison.

"Fustian!" Anna said out loud as she struggled back into her gown, muttering about buttons that were never designed for a lady to do up by herself. In the end she put on a short spencer jacket to cover the undone buttons at the back.

The mirror assured her that she was covered

neck to toe, and decidedly not the sort of appa-
rition likely to drive a man mad with love or
lust.

As the clocks in the house struck midnight,
she told herself that was how she wanted it and,
heart thudding, moved the bench so she could
return to number 10.

The lever worked without a sound, and the
door opened smoothly. She almost screamed,
however, to find the earl awaiting her in the bedroom.

"Ah," he said, investigating the doorway, "I
thought it must be in here, but I couldn't find
the secret to it."

Anna sidled away from him, shockingly aware
of the intimacy of being alone with an unrelated
man for only the second time in her life, and
certainly for the first time in a bedroom! At least
the place was still shrouded in Holland covers,
which in some irrational way made it less dangerous.

"Does the room make you nervous?" he asked
calmly. "Don't be. I have no wicked intentions.
But there are servants now, and to be wandering
around the house would be very dangerous."

Anna put down her unsteady candlestick, placing it beside his on a bureau. "What if the door
had not been in here, my lord? Then I would
have had to search the house for you."

He smiled. "You are charmingly forthright. I
gambled, but I also hedged my bets. There is a
note in the library asking you to come here. Will

you take a seat?" He indicated one of the two chairs bracketing the screened fireplace.

Both relieved and disappointed that there was no sofa, Anna perched on the chair. He relaxed into the other one and stretched his long legs so that his boots came perilously close to her skirts. "Damned uncomfortable, these chairs. I like ones with lots of padding. I see you feel the same."

"Me?" It came out as a squeak. Anna tried to relax, but it was impossible when this man was sitting so close, making her feel rather breathless. "I am just somewhat apprehensive, my lord. Do you intend to tell my parents?"

His brows rose in surprise. "What! That you sneaked into my house, where I mistook you for a serving maid and did my best to have my wicked way with you? Hardly."

"Oh. Then I don't suppose you are going to try and blackmail me, either."

"Is that what you thought? What was I going to blackmail you into doing? Oh, dear. Not into succumbing to my wicked way. You've been reading too much Mrs. Jamison, Pippin."

Smarting from his tone, Anna snapped, "Don't call me that! It's my father's pet name for me."

"Ah. I'm sorry then. It does suit you, though. And I have the greatest appreciation for juicy apples."

Anna could feel herself turning as hot as if there was a roaring fire in the grate. "Are you flirting with me, sir?"

His smile turned wry. "That would be most

dishonorable, wouldn't it, after I'd given you my parole. Very well, to business. The reason I requested this meeting, Miss Featherstone, is because you clearly know things that I do not. Such as the location of that secret door. I've been trying to find a way to speak with you for weeks, and have had to resort to this. Would you explain it, please?"

Anna felt very loath to tell him, loath to share her secret with anyone, but made herself say, "It's in one of the novels. *Forbidden Affections.*"

He sat up. "In a novel?" he said blankly. "Read by thousands?"

"Yes. You see, Dulcinea is kept in a room exactly like the one I have—it's very horrid—and Roland . . ."

He winced as if in pain. "Did that dreadful woman actually name a hero after me?"

Anna tried to assimilate the word "dreadful." It seemed to her that no one could refer to a lover as dreadful in quite that tone. "I'm afraid so. Roland of Toulaine."

"No wonder you reacted to my name the last time we met. And what did the noble Roland look like? Or can I guess?"

She nodded. "Just like you, I'm afraid. Or rather, more like you in that portrait."

His blue eyes opened wider. "You *have* been prying, haven't you, my dishonorable maid."

Anna was blushing again, this time with mortification. "I do beg your pardon. It was inexcusable."

"Hardly," he said, recovering his equanimity.

"I doubt I could have resisted the temptation, especially at . . . How old *are* you?"

"Sixteen, as I said."

"I was hoping you'd lied. *Hélas*. So, are there other aspects of this novel that relate to reality?"

"How should I know, my lord? You might read it for yourself. You do own a copy."

"The woman gave copies of all her works to my mother, who was too polite to refuse them but has never read a novel in her life."

"How sad for her," said Anna militantly.

Humor flickered in his eyes. "She has often declared that they turn young ladies into weaklings, inclined to faint at the slightest thing. I will delight in telling her how wrong she is."

"She's still alive?" Anna immediately regretted the question, but she was startled to find that the earl was not alone in the world.

"Yes, though she has not been hearty for years. She resides in Bath. So, come, tell me more about this novel so that we can see what parallels there might be."

"Why?"

"You are not a particularly biddable girl, are you? Because, Miss Featherstone, I am still suspected of having murdered Lady Delabury, largely because no one ever believed that she could have gained entry to this house in her very revealing nightgown—for, unlike you, she favored diaphanous silk—without me knowing. Since my friends vouched for me, this casts a shadow on their honor, too. I want the matter cleared up."

"After all these years? And . . ."

"Yes?"

Anna looked down. "I feel horribly selfish, but how can you tell the world about the door without involving me?"

She looked up to see him smile quite gently. "I'll find a way. You must trust me."

And she did. Yet again, relief was tinged with a little disappointment. She trusted him with her reputation, but she feared she could also trust him with her virtue. He wasn't going to seduce her, after all.

Oh dear, she was a perilously wicked creature!

"Anna?"

She started at his use of her name.

"Anna, tell me about the book."

And so she did, not making a great deal of it because it was quite a silly story. She told how Count Nacre had trapped poor Dulcinea on the very eve of her wedding to Roland, and hidden her in the deserted tower of his castle, where he intended to ruin her, thus forcing her to marry him instead.

"And each night he would come to her, intending . . ."—she was blushing again—". . . intending the worst. But something would always happen to disturb them." She found the courage to look at him. "It is a little like Scherazade, my lord, except that stupid Dulcinea does *nothing* to change her fate. She just faints and weeps."

His lips twitched. "Unlike you."

Anna's face was heating again. "I did. Weep."

"True, and most disconcerting it was, child. But you also smashed me on the head with a heavy glass. I'm sure Dulcinea could have done the same."

"Yes, she could. If I'd been her I would have waited by the door and hit him with a poker as he came in. In fact, I saw nothing in the book to suggest that Dulcinea couldn't have opened the door from her own side any time she wanted. But you see, she was afraid of the rats."

He laughed out loud. "Oh, the scorn! Are you not afraid of rats, Anna?"

Something in his manner was causing a new kind of heat, a warmth that came from his relaxed manner and smiling eyes, from his admiration. "I don't like them, my lord, but if it were rats or Count Nacre, I'd chance the rats."

"I'm sure you would. And so the fainting maiden waits patiently for Roland to arrive on his white charger and throw her over his saddle-bow."

"Hardly at the top of a tower, my lord."

"True. So what did happen?"

Anna settled to telling the story. "Roland confronts Count Nacre in his hall, where they engage mightily with their swords. The contest is equal . . ."

"How old is Count Nacre?"

"Oh, quite old. At least forty."

"Ancient," he remarked dryly. "But then the contest is unlikely to be equal. He probably has the gout."

"The count is a mighty warrior, my lord, champion of the king. May I continue?"

"I do beg your pardon," he said unrepentantly. "So they engage mightily with their swords. Do they batter themselves to simultaneous exhaustion?"

"Of course not."

"Why not? Ah, she frowns at me . . ."

Anna was indeed frowning, though she was hard-pressed not to giggle. "Because, my lord, the count suddenly comes to a realization of his own wickedness and throws himself upon Roland's sword."

He blinked. "How very disconcerting."

"Hush, my lord!" She bit her lip and pushed gamely on. "Roland races up the tower to Dulcinea . . ."

"Despite his wounds?"

"Heroes are *never* wounded. Or not seriously."

"Then they are hardly very heroic, are they?"

"Have you ever been wounded?" The words popped out before she could control them, fracturing the lighthearted atmosphere. Her eyes fixed on his scar.

"I'm no hero, Anna."

"You didn't answer my question."

"Villains get wounded, too. Proceed with your story or I'll show you my other wounds, which would move this meeting out of the field of honor, Miss Featherstone."

Anna was crushingly aware of having been relegated to formality, and swallowed a hint of tears. "Where was I, my lord?"

"Your hero was racing up the tower steps despite his many wounds, and muscles that burned and ached from the mighty battle."

"So he enters Dulcinea's chamber, causing her to swoon."

"Twit. You would have tended his wounds, wouldn't you?"

"My lord, he *wasn't* wounded!"

"How could she tell? He was doubtless covered by the evil count's blood."

Anna paused. "That's true, isn't it? I didn't say it was a *good* story, my lord."

"Just as well. So, what next? I suppose he has to carry her down the winding stairs. Tricky, that, I should think."

"Doubtless, especially as an earthquake starts just then . . ."

"An *earthquake?* The very earth protesting at the count's demise? Then he must be the hero, and Roland, vile Roland, a wastrel and a murderer."

"Nonsense. Roland is the very epitome of a hero. But the stones do begin to tumble around them, and the steps crumble beneath their feet . . ."

"Whereupon, he slaps her awake and makes her use her feet as they race to safety?"

"Of course not! In fact, she does come out of her swoon . . ."

"Thank heavens . . ."

". . . But by then they have rats swarming around them, which sends her off again. Please, my lord, don't make me laugh or I will never finish!"

"There's more?" he asked, straight-faced, but with eyes full of hilarity. He looked exactly like the portrait.

With difficulty, Anna gathered her wits. "It can hardly end then!"

"I don't see why not. They can be entombed together as an eternal monument to folly."

"They manage to survive. Just as they emerge, the tower crumbles, leaving only a heap of stones . . ."

"And a lot of homeless rats."

"I don't think that was mentioned," she said severely. "The king then arrives . . ."

"George III?" he queried in astonishment.

"No! King Rudolph of . . . Oh, I've forgotten the country. It's all made up."

He raised one brow. "You astonish me, Miss Featherstone."

A giggle escaped, but Anna struggled on. "The king has found out that Count Nacre is plotting treason and has come to execute him . . ."

"How very unlawful. Due process, my dear."

". . . But now he makes Roland Count of Nacre . . ."

"Whereupon Dulcinea breaks off the match because she refuses to live in a rat-infested castle."

"The *castle* wasn't rat-infested, my lord!"

"It will be now the rats don't have their cozy

tower to live in. Where do you think all those rats went?"

Anna succumbed to laughter. "Oh dear! It is all . . . all so silly, isn't it?"

He leaned over and passed her a handkerchief. "Very. Are you truly addicted to these novels, Anna?"

Anna controlled her laughter and wiped her eyes. "Most of them are not as bad as that. Even Mrs. Jamison's earlier ones were much better, though her heroines did tend to swoon at the drop of a pin."

"From the little I know of her, Lady Delabury was of much the same temperament."

Anna made a business of drying her cheeks, considering yet another statement that indicated that the earl and Lady Delabury had not been intimate. Then why on earth had the woman committed suicide in this very room?

He leaned back, sober again and thoughtful, and echoed her thought. "I see nothing in that silly story to explain why the author decided to commit suicide, or why she chose to do so in this room."

"Perhaps because she'd written such a terrible novel?" Anna clapped her hand over her mouth. "Oh, how uncharitable!"

He focused his serious features and amused eyes on her. "Quite. And Margaret Delabury thought every word she wrote absolutely perfect. She had just married Delabury, an excellent catch for her, and the poor man was besotted. She had everything."

He lapsed into thought, and Anna chanced a question. "What was in the note she left, my lord?"

"Some stuff about despair because she could not hold her husband's affection."

"He was unfaithful?" Anna asked, knowing she was turning pink at discussing such matters with a gentleman.

"Most unlikely. As I said, he was besotted. One reason I left the country was because fool Delabury was convinced I was his wife's lover and murderer. Having failed to get me sent to trial, he was intent on calling me out."

"Oh, my."

"I did hope that by now he'd found a new bride and no longer felt so keenly on the subject. I have just heard that he is on his way to town with dueling on his mind."

"Oh, dear!"

"Quite. Which is why I want to solve this mystery."

"I wish I could help. Truly. But I think I've told you all I know."

He rose to his feet. "I think so, too." He was suddenly standing quite close to her. "I have enjoyed this, though."

She looked up at him, delight at their shared amusement still fizzing in her. She had never known an instant bond such as this. "So have I, my lord," she admitted shyly.

For a moment she thought he had something important to say, but then he turned sharply away. "Would you permit me to glance into your room, Miss Featherstone?"

Anna swallowed her disappointment. "By all means, my lord. I've wandered all over your house, so it seems only fair that you should see a little of mine."

As they went through the door, he said, "It is not at all the same. You should not invite men into your bedroom."

She glanced back over her shoulder. "For fear that the very sight of my virginal couch will turn them into ravening beasts?"

"Something like that," he said vaguely, but he was staring around at the room. "Good God. The solution is obvious. The woman was mad."

"A convenient assessment, my lord, but hard to prove."

"This room is proof." He poked a finger into the grinning mouth of a gargoyle. "I suppose one could keep small coins and buttons in places like that."

Anna giggled, but placed her fingers over her lips. "Hush, my lord. I'm not at all sure your voice cannot be heard in other rooms!"

"And that would set the cat among the pigeons, wouldn't it?" he said softly. He turned to look at her. "Farewell, Anna."

Her heart skipped a beat. "No more secret meetings?"

"No more secret meetings. It would be very foolish."

"No one need know . . ."

"Except us."

Anna gripped her hands tight together. "I . . . I like you, my lord."

There was the merest twitch of his lips, but his eyes looked rather sad. "I like you, too, Anna Featherstone."

"Well," said Anna, after swallowing a lump in her throat. "I suppose if you marry Maria, we will meet occasionally."

"I have no intention of marrying your sister. I've only been paying court to her to get access to Maggie."

"Oh. And that was just because you wanted to know about the secret door."

"Exactly."

It was all rather deflating, but that magical time of intimacy and laughter could not be entirely dispelled. Anna gathered her courage and looked up at him. "If you were feeling grateful for my help, you might perhaps . . . might kiss me once, my lord, with kindness, before you go."

"Kindness? Was I not kind the other night?"

"It was hard for me to tell. I was very frightened."

"It may be hard for you to tell now. Why aren't you frightened?"

Anna considered it. "I trust you."

"If I were truly kind and trustworthy, Anna, I would leave." But he held out a hand.

Breath catching in her throat, Anna placed her hand in his, touching him for the first time in weeks. His hand was firm, warm, smooth . . . All in all, it would be extraordinary if it were anything else, and yet it seemed remarkable to her.

He drew her into his arms and inside she melted into a blend of sadness and wonder.

"It is so unfair," she said.

He tilted her chin. "What is?"

"That this is wrong."

She could not read his expression at all. "You do at least know that it is wrong?"

"To be kissing a man in my bedroom? And such a man? I'd have to be perfectly fluff-witted not to."

"And fluff-witted is the last description I would put to Anna Featherstone. Too clever by half . . ."

He kissed her simply on the lips. She was about to protest that the kiss was too brief when he returned to deepen it, teasing her mouth open and bringing the pleasure that had heated her dreams.

When he started to draw away from her, she tightened her arms about him. "Oysters," she said.

"What?"

"Kissing is like oysters. A bit unpleasant at first, but quite delicious when one is accustomed."

He laughed then, struggling to be quiet. He rested his head against hers, his shaking running through into her.

She moved her head so her lips found his and swallowed his laughter so that it changed into something else, something even better than before. Her body became involved in the kiss, moving against him as her hands explored—

He pulled away.

When she resisted, he used force.

Anna was abruptly mortified by her behavior, but at least he was none too calm either.

Then his expression became kind, and he brushed some hair from her face. "I do wish you weren't sixteen, Anna Featherstone." With that, he slipped back through the doors.

"I will get older," she whispered, but it was to a closed panel.

Anna undressed, aching with needs she had never imagined but understood perfectly well. He was right, though. The world would be shocked by such a match, and an eligible earl couldn't be expected to wait years until she was older, and "out." He would marry someone else, and Anna's heart would break. But at least it wouldn't be Maria.

That was cold comfort. Anna sniffed a few tears as she changed into her nightgown and climbed into her chilly, virginal couch.

In the next days, Anna could only be glad that her parents and sister were busily engaged in the height of the Season, for it was beyond her to behave entirely in her normal, prosaic manner.

She was foolishly, idiotically in love. Daydreams filled her head, wild sensations flooded her body, and she could hardly think of anything but the

Earl of Carne. She attempted drawings of him, and wrote his name endlessly on pieces of paper—which were hard to dispose of in warm weather when there were no fires except in the kitchen.

She spent entirely too much time sitting by windows hoping to catch a glimpse of him entering or leaving his house. Once or twice he looked thoughtfully at number 9, but she wasn't sure she could read anything significant into that.

To try to bring some order to her mind, she began again to consider the mystery of Lady Delabury's death. After all, if Carne was to be believed, the lady's husband could already be in town looking for an excuse to call the earl out, or perhaps planning to kill him in cold blood!

She was sitting in the drawing room one day scribbling random thoughts on a piece of paper when Maria came in, untying the ribbons of a very fetching blue silk bonnet.

"I confess I am beginning to weary of this constant social round," she said, with feeling. "We meet the same people everywhere, and everyone talks of the same things."

"It must grow tiring," Anna commiserated. "But it will be worth it if you find the ideal husband."

Maria sighed. "What is an ideal husband? This one is handsome, that one is rich, another is clever, another has exquisite taste . . ."

"Have you not found anyone to love?" Anna

asked. It seemed to her that falling in love was alarmingly easy.

"Oh, *love.* You are such a romantic, Anna! If you talk of that sort of foolishness, I perhaps favor Mr. Liddell, but he is impossible now his cousin is home, hale and hearty." She drifted over. "What are you writing?"

Anna said the first thing that came to mind. "A . . . novel."

When Maria picked up the piece of paper, Anna almost snatched it back, but she realized in time that to do so would alert her sister to a mystery. She hoped the scattered words would be meaningless. She hadn't used "Carne" or "Delabury." In fact, the names she had used had been mainly from *Forbidden Affections.*

"I'm trying to come up with the plot for one," she said. Maria did not read novels. She hardly read anything. Surely she wouldn't recognize the names.

Maria scanned the sheet and suddenly frowned. "It's not a *roman à clef,* is it, Anna?"

"No. Why would you think that?"

Maria lost interest and returned the sheet of paper. "Just the name of your hero. Count Nacre. It's an anagram of Carne. Count Nacre—the Earl of Carne. Since you seemed to take the man in aversion, I thought you might be planning a novel in which he came to a dreadful end. Mother would have the vapors." With that, she wandered away leaving Anna stunned.

Her brains must have been muddled for weeks not to see that the villain of *Forbidden Affections* had been the Earl of Carne, the present earl's father. She wondered if they looked the same, for that would clinch it.

She hurried down to visit the cook, and though it took time to turn the conversation to the old earl, she eventually confirmed her suspicions. The Wicked Earl's father had been a tall, barrel-chested, dark-visaged man who up to the time of his death had enjoyed hard riding and pugilism. He had been Count Nacre.

She retreated to her room to ponder the implications. Had Lady Delabury been in love with Lord Carne's son, Roland, and thwarted by the father? Had *Forbidden Affections* been a novel of revenge?

Or had the lady been trying to reveal to the world that the earl was creeping into her horrid chamber to terrorize her?

But that was nonsense! Lady Delabury herself had ordered the chamber made, and if the earl had come through the secret door—that peculiar secret door—she could easily have complained or nailed it shut.

So what if . . .

Anna's mind began to wander strange paths which seemed unlikely but were the only ones to fit the facts.

One thing was clear. She had to discuss this with the earl.

Anna could not be sure of the earl being in his house at any particular hour. She could only

plan to take up vigil once her family left for the evening, hoping to see Lord Carne come home before she fell asleep.

A snarl in this plan developed during the afternoon as her family sat together in the drawing room.

Her father addressed Maria. "We are well into June, my dear; and must soon be returning home. Is it not about time I started to encourage one of your eager suitors?"

Maria blushed. "I am undecided, Papa."

"I can quite see that you're spoiled for choice," he teased. "But the old saying is 'Out of sight, out of mind.' If we return home with you unspoken-for, they might turn their eyes elsewhere."

"If I am so easily forgotten, perhaps I should be."

Anna so heartily agreed with that sentiment that it took her a moment to realize how strangely it sat on Maria's lips, who thought no one should ever forget her. She looked up from her book and realized that Maria was quite agitated.

"Now, now, my love," said Lady Featherstone. "We do not intend to pressure you. But you must have some notion of where your favor lies."

Maria looked down and said nothing so that an awkward silence developed.

It was as much to break that silence as to tease that Anna said, "It seems to me that Maria favors Mr. Liddell if she favors anyone."

Maria's delicious color blossomed even as Lady Featherstone's face became pinched. Sir Jeffrey merely looked thoughtful.

"Maria!" exclaimed Lady Featherstone. "You have an *earl* seeking your hand. Surely you cannot be so foolish . . ."

"Hush, my dear," said Sir Jeffrey. "We do not look only at rank, surely. Maria, do you favor Mr. Liddell?"

Maria's fingers were knotted in the trim of her embroidered tunic. "I truly don't know, Papa. But . . . but I cannot seem to find interest in any of the other gentlemen, excellent though they are."

"Well, really!" snapped Lady Featherstone. "I never thought you to be so . . . so ungoverned in your affections! I have told you over and over that a girl can fix her affections where she should if she but puts her mind to it. I forbid it! I forbid you to even speak to the man again."

Maria leapt to her feet. "How can you be so cruel! If his horrid cousin had been dead, you would have been delighted to see me wed to him. How is it different?"

"It is a title and eighty thousand a year different, my girl! Believe me, Maria, you are not cut out to live in a cottage doing your own laundry."

"It would hardly come to that. Michael has nearly a thousand pounds a year."

"Michael, is it?"

"Hush, my love," said Sir Jeffrey. "Let us not wrangle over it. This requires thought and calm debate. Maria, I am saddened that you have tried to conceal the state of your feelings."

Maria was weeping now, very prettily. "Oh, Papa, I have not been deceitful. Truly I haven't. I thought I could grow fond of Lord Whelksham, or Lord Harlowe. It is only now in talking of it that I realize how I feel about Michael."

Her father rose to hug her. "It is well that we know the truth. Now, I'm not saying I will consent, for like your mother I have qualms. But we will all think over it. I am sure it will be wise for us to make our apologies and stay home tonight, and perhaps you and Anna would be better for having a quiet meal in your rooms."

Anna met her father's eyes with a quizzical expression, and humor tugged at his lips before being controlled. She dutifully accompanied her sister upstairs.

Maria collapsed into a chair. "Oh, Anna, what will become of me?"

"I suspect you'll end up married to Mr. Liddell if you truly want it."

"Mama will oppose it with all her strength!" Maria declared, reminding Anna all too much of Dulcinea in despair.

"Mama will come to see reason once the first shock is past. But have you truly considered the practicalities?"

"I love him!"

Anna felt like Horatio facing overwhelming odds, but she set herself to trying to lead Maria into a logical consideration of her future. "You have always wanted a fine country estate, Maria."

"I am sure Michael will have one in time."

"How?"

Maria's eyes shifted. "If his cousin should die . . ."

Anna's heart tightened painfully. "Lord Carne seems very healthy."

"Healthy men die. In duels, for example. I understand there may be a duel."

Anna moved slightly backward. "Maria, you *can't* wish for someone's death. That is wicked!"

Her sister's lips tightened. "He was supposed to be dead. And he is a murderer."

"Oh, nonsense."

"You can't know that. Why are you so hot in his defense?"

Anna controlled herself. "I feel sure that old story is mostly rumor and exaggeration. Maria, if you marry Mr. Liddell you must accept that you will be marrying him as he is, and as he can be. He seems personable and intelligent. I'm sure he can work his way up to a comfortable situation, perhaps even into being awarded a title one day."

Anna had not actually intended this to be a daunting speech—it wouldn't have daunted her—but Maria paled. "That could take years!"

"Yes."

"Oh, go away! I don't see that you have any right to lecture me so. You think you are so clever but you know nothing about the way the world works. Nothing!"

Anna saw that her attempts to help could drive Maria into the vapors, so she left and took up her post by her window watching number 10. More than ever she wanted a word with the earl. It clearly was important to try to solve the death of Lady Delabury, but she also wasn't sure it was beyond Mr. Liddell to plot his cousin's murder.

Lord Carne must be warned.

Unfortunately, what she saw was the earl leaving his house with a friend, dressed for the evening.

The two men waited at the curb, presumably for his carriage, for the earl wore only light shoes. He must be going to a ball later, perhaps after the theater.

Anna sighed, wishing she were going with him, trying to imagine what it would be like to dance with him. He was very agile and graceful, so he must be a good dancer. She imagined spinning in a waltz with him and then, at the end, being wickedly pulled into his arms and kissed. She was sure he was bold enough to defy convention in that way . . .

She sank her head in her hands, alarmed at the physical response she felt at the mere thought.

When she looked up, he was gone.

Doubtless he'd be out until the early hours. Anna took her dinner by the window; then when she was ready for bed she sat there to read a book, just on the chance that he would come home.

When he did, she almost missed him. He didn't return in the carriage, and she was absorbed by *Mr. Arnold's Travels in North Africa.*

Some sixth sense, perhaps, made her look up just in time to see Lord Carne turn toward his house and go in.

Anna's heart immediately started to pound and her hands went clammy. There was nothing she wanted more than to be with the earl again, but she feared he wouldn't be best pleased to see her, and wouldn't like the subject she wanted to discuss.

She must be resolute, though. She slipped into her gown and spencer, not forgetting the armor of stockings and shoes, and went to open the secret door.

The door did not move.

The other side was blocked!

She pushed harder and the door gave a little but was reinforced by an obstacle. The earl had done as she had once, and placed something against it. What, though? If it was an armoire, she would never get through.

She had blocked her door in fear of her virtue. She stifled a giggle at the thought of the earl barricading the door for the same reason. Then she decided it wasn't funny. He'd doubtless blocked the door because he did not want her to use it. He would not be pleased to see her.

Anna pushed again, increasing the pressure until the obstacle moved. Ah, not too substantial an object. Probably a very solid chair. As with her bench, its main deterrence would be noise, but unless the earl had moved into this room there was a chance that no one would hear it.

She pushed as hard as she could, and with a trundling noise the chair moved enough to let her through.

"Hah!" she said, and triumphantly moved the chair to another spot further down the wall. Then, breathing heavily from her exertions, she stopped to listen. She didn't think that noise would have alerted anyone, and in a moment, peace told her it had not.

Now her only problem was to decide how to find the earl in a house still awake and equipped with servants. She thought of returning to her room to wait for later, but she was afraid that Lord Carne might have only returned home for a short while.

So, she would have to be brave and venturesome.

Anna opened the bedroom door a tiny chink, feeling very different from that first time when it had all seemed like a wonderful game. The dangers were greater now, and she also knew this wasn't a game. She very much feared she had passed over into a new world, an adult world, where what one did could have grave consequences. With a sigh, she looked out into the corridor.

The landing around the central stairs was completely deserted, but the feel of the house was different. It was inhabited now. She heard the ticking of clocks and, faint in the distance, noise of the servants in the basement. On the end posts of the staircase, oil lamps flickered against the time when the setting sun brought gloom.

This part of the house seemed safe, but the earl was probably in his library, which meant she must go down to the lower floor. Anna crept along the carpet runner, praying that no board creaked. As she passed one door a noise froze her in midstep. Faint, slight, unidentifiable, it told her someone was there.

She let out the breath she had been holding. From her previous exploration she knew this was one of the major bedrooms, and likely to be used by Lord Carne. If someone was in it, it was either the earl or a servant. The chances were that it was the earl, though it easily could be both . . .

She contemplated the mahogany panels and decided that she must either open this door or return to her own room. No other choice was logical.

She turned the knob and walked in.

"What is it?" asked Lord Carne sharply, and turned.

They stood frozen for a second, he by her unexpected appearance, she by the fact that he was only wearing his tight dark pantaloons.

Then he moved swiftly past her to shut the door. "What the devil are you doing here?"

"I had to speak to you!" Anna swiftly turned her gaze to a still-life on the wall, but the image of his body was imprinted in her brain. She'd never seen a real muscular male torso before in her life, and the wonder of it had her dizzy—golden, contoured like the finest classical statue . . .

"Why?"

She had to turn back. When she did, he had
pulled on a shirt. That helped her equanimity,
but no one could think he was pleased with her.
"I . . . I've been thinking about Lady Delabury,
and the novel, and everything . . ."

"Yes?" Then before she could answer, he said,
"Damnation. It's not much past nine. Surely
someone might check on you."

"Not usually."

"It would be just our luck." He grasped her
wrist and pulled her toward the door.

"Stop! What—"

"Be quiet and come along."

Since he'd already towed her into the corridor,
Anna had little chance but to be quiet; however,
inside she was seething. He was going to throw
her back into her room and nail the door shut
without giving her a chance to explain her
thoughts.

At the secret door he stopped and let her go.
"All looks well."

"I told you so!" she snapped, rubbing her
wrist.

"Did I hurt you? I'm sorry. But I've no mind
to be entangled in another scandal." His tone
was courteous, but merely the courtesy he would
give a stranger.

An intrusive stranger.

Anna felt rather sick, but she spoke up. "I do
need to talk to you, my lord."

He leant back against the wall. "Talk, then.
But keep your ears open. If it seems anyone
might enter your room, dash in and shut the

door. If they see the door you can claim to have just discovered it."

Though she was still rather cross with him, Anna had to admit that made sense, and moved into her room. "Count Nacre is an anagram of Lord Carne," she whispered.

"Of course."

She stared at him. "Why didn't you say so?"

"It didn't strike me immediately."

Anna frowned at him. "And perhaps you didn't want anyone to know?"

He looked at her sharply, and he may even have colored, though that could just be the setting sun shining through her lace curtains. "You really are too sharp for your own good, Anna."

She swallowed and said the awful words. "Your father was Lady Delabury's lover."

After a moment he said, "Then why did she make him the villain of the book?"

Anna had worked out a rationale. "I think the affair must have been over, and it was a kind of blackmail. She was threatening your father that she had merely to direct her husband's attention to the novel for him to guess the truth. But she couldn't make him the hero. He was too old. So she made him the villain. I realized that was what was wrong with the book. Even though Count Nacre is supposed to be the villain, Dulcinea is . . . is too drawn to him. It's difficult to believe she truly wants to escape."

"Too clever by half indeed. How do you come to understand these things?"

"I read a lot."

"I always knew it was a mistake to allow women to read." But he smiled slightly and the barriers between them were lower.

"Did your father kill her?"

"It was looked into. He was in Norfolk at the time."

"Oh." Anna had forgotten that. Also, she felt she had walked into a wall, the wall of his reticence. She chipped away anyway. "Was it a true suicide, then? There was the note."

"A dose of laudanum and a note was exactly in Lady Delabury's style. Suicide wasn't. She thought herself much too important to leave before her time. Look, Anna, I know this must tantalize you, but I want you to leave it alone."

"But what of Lord Delabury? He's going to call you out!"

"He already has. That's why I came home. He threw a glass of wine at me in White's."

Anna gasped and clutched his shirt. "No!"

He touched her cheek fleetingly. "Hush. Our seconds did their appointed duties for once. We managed to have a discussion and it is all sorted out."

"Oh, thank God. But how? How did you convince him? Did you tell him about your father?"

He sighed and freed his shirt from her grasp. "He knew. Or suspected." He had not released her hands. "Delabury's belief that his wife was unfaithful had been a source of contention throughout their marriage, though his suspicions had naturally fallen on younger men such as myself, especially as such types were always the he-

roes of her novels. It was only after her death
that he began to wonder about my father. He
didn't want to accept it. He, too, is a bit of a
romantic and he doesn't much care for the fact
that his wife preferred a man twice his age,
and . . . My father was a hard-drinking, hard-
riding old rip, if you want the truth. Delabury
found a journal of hers. It named no names but
made it clear that part of the charm of her lover
was his domination and roughness . . . Good
Lord, I should not be speaking of such things
to you!"

He began to move away, but Anna held onto
his hands and he did not fight free. "Don't
worry, my lord. I have read Greek tragedies. I
suppose this explains why she was in your father's bedchamber. She wanted to frighten him
back into the affair. Or perhaps just experience
more of his roughness," she added thoughtfully,
causing Lord Carne to raise his brows. "But this
still doesn't explain why she died."

"Perhaps she simply miscalculated her
dose . . ."

"Or perhaps someone forced her to take
more. But who . . . ?"

He switched his grip so he was holding her
hands, controlling her. "The main thing is that
Delabury accepts that I lacked sufficient reason
to kill her."

"Sufficient? You lacked *all* reason!"

"Did I? The woman was flirting with me, and
generally doing her damnedest to make it look
as if we were having an affair. This and possibly

other suspicions were upsetting my mother, who was not well even then. That in turn was upsetting my father, for in his own way he cared for my mother. I suspect that was the reason he ended the affair, and that was why Lady Delabury staged her suicide. He was expected back that night and should have found her in his bed. But he took ill just before leaving home. My mother came back alone, since she had commitments in town. It was she who found the body."

A blinding certainty struck Anna. She stared at him, and even opened her mouth, but then balked at putting it into words.

"Wise Anna," he murmured.

She remembered the blithe young man of the portrait and wanted to cry. "But you went abroad. For so long!"

"It was no great hardship. In fact," he added with the ghost of a boyish grin, "I enjoyed it immensely. But you are right. In the beginning I left England to avoid Delabury, who was a lot less rational then than now."

"Because you knew that in such a case your mother would come forward—"

He laid his fingers over her lips. "Remain wise, Anna. It's over now. All it will ever be is an unsolved mystery."

"People will still talk."

"A fig for gossips." He moved away then, and began to leave.

"Can I ask just one more question?"

He halted warily. "Yes, though I don't promise to answer it."

"How did your father die? It was within days of Lady Delabury's death."

His features hardened. "The event killed him. Perhaps his sickness had been more serious than we thought, but I don't think so. As soon as he had word of Lady Delabury's death, he rushed to London. His heart gave out on the way."

"I have another question."

His lips twitched. "Why doesn't that surprise me?"

"I don't understand Lady Delabury. Her husband was apparently young, handsome, and in love with her. Why was she having an affair with an elderly man? And what did she hope to gain from her mock suicide?"

"I'm pleased to see that some human behavior still perplexes you, Anna. My father at the time was only forty-five. That may seem ancient to you, but he was a fine figure of a man. One could ask rather why she married Delabury at all." He looked into the distance. "She wanted marriage, I think. She wanted a title. I suspect she was rather naive. She lived quietly with her parents before her marriage, then married someone very like the heroes of her novels. I'm sure she thought she would find the blissful happiness that occurred at the end of her stories, but instead was rather disappointed. Then she met my father and discovered she was a woman who finds older men attractive. Moreover, she found adoration boring and challenge stimulating."

"That seems very strange to me."

He smiled at her. "So it should. You, of

course, have daydreams about handsome young gallants with pure hearts and the most noble of intentions."

She had daydreams about him, but she muttered, "I suppose so."

"Is the mystery solved to your satisfaction?"

Anna touched the door. "I'm still not quite sure how they had this made without raising suspicion."

"Delabury still has no idea about the door, but I asked him about the room. Apparently Lady Delabury asked that such a room be made and he agreed. She even specified the firm to do the work. That firm was the one regularly employed by my father, so it must have been collusion. He was clearly infatuated beyond all sense . . ."

When he broke off, she feared he would not complete the tale, but he carried on. "At the same time that this room was made, he had renovations done to his house, including his bedroom. I talked to the builder, who still has responsibility for the maintenance of the terrace. It was simply a matter of keeping mouths shut about a little extra detail in the work. Straightforward enough for the builder in return for the job of looking after all the earldom's property in London."

"Oh. It is rather disappointing that in the end everything turns out to be so rational and lacking in drama."

He shook his head, smiling. "There's been enough drama for me, I assure you. You would rather I be meeting Delabury at dawn?"

"No."

"Then what?"

"I suppose I'd rather there was a wicked villain to suffer an appropriately grisly fate."

"But this is life, not a novel, Anna, and there's trouble enough in the world without looking for more. Certainly no good would be served by dragging my invalid mother before the courts." He stepped backward. "Now, this time it really is farewell, Anna. I don't want to risk suspicion by having the builders in to seal this door, but I will if I have to. I want your word that you will not use it again under any circumstances."

Anna gathered her courage. "I love you, you know."

He met her eyes. "I hope you don't. It is—"

"Just infatuation," she completed bitterly. "A girl of my age is *capable* of love, you know. In the past, girls were married younger than sixteen!"

He put his hand hard over her mouth. "Hush. Unless it is your plan to have us discovered."

Anna went hot and red. "How dare you!" she whispered when he released her. "I would never sink to that."

"No, of course you wouldn't. My apologies, Anna. But you must recognize that the world would have a collective case of the vapors at the thought of our marriage. I'm fourteen years older than you, theoretically old enough to be your father, and have lived those fourteen years to the full."

"And do such things matter to you?"

"They would matter to your father, I'm sure."

"Are you saying you would marry me if my father consented?"

She did not see him move, but it felt as if he had stepped further away from her. "Anna, stop this. There is no question of marriage between us. Our meetings have been pleasant, but that's as far as it goes. You will get over your current insanity and in time you will meet a suitable young gentleman and be—"

To salvage some of her pride, Anna stepped back and closed the door in his face. Then she sat down and won a battle with tears. He was doubtless right. In time it would not seem so tragic. Thank heavens that she, unlike Maria, would have a few years to recover from her own forbidden affection.

She got up and blew her nose fiercely. In two years time when she entered Society with marriage in mind she would have entirely forgotten the Earl of Carne. It would be much more sensible anyway to marry a man closer to her own age. When she was in her prime, Lord Carne would be a gouty ancient.

She blew her nose again.

Then she heard the screams.

She dashed out into the corridor, then headed toward the noise coming from downstairs. A servant, she assumed, but in some terrible distress.

It was Maria—a tattered, bruised, hysterical Maria.

Lord and Lady Featherstone were already with her, helping her into the drawing room.

"He hit me!" she gasped between sobs. "He *hit* me!"

Sir Jeffrey glanced around. "Anna, get some brandy." He looked back to his older daughter. "Who hit you? Where were you? What have you been doing?"

"Hush, Featherstone," said his wife, dabbing at Maria's dirty, bruised face with her lace handkerchief. "Oh, poor darling. Water. We need water. Who did this to you?"

Maria stared at her mother a moment as if lost for words. Then she said, "Lord Carne! It was Lord Carne. I went out into the garden, and he tried to . . . I fought him . . . Lord Carne."

There was a gasp from the hovering servants. Anna gasped, too, then dazedly brought over the glass of brandy. Sir Jeffrey made Maria drink a little.

Anna studied her disheveled sister, wondering what on earth was going on.

Maria coughed as the fiery spirit went down, but it seemed to calm her, so that she could lie back on the sofa. With a chill, Anna saw that one of the sleeves of her sister's gown was hanging loose, and it seemed someone had slashed the front so that it gaped, almost showing her breasts.

A servant arrived with a bowl of warm water and a cloth and Lady Featherstone began to wipe her face. "Now, Maria, you must tell us exactly what happened to you."

Maria's eyes were still wide with what looked like terror. "He attacked me!"

"Lord Carne?"

Maria closed her eyes and nodded.

"When?" Anna demanded urgently. She couldn't believe he had done such a thing.

"Just now," Maria said. "What a stupid question!"

Anna had a moment to consider, to contemplate keeping silent. A moment to consider all the consequences. She swallowed. "Then it wasn't Lord Carne."

"Oh, do be silent, Anna," snapped her mother. "You can know nothing of all this."

"Yes, I can. Because just now Lord Carne was with me."

Everyone stared at her. Then her father said, "Anna, this is no time for fairy stories."

"It's not a fairy story, Papa. He was with me."

"Where? I do see that you are dressed for the outdoors rather than for bed."

Anna thought she'd considered the implications, but the avid looks on the faces of the gawking servants made her want to hide.

Her father went swiftly to close the doors. "Where, Anna?"

"In my bedroom," she whispered.

Lady Featherstone gave a small scream, and Maria said, "To speak of liars! How on earth would the Earl of Carne get into your bedroom, you foolish girl?"

"There's a secret door."

Her father shook his head. "Anna, my dear, I fear you are letting your imagination run away with you. This is not a novel but a very serious situation . . ."

"I'm telling the truth! If you come up to my room, I will show you. As for the earl, you will have to believe me. We did nothing wrong. We were discussing the mystery of Lady Delabury's death."

"Discussing . . . ?" Her father rose to his feet. "Very well, miss, I will come and see this secret door. But if it is not there, there will be no more novel-reading for you."

Anna knew that proving the door was real was the least of her problems, but she led the way through huddled, whispering servants to her room.

Having a man in her bedroom was enough to ruin her. It was enough to force a marriage . . .

Was her tiny thrill of excitement at that thought very wicked?

Yes, it was. She had never thought to trap the earl like that, and she would not let it happen.

Once in the room, Lady Featherstone shuddered. "Poor Anna. It is this room that has disordered your wits! I knew I should never have allowed you to sleep here."

"My wits are not disordered, Mama. This room is a replica of one in a novel called *Forbidden Affections* by Mrs. Jamison, who was also Lady Delabury . . ."

This summoned fresh exclamations from Lady Featherstone. Maria, however, was looking paler, and even more frantic.

"Oh, this is such nonsense," she gasped. "Don't listen to her . . ."

"In the novel," Anna continued, already having some terrible thoughts about her sister, "the heroine's room had a secret door. I looked to see if this one had the same door." She went to the fireplace and used the lever, then swung the door open. "And it does."

"Good Lord!" said her father. "But surely it doesn't . . ."

"It opens into the room where Lady Delabury died." Anna pushed open the door, noting sadly that the earl had trusted her word and not replaced the chair. At least he wasn't there.

Maria had collapsed onto the chaise, and both she and Lady Featherstone were staring at Anna in horror.

"How long have you known about this?" Anna's mother demanded.

"Since the first night we were here," Anna admitted.

"And you have left a way for that man to creep into this house without saying a word? You foolish girl. We could all have been murdered in our beds!"

"He didn't murder Lady Delabury!"

"Oh, you poor, misguided child. What has he been doing to you?"

"Yes," said Maria spitefully. "What has he been doing to you, since you seem so eager to lie to protect him."

"Well, Anna?" asked her father quietly as he closed the door.

"He's done nothing," Anna protested, determined to avoid entangling Lord Carne in just the scandal he'd wanted to avoid. "The earl didn't know about this door himself until I told him. And he didn't want me to use it. He even put a chair to block it, but I pushed it out of the way tonight because I wanted to talk to him about Lady Delabury's death. He made me promise never to use the door again."

"If true, that shows some sense. It would have been rather better, however, if the earl had come to me to tell me of this foolishness." He turned to Maria. "So, what does this make of your story, miss?"

"I've told the truth," said Maria stubbornly. "It's clear to me that Anna has been behaving most improperly. She's become infatuated with the earl and will say anything to protect him from the consequences of his wickedness. I don't believe for a moment that tonight was their first meeting."

Sir Jeffrey turned to Anna. "Well?"

Damn Maria. "I never said it was. I . . . I know it was wrong, Papa, but I couldn't resist exploring a little. When we first arrived here, number 10 was empty. Then the earl returned and caught me."

"Maggie!" exclaimed her father. "Did you really hit him with something, Anna?"

Anna hung her head and nodded, praying desperately that no one would ask why she had hit him.

"Why did you do such a thing, Anna?" asked her mother.

Anna tried desperately to think of a clever story that would cover all the elements of the situation, and failed. All she could do was mute the truth. "He . . . he thought I was a servant, and he was a little foxed. He tried to kiss me . . ."

"There, see?" said Maria triumphantly. "He is in the habit of attacking defenseless females. When I think on it, I smelled brandy about him tonight."

"Maria, he wasn't in the garden tonight," Anna said.

"So," said her father, "having escaped, you never went into the house again until tonight?"

Anna tried to pronounce the lie, but couldn't, and knew her color was betraying her.

"Anna. The full story, please. What has been going on?"

Anna sat down, for her legs were beginning to feel rather unsteady. "I did go into number 10 one other time to meet him. He asked me to."

"How, pray?" demanded Lady Featherstone. "How could you speak to such a man, or receive messages from him?"

"It was at the tea party when he was talking of maids-of-honor." She could see her mother did not understand at all, and looked at her father. "It was a sort of code, Papa. But I understood."

"But why would you think of going, Anna, when he had assaulted you?"

"He told me I could trust him."

Lady Featherstone exclaimed, but Anna saw some understanding in her father's eyes. "And what happened?" he asked.

"The earl had realized who Maggie must be, and that there was a secret door. He was trying to find out what had happened to Lady Delabury." Anna meticulously went through their discussion and conclusions.

"And that was all?" her father asked at last.

Anna nodded, but she could feel the betraying heat rise in her cheeks.

"Anna?"

She looked up. "He kissed me." When her mother exclaimed, she added, "I asked him to!"

"And is that all he did?" her father asked.

"Yes. Truly, Papa!"

He nodded. "I believe you. You have been very foolish, my dear, but the blame goes to him, a man old enough to know better who has taken advantage of your innocence."

Anna thought this dreadfully unfair, but knew that to say so would make matters worse.

"But you do see, Papa, that Maria must be mistaken, for tonight I was speaking to the earl here, in the doorway, when she thought he was attacking her."

Sir Jeffrey turned to Maria. "Well?"

"She's lying," said Maria mulishly. "She's lying about everything. He's probably ruined her."

Lady Featherstone added to this. "What reason

could Maria possibly have for lying? And it is clear that someone assaulted her."

Anna didn't want to do it, but she had to speak up. "I think it is something to do with Mr. Liddell."

Maria's face gave her away.

"Maria?" asked her father.

Maria sat in silence, hands clasped tight together.

"Maria?" asked her mother, disbelievingly. "Did Mr. Liddell do this to you?"

"It was Lord Carne . . . It was!" But then Maria took refuge in hysterics, and with an aghast look at her husband, Lady Featherstone led her away.

Sir Jeffrey looked at Anna. "You've been playing in deep waters, Pippin."

His disappointment brought tears to prick at her eyes. "I'm sorry, Papa."

"Are you really? If you had your time again, would you change your behavior?"

Anna considered it and sighed. "No, Papa."

"I suspect you fancy yourself in love, Anna."

Anna blew her nose. "It's all right, Papa. The earl thinks me every bit as much of a foolish child as you do."

"I doubt that, Pippin. If he did, he would surely have spoken to me about this."

Her father turned to leave, and Anna said, "Papa! You won't say anything to him, will you? It wasn't his fault!"

"I hardly think Lord Carne needs your protection, Pippin. This is a man's matter. I cer-

tainly will have to speak to him, since you un-
wisely spoke up in front of the servants. Moreover, I fear he may be in danger of mischief."

"Oh, yes, do warn him, Papa! And I thought
Mr. Liddell quite a sensible sort of man when I
met him."

"Young women like Maria can deprive the wis-
est men of their senses. It seems you have that
power, too." He opened the door, then turned
back, truly stern. "And you are not to use that
door, Anna. Not even to warn the frail and sensitive earl of the impending visitation of an irate
father. Yes?"

"Yes, Papa." They shared a smile, since it was
ridiculous to think that the earl could not handle her father's annoyance.

She ran into her father's arms. "Papa, I do
love you so. Many fathers might not have believed my innocence."

He hugged her back. "I know you, Pippin, and
I'm sure you're a match for any man, no matter
how rascally."

"He's not a rascal, Papa."

"We won't argue about that, if you please. But
he is not the man for you, my dear. You must
believe that."

"Very well, Papa."

As she prepared again for bed, Anna fought
against tears. She knew there was no hope that
Lord Carne would marry her, but that didn't
stop her heart from bleeding. She also felt as if
she had betrayed their secret, no matter how
good the reason.

Moreover, she and Lord Carne had parted coolly, with him out of patience with her. This turn of events would hardly improve matters. She did want him to like her at least . . .

But thankfully he would be warned about his perfidious cousin.

The next day, the Featherstone establishment was as somber as if a death had occurred. Maria remained in her room, attended by her mother and Martha. Sir Jeffrey paid a visit to number 10 and then retreated to his study. Anna attempted to lose herself in reading and failed miserably. A careful watch of the street did not catch Lord Carne leaving his house.

As the hours passed she lost patience and went to knock on her father's door. At his permission, she entered.

"Did you speak to the earl, Papa?"

Her father appeared abstracted and solemn. "Yes, Anna. He freely admitted his fault in encouraging you to use that door, and he was deeply shocked by his cousin's behavior."

"What will he do?"

Her father raised his brows. "He had no need to tell me that, and I no cause to ask. I am sure he is a man capable of handling these matters."

"Oh, poor Maria."

"Oh, poor Maria if she were to marry Liddell, Anna. Sit down."

Not liking his tone, Anna sat gingerly on a hard wooden chair.

"Anna, I have told the servants that you were out in the garden with Maria, and that you ventured into the mews and met the earl there. He agrees to support that story. Your rashness in speaking up before the servants could have caused a scandal, though."

"I'm sorry, Papa. But I could not let Maria's accusation stand."

"I realize that. With a little thought, however, you could have held your tongue until we were private."

"But then the servants would have believed her."

Sir Jeffrey shook his head. "The earl's reputation could bear another dent, I think. And if we continued on good terms, no one would believe the worst."

"But that wouldn't be fair, Papa!"

"Oh, Anna . . . Fighting for justice is very dangerous, you know."

"Do you say we shouldn't?"

He smiled. "No, I cannot say that. But any parent wants a smooth path for their children's feet. However," he said more briskly, "you need a stern talking-to, young lady. You are too trusting. The earl, had he been a different sort of man, could have abused you quite dreadfully, and your rash behavior would have largely been to blame."

Anna was inclined to argue on both counts, but decided submissive silence was the wise course.

"Mr. Liddell is a handsome man with a smooth social manner, and thus both you and Maria found him attractive and pleasing. The earl could well have been another of the same stamp."

"I wouldn't say Lord Carne had a smooth social manner when I first met him."

"The less said of that, the better, miss."

Anna blushed, wondering just what her father knew, or guessed. "I would like to know exactly what happened last night, Papa."

"I'm sure you would, Miss Curiosity." He flashed her an intent look. "The earl expressed a wish to meet with you in more normal circumstances, and he seemed to feel you were entitled to an explanation of it all . . ."

Anna's heart began to beat a little faster.

"I have been considering the matter, and cannot see that it will do harm. Do you wish to meet him?"

Anna suppressed a wild *yes* and said demurely, "I would dearly love to know exactly what went on, Papa."

Her father was clearly not bamboozled, but he wrote a brief note and rang for a servant to deliver it next door.

In a few minutes, Lord Carne entered the study.

Anna stared at him anxiously, wondering if he would be angry, but he smiled. "I understand I have to thank you for defending my honor, Anna."

Anna glanced between the two men, feeling the strangeness of the situation. "I'm sorry if it caused trouble."

"I'm sure it caused less than it saved. Your father was quite forbearing in the circumstances."

"Largely," said Sir Jeffrey, "because of my belief in Anna's good sense. Please be seated, Carne."

The earl sat quite close to Anna, reminding her of that meeting in the bedroom, when they had shared laughter and a depth of understanding that still lingered in her heart. She lowered her eyes to her clasped hands. *Don't make a fool of yourself, Anna. This is the end.*

She looked up. "So, my lord. You are going to explain it to me?"

"Can anyone explain the insanity of love? My cousin, desperate for your sister, decided to do away with me. His clever plan was to incite poor Delabury to challenge me. When that failed, he rushed over here, where he had arranged a tryst with your sister."

"Maria had arranged to meet him in the garden? She must have been besotted."

"How true. He needed some way to re-agitate Delabury, and hit upon the notion of having me supposedly attack Maria. Michael would inform Delabury, pointing out that my rank would prevent justice being done, but that he could rid the world of a villain. We'll never know if it would have worked, thanks to you."

"I could almost feel sorry for your cousin if he hadn't hit her."

"It does show a baser side, does it not? But it had a good effect in that it truly shocked your sister. She stuck with her story at first because

she could see nothing else to do, but I gather
she no longer wants anything to do with my
cousin. You'll be pleased to know he is to leave
England. I have some business interests in Mo-
rocco and he will take care of them for me. If
he does well he could make his fortune. If he
tries any tricks, I fear he will come to a sticky
end. As he will if he returns to England in the
next ten years."

"You're ruthless . . ."

"When I need to be, yes."

Anna stared at him, storing him in her heart,
for she could sense the farewell approaching like
a cloud on a summer's day.

The earl rose. "Any more questions?"

When will I see you again?

Do you care for me at all?

Are you hurting now as I am?

Anna shook her head and stood, too. "No, my
lord. I think all is finally explained."

"As I gather from your father that you will
shortly be leaving town, I think this is farewell."

Anna glanced at her father, who said, "There
is no purpose in staying, Anna, and Maria needs
the peace of the country, I think."

Anna turned back to the earl, and despite her
watching father said, "We have said farewell before, my lord."

"This time, it is real." He took her hand and
kissed it lightly. "Goodbye, Anna. One day, a
hero is going to be very fortunate in his heroine." With that he nodded to her father and
left.

The next day, as the hired chaise rolled away from number 9, Carne Terrace, Anna refused to look back, but she allowed herself to imagine the Wicked Earl emerging disheveled from number 10 to stare haggardly after the departing vehicle.

It helped Anna's sanity to be back home. There was nothing to remind her of Lord Carne, and if memories intruded, she could push them back with summertime activities.

She had her friends to visit again, and to tell of the excitements of London. Though it was tempting, she did not tell any of them—not even her closest friend, Harriet Northam—about the secret door and the earl. She did tell her that the house had once belonged to Mrs. Jamison, author of some of their favorite novels, and that was enough of a thrill in itself.

Since it was July, her brothers were home to bother and distract her, and the garden provided work. The Featherstone children were expected to help there, doing such things as picking fruit and weeding. Long days and good weather bred abundant social activities such as walking, riding, angling, and parties both formal and informal.

Maria soon regained her bloom, and being Maria, soon forgot the less fortunate parts of her London experience. Her spirits revived amazingly when Lord Whelksham contrived a visit to a nearby house, clearly with the sole intention of pursuing his ardent courtship.

Anna believed she had put folly behind her and achieved a return to her pleasant, unadventurous life until she was summoned to her father's study one morning.

"Yes, Papa?"

He was standing by the window, hands clasped behind his back, in his serious-consideration pose. He turned slowly. "Anna, we have a visitor."

Anna looked around, but saw no one.

"He is in the garden. It is the Earl of Carne."

Anna's heart immediately began a mad dance that threatened to deprive her of her senses. Six weeks of conscientious common sense were wiped away in an instant.

"What does he want?" she asked, compelled to sink into a seat.

Her father laughed and shook his head. "For an intelligent, mature man he was remarkably confused upon the subject. He claims to be only passing by, though I am not clear as to his destination. He wants to speak with you, though I don't know about what."

Anna bounced up again. "Then I should go into the garden?"

"I doubt that will do you any harm, my dear."

"Oh." Suddenly nervous, Anna straightened her skirts. She wished she were in something better than an ordinary printed muslin. She wished her hair wasn't in a plait . . . But her encounters with Lord Carne had not been marked by elegance, and he presumably didn't care what a schoolroom miss looked like.

She caught a twinkle in her father's eye and blushed. "What should I say, Papa?"

He frowned as if in heavy thought. "You could try, 'Good day, Lord Carne. How kind of you to call.'"

Anna giggled. "Papa, what does he *want?*"

"You'll have to ask him, Pippin. But if he asks you to marry him, you should know that I will not oppose the match, even though you are so young."

"Marry . . ." Anna whispered, her suppressed hopes bubbling wildly and turning abruptly into blind terror.

"You have been very sensible about it all, Anna, but I have no doubt you formed an attachment. The fact that the earl is here—and we are not on the road to anywhere of significance—implies that perhaps he has, too. You are young, but in many ways you are more mature than Maria. I leave the decision up to you. And I may be wrong, Anna. He may not put such a question at all. Off you go, my dear, and find out."

Anna wandered out of the room in a daze, half-tempted to run and hide under her bed to avoid a meeting for which she was ill-prepared. She didn't even know anymore if she wanted to marry the earl, who had become an almost dream-like person in her mind. Perhaps he wasn't as handsome. Perhaps they didn't share the same sense of the ridiculous. Perhaps he would seem old . . .

On such a sunny day, she really should find a

bonnet, but a part of her was so anxious to see him again that her feet found wings all of their own and fairly rushed her out into the gardens.

She found him in the rose garden by the sundial, standing quite still and gazing into the distance.

He was dressed very like he had been at their first meeting, without the greatcoat—in dark leather riding breeches and a dark jacket. He wore a beaver on his head and carried a crop. He must have ridden . . .

Anna was frozen, heart pounding, unable to move closer.

Suddenly, he turned and saw her. He looked rather rueful, but just as wonderful as always, and the feelings she remembered blossomed as freshly as the roses all around them.

At the slightest encouragement she would have run into his arms, but she would not make a fool of herself and walked forward calmly. If he had come, all confused, to ask for more information about Mrs. Jamison's novels, she would hide her hurt for later.

A few feet away she cleared her throat and dropped a curtsy. "Good day, my lord. How kind of you to call."

His eyes were intent as they traveled her. "Anna," he said at last, slowly, as if the word had great meaning. "Sunlight and roses become you."

She pushed some straying curls out of her eyes. "I should have a bonnet . . ."

"Do you fear for your complexion?" He

looked around. "There is a seat beneath that beech tree, if you would prefer it."

They walked over to the rustic seat built around the trunk of the spreading tree, and sat in the shade there, a proper few feet apart. Anna's rainbow exhilaration was fading to grey. He didn't seem confused. He doubtless was here on a very practical matter.

And there was nothing less practical than a marriage between a sixteen-year-old schoolgirl and a thirty-year-old rake, as both he and her father had so clearly pointed out.

She made herself look calmly into his face. "How can I help you, my lord?"

"I wanted to thank you again for stepping forward to deflect my cousin's malice. It must have been difficult."

"Not very. My parents are not ogres."

"No, they are not. But I am in your debt." He, too, appeared calm. Even bored. Was that truly why he was here? Obligation?

"Consider the debt forgiven, my lord. I am only sorry that Maria lent herself to such a scheme."

"My cousin can be a clever cozener."

"Has he left to take up his punishment?"

"Yes, appearing genuinely shaken by his own villainy. Perhaps he was turned mad by love."

Anna was beginning to feel rather bitter, and lashed out. "And what of your mother, my lord?"

"What of her?"

"It seems to me that she has avoided the consequences of murder."

He shook his head. "She suffered. She lost my

father far more absolutely than she would have done through his affairs with such as Lady Delabury. It is doubtful he would have died so soon if not for that disaster. And she lost me, both physically when I went abroad, and spiritually when I realized what she had done, and that she never made any attempt to clear my name. Will it distress you if I tell you that my mother has always been a selfish, small-minded woman?"

Something in his tone made Anna reach out to touch his hand. "I wish for your sake it had not been so, my lord."

"And for your sake?" He turned her hand to hold it. "A selfish mother and a philandering father. What does that make me?"

Anna felt the heat rise in her face, summoned perhaps by the look in his eyes. "I once confessed to . . . to finding you admirable, my lord."

"You might have come to your senses."

"I might," she said, unwilling to open herself to ridicule.

He released her hand and rose to swing his crop at an innocuous dandelion. "I have argued with myself about this for weeks, Anna. You deserve better. You deserve a young man with the bloom of innocence still on him, someone you can learn about life with, hand in hand. You deserve more years of girlhood before settling to domesticity. You deserve more balls, more parties, a Season in London, and the chance to have dozens of adoring suitors vying for your hand . . ."

Anna bit her lip. "My lord, are you saying you're not worthy of me?"

He flashed her a glance. "I suppose I am."

The laughter escaped. "Oh, I'm sorry, but I remember thinking that you would never act like a hero in one of Mrs. Jamison's novels. If you would care to get down on your knees and kiss the hem of my garment, the picture would be complete."

A flash of appreciative humor entered his eyes. "If I get down on my knees and raise your skirt, minx, it will be to enjoy the sight of your lovely legs. I was serious about what I said, though."

"I know. And it is very kind of you, but . . ." Anna grasped her courage and placed her heart before him. "It would be a dreadful waste of time to go through all those experiences when I only long for you."

He stared at her for a moment, then dropped his crop and drew her to her feet. "Are you sure? I am convinced I'm being a selfish brute."

"I'm sure. Even if you will be gouty when I'm in my prime."

His brows shot up. "What?"

Anna rested her hands on his chest, delighting in the fact that such intimacies might, perhaps, be no longer improper, and remembering a naked chest she very much wanted to see again. "I have already considered the practicalities, you see," she teased. "When you are fifty, I will only be thirty-six, and with luck I will still be in full vigor. But I will be most careful not to overexert you, my lord—"

Her mischief was silenced by his demanding lips, and she responded enthusiastically. When he finished, however, she rested against him, clinging to his lapels. "I am not sure I will be in full vigor after twenty years of kisses such as that."

"I hoped you'd realize that, minx. I will eat moderately and exercise frequently so as not to be a disappointment to you in my dotage."

"Oh, good." She ran her hand up over his starched cravat to his neck. "You're very hot."

"Quite natural in the circumstances, I assure you. Anna, you do realize that Society will raise its brows at our marriage."

"A fig for Society. Anyway, I am hoping that you will revive your love of travel and take me to Greece."

He captured her hand and kissed it. "It will be my delight to take you to Greece, and to Rome . . ." He turned her hand and kissed her palm. "And to heaven."

"Heaven?" Her knees were weakening again.

"You will see."

"Oh, you mean bed." Anna tried to sound prosaic, but it came out as a squeak.

He nipped the base of her thumb. "Yes, I mean bed, you outrageous child. And though it will be beyond me to deny myself your delights entirely, I will try not to get you with child for a while. I will try to give you some years of freedom."

Anna stared at him. "I didn't even know that was possible. How—"

He covered her lips with his fingers. "I will educate you after the wedding."

When he moved his fingers, Anna said, "But if there are such ways, everyone should know! When

I think of the suffering some women experience through unblessed or unwanted babies . . ."

He was looking rather harried. "Lord, I should have learned to keep my mouth shut with you, Anna. Don't go babbling of such matters. When you know all, perhaps you can pass the information on, privately. Many men do not approve of women having such knowledge."

"Many are villains, too." But then social issues were swamped by other thoughts. "Are we engaged to marry, then?"

He smiled, and there was a glow to it that warmed her heart. "I consider us to be so."

"Oh, good." Anna began to tug him back toward the house. "We must tell my parents. How soon can we be wed? I have this great thirst for education."

He laughed. "Soon, Anna. Very, very soon. I'm afraid that if I hesitate my better nature will resurface and I'll let you escape."

"Escape!" Anna halted to frown into his wonderful blue eyes. "If you try to renege, my lord, after raising my hopes so high, I will hunt you down and take terrible revenge upon your body!"

"Now that," said the Wicked Earl with a mysterious smile, "is almost sufficient enticement . . ."

Put a Little Romance in Your Life With
Janelle Taylor

Put a Little Romance in Your Life With

Jo Goodman

__**Crystal Passion** $5.50US/$7.00CAN
    0-8217-6308-3

__**Always in My Dreams** $5.50US/$7.00CAN
    0-8217-5619-2

__**The Captain's Lady** $5.99US/$7.50CAN
    0-8217-5948-5

__**My Reckless Heart** $5.99US/$7.50CAN
    0-8217-45843-8

__**My Steadfast Heart** $5.99US/$7.50CAN
    0-8217-6157-9

__**Only in My Arms** $5.99US/$7.50CAN
    0-8217-5346-0

__**With All My Heart** $5.99US/$7.50CAN
    0-8217-6145-5

Call toll free **1-888-345-BOOK** to order by phone, use this coupon
to order by mail, or order online at **www.kensingtonbooks.com**.

Name_____
Address_____
City _____ State _____Zip_____
Please send me the books I have checked above.
I am enclosing $_____
Plus postage and handling* $_____
Sales tax (in New York and Tennessee only) $_____
Total amount enclosed $_____
*Add $2.50 for the first book and $.50 for each additional book.
Send check or money order (no cash or CODs) to:
Kensington Publishing Corp., Dept. C.O., 850 Third Avenue, New York, NY 10022
Prices and numbers subject to change without notice.
All orders subject to availability.
Visit our website at **www.kensingtonbooks.com**.

Simply the Best . . .
Katherine Stone

__Bel Air
  0-8217-5201-4 $6.99US/$7.99CAN

__The Carlton Club
  0-8217-5204-9 $6.99US/$7.99CAN

__Happy Endings
  0-8217-5250-2 $6.99US/$7.99CAN

__Illusions
  0-8217-5247-2 $6.99US/$7.99CAN

__Love Songs
  0-8217-5205-7 $6.99US/$7.99CAN

__Promises
  0-8217-5248-0 $6.99US/$7.99CAN

__Rainbows
  0-8217-5249-9 $6.99US/$7.99CAN